*continued . . .*

"Quindicott's enigmatic townspeople come alive in this quirky mystery, and readers will eagerly anticipate future installments—and the continuing easy banter and romantic tension between Jack and Penelope."     —*Romantic Times*

"Ms. Kimberly has penned a unique premise and cast of characters to hook us on her first of a series."     —*Rendezvous*

"Part cozy and part hard-boiled detective novel with traces of the supernatural, *The Ghost and Mrs. McClure* is just a lot of fun."     —*The Mystery Reader*

"Charming, funny, and quirky . . . He is hard-boiled in the tradition of Philip Marlowe and she is a genteel Miss Marple . . . An explosive combination. Alice Kimberly definitely has a hit series if the first book is anything to go by."
                                        —*Midwest Book Review*

"What a delightful new mystery series! I was hooked from the start . . . I adored the ghost of Jack . . . Pairing him with the disbelieving Penelope is a brilliant touch."
                                        —*Roundtable Reviews*

To read more about the Haunted Bookshop Mysteries
or the Coffeehouse Mysteries, visit the author's website at
www.CoffeehouseMystery.com.

# The Ghost
## AND THE
# Haunted Mansion

# ALICE KIMBERLY

BERKLEY PRIME CRIME, NEW YORK

**THE BERKLEY PUBLISHING GROUP**
**Published by the Penguin Group**
**Penguin Group (USA) Inc.**
**375 Hudson Street, New York, New York 10014, USA**
Penguin Group (Canada), 90 Eglinton Avenue East, Suite 700, Toronto, Ontario M4P 2Y3, Canada
(a division of Pearson Penguin Canada Inc.)
Penguin Books Ltd., 80 Strand, London WC2R 0RL, England
Penguin Group Ireland, 25 St. Stephen's Green, Dublin 2, Ireland (a division of Penguin Books Ltd.)
Penguin Group (Australia), 250 Camberwell Road, Camberwell, Victoria 3124, Australia
(a division of Pearson Australia Group Pty. Ltd.)
Penguin Books India Pvt. Ltd., 11 Community Centre, Panchsheel Park, New Delhi—110 017, India
Penguin Group (NZ), 67 Apollo Drive, Rosedale, North Shore 0632, New Zealand
(a division of Pearson New Zealand Ltd.)
Penguin Books (South Africa) (Pty.) Ltd., 24 Sturdee Avenue, Rosebank, Johannesburg 2196,
South Africa

Penguin Books Ltd., Registered Offices: 80 Strand, London WC2R 0RL, England

This is a work of fiction. Names, characters, places, and incidents either are the product of the authors' imagination or are used fictitiously, and any resemblance to actual persons, living or dead, business establishments, events, or locales is entirely coincidental. The publisher does not have any control over and does not assume any responsibility for author or third-party websites or their content.

THE GHOST AND THE HAUNTED MANSION

A Berkley Prime Crime Book / published by arrangement with the authors

PRINTING HISTORY
Berkley Prime Crime mass-market edition / January 2009

Copyright © 2009 by Penguin Group (USA) Inc.
Cover illustration by Catherine Deeter.

ISBN: 978-0-425-22460-1

BERKLEY® PRIME CRIME
Berkley Prime Crime Books are published by The Berkley Publishing Group,
a division of Penguin Group (USA) Inc.,
375 Hudson Street, New York, New York 10014.
BERKLEY® PRIME CRIME and the PRIME CRIME logo are trademarks of Penguin Group (USA) Inc.

PRINTED IN THE UNITED STATES OF AMERICA

10  9  8  7  6  5  4  3  2  1

*For their "spirited" support over the years,*
*this book is affectionately dedicated to*
*the inspiring, creative, and dangerously intelligent*
*J. J. and Marcia Pierce.*
*Thanks for reading—and for caring.*

# ACKNOWLEDGMENTS

Once again, the author tips her fedora to
Wendy McCurdy, executive editor,
and
John Talbot, literary agent.
Class acts from start to finish.

And a very special thank-you to Allison Brandau
for her valuable editorial input.

# CONTENTS

Don't you see . . . if everyone rushes off at the slightest sound, of course the house gets a bad name. It's too ridiculous, really, in the twentieth century to believe in apparitions . . .

—*The Ghost and Mrs. Muir* by R. A. Dick
(a.k.a. Josephine Aimée Campbell Leslie)

# PROLOGUE

"So you're a private detective," she said. "I didn't know they really existed, except in books."

—*The Big Sleep*, Raymond Chandler, 1939

Third Avenue Lunchroom
New York City
September 10, 1947

"WHAT'S GOOD TODAY, Birdie?"

"It's all good."

"You say that every day."

"It's all good every day."

Jack Shepard tossed his fedora onto the dull green counter and stifled a yawn. It was close to noon already, but he'd been on a tail much of the night.

*One more cheating Charlie*, he thought, *only this time Charlie wasn't stepping out on his Park Avenue wife. This genius came all the way from Pittsburgh to sample the side dish.*

Jack had been hired by a PI in PA who didn't feel like riding the rails all the way to the Big Apple. Jack filed his report by phone and collected his dough by wire. Now the job was over.

*Another "happy" marriage right down the drain...*

At least the case was open-and-shut, which was fine with Jack now that he'd lost a night's shut-eye over it. Anyway, he had a payday in his pocket, he'd earned a night off, and he was hoping to spend it with something a whole lot softer than a whiskey bottle.

Jack dragged out a fresh deck of Luckies, shook one clear. While Birdie went for his coffee, he lit up and took a drag. Someone had left a *Times* behind and he skimmed the page one headlines—"Butter Rises to 90 Cents a Pound," "Truman Hails National Guard," "Long Island Fire Kills 8" . . .

"So what else is new?" Jack turned on his stool and cased the rickety wooden tables.

Same old tired crew, except for the little twerp from that Midtown blab sheet. Most days, Timothy Brennan drank his lunch at the hotel bar up the block. The newshound only showed here when he was down on his luck—or angling for a story.

"Hey, Shepard," Brennan called from across the lunch-room. "What do ya know, what do ya say?"

*To you? Nothing,* Jack thought.

The last time he'd answered "a few questions" for Tim Brennan about a case he was working, the little punk put it in print. Jack figured "off the record," "in confidence," and "private" were words the little snot-nosed scribbler had failed to learn at that upstate college. Brennan got a bonus for his article. Jack nearly got killed. So he made sure Brennan got an extra-special bonus from Jack personally: a nice black one around the vicinity of his eye in the blab sheet's back alley.

"Why aren't you at the Mayfair, kid?" Jack called. "Lose on the ponies again? Or was it the fights this time?"

"Got a hot tip, Jack?"

"Yeah, you're a degenerate gambler. Quit while you're behind."

"Thanks but no thanks, Shepard. I'll stop up to see you later."

"Sure, you do that," Jack called. *'Cause I won't be there.*

"So what'll you have today?" Birdie asked as she poured his coffee.

"Your Blue Plate."

"Wow, a big spender."

"Yeah, two whole bits for roast beef and smashed potatoes." Jack threw her a wink.

Birdie was new behind the counter. Jack liked her butterscotch curls and bluebonnet eyes. Only one thing bugged him: She grinned too much—like those Square Jane cheerleader types who didn't have a clue how the world really turned. For all their giggling, Jack found them about as much fun as a sober sunrise. But the last few days, Birdie had started glancing at him with a different kind of smile, flirty little flashes that promised a grown woman might be smoldering somewhere beneath that pink, frilly tent of an apron, one that came out when the sun went down.

"You're missing a real catch here, you know," Jack told her. "I just got paid."

"Is that right?"

"Sure. And I got big plans for us tonight. Interested?"

Birdie arched a blond eyebrow. "My friend Viv warned me about you, Jack Shepard."

"Viv?" he said, considering Birdie's bountiful curves—what he could see of them, anyway, on his side of the counter. "You mean Vivian Truby? The cocktail waitress at the Mayfair up the block?"

Birdie nodded. "She said she had a real good time with you, all right. But then after . . ." She shook her head. "You never called her again."

Jack worked his iron jaw. Dames never complained when they were with him. Why wasn't that enough?

"Tell you the truth, Birdie, I called Viv plenty. She just had the wrong idea about me."

"What do you mean?"

"I mean I'm a taxi, honey. I'll give you the best damn ride in the city. But you can't lock me up in your garage. Not with so many of you dolls needing my services around town. Just wouldn't be fair."

Birdie laughed so hard a few customers looked their way. "Jack, you're terrible!"

Jack shrugged his acre of shoulders. "Listen, honey, you want a proper boyfriend? Go find a nice church social, or better yet move to some little cornball town where the Alvins all buy you malteds and bore you to tears. But, honey, if you want a good time"—he threw her another wink—"you know where to find me."

By now, everyone in the building knew Jack's office was five floors up. He tipped his scarred chin north, just to remind her.

For a curious moment Birdie studied that dagger-shaped scar—a souvenir from his four hard years "over there" for Uncle Sam. Her gaze dropped down to the broad *T* of his shoulders, followed the line of his double-breasted as it tapered to his still-narrow waist. Finally her baby blues returned to the hard planes and angles of his nearly forty face.

"I'll think about it," she said, but the hot stare said something a whole lot more encouraging.

Jack almost smiled. Catching dames was no different than catching grifters. You just had to throw out your bait and wait. Birdie here was nearly ready to bite; she just wanted to be fed a few more lines. Jack was all set to oblige; then he'd reel her in with a nice, firm tug. He opened his mouth to make his play when the tug came to his coat sleeve instead.

"Hey, mister. You Jack Shepard?"

The voice was high-pitched, but it wasn't a dame. Jack turned on his stool to find a scruffy little runt standing behind him. The kid was young—eleven, twelve maybe. His freckled face could have used a good scrubbing. Ditto for his wrinkled clothes. And his shaggy brown hair was in sore need of a boot-camp razor. Jack recognized the kid from somewhere . . .

"You're a gumshoe, ain't you? You got an office right upstairs?"

"What's it to you, kid?"

"I need to hire a private dick. And you're as good as anybody. That's what my boss says."

"Your boss?" That was when the light dawned. This kid worked the corner, hawking headlines every afternoon.

"My boss is Mr. Dougherty," the kid said, pointing out the window. "He runs the corner newsstand."

"Sure, kid, I know Mac Dougherty. But I'm trying to get some lunch here." *Among other things . . .* "So do me a favor and shove off, okay? You can tell me to 'Read All About It' some other time."

Jack turned back to Birdie, but she'd disappeared on him. He glanced down the counter to find her five seats away, waiting on some salesman with a plastic grin and a dime-store tie. Jack cursed softly, stubbed out his cigarette.

"You got it all wrong, mister," the boy said.

"You still here?"

"I'm not trying to sell you a paper."

Not only did the kid fail to shove off, he climbed aboard the empty stool next door. "What's the big idea, junior? You're ruining a perfectly good lunch hour."

"I told you, Mr. Shepard. I want to hire you. It's a finder's job. Should be easy for someone like you. Mr. Dougherty said you used to be a copper. He said you was a war hero, too."

Jack looked away. "Gunning men down doesn't make you a hero, kid. Not in my book."

"I got money to pay, Mr. Shepard. It's not dirty or nothing, neither."

The kid gaped at Jack then, his big, brown eyes all puppy-dog expectant. Jack exhaled long and hard, drained his coffee cup, and set it down.

"Listen, son, I'm not in the business of finding lost poodles. Tack up some posters, maybe you'll get lucky."

"I didn't lose a dog, mister. What I lost was a person. She walked right out the door two weeks ago and never came back."

"Oh, yeah? And who would that be?"

"My mother."

# CHAPTER 1

## Final Destination

In the long run, we are all dead.

—John Maynard Keynes

**Quindicott, Rhode Island
June 9, present day**

"OH, NO. DON'T tell me . . ."

Since I'd crawled out of bed at seven this morning, I'd encountered setbacks galore: a stubbed toe, a misplaced wallet, a malfunctioning toaster, no milk for my son's cereal, and a kitty litter shortage. That was only the first hour.

Spencer was leaving for summer camp tomorrow and after I'd stuffed his clothes into our old washer, he told me about a list of things he was supposed to pack and didn't have. So I was off, shopping for a second pair of swim trunks, rubber flip-flops for the shared camp showers, and sunscreen with an SPF high enough to block a nuclear winter—not to mention the milk and kitty litter we'd just run short on.

(Until I got back, Bookmark had to make due with piddling on this week's *Quindicott Bulletin*, which was actually a pretty good use for it, considering the rumor-as-journalism philosophy of the town paper.)

Then Aunt Sadie called my cell to inform me the store

just got saddled with a triple shipment of stripper-turned-television-actress Zara Underwood's debut crime novel, *Bang, Bang, Baby*.

I knew the book was sailing on celebrity for most of the country. She received a huge advance, and there was a big, expensive publicity campaign with print and radio ads, but the review galley was written on the level of "See spot run." And since my customers actually liked to read the books they purchased, I figured we'd be lucky to sell five of the woman's books, let alone the eighty-four copies the publisher had shipped us mistakenly.

I raced back to the shop, and while Aunt Sadie rang up customers, I put together the cardboard dump (with the life-size standee of grinning "stripper-turned-actress-turned-writer" Underwood, who was practically wearing nothing but underwear), and then the store phone rang.

Soft-spoken shut-in Miss Timothea Todd was calling to politely inquire about her June 1 book delivery. It was now June 9, and my aunt felt so badly about the oversight that I'd agreed to do a quick, there-and-back run after our lunchtime business had died down.

*Quick* was the operative word until I'd hit the funeral cortege. Now I was trapped in my car watching a long parade of tiny black flags flutter on radio antennas behind a fully loaded hearse. Its final destination (pardon the pun) was the "Old Farm"—what we locals called Quindicott's nondenominational town cemetery, a manicured area of gentle Rhode Island hills situated between the central district and the secluded mansions of Larchmont Avenue.

The vast graveyard used to be part of the Montague family farm until the city forefathers bought the land one spring when a terrible fever ripped through the region and there were far too many dead for any one church to handle. (Seymour Tarnish, our shop's mailman and the local repository for all manner of trivia, insisted the phrase *bought the farm* actually originated in our little town with that plot purchase.)

Anyway, since Miss Todd lived on Larchmont, it was my destination—at the moment. I was well aware my *final* destination would be the Old Farm, too, since Quindicott's dead had been planted there for going on three centuries now.

I shifted in my car seat, watching the funeral party wind its way around a bend. All of the vehicles' headlights were on, a typical funeral procession tradition, but I hadn't noticed that fact until the caravan rolled under the dappled gray shadows of overhanging dogwoods. Funny, I thought, how something as bright as a headlight can be made to appear invisible by the glare of a sunny day . . .

As I contemplated tricks of light, beads of sweat formed on my neck and began trickling beneath my blouse. My black-framed glasses slipped down my slick nose. I pushed them back up. My Saturn was more than ten years old. Its air conditioner had sputtered into dysfunction last September, and I had yet to get it fixed.

I powered down the car's windows and tied my shoulder-length auburn hair into a ponytail. I was dressed for summer in flat leather sandals, beige capri pants, and a white sleeveless blouse, but now I was really beginning to bake. Sticking my head out the window, I longed for that fresh glass of Del's frozen lemonade Miss Todd would likely be whipping up for me, and considered passing the slow-mo procession.

Dogwood was a narrow route with the dark density of Montague's Woods on its left and the old graveyard's rustic, gray fieldstone fence on its right. There wasn't much of a shoulder on either side; and, unfortunately, the painted line running down the middle of the road's black tarred surface was solid yellow. This area was a no-passing zone.

But no one was coming toward me in the other lane (at least that I could see), and a quick glance in my rearview mirror told me there wasn't a police car around, either. In fact, there was no one behind me.

"Should I risk it?" I turned the wheel a fraction, ready to veer into the oncoming lane and put the hammer down. "Why not?"

*ARE YOU INSANE!*

The explosive masculine voice in my head was accompanied with a sudden decrease in the temperature of the warm car. The double whammy jolted me backward.

"Jack?" I called to the chilly blast of air. "Is that you?!"

*What do you think?*

"Where've you been all day?"

*With you, baby. Every step of the way. You've been blowing around Cornpone-cott at full speed so long you didn't notice.*

"It's Quindicott, Jack, not Cornpone-cott—and I was beginning to think you'd abandoned me . . ."

I once seriously considered therapy to sort out whether Jack was an actual ghost (i.e. spook, specter, spirit of a dead guy). I mean, a private detective named Jack Shepard was actually gunned down sixty years ago inside the bookshop my aunt Sadie and I now owned. Not long ago, a major mystery writer had revealed Jack's fate as a true-crime fact.

Still . . . I was the only one who ever heard the ghost, which sometimes made me question my sanity. I mean, add it up: I'd always been an admirer of the hard-boiled school of detective fiction. So Jack *could* be the equivalent of an "imaginary friend," created by my subconscious to help me (say) cope with life's relentless stresses. In that case, any shrink would probably just reduce Jack down to an alter ego with a fedora, ready to coach me through things my vulnerable self didn't think it could handle.

On the other hand, I had to wonder why my vulnerable self would use off-color language and slang so outdated I couldn't follow it. And if I really was a candidate for (as Jack once put it) "the cackle factory," would I even be able to rationally consider psychological options?

Tired of debating myself, I threw in the skeptical towel. There was, however, another key reason why I was determined to keep the dead gumshoe all to myself: my late husband's wealthy, well-connected family. Ever since my chronically depressed young husband had decided to stop taking his meds and instead take a stroll out the window of our New York high-rise, any hint of crazy from me was going to be enough for the McClures to put me away and ship Spencer off to boarding school (their original "suggestion" for me the summer after my husband killed himself).

That infuriating advice (more of a threat, really, if you knew the McClures) had been quite enough motivation for me to move Spence up here to my small Rhode Island hometown so we could both start over again. It was also more than enough reason to keep my mouth shut about Jack the PI ghost.

By now, I'd become quite fond of the ghost. We'd been through a lot together. His police and PI experience on the mean streets of New York had come in handy more than once. Even his supernatural chills turned out to be handy— particularly when riding around in a hot car with a broken air conditioner.

There was a downside to Jack, too, of course. His 1940s sensibilities weren't always, shall we say . . . *enlightened*?

"I'm glad to have you on board," I told the ghost. "I was beginning to think you'd stayed in the store to hang out in our new occult book section. I mean, given your own state, you might find some interesting reading."

*That hocus-pocus aisle is the last place I'd haunt. Have you seen some of the clientele it's bringing in? They've got more tattoos than a brace of Malay sailors. Some of them have pins sticking out of their ears, noses, lips, and a few other places your prim little eardrums wouldn't relish hearing about—*

"Excuse me, but—"

*For a second, I thought a tribe of New Guinea cannibals had come calling.*

"Oh, for goodness' sake! They're just college students, Jack! In a few years, their piercings will be gone and their tattoos will be covered up with button-downs and blazers. Some of them might even be scribbling PhD beside their names."

*In my experience, a few fancy letters behind some Alvin's name is like a vaccine against common sense.*

I shook my head and Jack fell silent for a few minutes.

The deep freeze had lessened into a pleasant coolness and the car's interior was much more comfortable now. Still, I frowned at the SUV bumper in front of me and checked my watch again. The funeral procession was moving with all the speed of maple tree sap.

A big, bronze vintage Harley blew by me in the opposite lane. Before I'd even caught a glimpse of Leo Rollins's shiny gold helmet, I would have recognized his uniquely customized engine by its odd high-low-pitched sound. Other than Leo, however, there was no one else. No other traffic was traveling back from Larchmont Avenue.

"If I floor the accelerator," I murmured, "I could pass this grim parade in about thirty seconds—"

*DON'T DO IT, SISTER!*

The ghost's angry blast of icy air had me shivering again. Now my goose bumps had goose bumps. "Jack! You're going to give me a heart attack!" I told the ghost. "Which means your little frights may just kill me quicker than an oncoming pickup!"

*There's nothing wrong with your heart, baby. But you'll flirt with a head-on collision over my dead body.*

"Very funny."

*What?*

"You're the first person I've ever heard say, 'Over my dead body,' who actually has a dead body."

*Listen, honey, you've been burning rubber all day. Until now, you haven't slowed down long enough to hear one word from me. So take a breather already.*

"But this is like watching paint dry. Can't you say something to the guest of honor in this parade to maybe get things moving a little faster?"

*You mean Mr. Room Temperature in the hearse up there? I've told you a hundred times, dollface, I can't talk to the dead. I'm just one of 'em.*

I sighed.

*Who is this Barney in a box anyway? You know him?*

"No. But I think this is the funeral announcement I read

about in this week's *Bulletin*." The Wolfe Construction bumper sticker on the last car in line had reminded me of the article.

"I'm pretty sure this is the guy who was electrocuted on a construction job. He was young, too, still in his twenties. A real tragedy."

I took a closer look at the SUV in front of me, more specifically at the back of the blond man behind the wheel, and realized it was Jim Wolfe himself driving. Just thirty-five years old and running his own construction company, Wolfe had won a number of bids on construction projects around our region. He wasn't a resident of Quindicott and he wasn't a reader, so Sadie and I never saw him in our bookstore, but he always said hello to us on the street. (It wasn't exactly a chore saying hello to James Wolfe. Aunt Sadie said he had the good looks of Ralph Meeker in *Kiss Me Deadly*. I thought he looked more like Kirk Douglas in *Out of the Past*, or even the *Vikings*—including the dimpled chin and the build to go with it.)

*So what's your big hurry, anyway?*

"I left Sadie alone at the store. And I'm trying to get Spencer off to summer camp, and . . ." I paused. "To be frank with you, Jack, I don't much *want* to stop and think today. I'm worried about Spencer going. He'll be gone for three whole weeks. And the last time I sent him to camp, well, you know how badly it went . . ."

*Relax, honey. The kid can take care of himself. He ain't the head case you sent off the last time.*

"I know he's better. He's been so happy this year at school. And he's been looking forward to this . . ."

*So it's all coming up roses, right?*

"Wrong. He's not even gone and I miss him already."

Jack went quiet a minute. Then across my cheek I felt a gentle wisp of cool air. *You're not alone, Penelope,* the ghost said softly. *You got Sadie. And you got me. I'll always be here when you need me.*

I smiled. "Thanks, Jack."

*Anyway, you're looking at this whole thing through a gloomy eye, instead of through a nice happy glass of cheap rye, as Curly the Bookie used to say.*

"You're going to have to translate that one."

*It's a good thing, Spencer going off to boot camp—*

"It's not the army, Jack, just cabins by a lake—"

*The boy needs a seventh-inning stretch is all I'm saying. And you do, too. A nice break from nagging the junior slugger about homework, taxiing the kid to and from Little League practice, and laundering his smelly gym shorts. No more of the kid sneaking out of bed to watch the all-night* Shield of Justice *marathon on the Intrigue Channel—*

"What?!"

*Uh . . . how about you strike that last comment from the record—*

"Wait until I get home—"

*Look, doll. All I'm saying is that you could use a break from the dull routine, too. Why don't you take me to the picture show, or better yet the races? I haven't seen the ponies trot in sixty years.*

I grunted, staring sullenly through the windshield. The scenery was passing by at a glacial pace.

*Where are we headed, anyway?*

"I have books to deliver to Miss Todd."

*That crazy old dame in the big house on Larchmont?*

"The same."

*Doesn't your auntie usually make that run?*

"She broke her glasses this morning and her spare pair has gone missing. Sadie doesn't feel confident enough to drive, even though she can see well enough without them."

*You're on the level there. Red bird's a real hawk-eye when it comes to spotting low-life grifters trying to snatch a tome—*

"Anyway, that's why I'm doing it. Miss Todd's a good customer and her delivery is over a week late."

*Why can't the old dame come down to the store and pick up her own books?*

"She never leaves her house. Hasn't for years, as far as I know. Except for Sadie's monthly visits to talk books, she has very little contact with the outside world. There's a cleaning service, and I understand most of her business is conducted through some law firm."

*Sounds like she's a little light in the head.*

"No, she's very sharp. She can be a little formal, but for someone with a reputation as a hermit, she's been awfully gracious to me and Sadie."

*Except for the wild hair, the nine-inch fingernails, and the fact that she hasn't bathed in years, she's a sweet old broad—*

I laughed. "Jack, you're terrible! She's not like that at all! In fact, she dresses better than me, always has her hair nicely done. She wears a lot of jewelry, too. Necklaces, rings, bracelets, earrings. Once she greeted Aunt Sadie wearing an elaborate silver crown. Sadie told me Miss Todd must have a thing for silver, because that's the only metal she'll wear."

*So what's this rich broad read then? I'll bet you even money it's little old lady mysteries:* Miss Petunia Finds a Body. Colonel Ketchup Kicks the Bucket. *Right?*

"Wrong. Miss Todd's a true-crime enthusiast. No murder is too grisly, no chain of events too disturbing."

*Sounds like she'd make a good morgue attendant.*

"Well, lately, she's widened her interest. After Aunt Sadie mentioned our new occult titles, the old woman began ordering books by the dozen. In fact, most of the titles Aunt Sadie boxed up for her today deal with psychic phenomenon, extrasensory perception, and a study on cross-cultural beliefs about the afterlife. Of course, I could save her the trouble of all that reading and just introduce her to you."

*Is that supposed to be a joke, dollface?*

We'd finally reached the entrance to the Quindicott Cemetery and the funeral procession veered off the main road.

"Thank goodness!"

The last of the vehicles rolled through the graveyard's open gates and I hit the gas. Feeling the breeze on my face again, I accelerated up Dogwood's long, slow grade until I was going nearly sixty.

I crested the high plateau and turned onto Larchmont. Unfortunately, I swerved straight into the sun's glare. For a few seconds, I was totally blinded. As I raised my hand to shield my eyes, a man's silhouette appeared framed by the brilliant light—right in front of my windshield.

"Oh, my God, I'm going to hit that man—"

*LOOK OUT, BABE!*

I slammed the brakes and cut the wheel at the same time. Both of my actions were too fast. I was thrown forward and my car began to fishtail on the pavement.

# CHAPTER 2

## *Hit and Run*

I looked at my face in the flawed mirror. It was me all
right. I had a strained look. I'd been living too fast.

—Philip Marlowe in *The Little Sister*,
Raymond Chandler, 1949

MOMENTUM PITCHED ME against the shoulder harness. My nose stopped short of merging with the steering
wheel and my vehicle simultaneously rotated, spinning me
around like a little girl on the Mad Hatter's teacups. I
swung left, then right, and back against the seat. Finally I
heard a disturbing *THUMP!* The car shuddered and came
to a halt.

In the eerie stillness that followed, I lifted a shaky hand to
shield my eyes from the sun. That awful *thump* was still
echoing through my system. Had I actually hit the man
who'd dashed out in front of me? Through the glare, I made
out a large figure rushing away. This time I saw the man for
more than a split second—and I recognized him.

"That's Seymour Tarnish!"

*Your letter carrier? The one who navigates an ice cream
truck in his spare time?*

I was about to call out, but the mailman was already
halfway through a gap in a low stone fence. A second later,

he melted into a thicket of trees. Before I lost sight of him, however, I'd spied a large, red blot on the back of his uniform's light blue shirt.

"A bloodstain," I whispered. "My God, I must have hit him!"

*Doubt it. If he was bleeding that badly, your postal pal would be flat on his back, not running as if a junkyard mutt were after him.*

In the quiet, my engine's purr sounded more like a menacing growl. I pushed up my black-framed glasses, unlocked my shoulder harness, popped the car door, and stepped out onto Larchmont Avenue.

This area of the town was situated at a higher elevation than the shopping district, allowing it to catch strong breezes, which often escaped Cranberry Street. Apart from the hot wind now whipping at my clothes and hair, however, there was no other movement or sound.

Thinking maybe a dog *had* chased my friend, I glanced around the neighborhood, but all I saw beneath the riotously swaying tree limbs were deserted streets and sidewalks. Not one resident even bothered to stick a head out a door or window at the sound of my screeching tires. Seymour was the only person I'd seen.

"So where was he going in such a hurry? And *why* was he going in such a hurry?"

*Maybe he's late for a liquid lunch. In my day, alkies moved like lightning when they needed their fix.*

"That can't be it, Jack. Ice cream's his fix. Seymour seldom drinks alcohol. I've certainly never seen him drunk."

I didn't know if it was the heat or the adrenaline, but I was beginning to feel queasy. The close call had shaken me. I checked the front bumper and tires. I found no dents, no scratches, no damage of any kind—and, thankfully, no blood, either. When I circled the car, I discovered the rear tire had skidded up against the concrete curb. That explained the thump I'd felt.

"I guess when the car fishtailed, I hit the sidewalk.

Doesn't look like any damage was done . . ." I opened the door and sat back down, clutching the steering wheel to steady my hand.

*Calm down, baby. You're in once piece.*

"So far . . ."

*Will you listen to me now and slow your motor already?*

"Okay, Jack. Okay . . ."

That's when my cell phone went off. I fished it out of my handbag. "Hello?"

"Pen. It's Bud—"

Bud Napp was the lanky widower currently dating my aunt. He also owned and operated Napp Hardware, and just the sound of his local twang made me feel better. Whatever he'd said *after* his name, however, was drowned out by the loud noise of heavy machinery.

"You'll have to speak up, Bud! Or turn off the machine you're using!"

The roar of a motor was the only reply. Suddenly the line went silent, and for a moment I thought I'd lost my connection.

"Pen! Can you hear me now?"

Actually, what Bud said was: "Can you *hee-ah* me *nowr*?"

(Having lived in *"N'yawk"* for years, I'd lost my Rhode Island accent some time ago. But a number of Quindicott's older residents still turned their *R*s into *Ah*s: "Pahk the *cah*." Replaced *W* with *R*: "*lahr* school." And generally pronounced certain phrases their own unique way: "Give me a *regla cawfee*." Of course not everyone in my home state could be heard using the local slang. Larchmont Avenue's tony residents, for instance, turned *R*s into *Ah*s about as often as they drove to Newport in dented, ten-year-old compacts with broken air conditioners.)

Anyway, I could finally hear Bud again. "You're coming through loud and clear," I assured him over my cell phone.

"I had to go in the john and shut the door to get some quiet!" he shouted.

"You don't have to yell anymore. What's going on? Where are you?"

"In my store. There's a (expletive deleted) of construction equipment parked on my sidewalk, blocking my loading dock, and even my front door. They're part of Jim Wolfe's crew working on the new sewage system."

"Tell them to move, for goodness' sake! Jim's a nice guy. Why would he do that to you?"

"I talked to Wolfe himself first thing this morning," Bud replied. "He apologized, but he said his hands are tied. He has to park some of his equipment on Cranberry to do the sewage job, and the town council gave him permission to park one place and one place only—in front of my hardware store!"

I sighed, rubbed my eyes. "By 'town council' I take it you really mean Marjorie Binder-Smith?"

"It's retaliation, Pen, pure and simple. That witch is trying to ruin my business because I'm running for her seat this November."

I couldn't disagree with Bud's assessment. The councilwoman Binder-Smith had done her level best to take the widower down, ever since he declared his intention to defend the small-business owners of Quindicott instead of sticking it to them with draconian parking regulations, littering fines, and ill-considered taxes. She began by targeting Bud's business through a legislative proposal called the "Binder-Smith Green Initiative."

On the face of it, the legislation sounded reasonable. I mean, everyone wants clean air, clean water, and clean sources of energy, and the woman's "Green Initiative" promised to deliver all of that in time. But when Bud read the fine print of Marjorie's legislation, he discovered that the councilwoman's "initiative" was placing a 10 percent surcharge on the sale of all "fossil fuel–powered lawn mowers, generators, heaters, and lanterns, as well as all propane gas and outdoor cooking and camping equipment." (Marjorie well knew that Bud Napp was Quindicott's only propane dealer and the town's first destination for outdoor cooking supplies, too.)

The *Quindicott Bulletin* fully supported these measures—actually, its longtime editor simply reprinted Marjorie's "press release" word for word. Thankfully, both proposals were ultimately defeated, mostly because Bud pointed out to the town's taxpaying consumers that they would be the ones hurt most by such legislation.

Bud also pointed out that Marjorie's primary rationale for the tax monies was to "discourage" the use of carbon-based products, and the money itself wasn't going directly toward alternative fuels, or planting trees, or anything specific. It was simply going into the city council's special slush fund to be used at the council's "study" of alternative energies.

Bud did a little *more* investigating and let the community know that this was the same "special slush fund" that the council had used for a junket to Marin County, California, the year before to "study solar energy at a national seminar." The seminar included trips to the local spa, and a tour of wine country in a rented luxury bus.

Bud pointed out that the carbon footprint for crossing the country on jet-fueled aircraft, not to mention tooling around in a gas-powered monster vehicle, was pretty major. In a self-distributed flyer (the *Quindicott Bullentin* refused to print Bud's findings, calling them "partisan"), Bud even revealed that the inn where the council members stayed included personal fireplaces in every room, and during their trip they'd had several gourmet dinners at an Italian restaurant with a wood-burning oven.

The political hypocrisy was off the charts. The town's citizens were furious. Bud became more visible, and even more popular with the locals.

Binder-Smith's initiatives also helped to forge an alliance between Bud Napp and his former business rival, Leo Rollins, owner of Rollins Electronics (and seller of gas-powered electric generators). Leo, the big, bearded Desert Storm vet, motorcyclist, and self-described loner, even joined the Quindicott Business Owners Association, an organization he'd shunned since he opened his store a few years ago.

"Apparently the councilwoman hasn't exhausted her bag of tricks," I said.

"I'm calling an emergency meeting of the Business Association," Bud declared. "When is your community event space available? I can't get anything but voice mail on your store's phone."

I chewed my lip, guessing that my aunt was too busy to answer. "That's a problem, Bud. The Yarn Spinners are meeting tonight—"

"Who?"

"The knitting-themed mystery enthusiasts. And Feline Friends are meeting on Wednesday."

"What? You're a pet store now?"

"They fancy cat mysteries."

"Okay. What about Thursday?"

"No good," I said. "We have an author signing, then the Culinary Cozy Crew meets, and Friday is the Hard-Boiled Buddies—those are the guys who read the gritty, alcoholic ex-cops-turned-private-investigators mysteries."

"Didn't that tough-guy reading group used to meet at the girly bar on the highway?"

"Yeah, they did. Until their wives found out."

Bud sighed. "Well, the weekend's no good. The store owners are too busy to meet on weekends. What about Monday?"

"We have the Seekers until nine or so. If you want, the Quibblers can meet after that, say ten or ten thirty."

"If we meet that late, we're sure to have a lot of no-shows. Who are these Seekers? Maybe you can convince them to reschedule or move their event."

"The Seekers are a new occult reading group, and this is their first ever meeting. I can't just kick them out."

In the background I heard the *beep, beep, beep*ing of heavy trucks backing up. "Okay, Pen. Monday at ten. I'll pass the word."

"I'm sorry about what's happening to you, Bud."

"Me, too, Pen. I thought we threw spiteful aristocrats the hell out of here two hundred years ago!"

Bud ended the call and I tucked the phone in my bag. "I really need some good news."

*The old girl might cheer you up.*

"Who?"

*The one you came all the way up here to see.*

"Oh, right! Miss Todd!" I threw the car into gear and started speeding away.

*Geez, Louise! Slow down, will ya?! You want to run over the milkman, too!*

Jack was right. I gritted my teeth and eased up on the gas.

*That's more like it . . .*

I rolled down Larchmont, the only moving vehicle in the exclusive neighborhood—the oldest and cheapest car, too, given the late-model Mercedes, BMWs, and sports coups parked in the half-moon driveways. No two dwellings looked the same on Larchmont and none of the homes was built later than the 1920s—mainly because once the Great Depression hit, no one in Quindicott could afford to build so lavishly again. Even today, they were occupied by the wealthiest residents in the area—lawyers, doctors, entrepreneurs, deans from nearby St. Francis College, and the children and grandchildren of those who'd inherited fortunes.

Despite the quiet luxury of manicured lawns and precisely pruned shrubbery, I sorely missed my Cranberry Street. The hustle and hum of life, albeit a hard-working one, was a much more appealing alternative to the stillness of this particular plot.

A few minutes later, I spotted our destination. "That's Miss Todd's mansion, up ahead." I nodded at the massive home on the high hill at the end of the development.

Though everyone referred to the Todd place by the catch-all term *mansion*, a more accurate term was "Second Empire mansard-style Victorian." (I'd picked up a few things about Victorian architecture from Fiona Finch, who ran the town's only bed-and-breakfast with her husband, Barney.)

Miss Todd's Second Empire was nowhere near as
cheery as the Finches' Queen Anne. It wasn't that the Todd
mansion was in disrepair. The place was in good enough
shape—although the overgrown grounds didn't appear to
be feeling the love from anyone. No, it was the overall
impression of Miss Todd's house that made me uneasy.

The Finches' Queen Anne began its welcoming impression with a wide, wooden wraparound porch. The colorful
flower boxes, stained-glass front door, and romantic corner
turret all extended the feeling of warmth and whimsy.

By contrast, Miss Todd's Victorian was a severe box of
cold gray stone. There were four floors total: a high attic
with dormer windows just under the mansard roof; a second
and third story with wrought-iron railed balconies; and a
grand first floor. The windows of the main floors were tall
and narrow, their stone arches overhanging the stingy plates
of glass like an old man's disapproving eyebrows.

The entire place appeared to be designed with off-putting
pretension. Take the cupola crowning the roof. I usually liked
cupolas. The doming tops of cathedrals always reminded me
of the top tier of a wedding cake. But the trapezoidal shape
of the cupola on the roof of this Victorian was an *Addams
Family* fright.

The worst detail was the decorative wrought iron, spiking
out of the roof's upper cornices like a punk rocker's
overgelled hair. Almost as bad, in my opinion, was the porch.

The Finches' wraparound veranda was as wide and
open as a grandmother's arms. The narrow deck of stone
on the Todd mansion appeared to be demanding refer-
ences. A pair of Ionic stone columns felt intimidating, and
the triangular gable that sat above them completed the sort
of formal, Greek Revival style one usually saw in government buildings. The effect was chilly and forbidding, a
theme echoed in the rusting, eight-foot fence built around
the perimeter of the large property.

Miss Todd's was the oldest house on Larchmont. Its
grounds were also the largest since it was built well away
from the rest of the neighborhood, the last home in the de-

velopment. Larchmont Avenue kept going after Miss Todd's place, wending its way down, down, down, the countryside, through a densely wooded area until it finally turned into Mill Run Road, and connected to a large highway, which led to Millstone, the next town over.

As we approached Miss Todd's drive, I took a closer look at the wrought-iron fencing around the property. The design in the fence always caught my eye—not because I liked it. The motif was one I'd never seen before or since: a continuous pattern of five-pointed stars, each with a fleur-de-lis in the center.

"You know, I've seen pentagrams before—especially in our occult book section. But I never saw one with a fleur-de-lis at its center. This is the only place I've ever seen that design."

*Oh, yeah? Well, I've seen it before.*

"You have? Where?"

*It's a long story, honey. Ask me when you have time to listen.*

Jack was right. I had books to deliver and errands to run, and I was already turning my car through the gated entrance to Miss Todd's mansion. The heavy iron doors were open wide, and I suspected they'd rusted in place. My car's tires bumped and rumbled up the cobblestones. I cut the engine and climbed out.

The wind was still strong, but it was a hot wind, offering little relief from the warm day. I redid my ponytail, securing the flyaway auburn strands. That was when I noticed the double doors at the front of the house standing wide open.

"I guess Timothea is expecting me."

Even as I said it, I found the sight of the open doors disturbing. But it was Jack who gave voice to my buried suspicions.

*Something's wrong, dollface. A dame who's got a phobia about going outside isn't about to leave her front doors like that.*

Deep inside I knew Jack was right. But a more shallow part of me wasn't in the mood to foresee gloom ahead.

"Maybe the house just got stuffy!" I chirped, electing to believe my sunny side. "It is awfully hot."

*Uh-huh. Sure you want to go in there?*

"Either that or I drove up here for nothing." I reached for the carton of books in the backseat, only to find they'd tumbled onto the floor. "Great."

*Leave the kindling. Keep your hands free.*

"For what?"

The ghost did not reply. With an exhale of frustration, I slung my bag over my shoulder and dropped my car keys into my pocket.

"Okay," I told the ghost, whether he was listening or not. "I'll come back for the books. But I'm sure nothing's wrong."

I reassessed that opinion a few moments later, after I passed through the towering Ionic columns of the formal front porch and discovered the mess inside the mansion's foyer.

*Not good, baby. Looks like signs of a struggle.*

Mail was scattered all over the hardwood floor, and a delicate little black-lacquered table had tumbled onto its side.

Nervous now, I remained outside and began ringing the doorbell. Its electronic buzz sounded from somewhere deep inside the massive house. I knocked loudly and called out: "Miss Todd!"

Silence.

"Jack?" I whispered.

*Go inside, honey, but be careful. Keep your peepers open.*

I took a deep breath and stepped over the threshold. "Miss Todd?" I called again.

My voice echoed back to me. I took another step, moving into the hallway. There was nobody on the staircase; nobody lying at the base of the steps, either.

"At least she didn't fall and break her neck," I murmured, recalling a terrible incident, not too long ago, involving an elderly Newport man.

I glanced into the dimly lit living room next, past the fireplace with the formal portrait of a heavyset man above it, past the Victorian clutter of dark wood furnishings, brass lamps, lace doilies, and knickknacks—and that was when I saw her.

Miss Timothea Todd was sprawled in the center of a plush, jewel-toned area rug. Crimson stained the bodice of her nightgown. Her hands, blanched almost as white as her gown, were covered with blood and still frozen into a position clutching at her throat. Bloody foam flecked the woman's pale, still lips, and her white hair seemed to be standing on end.

I stumbled backward. "My God, I think she's . . ."

*No thinking, baby. Look at her color. She's gone.*

I wanted to run, to flee, but I fought the urge, my fingers curling into hard fists. I took a breath and surveyed the scene. The most upsetting thing about Miss Todd's corpse was the obvious expression of stark fear on the dead woman's face. Her sightless eyes were wide and staring; her mouth twisted into a final, frozen scream.

"Look at her face, Jack," I whispered into the still room. "It's like . . . like . . ."

*Yeah, doll. It's like she's seen a ghost.*

# CHAPTER 3

## Cold Spot

Death tugs at my ear and says, "Live, I am coming."

—Oliver Wendell Holmes

I WAS NO stranger to the dearly departed. As a young widow I'd not only seen my share of death, I was beginning to consider myself a magnet for it. Certainly by now I'd witnessed more crime scenes than your average American single mom. So Jack's next piece of advice seemed almost unnecessary to me—if not a tad insulting.

*Scope the geography, but DO NOT touch a thing.*

"I know," I told the ghost. "You're not dealing with a rookie anymore."

*Don't get cocky, sister. And get out that Dick Tracy wrist radio of yours.*

"The wha— Oh! The cell phone!"

*Time to call Sheriff Cornpone and his Keystone Kops.*

"Right." I began fishing around my shoulder bag's less-than-organized interior.

*Your police chief's not exactly Boston Blackie, but he's the closest thing to the law you've got in this outpost.*

I shook my head at the sight of the poor woman, my eyes lingering on the blood, the horrible expression of dread frozen on her face.

"I can't imagine what Miss Todd experienced that terrified her so much . . ."

*I hate to bring up bad memories, baby. But being homi-
cided myself, I can tell you the business isn't a barrel of
laughs.*

"Right, Jack. Sorry."

*For what? You didn't plug me."*

That was when it happened. As my fingers closed around
the cell phone in my bag, a chill enveloped me. It was a sudden, disturbing sensation, and I knew one thing instantly:
This was *not* my ghost. No way. No how.

Jack Shepard's spirit, or aura, or whatever you wanted to
call his existence, fluctuated around me like a kind of energy
field. His typical "presence," for lack of a better word, felt
something like a pleasant spring breeze on a warm summer
day. It was always moving, swirling, or pulsing like a beating
heart. Jack felt like a field of *living* energy.

Sure, he occasionally blasted me with an arctic chill, but
it was always accompanied by an almost unconscious understanding of his mood. The cold I was experiencing now
felt totally dead, without sensation or communication, like
the lifeless chill of a coroner's morgue slab.

Whatever this was, it was disturbing. As soon as I felt
the anomaly, I cried out. My breath formed a little steamy
cloud, as if a New England winter had just descended inside the Second Empire's front parlor. I quickly moved
backward, toward the room's exit; and within a few yards,
the stifling heat of the June afternoon immediately returned.
Tentatively, I moved forward again and stretched out my
hand. Again I felt the cold air, as if I'd breached an invisible
curtain.

"Oh, my God, Jack. I don't know *what* or *who* this is—"

*Get out of here! NOW!*

Jack didn't have to tell me twice.

More than a little unnerved by the bizarre phenomenon—
not to mention poor Miss Todd's corpse—I waited until I was
outside before I made the call. But I didn't dial 911, or put a

call through directly to Chief Ciders office. Instead I called my friend Eddie Franzetti, *Deputy* Chief of the QPD.

Since I'd moved back to my hometown, Chief Ciders and I had clashed numerous times. At first, I thought the chief was nothing more than a tool of the small-minded town council, a body ruled by the manicured fist of Marjorie Binder-Smith, who had no love for me, my aunt, or our bookshop. But I'd since revised that opinion. Ciders's more recent animosity, I decided, was simply the result of my tendency to show up his police force.

Fortunately, Eddie Franzetti was different. Married with children, Eddie had escaped working in the family's pizza restaurant by joining Quindicott's finest instead. After a rocky start on the force, Eddie had helped me close a case or two. Consequently, when the Staties made him an offer, Ciders was forced to recognize his value and promote him to second-in-command.

Eddie was more than just deputy chief, however, he was also my late older brother's best friend. I was happy to call him my friend, too; and that was why, whenever I needed a cop, I called Eddie.

He answered on my second ring. "Pen! I know what you're calling about. I've been meaning to get to the store and pick up those Narnia books you're holding for my kids. I just haven't had the time—"

"This isn't about *my* business, Eddie. It's about yours," I interrupted. "There's trouble at Miss Timothea Todd's house. The address is 169 Larchmont—"

"I know where Miss Todd lives," he said, a note of irritation in his voice. "What's the problem this time?"

*This time?* Jack echoed in my head.

"She's dead," I told Eddie, ignoring Jack.

"Aww, no," Eddie said. "When?"

"When? I don't know. I just found her—"

*At least thirty minutes, but no more than three hours. That's my estimation by the look of the remains. Tell him.*

I did. "But, like I said, Eddie," I added, "I just found her. Listen . . . I think she was murdered."

"Are you there now?"

"Yes . . . I'm outside her house, in front of my car."

"Stay there, I'm on the way. And *do not* touch anything."

"I know! I'm not a rookie anymore, you know—"

Eddie hung up before I had a chance to ask about his previous encounters with Miss Todd. I closed the phone, shoved it into my shoulder bag, and thought again about that freezing curtain of air in Miss Todd's living room.

"There was definitely a cold spot in there," I told Jack. "In Miss Todd's house, I mean."

*Yeah? And?*

"And nothing. That's just what the phenomenon is called. I mean, according to those occult books in my store."

*It's a creaky old house. Could be all you felt was a draft.*

"You sure are changing your tune from a minute ago, when you ordered me to scram. Weren't you picking up anything? You know, like a psychic vibration of a fellow spirit?"

*I wanted you out of there for your own good. It's not too long a crap shoot that the murderer's still in that house.*

"Well, listen, okay. Unexplained cold spots are found in haunted places. *You're* a cold spot, for goodness' sake."

*Now ain't that a rotten apple to throw.*

Jack's irritation was easy to hear, *and* he got a whole lot colder. "You know, you have an awful lot of attitude for a ghost."

Wailing sirens cut off any reply from Jack. A few moments later, a Quindicott police cruiser was bouncing up the mansion's cobblestone drive, trailed by the volunteer fire department's ambulance. Jack noticed the ambulance the same moment I did.

*Your second meat wagon of the day.*

"Second?"

*What, you already forgot about that hearse train you ca-boosed onto?*

"Oh, yes." I closed my eyes, remembering the electro-cuted electrician, and took a breath. Death, death, and more death, I thought, then exhaled. "I'm really glad Eddie's here."

But when the cruiser stopped behind my compact, it was Chief Wade Ciders's bulky body that emerged from the passenger seat. His even bigger nephew, Deputy Bull McCoy, climbed out the driver's side.

"Where's Eddie Franzetti?!" I blurted out, rather undiplomatically.

Ciders's black boots clomped across the cobblestones until his giant shadow fell over me. He wasn't fat so much as large, with a broad nose, a jowly face, and a barrel chest that strained the shirt of his blue uniform.

The chief had been on the QPD going on thirty years now. He'd been happily married to the same bride for even longer. He had grown children and small grandchildren. But the pettiness of small-town law enforcement had taken its toll on the man (or at least that was my theory).

Decades of dealing with routine drunk and disorderlies, traffic accidents, and teen vandalism would have been enough to dull the edge of any gung-ho rookie. But Ciders's job as chief of police included years of butting heads with loud-mouthed City Hall bureaucrats, every one of whom had an opinion on how he should enforce the town's ordinances. By now, I could *almost* understand Ciders's knee-jerk reaction to any crime scene, serious or trivial: For him, it seemed to come down to how much time the confounded case was going to take away from his fishing trips and card games.

"I thought Eddie was coming," I said in a less hysterical tone.

Adjusting his ten-gallon chief's hat (the rest of the force had the regular flat-topped kind), Ciders regarded me. "I sent my deputy chief to fetch the *medicl 'xaminah*. Not that the management of my police *pahsonnel* is any of *yo-wah* business, Mrs. *McClu-wah*."

I winced. Here we go . . .

*Stiffen your spine, baby. This scowling speed-trap jockey has less than half your brains. And don't get me started on*

*his idiot nephew. That's who the big jerk is, right? Standing
there with that not-too-bright look on his face.*

"Yeah, Jack," I silently told him. Bull McCoy was essentially Chief Ciders's 2.0: a much bigger, much younger, much dumber version of the original model.

Ciders moved closer, until we were literally standing toe to toe. His grizzly-bear frame seemed to blot out the sun. "You said there was a body?"

"Inside." I pointed. "In the living room."

A pair of paramedics hurried past us, up the steps and across the entryway. They were followed by the stomping black boots of Bull McCoy, who entered Miss Todd's house with one fist closed on his gun butt. I felt like warning McCoy not to touch anything, but I bit my tongue, deciding that was Chief Ciders's job.

I looked up at the tower looming over me, and saw Ciders's suspicious frown. "You're pretty far away from your bookstore, Mrs. McClure. What were you doing at Miss Todd's residence?"

I told him about the book order and pointed to the box in the backseat. I explained that Miss Todd's front doors were wide open when I arrived and no one answered the door, even after I rang.

"That's when I went inside and found Miss Todd on the floor in the living room."

"Did you go upstairs?"

I shook my head.

"Did you see anything unusual on Larchmont?"

"Nothing," I said immediately.

"Nothing? Not one thing? Not one *person*. Think, Mrs. McClure. You're usually pretty observant," he said, "if not overly so."

Those last few words were muttered with naked condescension. I bristled, and Jack warned: *Steady, baby. Just answer the man's questions.*

"There was *one* thing," I told the chief. "Uh, I mean, person. I saw one person on the street."

The chief's bushy gray brows drew together over eyes the color of acid-washed denim. "Who?" he asked.

"Seymour Tarnish. He sort of ran across the street, right in front of my car. The sun blinded me for a few seconds, and I nearly hit him."

"But you didn't hit him?"

"No. I stopped just in time."

"So you saw Seymour, eh? And he was in some big hurry for no particular reason? Is that what he told you?"

I frowned. "Seymour didn't tell me anything. He didn't stop to talk."

"Sounds to me like he was fleeing the scene."

"Scene? What are you taking about? I didn't say he came from this crime scene. He was just in a hurry to cross the street for some reason. He *must* have been in a hurry, because he didn't stop."

"Uh-huh. Describe his appearance for me, Mrs. McClure. Tell me exactly what you saw. You claim you're observant. Prove it."

"I just caught a glimpse of him, really. He was wearing his blue postal uniform."

"Slacks or shorts?"

"Shorts."

"What kind of socks?"

"White tube."

"Anything else you can remember? Think."

I shook my head. "Just the stain . . ."

"What stain?"

"A red stain on the back of Seymour's uniform. I was worried for a minute that I'd hit him with my car. But then I realized he wasn't hurt, because if he was really that badly hurt he wouldn't have been able to rush off the way he did."

Ciders shook his head. "Let me get this straight. You saw a bloodstained man fleeing the scene of a crime, and you don't think there's anything to report?" The chief almost laughed in my face. "That's the best you can do, Mrs. Mc-Clure? *You*, with your bookshop full of fantasy detectives!"

"But Chief!"

"What?"

"Seymour Tarnish would *never* murder a poor, defenseless, little old lady! Seymour Tarnish wouldn't hurt a fly!"

A grunt sounded behind me. Without looking, I instantly knew Bull McCoy had come back outside.

"You lookin' at Tarnish for this, Uncle Wade—I mean, Chief?"

There was boisterous anticipation in Bull's tone, if not outright glee. Sure enough, I turned to find the giant in a uniform smiling. Bull never could stand Seymour, and the feeling was mutual.

"Pick him up, Bull," Ciders said. *"Now."*

"Chief Ciders, please don't do that!" I begged. "I'm sure you're jumping to the wrong—"

*Stop, baby!* Jack boomed in my head. *Take a breath.*

My fists clenched. "Why?!" I asked the ghost.

*Because you should let the big lummox bring in your pal, that's why. Maybe the letter carrier saw something you didn't. Can't be any harm in asking him to answer a few simple questions, can there?*

I exhaled, inhaled, exhaled. "No," I silently told Jack. "I guess a few simple questions can't hurt."

*For once, doll, I'm actually in agreement with Chief Cornpone.*

"About Seymour?"

*Admit it, honey. Isn't there some small part of you that's dying to ask the mailman how he got that red stain on the back of his blue shirt?*

"Maybe," I told the ghost. "But there's a much bigger part of me that's afraid of hearing his answer."

# CHAPTER 4

## The Chief's Suspect

You stand for your side of it and I'll stand for mine.
I didn't do it, and that's all I stand for.

—Frank Chambers, lying to the DA in
*The Postman Always Rings Twice*,
James M. Cain, 1934

FIFTEEN MINUTES LATER, Bull delivered my mailman to the Todd mansion. Chief Ciders escorted Seymour inside, sat him down, and started asking him those "few simple questions."

"Why'd you do it, Tarnish? Why'd you murder the old lady?"

Seymour leaped out of his chair. "Are you crazy?! I didn't murder anybody!"

I gritted my teeth. Sunlight was streaming in through Miss Todd's tall dining room windows. Ciders had opened them wide to air out the room, and a hot breeze was now making the sheer curtains billow violently. As far as I could see from my seat in the corner, an even larger amount of hot air was being produced by the humans in the room.

Seymour wagged his finger in the chief's face. "And another thing. I demand you return my uniform!" (Under Ciders's orders, Bull had already dragged Seymour into the kitchen and forcibly removed his shirt and shorts.) "That uniform is property of the Postmaster General of the U. S. of A.! And in case you need a refresher course in civics, the federal government supersedes your puny jurisdiction!"

"Sit down!"

For a few tense moments, Seymour refused to heed Ciders's command. I didn't think that was such a good idea. For one thing, Ciders was bigger than Seymour. Not that Seymour was a little guy. He was actually on the beefy side with heavy arms and a moderate belly (per his ice cream addiction) on top of sinewy chicken legs and bony knees (from his hikes carrying mail every day). At the moment, however, with Seymour's postal uniform impounded as evidence, he was dressed in nothing but his undershirt, a pair of Superman boxers, white tube socks, and black sneakers. Ciders, on the other hand, was packing a service weapon with (presumably) live ammo.

"I said, *sit down*!" the chief barked again. "Or I'll have you hauled off and booked right now!"

Ciders's voice was so loud it actually rattled the substantial collection of crystal displayed in Miss Todd's colossal china cabinet. I knew this because my chair was located right next to the mahogany showpiece.

Decibel level aside, I was seriously upset with Ciders's treatment of Seymour. Not only was it brutish, I didn't find it at all helpful to the investigation. I was also eager to question Seymour myself, but I knew Ciders well by now. If I made any trouble, he'd banish me from the house. The only reason I was allowed to watch this interrogation at all was to "finger" Seymour for the chief: Ciders told me that if he ran into trouble getting Seymour to "talk," he intended to use my "witness statement" to pressure the mailman into "confessing."

Of course, I had no intention of incriminating my friend. So I simply sat quietly in the corner, attempting to melt into the flocked and flowered Victorian wallpaper. (The entire dining room set appeared to be Victorian era. I was no antiques expert, but the heavy, carved, painstakingly polished pieces looked quite expensive to me. Miss Todd was certainly leaving behind a small fortune in this grand house and its contents.)

"You've got to believe me, Ciders," Seymour went on. "I didn't kill anybody. I didn't even know Miss Todd was dead until Deputy Dawg over here snatched me up and tossed me into his Batmobile."

"Deputy Dawg. Real funny, Tarnish." But Bull wasn't laughing. He was glaring. Then he was crossing his overly muscled arms and flexing his bowling-ball biceps, which I suspected contained more brain cells than his actual brain pan.

"Look, we know you did it," Ciders stated.

"Yeah, Tarnish," Bull added after a substantial lag. "So why don't you just 'fess up and make it easy on yourself?"

"'Fess up?" Seymour repeated. "Interesting interrogation technique, Bull. Where'd you learn it? The Disney Channel?"

The hulking deputy stared daggers at Seymour, obviously straining—and failing—to produce a retort. With an exhale of disgust, Seymour shifted his gaze to Quindicott's chief of police.

"I'd like to lawyer up now."

Ciders blinked, surprised. "Who's your lawyer?"

"I don't have one."

Ciders's jaw worked. "I liked it better when you were threatening to report me to the Postmaster General."

I silently groaned. "Are you listening to this, Jack?"

*I'm with you, doll. Don't panic.*

"I'm not panicking," I told the ghost. "I'm just frustrated with the chief. His 'interrogation' is going nowhere."

Seymour tried to rise again, but Bull McCoy stepped up and pushed him back into the chair. "Didn't you hear the chief? Sit!"

"Check your gorilla, Ciders," Seymour snapped. "I didn't do *anything* wrong, so I don't have to take any brutality from Barney Fife on steroids over here."

"He isn't hurting you, Tarnish."

"Says who? In my opinion, being in Bull's presence is cruel and unusual punishment."

"Stop ducking my questions," Ciders said. "We've already determined you were in this house earlier today. You're Miss Todd's mailman, and the mail was delivered, which means you were probably the last person to see Miss Todd alive."

"I was here, but I didn't see Timothea. Not today," Seymour insisted.

Ciders bent down until his broad nose was an inch from Seymour's. "Did the old lady piss you off, Tarnish? Did she complain about lousy mail delivery, maybe?"

Seymour shook his head. "Miss Todd was a nice person. She never complained about anything—"

"Did the struggle begin in the foyer? Why did you drag Miss Todd into the living room? So no one could see you while you strangled her to death?"

Seymour's eyes bulged. "You're crazy, Chief. I didn't do a thing to Miss Todd. You've got to believe me!"

"Explain the bloodstain on your uniform then," Ciders barked.

"I told you already," Seymour said. "I told you *ten* times. That's not a bloodstain!"

Ciders folded his arms. "It's clear to me the initial altercation broke out in the foyer."

*Not to me.*

"What?" I asked Jack. "You don't think the altercation began in the foyer?"

*No. I'm not so sure there ever was an altercation in the foyer.*

"I don't understand. You saw the mess. The mail was everywhere and that little antique table was knocked over."

*But there was no blood in the foyer or on the floor leading to Miss Todd. There was no blood anywhere but on the corpse itself. Meanwhile, look at that open window, doll. See the curtains? See the way they're blowin' around in the wind?*

"Yeah, it's blustery today—" I closed my eyes. "Oh, God. The wind."

*It's possible there was no struggle. Don't you remember what you did before you went in the house?*

"I retied my ponytail."

*Because the wind was so strong.*

"Right."

*Well, if the door latch didn't click properly, a strong gust could have blown the old lady's doors in, knocked down the mail, and overturned the little table.*

"But why wouldn't Miss Todd have latched her doors properly? Unless . . . maybe the killer was leaving in a hurry and didn't close the doors all the way—"

Just then I heard a door close, a car door. I rose up, hoping to catch a glimpse of Eddie and the medical examiner, but it was just two more of Ciders's regulars. With a sigh of disappointment, I sat back down.

"Okay, Tarnish. Let's change the subject," Ciders declared. "Tell us what you were doing last Tuesday night."

Seymour blinked. "Huh? What night?"

"Last Tuesday," Ciders said. "On most weeknights, your ice cream truck's parked down at Quindicott Pond. But for some reason, you weren't there last Tuesday."

"Wow," I whispered to Jack. "Guess I haven't been giving Chief Ciders enough credit for his powers of observation."

Jack laughed; his cool aura fluctuated colder for a moment. *I wouldn't jump to that conclusion so quick, doll.*

Gaping, Seymour looked impressed, too. "How do you even *know* that?" he asked the chief.

Ciders shrugged. "My two granddaughters wanted ice cream cones. You weren't there. It ticked me off."

"Let me guess why you were ticked," Seymour said. "You had to drive all the way up to Cold Stone Creamery on the main highway. Well, boo-hoo."

I rolled my eyes. So much for Ciders's powers of observation.

"Where were you, Tarnish?" Ciders barked.

"I took the night off, okay? So what?"

Ciders glanced at Bull. "You tell him."

Seymour smirked. "Tell me what?"

"Funny thing happened that very night. We got a call from

Miss Todd. She wanted us to investigate strange noises." Bull put air quotes around the words *strange noises*.

"What's that supposed to mean?" Seymour said, imitating the air quotes.

"It *means* the old lady probably heard someone trying to break into her house," Bull replied. "That's what it"— (air quotes again)—"means!"

Ciders rubbed his jowly jawline. "My men did a routine investigation. They didn't come up with anything, but it seems pretty clear that someone was harassing Miss Todd. She reported 'strange noises' again a number of nights after that first report. Since her doors and windows never showed any attempt at forced entry, I figured it was just pranksters— local teenage crap. But seeing what you did to Miss Todd, I'm thinking there was a pattern here."

"What *pattern*?" Seymour threw up his hands. "And how the heck did you find a way to shoehorn me into it?"

"You're sitting here without a solid alibi for why you weren't working your ice cream truck last Tuesday."

"Oh, for pity's sake. I *have* an alibi! The brakes on my truck were on the fritz! Cost nearly a grand to get them fixed, too. Call Patrick Scotch at Scotch Brothers Motors if you don't believe me. It was Paddy who did the scalping."

Ciders shook his head. "Miss Todd made a number of noise complaints, all of them at night. I think it might prove interesting to match the dates of those calls against the receipts from your ice cream truck."

"Oh, you'd love that, wouldn't you?" Seymour replied. "Prying into my private life like jackbooted fascists!"

In a disturbing coincidence of timing, the *clomp-clomp-clomp* of heavy boots sounded in the foyer. Eddie Franzetti entered the dining room a moment later, wearing his perfectly pressed blue uniform.

Eddie was more compact than Bull. He had a runner's physique with leaner muscles and a smaller stature, but his expression was light-years sharper. Under his flat-topped cop's hat, he had a thick head of black hair, like all the

Franzettis. His complexion always appeared lightly tanned, even in the winter. And when he walked in the room his big, long-lashed, cow-brown eyes (the ones that made all the girls swoon in high school, including the girl he married) surveyed the room in a microsecond. The first thing he did was nod to me. I silently waved back.

Ciders appeared to notice Franzetti's arrival and the fact that I was still in the room at the same time. His face darkened when he glanced at me. Then he directed his words to his deputy chief.

"Where the hell have you been?"

Eddie shrugged. "You told me to find the medical examiner. The man was out of cell phone range, so I had to track him down. It didn't take me two guesses to figure out where to find Dr. Rubino."

"At Mullet Point," Ciders said.

Eddie nodded. "He's going for your fishing championship title, for sure."

Ciders waved that comment aside. "So where's the good doctor now?"

"In the living room with the victim. He's already begun his examination," Eddie said.

The chief pulled out a handkerchief and dabbed the sweat off his neck. "Do you have an evidence bag, Franzetti?"

Eddie put his hands on his hips. "Sure, Chief, in my car."

"Get it. Seymour's clothes are on the kitchen table and there's blood all over them. I want you to bag them up for the state forensics team."

Eddie ducked out to his car, came back in, and crossed to the kitchen. He glanced at me again on the way. I nodded again but continued to keep my mouth shut. My mind, however, was still working.

"Jack," I whispered to the ghost, "do you really think Ciders can pin this on Seymour?"

*If he can, he will, and he's not about to lose sleep over it, either. In case you haven't noticed, your postal pal ain't so popular with the local law enforcement.*

"There's got to be something we can do."

*Sure, baby. Put your palms together and pray for a miracle.*

Eddie emerged from the kitchen a few seconds later, holding up Seymour's shirt. The red stain was impossible to miss.

"Hey, Chief, we got a problem."

Ciders scowled at Eddie when he saw the uniform. "I thought I told you to bag that up!"

"But, Chief, I don't see why. There's no blood."

Ciders's bushy eyebrows leaped north. "What?"

"There's a big red stain, all right, but it isn't blood—"

"I tried to tell you, Ciders!" Seymour said triumphantly.

Bull pointed a finger. "Shut up, mailman!"

Ciders stepped up to Eddie. "Since when did you become a forensics expert?"

Eddie rolled his eyes. "I don't have to be a forensics expert to recognize my own family's pizza sauce!"

# CHAPTER 5

## The Postman and His Second Slice

Do you realize what you've done? . . . You, with your sloppy mass of misinformation, your atrocious taste, and your idiotic guesswork?!

—"It's So Peaceful in the Country," William Brandon, *Black Mask* magazine, November 1943

CHIEF CIDERS SNATCHED the shirt from Eddie's hand and put the cloth to his nose. With a grunt he turned to glare at Bull McCoy.

"I thought you said these clothes were covered in blood!"

"It . . . It looked like blood to me—" Bull said.

"It reeks of garlic and oregano, you knucklehead!"

"Sheesh, Uncle Wade! You didn't expect me to actually *sniff* it, did you?"

Seymour stepped forward. "Can I have my clothes back now?"

"No," the chief said. "They're still going to the state's forensics people. If there's any blood, fibers, or anything whatsoever incriminating on here, they'll pick it up, and I'll want to know about it."

Ciders shoved the shirt back at Eddie, who shrugged and stuffed it into a plastic evidence bag.

"Damn pizza stains," Seymour muttered, folding his arms. "That uniform's ruined anyway."

"Wash them in white vinegar and cold water," Eddie suggested. "Works every time."

Ciders shot his second-in-command a nasty look. "You a law enforcement officer or a spaghetti bender?"

"Family traditions die hard. Here, Seymour, I had these in my trunk." Eddie tossed the mailman a pair of navy running shorts and an extra-large white T-shirt with HOT PIZZA! emblazoned on the front and WE DELIVER! on the back along with the phone number of his family's restaurant.

Seymour stuffed his chicken legs into the running shorts. They looked pretty tight over his boxers, even with the elastic band, but he didn't have much choice in attire at the moment. He pulled the T-shirt on next. Then he pointed to Ciders.

"Listen up, Chief. I don't have a lawyer yet, but I'm going to hire one. A *civil rights* attorney who's gonna sue you and this whole stinking town for false arrest!"

Seymour started for the door. Ciders blocked his exit.

"Where do you think you're going, Tarnish?"

"Leaving!"

"You're not going anywhere," the chief said. "You're not out of hot water yet."

"Oh, yes, I am."

Seymour stepped to the right. So did the chief. He stepped to his left. The chief followed. I knew this dance wasn't going to go on much longer. For one thing, Bull's fingers were moving toward his nightstick.

"Crap," I muttered, feeling guilty for getting Seymour into this mess. Then I launched myself between the two angry men.

"Stop it right now!" I cried.

*Baby, are you nuts?!*

"You're both acting like children!" I added, ignoring the ghost.

I pushed at Ciders, but it was my flat leather sandals that went skidding across the polished hardwood. Then Seymour charged and I was shoved in the opposite direction. Before I knew it, I was pressed against Chief Ciders's chest, his cold badge digging into my cheek. Somewhere in my head, I heard the ghost cursing.

*What do you think you're doing, sister?! Get the hell outta there!*

"That's enough, guys! Break it up!" I yelled.

The men finally broke their clinch so suddenly I nearly dropped to the hardwood. Ciders reached out to steady me. Meanwhile, to my surprise, Seymour turned his rage on me.

"Don't think I'm going to forgive you, either, Pen! You're the rat fink who fingered me! Bull told me. Making up a crazy story about how I was covered in blood. You should be ashamed of yourself!"

*Aw, blow it out your mailbag, you stupid—*

"How could I know what you were covered in, Seymour! You didn't even stop after I almost ran you down. You just took off! Why did you run away?"

Seymour blinked at my question. "It . . . It was that darn pizza," he said, the bluster going out of him. "I brought four slices up to the mansion today. Two for me, two for Miss Todd."

"You brought lunch for her?" I locked eyes with Seymour. "Just how well did you know Miss Todd?"

He shrugged. "Pretty well now. I've been delivering her mail for a decade. At first I never saw her. Then one day, a few years back, I delivered something she had to sign for. Miss Todd answered the door with a book in her hand, and we got to talking about it."

"What book?" Ciders demanded.

Seymour swallowed hard. "*The Boston Strangler*."

Ciders narrowed his eyes on Seymour. "Didn't the Boston Strangler break into homes and *kill* old women?"

"Yeah," Bull said. "The Boston Strangler killed a whole *bunch* of women, Chief. Tony Curtis didn't even know he was the strangler until Henry Fonda hypnotized him. I saw it in the movie. He was like some kind of split personality." Bull lowered his voice and sidled up to his uncle. "Maybe

Tarnish here's got a split personality, too. Did you think of that? Maybe that's why he can't remember killing the old lady!"

*Oh, brother,* Jack said.

"Oh, jeez," Eddie muttered.

Ciders rolled his eyes. "That's enough, Bull."

I stepped closer to Seymour. "Tell us more."

*That's it, baby. Get some useful information out of him. 'Cause Chief Cornpone here sure can't.*

"Tell you more about what?" Seymour said. "I don't understand."

"You were saying that Miss Todd talked about books with you," I said. "How often did you two chat?"

He shrugged. "Two or three times a week. Sometimes we'd have lunch together. We traded books, too. She was a very nice person." Seymour shook his head. "I'm really sorry to see her gone. I'm going to miss her."

"But what happened today?" I pressed.

Seymour sighed. "When Miss Todd didn't answer the door, I let myself in and put the mail on the table in the foyer and left. I figured she was sleeping late or something. She did that sometimes when she stayed up late to see an old movie on cable."

"You said you let yourself in?" I pressed. "So she left the door unlocked?"

Seymour nodded. "She has a mailbox by the front gate, but she doesn't like to walk down the drive. So as a favor, I always take the mail to her door. She's usually there to answer, but she told me that if she ever doesn't answer, I was supposed to just set the mail on the foyer table for her. Frankly, I never bought the reason she gave me for not answering the door."

"What do you mean?"

"I mean she told me that she couldn't always hear the doorbell and that's why I was supposed to leave the mail without seeing her, but . . ." Seymour shrugged. "I just think that some days Miss Todd wanted company and some days she didn't. On the days she didn't, she'd just leave the door open and ignore the bell. No big deal."

"When you opened the door and stepped inside, did you hear anything in the house?" I asked. "Did you see anyone at all in the vicinity?"

Seymour shook his head. "No. And that's nothing new. Larchmont's like a ghost town when I deliver the mail in the late morning. The hotshots are already at work, their kids are either in school or at some exclusive horsey summer camp, and the ladies who lunch don't exactly do their own yard work. Sometimes I'll see a maid or a gardener, but there wasn't anyone on the street during my rounds today."

"So what happened after you left Miss Todd's house?"

Seymour scratched his head. "Well, I didn't leave right away. I was really hungry by then, and that delicious pizza smell was driving me nuts, so I sat down under that big oak tree in her front yard and ate my lunch. And then I ate the cheese off of one of Miss Todd's slices—waste not, want not, right?"

"You said you were really hungry?"

"Starving."

"Then you must have been in a hurry to eat, right?"

"Right."

"Were you in enough of a hurry to neglect latching Miss Todd's door properly?"

Seymour closed his eyes. "Oh, damn. I did that once before."

"Okay, so that's why the doors were opened. The wind must have blown them in and knocked down the mail and overturned the little table."

"That's a stretch, Mrs. McClure," Ciders said.

*Tell him, doll.*

"There wasn't any blood in the foyer—not on the mail or the floor leading up to the corpse. So the 'signs' of a struggle are suspect if there's another explanation, right? Wouldn't a defense attorney argue that?"

Ciders scowled. "You're reaching."

I turned back to Seymour. "What happened after you ate your lunch?"

"I was full and it was a hot day," Seymour said. "I kind of nodded off. When a squirrel ran across my chest, I finally woke up."

"And that sauce on your uniform?" Eddie prompted.

"The squirrel spooked me, and I rolled over Miss Todd's two slices. Got the sauce all over me. But that isn't why I was running—"

Bull McCoy snorted. "What? You're afraid of squirrels?"

"When I woke up, I realized I was late making the rest of my deliveries. Real late. Last month, I got slapped with a reprimand, and I didn't need another one on my record."

Seymour looked at his Wonder Woman watch, then openly glared at Bull McCoy. "I'm *still* not done with my deliveries, thanks to Deputy Dawg here."

Bull's face flushed. "Watch your mouth—"

Seymour smirked. "Bite me, Bull!"

Bull stepped forward—and suddenly there I was again, mashed between two angry men. This time the ghost wasn't cursing. He was laughing.

"You're not helping, Jack!"

*Oh, yeah? Watch this—*

A brisk, cold breeze suddenly banged the dining room window so hard the two men started. I heard another bang and realized Jack had blown in the front doors, too. (Nothing like making your point!)

"Calm down!" I shouted, taking advantage of the momentary surprise. I pushed against them until I held the two at arm's length. "You have to get a grip, Seymour." Then I shifted my gaze to Bull McCoy and Chief Ciders. "And you both know Seymour's innocent. Why don't you let him go?"

Chief Ciders shook his head. "Pizza sauce or no pizza sauce, he's still my prime suspect in this murder—"

"Sorry, Chief, but I don't think so."

The deep voice that interrupted was new to the gathering.

All eyes shifted to the doorway, where Dr. Randall Rubino was now standing.

A divorced Bostonian, Rubino had moved to Newport to start his life over. A few months back, he'd agreed to remain on-call for Ciders whenever the town of Quindicott needed an official medical ruling on a death. Then just a few weeks ago, Rubino decided to make another move—to Quindicott itself. Now he lived on the other end of Larchmont Avenue, where he was preparing to take over the practice of our local GP, who was retiring to the Florida Keys in another month.

Rubino wasn't anything like the town's longtime physician, a short, lean, balding sixty-eight-year-old. The young doctor was more like one of those physicians you saw on the daytime soaps—tall, fortyish, with darkly handsome features and a toothpaste-commercial smile. Between his good looks and impressive profession, he'd become a pretty popular guy with some of the locals (most of them female).

Today Dr. Rubino was dressed in wrinkled, salt-stained khakis and scuffed deck shoes. The man had a private boat and a passion for fishing, so I wasn't surprised when Eddie mentioned picking him up at Mullet Point, which had some of the best ocean fishing in the state. Rubino's tanned face had just the right amount of weathering, and his wavy brown hair had been raked by the wind.

*Whoa*, I thought, *the man even smells like the sea.*

*You mean he reeks of fish?*

"Easy, Jack. Don't go getting jealous on me."

Jack grunted—and got a whole lot colder. With a little shiver, I rubbed my bare arms.

The chief turned to Rubino. "Okay, Doctor, I'm listening. Explain what you mean."

"I mean Miss Todd wasn't murdered."

"Go on," Ciders said.

"It's simple," Rubino said. "Miss Todd died of natural causes, not foul play. In my opinion she suffered a massive and instantly fatal cerebral hemorrhage. I can't be certain, of course, until I conduct an autopsy, but—"

"What about the blood?" Ciders broke in. "The victim was covered with it. Blood was all over the place."

"Well, it was a *hemorrhage*, Chief, and that means there's bound to be some blood. When the vein in her neck ruptured, Miss Todd started to bleed from her nose and ears. This is not an uncommon occurrence."

*You notice Doc Heartthrob still isn't saying what caused the old dame to pop a pipe.*

"You're right!" I told Jack—but it was Rubino who answered.

"What's that, Mrs. McClure? You agree?"

"Uh . . ." I stared at the man. "Did I say that out loud?"

Dr. Rubino frowned. "Say what?"

Now everyone turned to stare at me. "Actually, Doctor, I have a few questions."

*Atta girl, Baby Ruth. Swing away.*

"What questions do you have, Mrs. McClure?" The tone was mildly patronizing. I pressed on.

"The expression on Miss Todd's face," I said. "She appeared to be positively *terrified*."

"You would be, too, if you felt a twinge in your neck and blood began to pour from your nose and mouth. You must understand that Miss Todd suffered a sudden, terrible trauma before she died."

I thought of that cold spot and the strange noises she'd reported. "But there could have been something else that may have frightened her, right?"

The doctor folded his arms. "The only explanation I can offer for her frightful expression is medical."

"I have a question," Ciders said, glancing at me, then back to the doctor. "We've had several complaints from the deceased in recent weeks. Miss Todd claimed she heard noises inside and outside her home."

*Thank you, Chief!* I thought.

"I see," Rubino said. "And did you find the source of these noises?"

Ciders shook his head.

"Well then, Miss Todd was probably suffering from some

form of mild dementia," Rubino replied. "She was quite old and very reclusive. On top of that, I doubt she'd had a medical checkup or a psychological evaluation in decades."

"Not everyone gets a psychological evaluation as a matter of course," I noted.

Rubino nodded. "True, but living alone like this . . . her physician probably would have ordered one. She could have been experiencing paranoia. Delusions. The onset of audio hallucinations—"

*Audio hallucinations!* Jack laughed. *Hear that, doll? That's what you thought I was!*

"Excuse me," Seymour interrupted. "But Miss Todd wasn't suffering from any sort of delusions, audio or otherwise. I spoke with her nearly every day."

"And I spoke with her over the phone earlier today," I added. "She sounded perfectly normal to me."

"Selective observations are far from conclusive," Dr. Rubino said. "Neither of you are medical professionals."

"But still . . ." I paused. "Don't you think it's at least remotely *possible* that Miss Todd was frightened to death?"

Dr. Rubino gave the notion about two seconds' worth of consideration before laughing out loud.

I shifted with embarrassment.

*You got nothing to be embarrassed about, baby. You asked a question. You deserve an answer. So tell him!*

Jack was right. I cleared my throat—loudly. "Isn't it true, Doctor, that under certain circumstances strong emotions like fear or stress can initiate the onset of a stroke, a heart attack, or a hemorrhage?"

Ciders stared expectantly at the doctor and so did everyone else in the room. Now it was Dr. Rubino's turn to shift uncomfortably.

"It's possible, Mrs. McClure. Yes, I suppose. But dying of *fright* . . ." He shook his head. "That's far from an *official* cause of death. Do you understand my meaning? It's not something I'm going to rule."

Seymour loudly exhaled. He'd obviously heard enough. "I'm out of here!" he announced. "This is a bummer, you know. I was Miss Todd's friend . . . and anyway I still have mail to deliver, too—if I'm not fired already!"

Ciders stared at the mailman through furrowed brows. "I still suspect you, Tarnish."

"Of what?!"

"Of causing those noises Miss Todd reported. I don't know why you'd want to scare the old woman to death, but I'm keeping my eye on you."

"You're crazy, Ciders. Why would I want to scare a nice old lady like Miss Todd?"

"Who knows why you do anything, Tarnish. You've been a bad seed since I hauled you in for setting Montague's Woods on fire—"

"I was in the eighth grade! Me and Keith Keenan were shooting off bottle rockets. One of them got away from us!"

"You started an illegal fire, drank beer while you were still underage, and you were in possession of pornography—"

"Porno? It was a *Playboy* magazine me and Keith found in the trash, for cripes' sake!"

"Plus you were cutting school."

"Just gym class," Seymour said. "It sucked, and do you know why?" He stepped up to Chief Ciders and poked his finger into the man's barrel chest. "Because it was full of a-holes like your Neanderthal nephew over there! And that's the problem with bullies like him—and *you*—more brawn than brains. Just think about this logically for a second. What possible motive would I have for frightening poor old Miss Todd to death?"

Ciders's face reddened. He didn't have an answer. The room fell silent. No one moved. And then the doorbell loudly buzzed. We all tensed. Ciders gestured to the front door with an angry jerk of his thumb.

"Eddie! See who that is!"

He did. And a moment later he reappeared with a small, middle-aged man at his side.

Ciders faced the newcomer with zero patience. "Who are you and what do you want?!" he roared.

"My name is Emory Philip Stoddard, Esquire," the little man said, clearing his throat. "I am, or rather . . . I *was* Miss Todd's legal representative. I received a call from your dispatcher to come immediately—"

Ciders cursed. "Sorry, Mr. Stoddard. Sorry about the yelling there. My bark is worse than my bite sometimes. I forgot I told Joyce to call your office."

Seymour rolled his eyes. "I get strip-searched, falsely accused of murder, and prevented from doing my job, but the *lawyer* gets a formal apology over a little harsh language?"

Ciders shook the lawyer's hand, and introductions were made all around—though the chief pointedly neglected to introduce Seymour.

As I greeted the man, it occurred to me that Mr. Stoddard was the polar opposite of Dr. Rubino. Where the doctor was a tanned, toned *GQ*-type clad in rough-looking outerwear, Mr. Stoddard was a rough-looking character swathed in a *GQ* package.

About five-foot-two, he had a ruddy complexion with a receding blond hairline, a hawkish nose beneath smallish light eyes, and a pudgy body immaculately wrapped in a tailored cobalt suit. His Windsor knot was perfect, the thin silver bar gleaming as it held his Italian silk tie firmly in place along his opalescent dress shirt. He wore matching cuff links, too, with which he continually fidgeted.

"I guess Joyce explained the situation," Ciders said.

Mr. Stoddard nodded. "I understand that Miss Todd has passed. Can you tell me what happened?"

"Yeah, Chief," Seymour piped up. "Tell the man what happened."

Ciders scowled. "Mr. Tarnish here was just *leaving*."

"Tarnish?" Mr. Stoddard repeated. "Are you by any chance Mr. *Seymour* Tarnish?"

Seymour nodded. "The one and only. What's it to you?"

"It so happens that you're mentioned in Miss Todd's last will and testament," Mr. Stoddard replied.

Seymour's jaw went slack. "Huh?"

"You're a beneficiary, man."

Chief Ciders's eyes widened for a moment before narrowing down to tiny pinholes. "Tarnish here is *inheriting* something as a result of Miss Todd's death?"

Mr. Stoddard nodded. "And so is Mrs. McClure and her aunt. I'll be holding a meeting in my office forthwith."

"What exactly is this man getting?" Ciders asked with naked suspicion.

"Oh, I *am* sorry, Chief, but for now that's confidential."

Ciders folded his arms and smirked. "Well, whatever the hell Miss Timothea Todd left her mailman, it better not be valuable. Because if Mr. Tarnish here winds up inheriting anything more than a souvenir ashtray and some dusty old books, I'd say that's a motive for murder."

# CHAPTER 6

## Beneficiaries

I loathe these dives . . . They look as if they only existed after dark, like ghouls.

—Raymond Chandler, "Blackmailers Don't Shoot,"
*Black Mask*, December 1933 (Chandler's debut short story)

AFTER LEAVING MISS Todd's mansion, I'd watched clouds roll in all afternoon. Now it was twilight and darkness descended with more murk than usual for a warm June night.

Heeding Mr. Stoddard's official request to appear in his Millstone office at eight P.M., Aunt Sadie and I closed the bookshop early, leaving the Community Events room in the trustworthy hands of the Yarn Spinners reading group as well as our young part-timer, Bonnie.

Seymour Tarnish picked us up in his pristine, vintage 1975 lime green "breadloaf" Volkswagen bus. We piled in, dropped off my son, Spencer, at the home of his best buddy, Danny Keenan (the son of Seymour's old friend, "Bottle Rocket Keith" Kennan), and then headed for the highway.

Seymour didn't say much as he drove us to Millstone, which was unusual for the loquacious mailman. Wearing a slightly wrinkled blue suit, white shirt, and Mighty Mouse tie wide enough to double as a lobster bib, he stared at the road ahead, seemingly lost in his own thoughts.

*Your postal pal looks nervous,* Jack said.

"Can you blame him?" I whispered in my head. "Given the day he's had?"

Back at Miss Todd's mansion, Chief Ciders had wanted to continue detaining and questioning Seymour, but with Dr. Rubino refusing to rule the scene a homicide and Eddie calmly suggesting that they wait for autopsy and forensic results, *and* Seymour threatening to hire Emory Stoddard on the spot to represent him, Ciders finally backed off.

Seymour stormed out of the mansion, and I followed, eager to smooth things over. He let me drive him over to Cooper Family Bakery, where I treated him to coffee and a few of Milner Logan's lighter-than-air doughnuts. Once he calmed down, Seymour assured me (through gulps of Mocha Java and soothing mouthfuls of glazed fried dough) that I was forgiven for my part in the ugly incident, though he refused to give Chief Ciders and Bull McCoy, "the Boy Moron," a pass for the nasty way they'd treated him.

"There's the turnoff for Millstone," I gently told Seymour, pointing to the ramp ahead.

"Oh, yeah . . . Thanks, Pen."

Seymour was more than familiar with the way to Millstone, but he was looking so spaced-out I thought he could use the reminder. He drove his VW Bus up the steep ramp and turned at the top of the high hill. Skirting the back end of Prescott Woods, we continued to ascend the two-mile grade that led to the town's center. Millstone's main street was called Buckeye Lane, but it projected a substantially different atmosphere than Quindicott's Cranberry Street.

The grand reopening and expansion of our Buy the Book shop a few years back had sparked a real boom in our little town. The new customers we'd attracted with reading groups, author signings, and book events came from all over the region, and before or after their visit with us, they began patronizing stores close by. Soon Napp Hardware, Cooper Family Bakery, Franzetti's Pizza, Mr. Koh's Grocery, Donovan's Pub, the Seafood Shack, and a half dozen other shops were able to invest in new awnings, improved interiors, and local advertising, which helped spur even more commerce.

The Finches became successful enough to convert the condemned Charity Point Lighthouse into an extension of their bed-and-breakfast business. They'd even fulfilled a longtime dream of opening the town's first and only gourmet French restaurant, Chez Finch, next to Quindicott Pond.

Our town's latest story of commercial resurrection involved the (formerly) broken-down, boarded-up Movie Town Theater. Its grand reopening was just last month. Not only did the restoration of the old theater's Art Deco façade and plush interior earn it landmark status from the local historical society, but its weekend film-and-lecture series were also drawing huge crowds of students from nearby St. Francis College.

The increased sales taxes had allowed the city government to upgrade the public commons, paint and repair the bandshell, and reinstitute Sunday summer concerts.

Sadly, however, all of this burgeoning new capitalist life had yet to benefit the dead little burg of Millstone— "the Hinterlands," as some in Q had dubbed it. More than a decade ago, Millstone's major employer, a textile plant, had shut its doors. A handful of politicians had attempted to revive the town with fresh ideas; but like a depressed neighbor who no longer sees much point in getting out of bed, the people of Millstone were unwilling to rally. No one wanted to take a chance, to invest in anything, not even their own businesses.

The mood was routinely gloomy in Millstone, and the waning summer sunlight hadn't improved its atmosphere. As Seymour rolled down the town's pothole-peppered main drag, we passed storefront exteriors in need of repair. But those were the lucky ones. Boarded-up windows and GOING OUT OF BUSINESS signs reminded me of the bad old days in Quindicott when Sadie was about to end the life of the family's bookstore.

The law offices of Emory Philip Stoddard were located

on Whippoorwill Road at the edge of the business district. We turned off Buckeye Lane and searched for the doorway marked 919. Unfortunately, there were a lot of residential buildings on this street and a lot of parked cars. Seymour's VW Bus was too big to fit into the only two curbside spaces available.

"You two go ahead," Seymour said. "I'll drive around the corner and find someplace to park."

Stoddard's office occupied the ground floor of a three-story, Federal-style walkup. The red bricks were dingy, the white paint on the window frames flaked and peeling, and the plate-glass window had a hairline crack. Even the sidewalk was pitted, with dried leaves and stray candy wrappers littering the curb.

As we approached the front door, it opened abruptly. A seventysomething woman stood staring at us with chilly blue eyes. Her finely tailored suit and quilted leather handbag certainly didn't fit the depressed neighborhood. She was a bit heavy, with full hips and thick legs. Her short brown curls were shot with gray, her patrician features buried in a fleshy face polished up with base, blush, and lipstick.

Sadie smiled and nodded a polite greeting. I said, "Hello. Are you a client of Mr. Stoddard's?"

"Good evening," was all she said in return, rather coldly. Then she swept past us toward a silver luxury sedan parked across the street. Until now, I hadn't noticed the Mercedes idling there. A middle-aged man with dark hair, a mustache, and Hispanic features sat in the driver's seat wearing a chauffeur's uniform.

"Do you know that woman?" I asked Sadie.

"Never saw her before." I shrugged, figuring she was just another client, and we stepped inside.

The interior of Stoddard's office was even less impressive than the exterior. What passed for a waiting room consisted of five steel folding chairs on a threadbare beige carpet. The faux wood paneling covering the walls appeared badly scuffed.

*Strange,* I thought. *These aren't the sort of digs I expected for the immaculately dressed Mr. Stoddard.*

*The man's a lawyer,* Jack said in my head.

"So?"

*So expect two faces.*

The drab space was so poorly illuminated that at first we didn't notice the slender young woman sitting in front of high metal filing cabinets and behind a computer screen on a dented steel desk. The girl was college-age, maybe a little older, and like the client who'd just left this office, she wasn't dressed anything like the few girls we'd passed on Millstone's sidewalks with their cut-off shorts and denim skirts.

This girl's sleeveless dress of black summer silk was finely tailored. Her head was bent over a thick book. She wore a chain of gold links and her long, sleek, precisely cut raven hair spilled down around her shoulders. When she moved, I could see the flash of a gold tattoo on her pale upper arm. It appeared to be some kind of cross, but I couldn't really tell. Her dark veil of hair was too quick to cover it.

"Excuse me, miss?" Sadie said. "We're here to see—"

"Mr. Stoddard. You have an appointment," the young woman replied, finishing my aunt's sentence for her. She didn't smile at us, just stared intently, her liquid dark eyes squinting slightly behind small, rimless glasses. Her focus moved slowly from Sadie to me, then down to the desk. She pressed the intercom button.

"Excuse me, Mr. Stoddard," she said, "your eight o'clock appointment has arrived. Sadie Thornton, her niece, and the gentleman."

Sadie glanced back at me. I shrugged. Seymour hadn't actually arrived yet, but he'd be here any minute.

"Thank you, Miss Tuttle! I'll be right out."

The storefront office was so small I could hear Mr. Stoddard's voice coming from behind the thin door to our right as well as the intercom's speaker.

Miss Tuttle waved her hand. "You three can go in now."

Glancing at me again, Aunt Sadie wrinkled her forehead. "Three?"

The door opened and Mr. Stoddard stepped out. When his delicate, small-boned hand shook mine, I noticed a bulky gold ring on his right middle finger. I glanced at it, expecting to see a university insignia, but it was engraved only with a stylized cross, the top of which appeared open, like a sewing needle.

"Is that an Egyptian ankh?" I asked. "On your ring?"

A flash of annoyance momentarily soured Mr. Stoddard's welcoming expression. "How nice of you to notice," he said after a pause, but his tone didn't sound pleased. "A gift from a client. Sign of good luck, I believe."

While the man spoke, he deliberately twisted the gold circle, hiding the ankh design on the palm side of his hand.

*Odd,* I thought. Jack agreed.

*You said it, honey.*

After greeting my aunt, Mr. Stoddard looked around the small waiting room. He glanced at the young woman in the black dress.

"Miss Tuttle, you said over the intercom that all *three* had arrived? Where is Mr. Tarnish?"

The young woman smirked at Stoddard, as if he were being ridiculous. "There's a third with *her.*" She pointed at me, her tone implying this should have been obvious to everyone. "The man wearing the fedora and the double-breasted suit."

I held my breath as the girl stared at me.

"Jack?" I silently whispered. "Can she *see* you?"

*How should I know? Ask her!*

The moment Jack spoke in my head, the young woman's annoyed expression changed to surprise. "Oh," she said, shifting her focus back to the lawyer. "It's not Seymour Tarnish. Excuse me, Mr. Stoddard, but I was mistaken."

"No harm done," Stoddard replied.

Aunt Sadie shot me a *that-was-weird* look. I shrugged, trying to look clueless, but I couldn't shake the young woman's penetrating gaze. Like a high-intensity floodlight, I continued to feel Miss Tuttle's focus on me as Mr. Stoddard ushered us into his small office. Frankly, I was relieved when Stoddard closed his door and cut off the girl's vision.

"Seymour Tarnish is on his way," I assured Mr. Stoddard. "He gave us a ride over, but he couldn't find a large enough space for his VW bus."

"He has a VW bus?" Stoddard asked curiously as he moved around his desk.

I nodded. "Lime green."

"What year?"

"From the seventies," I said. "You should ask him about it. He's very proud of it; keeps it in perfect running order."

The décor in Stoddard's office was fractionally better, with expensive-looking red leather chairs instead of the folding variety in the waiting room. The cheap paneling might have made the room as unappealing as the waiting area, but Stoddard had hidden most of the scuffed wood behind elaborately framed original artwork as well as diplomas, award plaques, and certificates.

As we took our seats, Stoddard sank into a high-backed executive chair of quilted leather. It looked costly and brand-new—unlike the dull, nicked surface of his walnut desk. Before we could exchange more than a few words, a strident buzz interrupted us.

"Seymour Tarnish is here now," Miss Tuttle announced, loud enough to be heard without the intercom.

Seymour entered a moment later. He nodded at us, shook Stoddard's hand, and sat down in the chair next to mine.

"Let's begin, shall we?" Mr. Stoddard said. "All three of you are here because you're specifically mentioned in the last will and testament of Miss Timothea Todd, amended for the final time on March 24 of this year."

Stoddard steepled his fingers. "This won't be a formal reading of the will because other beneficiaries are also mentioned in the document, and for now those sections will remain confidential."

"Other beneficiaries?" I silently repeated. "I wonder who they are."

*So do I,* Jack said. *And why all the hush-hush? Why are you three the only ones invited to this party? Didn't the old dame have any relatives?*

"I don't think so, Jack. Not living, anyway. I asked Aunt Sadie that question, and she said Miss Todd never married or had children; never mentioned any other family, either."

Stoddard swiveled his chair slightly to face Sadie and me. "As the owners of Buy the Book on Cranberry Street, the two of you have supplied Miss Todd with reading material for many years. She wanted to return the favor after her passing, so Miss Todd has bequeathed your store the entire contents of her large and varied library."

"Mercy!" Sadie exclaimed.

"Wow," I said.

"That's really nice," Seymour agreed.

"Every book in the Todd mansion is yours, ladies, with the exception of one special volume located in the master bedroom, which is to go to Mr. Tarnish as part of his inheritance."

"What do you know," Seymour said, glancing at me and Sadie. "She left me a book, too."

"That's not all she left *you*, Mr. Tarnish." The lawyer swiveled his chair again and met Seymour's eyes. "You have also inherited *all* of Miss Todd's property in Quindicott."

Seymour stared. "What?"

"You have inherited the property on Larchmont Avenue and everything inside it. You have also inherited the land the structure is built on, as well as the two outbuildings."

"Holy cow," I whispered.

"Heavens to Betsy," Sadie rasped.

Seymour still hadn't uttered a word. He simply sat stiff as a cold corpse, his eyes bugging out.

"Mr. Tarnish," Stoddard said, "do you understand what I'm telling you? You are the primary beneficiary of Miss Todd's estate. You have just inherited her Larchmont Avenue mansion."

"Seymour?" Aunt Sadie called. "Did you hear the man?"

Seymour failed to respond.

*Will somebody shake that lug already! He's staring into space like a beached sperm whale.*

"I think we should get him some water," I announced.

Mr. Stoddard buzzed his receptionist. The young woman in the black dress strode in with a bottle of water and a paper cup. We all waited for Seymour to take a long drink and get a grip. I tried not to look at the girl, who continued to stare at me through her rimless glasses.

*What's with the chippy in black over here? Can she see me or not?*

"I can't even see you, Jack. I can only hear you."

*Well, can she hear me then?*

"How should I know," I told the ghost. "Why don't you ask her—"

*Okay, baby, if you insist.*

"Wait, Jack, maybe that's not such a—"

*HEY THERE, SISTER! WHAT DO YOU KNOW, WHAT DO YOU SAY?!*

A frigid blast of air swirled through the room. For a moment, I sat unmoving; then with emotions somewhere between dread and curiosity, I forced myself to look at the young woman. She folded her arms, arched a jaded eyebrow, and smirked in my direction. That's when Jack spoke again—

*BOO!*

The girl rolled her eyes. "Is he serious?" she mouthed to me.

"Oh, my God, Jack," I told the ghost. "I think she can see you *and* hear you."

*Gee, ya think so?*

"Yes, and I hate to break it to you, but I don't think you're the first spook to say *BOO* to her, either."

"My, there's a chill in here all of a sudden!" Aunt Sadie rubbed her arms. "Is your air conditioner broken, Mr. Stoddard? We have that same problem in our building all the time."

"I don't know." Mr. Stoddard scratched his receding hairline. "I'll have to have it checked."

Sadie turned to our mailman. "Are you okay to continue, Seymour?"

Seymour nodded mutely.

Mr. Stoddard glanced at his young secretary. "That will be all for now, Miss Tuttle. In fact . . ." He checked his watch. "Why don't you head home now? I'll see you in the morning."

Miss Tuttle nodded and strode out of the room, shaking her long curtain of raven hair as if she were completely unimpressed by my ghost's little display.

# CHAPTER 7

## *Change of Fortune*

If stirring things up is your system, I've got a swell spoon for you.

—*Red Harvest*, Dashiell Hammett, 1929

MR. STODDARD WENT back to explaining the terms of Seymour's inheritance, but I couldn't focus on the legal business. Not right away. My eyes glazed over as I tried to process the fact that another living human being had seen and heard the ghost of Jack Shepard.

Or had she?

*Now you're just second-guessing yourself.*

"She really did see and hear you, didn't she?"

*What's the matter, baby? Jealous?*

"Jealous?! Me? Of what?!"

*If this keeps up, you might have to share me with some other dames. You won't have me all to yourself anymore.*

"I doubt that."

The ghost's deep laugh echoed through my head.

"Quit gloating."

"Excuse me?" Seymour said, turning to stare at me.

I cleared my throat. "Uh, what?"

"I'm not gloating, Pen," Seymour said. "At least I wasn't. But you know, after the way Ciders and his moronic nephew treated me, maybe I *should*."

Sadie and Mr. Stoddard frowned at me. I shrunk a little farther into my red leather chair.

"I'm sorry for the interruption. I didn't mean it," I said quickly, silently adding: *except where it concerns a certain self-satisfied specter*!

"Please continue, Mr. Stoddard," Sadie said.

Stoddard cleared his throat and turned toward Seymour. "As I was saying, Miss Todd has established a trust fund for you, Mr. Tarnish. It will pay for all state and federal taxes for the foreseeable future, along with the legal cost of transferring the title of the house to you, which will take anywhere from six to eight weeks— although you may take physical possession as soon as tomorrow if you like."

I marveled at Miss Todd's thoughtfulness. Seymour probably hadn't even considered the burden of property taxes, having been a house renter his whole adult life.

"Wow, that's . . . that's really incredible," Seymour whispered.

"Mr. Tarnish, I'd like to ask you a question, if I may?" Stoddard said. "Do you have any idea why Miss Todd bequeathed her properties to you?"

Seymour shook his head. "Not a clue."

"You never spoke of the house or the property with Miss Todd?"

"I always told her that her house was great," Seymour said with a shrug. "Like something from *Dark Shadows*— you know, that gothic melodrama? Turns out she loved that old TV show, too. I lent her my videotapes so she could re-watch all the episodes." He glanced at me and Sadie. "I taped them off cable last year when they ran that *Dark Shadows* marathon. Did you know they used a mansion over in Newport for the exterior shots?"

Stoddard frowned. "Mr. Tarnish, are you aware there's a stipulation in Miss Todd's will that states you are not permitted to alter the house in any drastic way?"

"I wasn't aware I'd inherited the house in the first place, until you told me. So the answer to that would be *no*."

"Well, it is my duty to inform you that if you do alter the

house, you forfeit the trust fund that pays the mansion's property taxes, which are considerable."

"That's not a problem," Seymour said. "Like I said, I like the house the way it is, so—"

"Nor are you permitted to lease the property," Stoddard continued, his gaze intensely studying Seymour. "Does that bother you?"

"No. Why would I want to rent the house out?" Seymour glanced at us again. "I've wanted to live on Larchmont my *whole* life. This is like a dream come true! I mean . . . I'm sorry Miss Todd had to pass for this to happen, but can you believe it? I'm going to be 'Seymour Tarnish of Larchmont Avenue'!" He clapped his hands and rubbed them together.

"Holy Cannoli, Batman! This is hard to believe!"

"Yes," Mr. Stoddard said, an eyebrow arching. "It's hard to believe, all right."

*Those tony new neighbors of Postal Boy here are in for a shocker, aren't they?*

"I think so," I told the ghost.

Sadie exchanged a look with me, and I bit my tongue to keep from laughing.

"Wait till I tell Brainert!" Seymour grinned at us with the thought. "I'm going to be neighbors with half the St. Francis deans! That little academic snob will turn pea green with envy!"

Mr. Stoddard fingered his cuff links. "So, Mr. Tarnish, let me confirm. You *aren't* interested in renting the property? Is that right?"

"That's right."

"But what about selling it?"

"Selling it?"

"Yes, take a look at this."

Stoddard opened a manila folder on his desk. Then he turned it around so Seymour could read the document filed inside. The expensive stationery bore the gold-embossed letterhead of The Lindsey-Tilton Partnership, LLC.

"As Miss Todd's legal representative, I received this offer early in the year. As you can see, it is quite generous—"

Seymour whistled. "They offered Miss Todd a million bucks for that old house?"

Stoddard nodded. "An executive from the Lindsey-Tilton group has been tracking the steadily growing success of the Finch Inn, and planned to turn Todd Mansion into the town's second bed-and-breakfast. The Larchmont address affords easy access to the hiking and birder trails in Montague's Woods, and is additionally a quick trip to the fishing at Mullet Point. Your town's restored Art Deco cinema and its well-publicized film programs are creating quite a sensation in our region, and Chez Finch just got that rave review in the Providence paper."

"How did Miss Todd respond to this offer?" Seymour asked.

"As you know, Timothea was getting on in years and was not in the best of health. I tried to convince her to take the deal, move to a beautiful seaside retirement home in Newport, but she refused."

Stoddard placed his palms down on the desk and leaned forward. "In fact, it was shortly after this letter arrived that Miss Todd altered the will in your favor."

"Who was to inherit the house before the amendment?" I asked.

Mr. Stoddard's gaze shifted to me. "Miss Todd has a surviving sister, who was originally named in the will."

"A sister?" I said. I turned to my aunt. "Did you know Miss Todd had a living sister?"

Aunt Sadie shook her head. "She never mentioned one."

I recalled the well-dressed older woman we'd passed on our way into Stoddard's office—the one with the Mercedes, the chauffeur, and the chilly attitude. I leaned toward the lawyer.

"Who is this sister? What's her name? Was it the older woman who had the appointment before ours?"

Mr. Stoddard frowned. "For now, at her request, the identity of Miss Todd's sister is to remain a private matter." He turned to Seymour. "Of course, the terms of Miss Todd's will are quite restrictive, and quite clear. You are not to sell or lease the house, lest you risk losing the monies from the trust fund. *However . . .*" The lawyer paused. "If you actually *did* wish to sell the property for the million-dollar offer, the money from the trust fund would become moot, anyway. Clearly, you would no longer need it."

"Yeah," Seymour said, nodding. "I understand."

"So, although Miss Todd wanted you to keep the house, it's really up to you, Mr. Tarnish. Once the title is legally transferred—as I mentioned, in six to eight weeks—you are free to ignore Miss Todd's wishes and dispose of the property in any way you see fit. And, of course, I'm in a position to expedite the tangle of legal issues and paperwork. I am at your service."

"Thanks, Mr. Stoddard," Seymour said. "I mean, if I decide to sell, you'll be the guy I call—seeing as how you're the only lawyer I know!" He laughed. "But like I said, there's no way I'm going to pass up this chance to be part of the Larchmont set."

A gust of chilly air tickled the nape of my neck.

*Just like a slip-and-fall school graduate to talk out of both sides of his mouth.*

"It does sound like Mr. Stoddard is pushing Seymour to sell," I quietly told the ghost. "And with Seymour knowing nothing about how to broker a sale, he'd obviously hire Stoddard to handle the Lindsey-Tilton bunch—for a sizeable commission."

*Didn't I warn you? Lawyers are always figuring the angles. And by the look of this dump, I'd say Mr. Stoddard isn't exactly prosperous, which probably rankles him plenty, seeing as how he's dressed for success.*

"I think he was at one time. Successful, I mean. Look at the expensive leather chairs in this room, the framed paintings. He obviously brought these from another location. And did you notice there isn't any signage with his name on it? The building is just marked with a numbered street address. I'm sure this is some sort of hastily thrown-together office."

*I think you're on to something there, honey. I mean, Girl*

*in Black out front—does she strike you as your average legal secretary?*

"Not even close."

*Well, his downgrade in digs was pretty recent. That's clear.*

"What's not so clear is whether the man was desperate enough for money to commit murder."

*Keep your peepers open, doll. And find out one more thing.*

"What?"

*If Seymour's getting the property, then someone else is getting the shaft.*

My eyes opened wider at that. "Of course—Miss Todd's sister."

I cleared my throat. "Mr. Stoddard, I have a question. Isn't Miss Todd's sister upset about not being left the Larchmont property? I mean, can't she contest the will?"

Stoddard nodded. "The woman could take legal action, but I doubt she will. You see, Miss Todd and her sister were estranged for decades—and the sister has told me she wants nothing to do with the house. Although if Seymour were to die before the title is legally transferred, the property would automatically revert to Miss Todd's closest living relative, which would be her sister."

"Why doesn't the woman want anything to do with Todd Mansion?" Sadie asked.

"It's quite silly, really. You see, she believes that Todd Mansion is, well . . ."

"Yeah," Seymour piped up. "Todd mansion is *what*?"

"Cursed."

"What do you mean 'cursed'?" Seymour asked.

"Haunted would be more accurate," Stoddard said. "Haunted by evil spirits."

For a few seconds no one made a sound. Then I watched Aunt Sadie's eyebrows lift and Seymour's jaw literally drop open. My own mind raced back to the expression of mortal dread on the face of Miss Todd's corpse, along with that chilly cold spot.

Seymour cleared his throat. "Look, Mr. Stoddard, I know you're a smart guy and all, but I have a suggestion for you. Don't *ever* take up real estate as a profession, 'cause you don't know the first thing about pumping up the property to a prospective owner!"

Stoddard sat back in his leather chair and folded his hands over his belly. "You must understand that I don't put much stock in Timothea's sister's opinion. I merely mentioned the woman's theory in answer to *your* question. Remember, Mr. Tarnish, the sisters were estranged for many years. Why, I doubt that Mrs."—Stoddard caught himself—"excuse me, that *Miss Todd's sister* has set foot in the mansion for decades."

*Get her name, baby.*

"Excuse me," I interrupted. "I'm just so curious . . . Can't you tell us the woman's name? We'll keep it confidential."

"I'm sorry, Mrs. McClure. It's a matter of trust. Miss Todd's sister insists on privacy. Of course, once I've finished executing the will, it shall enter the public record—"

"When will you finish executing the will?" I asked, maybe a little too urgently. Mr. Stoddard's neutral expression changed.

"Hard to estimate at this time," he replied, his eyes narrowing on me with open suspicion. "Could be three months, maybe six. There's quite a bit of paperwork; transfers; and, of course, federal, state, and local taxes to be handled."

Seymour loosened his Mighty Mouse tie. "What makes Miss Todd's sister think the mansion is haunted?"

"I really couldn't say." Stoddard shrugged. "I mean, Miss Todd dwelled in that house for years without complaint."

I frowned. "But Chief Ciders told me that Miss Todd summoned officers to her home a number of times in recent weeks. He said she was complaining of hearing strange noises."

Stoddard sighed. "Miss Todd discussed the matter with me, as well. She seemed genuinely frightened, though I did my best to soothe her fears. And I believe fears were all they ever were. You see, Timothea's behavior had become increasingly erratic since a trivial incident that occurred last summer."

"What incident?" I asked.

Stoddard waved his hand as if dismissing the subject. "It doesn't much matter now."

*Jump on that, doll. Push him for more. But don't make him nervous. Keep it conversational.*

I cleared my throat, wrinkled my brow. "But I'd like to know," I said. "Wouldn't you, Aunt Sadie?"

"Well, yes," said Sadie. "I suppose so—"

"It was just a problem with the gas main on Larchmont," Stoddard said.

"Oh, I remember that!" Seymour turned to me and Sadie. "That Wolfe Construction crew resurfacing Larchmont dug a little too deep. A backhoe ruptured the gas main—"

"Yes, I remember, too," Sadie said. She shook her head. "That's the same construction company that's been blocking Bud's hardware store."

"They win a lot of the bids for the city," said Seymour.

Sadie turned to Stoddard. "Weren't some of those big houses on the avenue evacuated when that gas main was broken?"

"Only one, I'm afraid," Stoddard replied. "The damaged gas main was right in front of Miss Todd's gate, so she was forced to leave her home for almost ten days while the leak was capped and the pipes repaired."

"That would have been a terrible inconvenience," I conceded. "But why would that have affected Miss Todd?"

"She had a psychological attachment to the mansion," Stoddard said. "Leaving caused her distress." Stoddard sighed and looked down, studying the nicked desk. "At first she wouldn't leave, despite the danger. Volunteer firemen literally had to drag her out. I convinced Timothea not to return for her own safety."

"Where did you take her?" Sadie asked.

"The Finch Inn was booked, so I found a nice room at a hotel in Newport. But the drive there was difficult. Timothea hadn't been inside a car in decades, and the farther from Quindicott we traveled, the more agitated she became."

Sadie sighed. "The poor woman."

"When we arrived at the hotel, I did my best to make Timothea comfortable, but she nearly suffered a nervous breakdown. I finally called in a physician. He thought it best to sedate her. Miss Todd spent most of that time in bed." Stoddard shrugged. "But once we got Miss Todd back home, things returned to normal."

"Except that she began to hear strange noises," I said.

"Actually, that was many months later, Mrs. McClure."

"What kind of noises did she hear?" I pressed. "At what time of day or night did she hear them? In what part of the house?"

*Easy, baby! Slow down! You're spooking him!*

Annoyance flashed across Stoddard's face. "I really don't know."

"Surely Miss Todd must have mentioned—"

Stoddard shifted in his chair, glanced at his watch. "I do apologize, but we're going to have to cut this short. Mr. Tarnish and I still have plenty of work to do."

I gritted my teeth.

"Don't worry, Pen," Seymour said. "I know just what I'm going to do about those 'strange' noises."

Stoddard leaned forward. "What's that, Mr. Tarnish? Sell?"

"Heck, no! I'm going to call the Spirit Zappers!"

Sadie and I exchanged glances. "Who?" I asked.

"The Spirit Zappers!" Seymour repeated. "Oh, come on! Don't tell me you never saw their cable TV reality show?"

I glanced at Stoddard. He shrugged. I turned to Seymour. "We need more."

Seymour rolled his eyes. "*Spirit Zappers* is a hit prime-time show on the Alternative Universe network."

"Oh, yes!" Sadie said. "You remember, Pen. Spencer had us watch the *Secrets of Pompeii* last week on that network. Very interesting."

"Not half as interesting as their other programs,"

Seymour said, "like *Big Bill Big-Foot Hunter, U.F.O. Sightings: We Believe You!*, and, of course, *Medium at the Mall*—a psychic reads the minds of random shoppers at gallerias across America. But my all-time favorite has to be *Exorcise My Child.*"

"What's that show about," I asked, "fighting childhood obesity?"

"No, Pen, not exercise. *Exorcise!* It's kind of like *Super-Nanny* but with demonic possession."

Sadie appeared horrified. I was still confused: "So what do the Spirit Zappers do exactly?"

"They pretty much zap spirits like an exterminator zaps bugs. They *de-haunt* houses, Pen! I'll call them up tonight and make an appointment for them to zap Miss Todd's mansion. Hey, you know what? While I'm at it, I'll ask them to zap the entire town of Quindicott! Fiona says Finch Inn is haunted and your bookstore is supposed to be haunted, too, right?"

"NO!" I said, a little too forcefully.

Seymour stared. "Why the heck not? Listen, after they banish the 'spirits' from your bookstore on national television, you'll be swamped with new customers!"

Jack's chilly presence was getting colder by the second. *Will somebody tell this Alvin to put a sock in it.*

As if he'd heard Jack, too, Stoddard loudly cleared his throat. "Yes, well, let's move on, shall we?" He reached for a second file and handed it to Sadie. "This is a list of the books Miss Todd has bequeathed you. There are several hundred first-edition mystery novels and true-crime volumes dating back to the 1950s. I've made arrangements to have them boxed and delivered to your store by the close of business this Friday."

Sadie placed the file in her lap. "Thank you."

"I see no reason to dally, do you? Miss Todd's wishes were clear."

"Funny," I told Jack. "Her wishes were clear about the disposition of the house, too, but Mr. Stoddard seems willing to forgo that."

*Yeah, baby. He does.*

"It's obvious Miss Todd didn't want her house sold to strangers. Yet Stoddard's ready, willing, and able to broker a deal for Seymour."

*There's a lot less bucks in old books than in hot real estate.*

"And Stoddard keeps pretending the mansion isn't haunted. But I felt that cold spot myself. Do you think it's possible for a living person to manipulate a ghost into scaring someone to death?"

Jack didn't answer.

Emory Stoddard checked his watch again. "That concludes my business with you ladies," he said, punctuating the point by rising from his executive chair. "I think it would be best if you both departed now and allowed Mr. Tarnish and I to finalize the paperwork. We have several documents, title, and transfers to review, sign, and notarize."

"But we came with Seymour," Aunt Sadie said. "He gave us a ride over."

"Oh, in that case, let me call you a cab," Stoddard said, reaching for the phone.

"Don't bother," Seymour said, rising, too. "This time of night, you can't get a car service out here in under an hour." Seymour dug into his pocket for car keys and began to work one key off of it. "Here, Pen, take my extra key and drive the bus back to the bookstore. Just park it by a curb on Cranberry. I'll take the cab and pick it up when I'm done here."

"That won't be necessary, Mr. Tarnish," Stoddard insisted. "I'd be happy to drive you back to Quindicott once we're finished here."

"Great," Seymour said. "It's settled then."

I took the keys. "Okay, Seymour, if you're sure?"

Seymour nodded and Stoddard extended his hand. I shook, feeling the hard square of his reversed gold ring pressing into my palm.

"Good evening, Mrs. McClure, Ms. Thornton."

Seymour sat back down and smiled up at us. "Listen, you two, keep this Saturday night open, okay?"

"Why?" I asked.

"I'm holding a wake in honor of Miss Timothea, that's why! I'm not a guy who likes to waste time. I'm moving in ASAP. You're invited, too, Mr. Stoddard. And so is that cutie secretary of yours!"

"Thank you, I'm sure, Mr. Tarnish," Stoddard said. "Saturday evening, you say? I'll see what my schedule is like."

# CHAPTER 8

## Road Trouble

Trouble. Like the smoke over a cake of dry ice. You can't smell it but you can see it and know that soon something's going to crack and shatter.

—Detective Mike Hammer in *Kiss Me, Deadly*,
Mickey Spillane, 1952

LEAVING MILLSTONE'S DEPRESSED business district was like emerging out of a godforsaken mausoleum. Aunt Sadie and I didn't say much as I started up Seymour's VW bus and rolled through the town's shadowy lanes. I was still processing everything I'd heard in the lawyer's office, and I could see my aunt was engrossed in thoughts of her own. Even Jack had gone quiet. After a few minutes, however, my aunt broke the silence.

"That young woman," she said, her voice sounding almost disembodied in the large, dark vehicle. "She was acting oddly, don't you think?"

"Who?"

"Mr. Stoddard's receptionist, or assistant, or whatever she was. You know who I mean: the girl in the black dress."

"Miss Tuttle?"

"I can't get over how she stared right at you and said there was a man with you."

Behind the van's big steering wheel, I shifted uneasily. "Oh, she probably just noticed Seymour dropping us off."

"No, that can't be it. She was engrossed in her book when we walked in. And she was very specific about her description. She said a man in a fedora and double-breasted suit was with *you*. She was extremely clear about that point."

I forced a laugh—which sounded only slightly less phony than it actually was. "Probably just has an active imagination."

"You know, I hope she does come to Seymour's party. I'd like to ask her about that."

"I wish you wouldn't, Aunt Sadie. Tonight I found something a lot more disturbing than Miss Tuttle's confusion."

"You did?"

I nodded. "Mr. Stoddard's behavior."

"Mr. Stoddard was a perfect gentleman, dear. What are you talking about?"

"I'm talking about Stoddard pressuring Seymour into selling Miss Todd's home."

"You call that pressuring?" In the dim light of the car, I could see my aunt shaking her head. "It sounded to me like Stoddard was simply explaining that option to Seymour—and he rejected it pretty firmly, too. But, you know . . . maybe Seymour should sell."

"Why? Do you think Miss Todd's house really is haunted?"

"Heavens, no." Sadie waved her hand. "But even if it were, that's nothing to cause alarm. My word! Look at Finch Inn. It's supposed to be haunted, yet Fiona and Barney have never seen an apparition. And half the inns in Newport have ghost stories attached to them, not to mention the landmark buildings. Fiona tells me the stories are good for business. And you know that's one reason we started our occult book section."

"I know."

Sadie laughed. "Why, I've heard stories that parts of this very road are haunted. Some phantom car, which was run off Buckeye Lane years ago, supposedly comes back to haunt random drivers. And don't you remember, dear, what Seymour said about our very own bookshop? It's supposed to be haunted, too!"

"Ah, yes. I do seem to recall something like that—"

"When you first moved in with me, you did mention some strange things happening."

"True."

"But then you settled in and that all went away. Now, I'm sure if you actually saw a ghost in our bookshop, or continually heard strange noises, you'd tell me, wouldn't you?"

"Um—"

"Of course you would! And I'm sure Timothea would have told me if she was afraid of a ghost in her home. No, I'm sorry to say I think the noises she heard were a form of dementia."

"But I still don't understand, Aunt Sadie. If you don't think the mansion is haunted, then why should Seymour sell?"

"Because he's a bachelor. What's he going to do all alone in that huge house? His father passed away years ago and his mother's happy as a clam since she moved to the Florida coast."

"You don't think she'll come up to live with him?"

"Judy Tarnish never did get used to our New England winters. She was raised in the South, and after her husband died, she couldn't get out of Rhode Island fast enough. In fact, I remember her telling Seymour that the only way she'd come back up here is to attend his wedding."

"Seymour a groom?" I smiled at that idea. "Can you imagine?"

"You know what they say, Pen. There's someone for everyone." Sadie paused and leaned back in her seat. "Now that you mention it, didn't you get the feeling Seymour was kind of sweet on that strange Miss Tuttle?"

"I'm glad there's no traffic tonight," I said, attempting to change the subject while *still* trying to get used to the acre of distance between me and the road. My compact car was a lot smaller than Seymour's VW bus. Between the mass of lime-green metal around me and the height of the front seat, I felt like I was steering an army tank down Buckeye Lane.

"Traffic's never a problem around here anymore." Sadie peered out the side window. "It's sad what's happened to Millstone." She shook her head at the empty storefronts, the GOING OUT OF BUSINESS signs. "When I was a little girl, this town was such a pleasure to visit, so alive."

I slowed to a stop at an intersection, although there was no need. The crossroads were empty. I forged ahead, the tarred road getting blacker by the yard. Not only were storefronts dark; corner streetlamps weren't always working. Every few blocks, one was either flickering or entirely burned out, which certainly didn't help the sense of bleak gloom. The uncertain light didn't make driving Seymour's VW bus any easier, either.

"This thing is so much harder to handle than my little Saturn."

"Just go slow, dear. There's no one behind us." Sadie glanced into her sideview mirror. "Oh, I'm sorry. I spoke too soon. Someone's coming up on you now."

I glanced in the rearview and saw a sedan with a single person visible in the car. I barely glimpsed the driver's shadowy silhouette before a brilliant light blinded me.

"That driver's turned on the car's high beams!"

We were just entering the two-mile stretch that led from the town to the highway's onramp. Averting my eyes from the mirror, I stuck my hand out the window and waved the car forward. But the stubborn driver just kept rolling along behind me, blasting those high beams.

"What's that idiot doing?"

Sadie glanced in her side mirror. "I can't see a thing. Those high beams are too bright!"

I waved again and even hit the horn, but the sedan refused to pass.

"Maybe the driver's afraid of passing here," Sadie said.
"Fine then."

I pressed harder on the gas pedal, increasing my speed to put more distance between Seymour's vintage van and the tailgater with the high-beam issue.

Sadie leaned over to check the speedometer. "I thought you said you weren't comfortable driving this thing?"

"I'm not! But Speed Racer here is breathing down my tailpipe!"

Sadie glanced in the mirror again. "Be careful, Penelope. Never let someone else drive your car for you."

*Listen to your auntie, baby. Slow it down.*

"Jack! Where've you been?" I asked the ghost.

*Right here, doll, listening to your auntie's theories on the haunting racket. Did you hear me? Slow down—*

"Okay, okay."

For the last two miles, we'd been on a long, slowly descending grade, and I'd picked up a lot of speed. Ahead was the onramp to the highway, a steep, hilly decline, so it made sense to slow down anyway. I pulled my sandal off the gas, shifted my foot to the brake, and pushed down on the pedal—

"Why is it so spongy?" I muttered.

"Spongy?" Aunt Sadie echoed. "What do you mean?"

I pushed the brake pedal again, but there was too much give to feel right, and the bus was failing to slow.

"Penelope, we're going awfully fast." I could hear the tension in my aunt's voice. "I think you better slow us down."

"I'm trying!" I slammed the pedal as hard as I could, but it was no use.

*Pump the pedal, baby!*

I did, but that didn't work, either. "The brakes are out!"

"Out?!"

"Gone, Aunt Sadie! They're not working!"

My fingers tightened on the VW's wide steering wheel. We were well beyond the town's buildings now and there were no street lamps out here. I flipped on my high beams.

The brilliant light illuminated the black tar. In the twin moving spotlights I saw the angle of our descent was quickly getting steeper. Ahead of us the road was beginning to bend.

I had two choices: turn with the road or plow straight into the back end of Prescott Woods. There were no airbags in this vintage bus, and a head-on collision with a three-hundred-year-old tree trunk probably wasn't survivable. If we wanted to live, there was only one way to go—

*Turn, doll! Turn now!*

The trees came up faster than I anticipated. I cut the wheel, felt the VW shudder. Tires squealed and Sadie and I screamed as the bus tipped slightly. Sadie's palms flew up to the roof for balance. I gripped the wheel, certain we were going to roll over, but then the heavy vehicle righted itself. With a loud *thud,* we dropped back to four wheels again.

"Oh, my goodness!" cried my aunt.

I tried the brakes again—and again and again and again.

"I can't slow us down!"

"Oh, my goodness!"

"You said that already!"

*Don't panic, honey.*

"I'm not panicking!"

"I didn't say you were panicking!" my aunt shouted.

*You can handle this, Penelope. Calm down, use your head.*

I felt my aunt's hand on my shoulder. "Keep the wheel steady, Pen." Her voice was much calmer all of a sudden. "Keep your eyes on the road."

"Okay."

My fingers were wrapped so tightly around the steering wheel, my knuckles looked white in the VW's dim interior. My face was probably just as blanched. But this trip wasn't over. We were speeding along at close to fifty, and that last turn put us down the steep hill that served as the highway's onramp.

I could see the heavy traffic just ahead. "There's no shoulder! I'm going to have to get on!"

"Activate your emergency flashers," said Sadie, her voice still amazingly steady.

I glanced down for a moment, pushed the hazard button. "Okay! They're on!"

"Good," Sadie said. "Just do your best to merge into the highway traffic. The van will slow down on its own as soon as we hit level ground."

That sounded all well and good, but there was no place to merge. We blew right by the YIELD sign and were now speeding toward the highway's crowded right lane.

*Honk the horn, baby! Warn these people away from you!*

Good idea! I pumped the horn, sent out a succession of nasal VW beeps.

For a second, the lane showed me an opening, and I thought we were in the clear. Then I saw it: a giant Mac tractor, pulling a dozen cars on its ten-ton trailer. There was no way this massive truck could slow down fast enough. A foghorn bellow blasted my eardrums.

"Oh, my goodness!" Sadie shouted again. "Look out!"

The onramp ended and the truck's stack of new cars filled the windshield of the VW. *We're dead,* I thought, bracing for the crash—

But it didn't come.

The wheel in my hand cut sharply to the right. Beneath my fingers, it kept on turning. The stacked cars disappeared as the van's high beams illuminated high weeds and brush. We bounced so violently, my head bumped the van roof. The turn had slowed us, but we were still moving fast. My hands were still on the wheel but some other force was handling it now, steering the van up a bumpy hillock. The wheel turned again to prevent us from plummeting over the other side.

For a few yards more, we rolled along the high, narrow strip of brush-covered earth, parallel to the highway. Then like the end of a roller-coaster ride from hell, we finally came to a full stop.

I closed my eyes. "Thank you, Jack," I silently whispered.

*My pleasure, baby.*

I turned to my aunt. "Are you okay?"

Aunt Sadie's hand was on her chest; her eyes open wide. "What a ride!"

A few seconds later—after we both assured each other that nothing on either of us was bruised or broken—I unlocked my shoulder harness and tried to pop the door.

"It won't open! My door's wedged against some high brush. Try your door."

"Oh, dear. Mine will only open about five inches."

Just then, I noticed someone had stopped to help. There was no shoulder on this stretch of road, just a narrow strip of weeds below the steep embankment on which we were now stranded. The driver of a car or van couldn't fit on the thin strip of land below us, but a motorcyclist could—and that was exactly who'd pulled over.

"That's Leo Rollins's motorcycle," Sadie said, pointing.

I recognized the big bronze Harley. Then Leo lifted off his shiny gold helmet and I knew it was him for sure—no one else in the area had Leo's shaggy yellow hair and dark blond beard. Leo's mountain-man build was a giveaway, too; and for a big man, he climbed the steep, uneven embankment with surprising agility.

I rolled down the window. "We need help!"

"I can see that," he said. "You hurt?"

Leo was a man of few words and when he did speak his voice was so low and deep, I expected the floor to tremble, like it did for those sub-woofers he sold in his electronics store.

I didn't know the man very well; Sadie didn't, either. Ever since he moved to our town a few years ago, he pretty much kept his own counsel. The man's beard was more famous around town than anything he'd ever done or said. It grew in inverse proportion with the length of the New England days—the shorter the days, the longer his beard. By the time Christmas came around, and his whiskers were about down to his pectorals, he always put in a book order with us. Last year's included Lee Child's and Michael Connelly's entire backlists. We fulfilled it the last week of January and by the first week of February he was holed up alone in his Vermont cabin till March. For the past few years, he'd gone every year like clockwork.

"We're okay," I assured Leo. "Just a little shaken up."

"Thank you for stopping," Sadie called from the passenger seat.

"I saw the whole thing," Leo told us, pointing to the end of the onramp. "Seymour almost T-boned that Mac truck's trailer. Where is he?" Leo glanced inside the vehicle.

"Seymour wasn't driving," I said.

Leo frowned. "But this is his breadloaf bus."

"He lent it to us to get home."

"I'm phoning Bud," Sadie called to us, pulling out her cell phone. "He can pick us up and take us home. And he'll know who to call to tow this thing."

"Good idea." While Sadie placed her call, I turned back to Leo. "Can you help me get out of here? The door's wedged shut."

Mutely, Leo nodded his shaggy lion head. He bent over and lifted up his right pants leg. Strapped around the upper part of his black boot was a leather sheath. He pulled free a fancy-looking dagger and used it to slash at the brush wedged against my door. I pushed the door harder, forced it half open, and squeezed through.

"You said you saw the whole thing, right?" I asked, stumbling out onto the rocky hill.

Leo caught me. "Yep."

"Then you must have gotten a good look at the car right behind us?"

Leo's brows knitted. "A car? Behind you?"

"Yes, a dark sedan started tailgating us as soon as we left Millstone. There was just one driver, but the car's high beams were on, so I couldn't tell whether it was a man or a woman. I was hoping you could help me out there. Did you get a look at the car and the driver?"

Leo scratched his temple. "A car? Behind you?"

"Yes! The sedan was right behind us when we turned onto the onramp, so it must have been right behind us as we merged onto the highway. Did you see the driver?"

"I didn't see any driver, Mrs. McClure, 'cause I didn't see any other vehicle. The only thing that came hurtling down that onramp was Seymour's ride here."

I frowned at that, unable to comprehend how that could possibly be true.

"Pen!"

I wheeled. "What is it, Aunt Sadie? Are you okay?"

Sadie had finished her phone call to Bud and now seemed to be struggling inside the VW. "I can't unlock my seatbelt. It's jammed!"

"Here," Leo said, holding out his knife for me. "Cut the strap and get her out."

I nodded, took the dagger, and squeezed back into the front seat.

"Oh, thank you!" Sadie said as I easily sliced the thick seatbelt strap.

"Don't thank me. Thank Leo for keeping this blade of his razor-sharp." I smiled at Sadie and she glanced at the weapon. The steel blade felt heavy in my hand; the hilt slightly bumpy, as if it had been embossed with a design.

*Take a closer look, baby.*

I heard the ghost's cool whisper in my head, but I didn't know what he meant. "A closer look at what?"

*That fancy gut-ripper, what do you think?*

It was too dark in the front seat of the VW to see it clearly, so I leaned forward, opened the glove compartment, grabbed the flashlight inside, and turned it on.

"Penelope?" Aunt Sadie said. "What are you doing?"

"Just taking a look at Leo's knife," I whispered, flipping on the light. I directed the bright beam onto the blade and my brows drew together.

*Strange coincidence, don't you think?*

"Yes," I told the ghost.

*If it is a coincidence.*

Under the white beam of the flashlight, the hilt of the steel dagger appeared distressed, like a decades-old antique. Embossed on the metal surface was a five-pointed star with a fleur-de-lis at its center. I'd only seen the design once before—on the gate of Miss Todd's mansion.

*I saw that design before, too, baby, a long time ago.*

"Where?" I asked the ghost. "And when exactly? Who had it? And what does it mean?"

But the ghost didn't have time to answer any of my questions. An approaching siren on the highway interrupted our little supernatural chat.

"Staties here!" Leo called from the hillside.

The patrol car arrived a few moments later, carrying two well-pressed officers beneath matching Smokey the Bear hats. It was time to explain this "accident" to the Rhode Island State Police.

# CHAPTER 9

## *Who's Got Her Covered?*

She had the look around the eyes and a set of the
mouth that spelled just one thing: She was for sale
cheap.

—*My Gun Is Quick*, Mickey Spillane, 1950

BY THE TIME Bud Napp turned his van onto Cranberry
Street, it was close to ten thirty in the evening. Compared to
the dead village of Millstone, the hustle and hum of Quindicott's shopping district, even at this late hour, felt like another
world—and I was extremely relieved to be back in it.

A screening had just let out of the Movie Town Theater
and small, laughing clusters of people were heading for
Franzetti's Pizza, the Seafood Shack, and Donovan's Pub.
Young couples were cuddled up on benches along the commons, where the Chamber of Commerce had just installed
new faux Victorian street lamps. Older pairs were mean-
dering down sidewalks, gazing into store windows, many
of which were still glowing brightly as shopkeepers completed their final transactions on this lovely summer night.

I glanced at my aunt, who was sitting snugly between
me and Bud in his van's front seat. Relief was evident in
her face. Sadie was glad to be home, too.

As we rolled up to 122, I checked my watch. We'd
closed our bookstore early, but the Community Events

room in the adjoining storefront was often occupied at this hour.

"Do you think the Yarn Spinners are still meeting?" I asked my aunt.

"Doubt it," she said. "I know most of those ladies from church. They're early risers."

We'd already phoned Seymour to give him the bad news about his vintage VW bus. He was relieved that we were okay but furious about the brakes failing. Cursing a blue streak, he vowed to us he'd just had the thing inspected at Scotch Brothers Motors.

"Wait till I get my hands on Patrick Scotch!"

"Don't be too sure it's Patrick's fault," I told him.

"Why?" Seymour asked. "What do you mean?"

"I mean, I think it's awfully coincidental that your brakes failed right after you inherited Miss Todd's mansion. That's what I mean."

Seymour told me to chill out. "Don't go all conspiracy theory on me, Pen. The bus is pretty old."

"But you just had it inspected, didn't you?"

"Yeah, *supposedly*," Seymour said. "But Patrick Scotch is turning into a real rip-off artist. He charged me an arm and a leg for dubious repairs to my ice cream truck, and I wouldn't be surprised if his inspection on my breadloaf was slipshod. It's time for me to find a new mechanic."

"But it is suspicious. You have to admit."

"I'll only admit I need to get someone *reliable* to overhaul my VW's brakes."

Bud and the tow truck had arrived by then. Leo Rollins was already gone. He'd stuck around only long enough to give his statement to the Staties—which, unfortunately, contradicted our statement since he'd said that he sure didn't see any sign of a sedan behind us. Then he'd rumbled away on his bronze Harley.

Before Leo departed, I'd asked him about the strange design on the hilt of his dagger. He'd claimed he didn't know anything about the design or what it meant—just saw it in the window of a Newport antiques shop one day and picked it up for a steal.

*You believe that?* Jack had asked.

"What else should I believe?" I'd told the ghost. "You still haven't told me your own connection with that odd design."

Once again, the ghost clammed up.

Now we were back home, and Bud was pulling up to the curb in front of our bookstore's front window. I jumped down from the van to give my aunt and her sweetheart some privacy for their goodnight. Then she climbed down, too. Bud drove off, and together we pushed through our shop's front door.

Not bothering with the lights in the main store, I moved through the archway, entering the sizeable space we used for reading groups and author appearances. My aunt was right: I could see right away that the knitting-mystery enthusiasts were gone. Only Bonnie was left.

"Hi!" she said, glancing up from her floor-sweeping with the apple-cheeked enthusiasm of the unburdened young.

Like her brother, Bonnie Franzetti had thick, black hair, but where Eddie's was straight, hers was curly. She wore it just past her chin, which flattered her heart-shaped face and big, brown, long-lashed eyes (like her brother's, too). She'd just turned seventeen and her youthful energy, even at this hour, radiated with almost palpable warmth.

"How was your evening?" she asked.

"Good," I croaked out, trying to sound pleasant, even though the stress of the failing brakes (not to mention Miss Todd's death, Seymour's near arrest, and the strange meeting with Stoddard) was settling into my bones. "How was yours? Any problems?"

Bonnie tensed. "Not really. I mean, that depends."

I frowned, jumping to an unhappy conclusion. "Where's Spencer? Did he come home yet?" I checked my watch again.

Mr. Keenan was supposed to have driven Spencer back home when the boys were finished playing their video game. For a second, my heart started racing again, and then—

"Hi, Mom! Hi, Aunt Sadie!" My redheaded eleven-year-old strolled into the room from the back hallway.

"Spence was helping me," Bonnie explained. "He carried the garbage bag to the cans out back."

"Oh." I exhaled. "Okay."

"Thanks, Spence," Bonnie said.

"No problem." My son's lightly freckled face reddened slightly.

Okay, I thought, this is new: the obvious blushing, the shy smile, the hands nervously shoved into pockets, the swaying from foot to foot.

*Looks like Junior's sweet on someone.*

"Oh, great. So now you're going to speak up?"

*It's my prerogative, baby. I'm haunting you, remember?*

I gritted my teeth. Not unlike your average, obstinate *living* man, my dead guy maintained his own rules—which sometimes left me struggling to maintain my equanimity. What was I going to do about it? *Miss Manners for Ghosts* had yet to be written, although I was seriously considering self-publishing.

"Spencer can't be sweet on Bonnie," I silently told the ghost. "She's been his babysitter for three years. Consider the first word please: *baby.*"

In my head, Jack laughed. *I hate to break it to you, doll-face, but your boy's not in diapers anymore. He's about to go off to boot camp.*

"It's not GI training, for goodness' sake! I told you: It's just a kids' summer camp! Oh, forget it." My shoulders slumped. "I just thought I had plenty of time before Spencer started showing an interest in girls."

*Time's up. And take it from me: Until they get a clue and wise up, boys'll do just about anything for the girl they're sweet on.*

"Don't remind me."

My older brother's crush on a girl was what led to his

showing off in a drag race. But Peter never finished that race. When his souped-up GTO crashed, he hadn't survived.

"Anything else you need?" Spencer asked Bonnie, his eyes darting back and forth from the pretty teenager to the hardwood floor.

"No, thanks," she said brightly. "I'm almost through."

"Oh, that's all right, Bonnie," Aunt Sadie said, waving her hand. "You've stayed late enough. Get home safe now. We'll lock up."

"Okay. If you're sure?" Bonnie said. She put the broom away and headed for the door. "Well, goodnight, everyone!"

"Wait a sec there, Bon," I called. "Just one last thing. What did you mean when I asked you if there were any problems tonight?"

Bonnie tensed as I walked up to her.

"You said, 'not really, that depends,' " I reminded her. "You want to elaborate on that?" (I didn't like putting the girl on the spot. But given the day I'd had, I wanted to be as fully prepared as possible for any unpleasantness coming our way.)

"Well, something did happen, uh, while the Yarn Spinners were meeting," Bonnie replied.

Her tone wasn't jocular, but Spencer suddenly started giggling. He exchanged a look with Bonnie and she bit her lip—apparently to keep from laughing, too.

I folded my arms. "Okay, spill it. What happened tonight?"

"It's the display," Bonnie said. "The Zara Underwood standee."

"Uh-oh." Sadie shook her head. "Here we go again."

"Again?" I frowned at my aunt. "What's wrong with the standee?"

Sadie shrugged. "One or two people complained to me about it earlier today."

"Complained?" I said. "About a cardboard cutout? What's the issue?"

Spencer started laughing harder. In fact, he laughed so

hard he doubled over. Then I heard a deeper voice laughing inside my head. "Jack!?"

*Great,* I thought, *even the* ghost *knows what they're talking about!*

"Okay," I said. "Will *somebody* tell me what's so funny?"

"Just *look,* Mom! Look for yourself!"

I followed my son's pointing finger, striding back through the archway that led to the bookstore's dark aisles. I flipped on the lights, which not only activated the recessed lighting but also turned on the many floor lamps throughout the aisles.

The lamps were actually a part of our business strategy. When I'd first moved back to Quindicott from New York City, I'd used my late husband's life insurance check to completely remake the dusty old shop. Sadie had been all for it, so we'd replaced the heavy metal shelves with hardwood bookcases, restored the woodplank floor, added colorful throw rugs, and placed easy chairs, Shaker-style rockers, and a variety of floor lamps throughout the shop. Jacking up the "comfy" factor had increased shop traffic significantly. Tourists found the bookstore "quaint," like stepping into a New Englander's private library, and locals found the atmosphere so comfortable they browsed longer and bought more.

For all of the store's casual coziness, however, we were still a business. We used display tables, cardboard book dumps, window clings, shelf-talkers, eye-catching standees, and signage near the picture window to inform local customers and window-shoppers alike what was new in stock.

As I stepped past the cardboard displays for the newest front-list releases from Dean Koontz, Jacqueline Winspear, and Alexander McCall Smith, I finally saw the Zara Underwood standee.

I'd put the thing together, and I well remembered what the two-dimensional cutout of the stripper-turned-actress-turned-writer was *supposed* to look like. The big-breasted blond had posed holding a revolver against her thigh. She wore high heels, white stockings held up with a garter belt, a powder-blue bustier, and matching frilly panties. The outfit was the exact same one described in a key scene of *Bang, Bang Baby*, Zara's debut crime novel.

At the moment, however, I couldn't tell what the woman was wearing. Her entire body from her neck to her ankles had been wrapped like a mummy in four different kinds of yarn.

"Oh, for pity's sake."

Bonnie quickly stepped up. "I'm sorry, Mrs. McClure. But I couldn't stop them."

"*Them* being the Yarn Spinners?" I pointed to the fuzzy threads of lemon yellow, turquoise blue, neon pink, and white cashmere crisscrossing Zara Underwood's cardboard torso. "I mean, who else, right?"

Bonnie nodded and Jack started laughing again in my head.

"What's so funny?" I silently snapped.

*The cardboard dame's holding the rod. But she's the one who got covered!*

"After the Spinners left," Bonnie said in a rush, "I tried to undo it and pull it all off, but those ladies are really good at making knots! I didn't want to risk damaging the standee, so I just left it—"

"It's okay." I patted her shoulder and dug out my keys. "Spencer, unlock the stock room and bring me a box cutter."

"Okay, Mom," Spencer said, stifling giggles as he hurried away.

Bonnie went home, and Spencer returned to the front of the shop not only with the box cutter but also with an armload of *Bang, Bang, Baby*.

"The dump's almost empty, Mom."

"Thanks, honey. I'll take those." I grabbed the stack of hardbacks. "Now go upstairs and get ready for bed. You have a big day tomorrow. Your bus for camp leaves at nine."

"I know, Mom."

When Spencer was finally out of earshot, I faced my

aunt. "Why didn't you tell me there were complaints about the standee?"

"Because they weren't worth wasting my breath over. This is a mystery bookstore, not a monastery. The standee's racy, but so what? So is the book. So are a lot of the crime novels in our stock. That standee is appropriate advertising for the product. It lets readers know what's on sale and what to expect from the book they purchase."

I shook my head as I bent down to refill the display. "It *is* a terrible book."

"Maybe to you, Penelope. But did you know that Bud is reading it right now and enjoying it?"

"He is? Really?"

"Yes! He thinks it's a hoot. And before you let a few opinionated customers tell you how to run your business, I suggest you check today's receipts. We've sold more copies of *Bang, Bang Baby* than any other hardcover front-list book in the store."

"You're joking."

Sadie folded her arms. "I've been in this business a lot of years, dear. And when a loudmouthed customer complains about a book I'm carrying, do you know what I ask myself? 'Sadie, are you a literary critic or a bookseller?' "

"But look at her!" I pointed to the yarn-wrapped card-board. "She's practically mummified!"

Sadie shrugged. "We've gotten complaints about our new occult books, too. Over the years I've gotten complaints about any number of authors: James Ellroy, Philip Pullman, even Mickey Spillane. Do you remember what CNN said about Spillane the day he died?"

"Yes, I remember," I said with a sigh. "Nobody liked him—except the reading public."

"And our reading public—our customers—are the ones who'll tell us what they want through their purchases."

"But the people who complained about *Bang, Bang Baby* are our customers, too!"

"And they're perfectly free to purchase what they like to read. In this store everyone is, and no one will ever be made to feel bad about reading whatever speaks to them, whatever makes them happy. Did you know a St. Francis Ph.D. candidate once asked me in serious, earnest tones why I sell *cozy* mysteries?"

"What?!"

Sadie snorted. "Apparently this young man hadn't heard that Agatha Christie is one of the most widely read authors in the English language, and the genre in which she excelled is still very much alive and loved, not to mention one of our most popular sales categories."

She shook her head and continued. "Should I stop selling the Yarn Spinners their favorite books because some young man, paying oodles of money to read a professor's syllabus, has an opinion about what some of my very best customers 'should' be reading?"

"Of course not. That's ridiculous."

"I'm not saying Zara Underwood and her ghostwriter are geniuses, or even that this year's roster of bestselling authors will stand the test of time. But, you know, the novel itself was once considered a 'disreputable' genre; and some of the greatest books ever written—in my humble opinion—would be dismissed today as 'popular' fiction, given the literary theories of the moment. And I do mean *moment,* dear."

"You don't have to tell me. Brainert Parker's made the point dozens of times. He still hasn't gotten over the *Norton Anthology* leaving out Robert Louis Stevenson from 1968 to 2000."

"My point exactly! Academia can be as changeable and trendy as the rest of society in what it decides to deem worthy, and people who go out of their way to make others feel bad about their enjoyment of a particular book, even an entire genre, are missing the bigger picture."

"Which is?"

"At a time when fewer and fewer adults are reading anything, we should be celebrating enthusiasm, not condemning it."

Flipping the trigger on the box cutter, I exposed the

sharp razor. Now I could easily slice through the tangle in front of me.

"Be careful, Penelope. *'My* books are good and *yours* are bad'* is a dangerous *Animal Farm* game . . ." Sadie's voice drifted off as she moved to lock the front door.

"What do you mean?" I called.

"For some people, 'erudition' is nothing more than a vehicle for hostility and arrogance; 'good taste' merely an excuse for condescension—or worse, censorship."

# CHAPTER 10

## *Tossed and Turned*

Stories of rugged Adventure, and real Romance,
rare Western yarns, weird, creepy Mystery tales and
the only convincing Ghost Stories to be found anywhere.

—Opening editorial, *Black Mask* magazine, October 1, 1923
(The same issue that published "Arson Plus,"
the first Continental Op story by Dashiell Hammett)

"BE CAREFUL, PENELOPE."

"Careful of what?"

It was nighttime, and I couldn't see much: a shadowy
dashboard, part of a windshield, gray landscape speeding
by like frames from a film noir reel. I was sitting in the
front of a large van, but I wasn't driving.

"Be careful, Penelope," the voice repeated. It was a
male voice. Beyond that, I didn't recognize it.

I tried swiveling my head toward the driver's seat, but
my neck refused to obey; I turned the other way instead.
Now I was looking out the passenger side window, at trees
and brush; at weeds flying by.

A large mirror was mounted to the door. High beams
appeared in its reflective glass. The glare of headlights was
coming up fast.

"Be careful, Penelope," the voice repeated. "Never let someone else drive your car for you."

I faced front again, saw a massive tree trunk looming like a solid, black wall.

"Stop!" I shouted. "We're going to crash!"

Tires squealed like a woman screaming. Then I started screaming and—

My eyelids lifted.

I was lying down. The room around me was small and dark. My own bedroom. "A dream," I whispered. It was just a dream. Yet it felt real enough to make my heart race.

I swallowed, licked dry lips, kicked off bedcovers. I sat up, chugged spring water from the bottle on my nightstand, forced myself to take conscious deep breaths. Finally I calmed.

Two hours ago, before I'd climbed into bed, the evening breeze had been gusty, ruffling my window curtains, cooling the air; but the night had gone still. Now the room felt warm. The bedside clock read 2:15. I punched my pillow and flopped back down.

I tried to relax but my mind was too active. After a few minutes, I heard footsteps. My aunt was walking into the kitchen. She ran water, jostled pans.

"Must be having trouble sleeping," I mumbled.

*Like you.*

The cool air against my warm cheek sent a shiver through me. "Jack?"

*Well, it ain't Humphrey Bogart.*

I smiled against the pillow.

*Why's your auntie making a racket in the kitchen?*

"Probably brewing some chamomile tea."

*That's not what I meant.*

"If I didn't know her better, I'd say she's as disturbed as I am about our close call on the highway."

*She's not?*

"No. I'm sure it's that stupid standee that's still got her riled."

*The cardboard cutout?*

"Sadie never could put up with being pressured or bullied into what to think, say, or read. It really makes her blood boil."

I considered getting up to join her, but I turned over instead. As much as I admired my aunt's spirit of independence, the right of our customers to purchase *Bang, Bang Baby* was pretty far down on my list of worries right now, and I had a lot of thinking to do.

*You want some help in that department, baby?*

"Absolutely."

*Okay, doll, shoot.*

I exhaled warm air into the newly cooled room. "Leo Rollins said there was no car behind us tonight. But I saw it in the mirror. A luxury sedan was tailgating us. Sadie saw it, too."

*And Leo didn't?*

"He said he didn't. But the sedan was right behind me when I turned onto the highway's onramp—and that road doesn't lead to anyplace but the highway. So where did the tailgater go?"

*You're sure the car didn't crash?*

"That's what I thought. But one of the state police officers who took our statements went back up the ramp to check the road and woods nearby. He said there was no crashed car. And nobody else reported seeing an accident, either. That car just vanished. And don't you find it *a tad* suspicious that the brakes on Seymour's VW failed right *after* he inherited Miss Todd's mansion?"

*Hey, maybe it was just a coincidence.*

"You're kidding, right?"

*Only your postal pal's mechanic can tell you whether his brakes were tampered with. If he finds no physical reason, then you'll have to consider other theories.*

"Like?"

*Like you said it yourself. The car vanished. What else vanishes?*

"I don't know what you mean."

*Didn't your old auntie say something about that road being haunted?*

"The phantom car story?"

*Seems to me I'm not the only spook in this neighborhood.*

I groaned and pulled a pillow over my head. "Are you telling me a phantom driver in a phantom car made Seymour's brakes fail?"

*You may not want to consider it—I know I didn't, back in my day. But on one of my cases, I had to consider it.*

"Consider what?"

*You'll see. It was part of my case.*

I pulled the pillow off my head. "Which case? Tell me."

*Close your eyes, baby. Go to sleep . . .*

"No. First tell me about your case."

*I'm going to show you. Close your eyes.*

"Jack, I really don't think that's going to work tonight."

*Why the hell not? We've done it before.*

"I know. But right now I'm just too wired. There's no way I'll be able to nod off."

Deep male laughter resounded in my head, loudly at first; then it slowly faded, getting weaker and weaker until it diminished completely. Jack's cool presence receded along with it, and the room became warm again.

I sighed and turned over, feeling frustrated and alone. Lying still in the darkness, I replayed the long day's events—thought about Seymour and Miss Todd, Mr. Stoddard and his strange assistant, Leo and the failed brakes. Disembodied heads floated in my mind like pieces of a puzzle, but I couldn't fit them together. As I groaned and turned over again I realized a cool breeze had begun to circle my bedpost. I glanced at the window. My curtains weren't moving. Neither were the tree limbs outside.

The breeze grew stronger, lifted strands of my auburn hair. I felt the energy, the familiar presence.

*Close your eyes, Penelope . . .*

"I told you already, Jack, I'm too wired. I can't fall—"

*Don't argue.*

"Fine!" I said, humoring the dead man. "Okay, they're

closed! But I told you—" I paused to yawn. "I'm not at all"—*yawn*—"sleepy . . ."

I OPENED MY eyes.

"Ordering! Two Blue Plates; one ham and Swiss, whiskey down; one bowl of red, make it cry; and burn the British with two eggs—wreck 'em!"

I was sitting on a stool at the counter of an old-time diner. Let me be clear: This was not some retro eatery in a suburban strip mall—a diner built two years ago to *appear* old. This place actually *was* old. The olive-green linoleum counter was wash-worn, the tables and chairs visibly rickety. Behind the counter a Caucasian waitress was shouting orders to two black cooks in grease-stained aprons, their white cardboard hats bobbing back and forth in the ordering window like props in a foodie puppet show.

Up front the customers in the place were mostly white men in suits. The few women in the diner wore hats and belted dresses, which fell past their knees. I glanced down at myself and saw that I was dressed just like them—in a light green print dress with short sleeves and a thin, black patent leather belt. I felt stockings on my legs and saw peep-toed pumps on my feet. Someone had given me a pedicure, too, with deep red polish.

I checked my fingers but couldn't see the nails. My hands were sheathed in white cotton gloves. A patent leather pocketbook with a little black strap sat primly on my lap. I noticed a mirrored case behind the counter, which displayed desserts. I caught a glimpse of my reflection between the cream pies and fruit tarts. My auburn hair, which I usually wore tied back into a no-fuss ponytail, was now hanging down to my shoulders in a sleek, glossy pageboy, the bangs rolled as perfectly as Barbara Stanwyck's in *Double Indemnity*. My cheeks were rouged, my eyes (sans glasses) were heavily made up, and my mouth outlined with a lipstick redder than a hazard light. As my finely plucked eyebrows rose, I heard a child's high-pitched voice ask—

"Who's *she*?"

I glanced at the counter stool next to mine, half expecting to see Spencer, but it was another little boy sitting there—one I'd never seen before. His freckled face needed a good washing and so did his clothes; and his brown, shaggy hair looked like it could use a good trimming.

The boys in Quindicott wore T-shirts and jeans, almost exclusively. This boy wore a collared shirt tucked into belted and cuffed gabardine slacks. He didn't appear older than twelve, yet his frank, appraising brown eyes were staring up at me with an expression older and harder than any twelve-year-old's I'd ever seen.

"Did ya hear me, Mr. Shepard?" the boy asked. "Who's *she*?"

"She's going to help me with your case, kid. That's who she is." The voice was deep, gravelly, and intimately familiar.

I looked past the boy and saw the man. "Jack."

It took me a minute to get used to the realness of him—the fortyish face with its hard planes and angles; the flat, square chin with its daunting dagger-shaped scar. His sandy-haired head was bare at the moment, but I noticed his gray fedora sitting on the counter in front of him. The double-breasted suit looked familiar, too, with its lines tightly tailored to his broad shoulders and narrow waist.

"Hiya, baby. Welcome back to my world."

He was gazing at me now, over the boy's shaggy head, with a kind of bemused expectation—as if waiting for me to react to this trip back in time, back to the world of his memories.

I tore my gaze away from his intense granite eyes to check out the scene beyond the diner's front window. I could see it was daytime, the sidewalk crowded with pedestrians in '40s-era garb—men in suits and hats, women in calf-length skirts and dresses. Not one pair of distressed jeans. No flip-flops, T-shirts, tattoos, or piercings. The cars looked like something from a Smithsonian display: heavy metal dinosaurs spewing leaded fossil fuel. A few stories above, the steel-girder framework of an elevated train muted the midday light, dappling the otherwise sunny day with gray shadows and blue shade.

I glanced back at my PI. "What year is it exactly?"

Jack slid a newspaper across the dull olive counter. I skimmed the *Times* headlines—"Butter Rises to 90 Cents a Pound," "Truman Hails National Guard," "Long Island Fire Kills 8." My gaze searched page one for the date: September 10, 1947. Two years before a bullet sent Jack Shepard to an early afterlife.

"She got a name, Mr. Shepard?" the boy asked.

"She does," Jack replied, throwing a wink down the counter at me. "But it's Mrs. McClure to you."

The boy whistled. "She's a good looker. She your girl?"

"I'm not his girlfriend," I said. "I'm his—"

"Secretary," Jack said.

"Partner," I corrected. "Remember?"

"We'll see," Jack murmured, patting his pocket.

*"We'll see?"* I repeated.

"Case by case, honey. Case by case."

Jack pulled out a pack of cigarettes, shook one clear. I stared in shock as he dared to light up inside the restaurant. "Are you crazy?" I said, expecting the restaurant manager to rush over immediately and kick him out. And then I remembered.

"What's with the face?" Jack asked. "Oh, sorry. You want one?" He offered me the pack.

I shook my head.

"Oh, yeah." Jack laughed. "Forgot. You're one of those good-girl, do-right, no-smokin' Janes."

"Nicotine's a terrible carcinogen, Jack. That's why smoking's been banned almost everywhere in my time."

The PI blew a smoke ring. "Well, we're not in your time."

"I'll have hers!" In the space of an eyeblink, the little boy had grabbed a cigarette from the pack and shoved it between his lips. "Got a light?"

I plucked the Lucky from the kid's mouth, shoved it back into Jack's pack, and slid it back to its owner.

"Hey!" the boy cried. "What's the big idea?!"

"Your health's the big idea, young man. Haven't you heard that smoking causes lung cancer?"

"Lung what?" The kid turned to Jack. "Jiminy crickets, what's she talking about!"

Jack took another drag, blew it out. "She's saying you're too young to smoke. *That* I happen to agree with."

"I'm twelve years old!" the boy cried, as if that were plenty old enough.

"You shouldn't start smoking at *any* age," I said.

Jack threw me another bemused look, and I realized with a start that whatever this boy did back here wouldn't matter anyway. These were Jack's memories, his long-past memories. This little boy, whoever he was, might very well be deceased already. Feeling like an idiot, I closed my eyes.

"Easy, baby," Jack whispered. "We're here for a reason, remember? Your case—and mine."

My eyelids lifted. "This boy is your case?"

Jack nodded.

"What's his name?"

"John James Conway's the name," the boy announced loudly between us. "But you can call me J. J."

I looked back down at him. "Okay, J. J. Maybe *you* can tell me what I'm doing here?"

"That's easy. I just hired Mr. Shepard for a finder's job."

I smiled at Jack. "Lost dog?"

Jack shook his head. "Mother."

My face fell. "His mother's missing?"

"She went off to work two weeks ago and never came home," J. J. said.

"Where does she work?" I asked.

"At a school uptown. She's a teacher."

"What school exactly?"

The boy shrugged. "She never told me."

"Where's your dad, J. J.?"

"What dad?"

I met Jack's eyes above J. J.'s head. "What do I need to know here?"

"His mother's a schoolteacher. She went off to work uptown, never came home. Kid doesn't know where she teaches. Mother never told him."

My lips pursed. "I know that already. The boy just informed me of those facts."

"And?" Jack took another drag on his cigarette, blew it out. "What's your next step?"

"*My* next step? This was *your* case."

"Not anymore, baby. If you're bucking for partner, you're going to have to show me what you got."

# CHAPTER 11

## *Lost and Found*

Listen, darling, tomorrow I'll buy you a whole lot of detective stories, but don't worry your pretty little head over mysteries tonight.

—Detective Nick Charles to his wife, Nora, in *The Thin Man*,
Dashiell Hammett, 1933

I DRUMMED MY white-gloved fingers on the dull green countertop and considered my options. "Just tell me one thing, Jack. What does this case have to do with what's happening in my time?"

"That's for me to know and you to find out." He picked up his coffee cup and threw me a wink. "If you're up to it."

"Who's *she*?"

Once again, it was a high-pitched voice asking the question, only this time it wasn't a boy's. This voice belonged to a grown woman—very grown.

Standing in front of Jack, holding a plate of roast beef and mashed potatoes, was a waitress wearing a pink apron. The woman was young—probably mid-twenties. She was also quite tall and, much like our Zara Underwood standee, built with conspicuously above-average lung capacity. Beneath her little pink waitress hat, her face was roundish, her features handsome. She wore her light blond hair in curls, and her big blue eyes were presently glaring at me.

It was painfully obvious the waitress was unhappy to see some other female on the receiving end of a Jack Shepard wink. She banged the plate of food down on the counter in front of the PI and pointed.

"She your sister or something?"

Jack tossed an amused glance at me. "Or something."

The waitress scowled, sizing me up.

"That sure smells good," J. J. announced, eyeballing the Blue Plate special.

Jack observed the boy. "You hungry?"

J. J. nodded.

"Well, that's good. 'Cause, come to think of it . . ." Jack scratched the back of his head. "I'm not that hungry after all."

"No foolin'?"

"No foolin'. So help me out, kid." Jack slid the plate over. "Take this off my hands, will ya?"

"Sure thing, Mr. Shepard!"

J. J. dug in, shoving the potatoes into his mouth like he hadn't had a hot meal in days. I met Jack's eyes again. He shrugged, looked away.

The waitress was still standing in front of him. She propped her shapely hip and put a hand on it. "So what about those big plans of yours, Jack Shepard? The ones you had for *us* tonight?"

Jack glanced at my raised eyebrow and shifted on his stool. "We'll have to make it another night, Birdie. See, I just took on a case." He gestured in the general direction of J. J. and me.

"Oh." Birdie's arm fell off her hip and her scowl relaxed into the semblance of a sympathetic frown. She lowered her voice. "The dame and her kid your new clients, huh?"

"Yeah, Birdie, something like that."

J. J. snickered between bites of roast beef. Jack lightly

elbowed him. The waitress caught the exchange and looked me over again.

"You gonna have anything, sister? Or you just gonna sit there takin' up a seat at my counter?"

"Um—"

"Do me a favor, doll," Jack murmured. "Don't order a damn Vesper this time. Go for something that's been invented in this century."

"The Vesper *was* created in this century, Jack. Don't you remember? *Casino Royale*, Ian Fleming, 1952."

"At the moment, dollface, 1952 is still five years away."

The waitress put a hand on her hip. "Lady, are you gonna order or what?"

"Yes," I said. "A cup of coffee, please."

The waitress shook her head. "Big spender," she muttered, then sashayed away, putting far more swing into her hips (in my opinion) than was necessary for simple locomotion to a coffeemaker. I glanced down the counter and sighed. Jack's gaze was exactly where I figured it would be—glued to her caboose.

*"Ah-hem!"* I said.

"Yeah, baby?" Jack asked without breaking his focus. "You got something to say?"

"Yes. Were you *often* in the habit of picking up luncheonette waitresses?"

Jack smirked my way. "You got something to say about *the case*?"

"As a matter of fact, I do. I think we should begin our investigation by calling New York's Board of Education. If the little boy here doesn't know where his mother teaches, then we can ask them to look up her name. Next we go to the woman's school and question her boss and coworkers, find out what they know."

"Uh-huh." Jack lit a second cigarette. He didn't appear impressed with my logic.

"What's wrong?"

"Plenty." Jack said, blowing out a snow-white cloud of carcinogens. "Your first and best witness is sitting right beside you. Don't you want to find out what else the kid knows before you start charging up my phone bill?"

"Oh. Right. Of course." I turned to the little boy who'd just about licked Jack's plate clean. "J. J., what else can you tell me about your mother?"

"What else you wanna know?"

"Well . . ." The waitress returned with my coffee and a little air-kiss for Jack before sashaying away again. I concentrated on my young client. "Did she say anything special to you on the morning she disappeared?"

J. J. shook his head. "She just went off to work as usual."

"Did she have any special friends?"

J. J. shrugged. "Just Frankie."

"Frankie?" I repeated. "And who is he?"

"Frankie Papps. He's her boyfriend."

"Do you know how to reach this man? Where he lives? What he does for a living?"

J. J. shook his head. "I don't know where he lives. But my mom told me he's an electrician."

I motioned to Jack, then leaned around the boy's back to whisper: "Shouldn't we go to the police with this?"

"Police!" J. J. cried. "Hey, what's the big idea, Mr. Shepard? No police. You promised!"

"That's right, kid, take it easy." Jack met my eyes. "He says he'll run away if we bring the police in. He doesn't have any other family and he knows they'll stash him in an institution if they find out he's living on his own."

"But, Jack," I whispered, "he's only twelve."

"I can take care of myself!" J. J. declared. "I've got a job at the newsstand and everything. Jiminy crickets, Mr. Shepard, I already paid you twenty dollars. You're not going back on your promise, are you?"

"No, kid, I'm not. We'll find out what happened to your mother."

I frowned at Jack. "You took twenty dollars from this little boy?"

"Sure," Jack said, stubbing out the butt of his cigarette.

"I've got bills to pay, you know. I can't let it get around that I do charity work."

"Well, it's not very nice."

*"Nice?"* Jack grunted. "On these streets, baby, a 'nice guy' rep will land you six feet under. Wake up and smell the coffee."

I knew Jack wasn't being literal, but at the mention of coffee I remembered my cup. Birdie had served it to me black, and I really preferred milk and sugar. I was about to ask for some when Jack lifted his scarred chin and yelled—

"Hey, Birdie! Check!"

The PI reached for his wallet and Birdie sashayed back over, scribbling as she walked. "There you go, Jack," she said, sliding the check to him facedown.

As she sauntered away, I noticed something was written on the back.

"What's that she wrote?" J. J. asked, curiously craning his neck. "Plaza-3367."

Jack slapped down a dollar bill, picked up the check, folded it neatly, and tucked it into his breast pocket.

"What's Plaza-3367?" I asked. "An address?"

The little boy turned to Jack. "For a lady shamus she sure is slow."

Jack grabbed his fedora and rose from his stool. "Take it easy on her, kid. Where she came from, they do things different."

"Oh, I get it!" The boy faced me. "You're from Canada or something, huh?"

"Or something," I said.

"Come on, gang. Let's blow this joint." Jack began to herd us toward the door. J. J. skipped ahead. I was right behind.

"So what's Plaza-3367 really?" I pressed. "A clue?"

Jack's eyes were laughing. "You could call it that."

"Excuse me?" I said.

J. J. swung around. "Jeez, Mrs. McClure, it's a cinch!" he announced loud enough for half the diners to hear. "The waitress gave him her phone number!"

Jack turned the boy back around and pushed him through the front door. "Okay, kid. I think she finally got it."

I followed the pair onto Third Avenue's crowded sidewalk and noticed the busy newsstand on the corner. Reaching up, I tapped Jack's cementlike shoulder. "Hey!"

"Easy, baby. Don't go getting jealous on me—"

I rolled my eyes. "I'm *trying* to tell you that I just changed my investigation strategy."

Jack put the fedora back on his head and gazed down at me. "To what?"

I pointed to the newsstand. "Didn't J. J. say he works at that newsstand?"

"Yeah, he did."

"So we should speak to his boss. He might have some more coherent idea of what happened to his mother."

"Think so, huh?" Jack's eyebrow arched. "That's what I thought, too." He grabbed my arm. "Come on."


WE SPOKE WITH Mac Dougherty, the newsstand owner who employed J. J. He was thirty-two and blinded in one eye from a grenade battle in Germany's Hurtgen Forest. Jack had been one of the commanding officers in the field. He clearly thought the world of Jack, but he said he'd never met J. J.'s mother. The only things he knew about the woman were what J. J. had mentioned to him—she was a schoolteacher who taught uptown.

Jack mentioned the possibility of J. J. staying with him, but Dougherty shook his head.

"Wish I could," he said. "But the wife and I, we already got four mouths to feed and one on the way in a two-bedroom flat. We're full up. And anyway, J. J. has a place all to himself now, says he can take care of himself."

I was about to argue but bit my tongue. This was 1947. A man like Mac Dougherty, half-blind, his head already half-gray, had probably grown up fast in the middle of the Depression. J. J.'s situation wouldn't look the same to him as it did to me.

Jack pulled me to the side. "Okay, baby, what's your next move?"

I chewed my glossy red lips. "We need to find this Frankie Papps. If he's the woman's boyfriend, then he either has a clue to where she went, or else he had something to do with—" I glanced back to the newsstand, made sure J. J. was out of earshot. "I hate to say it, but this Frankie person might have had something to do with 'disappearing' the boy's mother."

"And how will I find Frankie?"

"Phone book?"

"I'll save you some time, doll. Frankie wasn't listed. Probably didn't even have a phone."

"What about your cop friends? You used to be on the police force, didn't you? Before you joined up and went off to fight the Nazis."

"No record for a Frankie Papps. No driver's license, either—not under that name."

"What do you mean *that* name? Are you saying—" A mechanized roar suddenly drowned out my words. I felt the vibrations of the girders around me and realized a train was passing on the elevated tracks overhead. I waited for the noise to subside. "Are you saying he was using an alias?"

"It's always a possibility, isn't it?" Jack folded his arms. "Come on, baby, what's your next step? We haven't got all day."

"You mean night, don't you?" I glanced around. Everything seemed real enough—the roar of the el train, the snap of high heels on pavement, the rank smell of leaded gasoline, the coolness of the dappled shade beneath the raised subway tracks. "This is all just a dream, isn't it?"

"It's more than that and you know it. Come on, honey. *Think.*"

"Okay. I guess we should search the missing woman's residence next, look for leads there."

"Bingo."

A minute later, Jack was herding us again—this time we

were heading downtown. Despite the slight limp from his old war wound, Jack guided us smoothly through the crowds, maneuvering our little group around men in fedoras, ladies in hats and round-toed pumps.

The Big Apple's blocks were lined with restaurants, bars, and stone stoops leading up to residential buildings—places that looked much the same as they had during my own years working in the city. But there were other sights, too, things I'd never seen in my time: an antiques store with a wooden Indian chief standing guard, a barber shop with an old-fashioned candy-striped pole, a rustic food stand with fruits and vegetables displayed in wooden crates, and the kind of corner drugstores that had lunch counters and soda jerks.

I noticed sidewalk shoeshine booths, too, and a hardware store with a dozen cast-iron potbellied stoves sitting out front. At the sight of them, I stopped and pointed.

"Why in the world would a New Yorker need one of those?"

A wood- or coal-burning stove might be useful in the country to warm a small unheated cabin, but this was the middle of Manhattan.

Jack laughed. "Cold-water flats, baby. We still got 'em back here."

J. J. Conway's residence turned out to be one of them. His building was a six-floor brownstone walkup—although we didn't have to walk *up*. J. J. and his mom were renting a basement apartment

We moved along a dimly lit hallway, then down an even more dimly lit stairwell. There were only four doors along the basement corridor. J. J. pulled a key from the pocket of his wrinkled gabardine slacks, stepped toward the door marked B2, and froze.

"That's funny," he said.

"What's funny?" I asked.

"Door's already opened."

I looked at the knob and lock. They were intact and unmolested. There was no break-in here. Someone had used a key. I began to hear sounds inside the apartment. Someone was loudly opening drawers, one after another. I put a hand on J. J.'s shoulder.

"Maybe it's your mom. Maybe she's come back."

The boy stared up at me like a hopeful puppy. "You think so?"

I moved forward, my hand reaching out to push the door all the way open, but I was suddenly jerked backward by a sharp tug on my elbow.

"Jack! What are you—"

"Stay quiet," he whispered, glancing down. "Both of you." His long left arm marshaled us behind him while his right hand dipped into his double-breasted jacket.

"What are you doing?" I whispered.

"You blew the call, honey." He pulled his .45 free of its shoulder holster.

"Wow." At the sight of Jack's gun, J. J.'s eyes went wide. "Lemme see!"

"Shhh." I grabbed J. J.'s small shoulders and maneuvered him behind me. "Jack, what's going on?"

"Those aren't the sounds of some dame moving around her own apartment, baby. Someone's tossing this place."

"Tossing?"

"Ransacking it."

Jack held his gun with two hands. As he slowly pushed the door open with his foot, he brought the weapon level in front of him, quickly sweeping the room with the sight until—

"Don't move!"

Jack stepped into the apartment.

"Stay here," I whispered to J. J., then followed Jack in.

The basement room was small, dark, and sparsely furnished—a threadbare sofa and a scuffed wooden table with two unmatched chairs. The only natural light came from two barred windows high on one wall. A black potbellied stove stood off to the side, near a small white sink. Next to it, a line of cupboards and a closet stood with their doors wide open, their contents scattered. Through the open bedroom door I noticed a dresser with its drawers pulled out.

Jack's large body was closing in on a young man now stepping out of the bedroom. The intruder had olive skin, dark hair, and his frame was just about as skinny as the living room's floor lamp. He stared at Jack with hard eyes, his hands holding a pillowcase stuffed with bulky items—presumably stolen from this apartment, but I couldn't imagine what there was of value to steal.

"Drop the bag," Jack commanded, "and put your hands up."

The young man didn't obey; he just kept moving away from the PI. The intruder didn't appear armed, either, and I couldn't imagine Jack would actually shoot an unarmed young man.

Jack took a step closer. "Do you speak English?"

The young man said nothing. And then, in an explosive motion, he swung the bulky pillowcase at Jack's gun. Jack reared back and in the second it took to regain his balance, the young man vaulted for the apartment's front door. Out in the hall, J. J. stuck his leg out. The burglar tripped, sprawling across the cold concrete. He got up a split second later.

By now Jack had recovered. "Stop!" he yelled. "Stop or I'll shoot!"

The young man didn't stop—but he didn't get away clean, either. During his fall, the pillowcase had spilled its contents, and he didn't have time to gather anything up. He raced for the stairs. Jack stepped into the hall, leveled his gun at the intruder's leg, and fired. The shot just missed, lodging into the back wall while the intruder disappeared into the stairwell.

Jack followed with surprising speed, forcing his bad leg to move faster than it had on Third Avenue's sidewalk. I kicked off my peep-toed pumps and ran after him. By the time I reached the front steps of the apartment house, however, Jack was already holstering his weapon.

"Where did the guy go?" I asked between deep breaths.

"Getaway car."

"What?!"

"He sprinted a block"—Jack pointed up the avenue—"then jumped in the back of a black Packard."

"Did you get a license plate?"

"Half of it."

"The getaway car makes no sense. I mean, for a bank robbery maybe. But that apartment's not exactly Fort Knox. What could there be to steal that's of any real value?"

Jack folded his arms. "Good reasoning, baby. What else do you think? What did you notice?"

"The door wasn't damaged. The burglar had a key."

"Or he was an expert at picking locks."

"But why that lock? Why not any other apartment?"

"Let's go."

Jack led me back to the basement where we found J. J. on his hands and knees in the hallway, stuffing items back into the pillowcase. We brought the case and J. J. back into the apartment and spread the almost-stolen booty on the scuffed wooden table.

I expected to see cheap things that could be pawned—clothes, hats, shoes. What I saw instead left me gaping in confusion: tarot cards, a Ouija board, a large purple fur-lined cape, books about fortune-telling and séances, a cheap crystal ball, a costume jewelry tiara, and one more thing—

"Oh, my God. I don't believe it." I picked up the polished steel dagger. On the hilt was a familiar embossed design—the same design I'd seen on the wrought-iron gate of the late Miss Timothea Todd's Larchmont Avenue mansion.

I ran my hand along the raised lines of the five-pointed star with the fleur-de-lis at its center. "It's exactly like the one Leo Rollins handed me beside the highway. Except this one's brand-new. It isn't an antique."

"Not yet," Jack said.

"Who's Leo Rollins?" J. J. asked.

I glanced up at Jack.

"Nobody, kid," he replied. "Did you get a look at the bag man?"

J. J. nodded.

"Did you know him?"

"Nope. Never saw him before. Did you shoot him, Mr. Shepard?"

"Naw," Jack said. "Too many bystanders."

"Awww, too bad!"

Jack pointed at the occult items spread out on the table. "So what's with all the fortune-telling gewgaws?"

"You said exactly what I was thinking," I murmured.

Jack smirked. "Ain't that a switch."

"This is my mom's stuff," J. J. said.

I frowned. "I thought you said your mother was a schoolteacher."

"She is," J. J. said. "But about a month ago, she said she hit her head and now she can see weird stuff, like promotions of the future."

"Don't you mean *premonitions* of the future?"

J. J. rolled his eyes. "That's what I said, didn't I? Mom told me she can talk to dead people now. You know, ghosts and stuff."

I exchanged a glance with Jack (sounds familiar, huh?), then picked up one of the occult books on séances, which included illustrations, case histories, and step-by-step instructions on conducting them.

"My mom said the books were going to help her learn more about her new abilities and help her get better at using them. Some other people were helping her get better at it, too."

"People?" I shut the book. "What people?"

J. J. shrugged. "She never told me. But she did practice an awful lot with the crystal ball and the Ouija board."

I examined the items, one by one, but there were no clues to where they came from—no names or addresses. I pulled Jack aside. "The best lead is still the boyfriend."

Jack nodded. "So how are you going to find him?"

"I'll bet I can find a clue in here somewhere . . ." I paused and tried to think like a woman—not a stretch since I was one. "J. J., where do you and your mom sleep in this apartment?"

"I use this sofa." He pointed. "And Mom uses the bedroom."

I went into the small room and began to search it. The burglar had already tossed the drawers; the contents were scattered on the bed and floor. I looked for an address book or letters or a diary—and came up with nothing. I searched a worn handbag but found only white gloves, tissues, and an old lipstick.

Finally I located what would have been the contents of the woman's lingerie drawer and started pawing through her underthings. "Got something!"

"What, baby?" Jack moved in.

I held up a small gift box. I opened it and found a business card and a velvet-lined jewelry box with nothing inside. Jack watched me closely. "Now what, baby?"

I went to J. J. "What was in this jewelry box?"

"Pearl earrings," the boy said. "I pawned them for twenty dollars, to pay Mr. Shepard."

I fingered the small cream-colored card. "BROADWAY'S BEST JEWELRY," I read. The address was near Times Square and the Theater District. "Happy Birthday! Love, Frankie."

I waved the card at J. J. "The earrings were a gift from your mom's boyfriend? Frankie Papps, right?"

J. J. nodded. "My mom's had a lot of them. Boyfriends, I mean, but she's been with Frankie the longest—almost six months now."

I exchanged glances with Jack and waved the card again. "I think we should talk to this jeweler."

Jack gave me a nod of approval. We finished up with the apartment search and then Jack told J. J. to pack a bag with his clothes and underwear and anything else he might need for a little trip.

"Where am I going?" he asked.

"Don't give me any lip, kid. If you want me on your case, then just do as I say."

Jack took us back up on the street, hailed a cab, and had the driver take us to a building on Second Avenue. He left us on the stone stoop for a few minutes while he walked upstairs to have a word with somebody. When he came back down, his previously grim expression appeared a little lighter.

"Come on up," he said.

We walked up three flights and paused by the open front door of a plump, middle-aged woman wearing a housedress and glasses. She had a kind face with a gently creased olive complexion and black curls threaded with gray.

"This is Mrs. Dellarusso," Jack told J. J. "She says she'd be very pleased to look after you."

"That's nice, but I don't need lookin' after," J. J. whispered.

Mrs. Dellarusso smiled and bent down closer to J. J. "You don't want to taste my spaghetti and meatballs? Or my fresh blueberry pie?"

J. J.'s eyes went wide. "Blueberry pie?"

"Sure. And with ice cream, too. And you can listen to any show you like on my radio."

"You have a radio?"

Mrs. Dellarusso stepped back from the doorway. "Come on in and look."

J. J. glanced at Jack. "Just for a minute . . ."

A minute later, J. J. was shoveling blueberry pie and ice cream into his mouth. Then he checked out the big bedroom Mrs. Dellarusso said could be all his for as long as he wanted—the one with a large window looking out on Second Avenue.

"Jiminy crickets, what a view! You can see all the way down the block!"

When it was finally decided that J. J. was going to stay with Mrs. Dellarusso until Jack could find his mother, we headed for the door. I noticed Jack handing the woman something and realized it was the twenty dollars J. J. had paid him for his PI services.

"That should help with the food and the rent for the boy," Jack said quietly.

"You don't need to give me anything, Mr. Shepard," Mrs. Dellarusso insisted. "Not after what you did for my son."

But Jack pressed the money into her hand.

"Who's the woman's son?" I asked as we descended the stairs.

"A young sergeant I knew over there. I just made sure she got his last letters and personals, that's all."

"*Was* her only son? You mean he—"

"Caught a round in the guts. Bled to death in the field."

I thought of my own son and felt the air go out of my lungs. In almost the next second, I reconsidered the bright look in the woman's lined face when she first laid eyes on the scruffy, smudged-face J. J. Conway.

"You did a nice thing there," I told Jack when we reached the building's small, tiled lobby.

He shrugged it off. "Had to stash the kid somewhere. I knew somebody sent that burglar. I figured whoever wanted that junk was going to come back for it again."

"Do you think that burglar had the mother's key, Jack?" He nodded.

"Well, I'd like to know where J. J.'s mother got that dagger with the Todd Mansion design on its hilt. Is it just some random purchase? Or did someone give it to her? And who are these 'people' that J. J. mentioned, the ones supposedly helping his mom with her new occult powers? Did they give her the dagger? The boyfriend is bound to know more."

Jack folded his arms and gazed down at me. "So what's your next step?"

"We go to the Broadway jewelry store and find out if anyone knows Frankie Papps."

With a single finger Jack pushed back the brim of his fedora. Then he rested an arm on the wall near my head. "It's pretty late, honey. Store's probably closing up by now. How about you and I go back to my place and"—he winked—"wait till morning."

I raised an eyebrow. "Is that what your big plans were with that well-endowed luncheonette girl?"

"Aw, baby, that was a long time ago . . . *before* I met you."

"Aw, Jack. Are you going soft on me?"

"Naw, sweetheart." He smiled. "Must be your imagination."

Maybe this was just a dream, but Jack sure felt real, standing close, leaning closer, until I felt a hard tug on my arm.

*What the . . . ?*

Another tug.

"Mom!"

A child's voice. A boy was calling for his mother. Was it J. J. calling?

"Mooooom!"

I opened my eyes. My son was standing next to my bed.

"Get up, Mom!"

"Spencer?"

"You have to drive me to the bus by nine, remember? I'm going to camp today!"

# CHAPTER 12

## *Limbo*

After that nothing happened for three days. Nobody slugged me or shot at me or called me up on the phone and warned me to keep my nose clean. Nobody hired me to find the wandering daughter, the erring wife, the lost pearl necklace, or the missing will. I just sat there and looked at the wall.

—Philip Marlow in *The Long Goodbye*, Raymond Chandler, 1953

THAT MORNING'S EVENTS blew me around like an Atlantic gale. After getting Spencer packed off to camp, I drove back to the store to find a waiting sales rep from a new regional publisher. I'd no sooner said goodbye to him than a female customer—one I hadn't seen in months—began loudly complaining about the Zara Underwood display. After finally calming her down, a bestselling author dropped in unexpectedly to sign all of her stock and I had to run to Cooper Family Bakery to pick up refreshments for the Tea and Sympathy book club—a local group of working women who met during lunch breaks to discuss British mysteries. Next a cluster of touring seniors descended on me with dozens of questions about our events schedule while a rather large group of men I'd never seen before lined up to buy *Bang, Bang Baby.*

All of that took place amid the typical increased traffic

Sadie and I handled this time of year of young people in search of beach books, and loyal customers wanting advice for vacation reading.

My few minutes of free time I used to search the Internet for any image matches on the Todd Mansion pentagram. Unfortunately, I could find nothing that even came close to matching the unique design.

By seven o'clock, Sadie was more than ready for her dinner date with Bud and I was holding the literary fort with Bonnie Franzetti and our new part-timer, Dilbert Randall, a St. Francis history major with brown wavy hair, an easygoing smile, and glasses of the small, round, Harry Potter variety.

As far as I could tell, Dilbert's entire wardrobe consisted of worn blue jeans, Hush Puppies, and pastel-colored Izod shirts. His passion for historical mysteries, on the other hand, ranged from Lynda S. Robinson's lively Egyptian mysteries—set in the time of Tutankhamun—to Ellis Peters's twelfth-century Brother Cadfael chronicles and the Victorian cases of Anne Perry's Inspector Thomas Pitt.

More than once during my crazy-busy workday it occurred to me that Jack Shepard hadn't said *boo* to me. But then I remembered what the ghost had told me the day before in my car—that I'd been moving too fast to hear him—and I began to think the communication problem was mine.

I was just about ready to take a short break and *finally* slow down enough to maybe hear my ghost's voice when a hip, young, bohemian crowd descended on us. They'd just exited a showing of *Mulholland Drive* at the Movie Town Theater's David Lynch retrospective and flooded the aisles to check out the stock. Even after viewing the surreal Lynch film, however, the sight of an overexcited Fiona Finch rushing through the front door in an atomic yellow pantsuit managed to attract a few stares.

Fiona's eyes flashed wildly as she began to shout, "Pen! Pen!" while waving her arm so frantically she scattered the pack of teenage boys that had gathered around the Zara Underwood dump.

"Where's Sadie?!" she asked breathlessly after finding me behind the check-out counter.

"Sorry, Fiona," I said, ringing up the next customer. "Sadie's at the Seafood Shack having dinner with Bud. What's got you so excited?"

"I just heard about Miss Todd's legacy! She left you mystery and true-crime first editions dating back to the 1950s?!"

Frankly, I was surprised it took Fiona twenty-four whole hours to uncover what was supposed to be completely confidential information.

"I simply must see that list!" Fiona gestured so suddenly that the crested cockatoo brooch pinned to her lapel nearly took flight.

"It's upstairs, Fiona. Sadie's still going over it. I'm sure she'll share it with you when she's ready."

"So is it true what else I heard? Has Seymour Tarnish actually inherited the Todd place?"

I handed the change back to my customer, bagged up her purchases, and turned to Fiona. "Miss Todd left him her house, everything inside it, the land around it, and the two outbuildings."

"That place is a wholly unique Second Empire. I'm dying to see the interior. You've been there. Do think the furniture is authentic Victorian?"

"Looks like it to me, but I'm no antiques expert. I'm sure Seymour will be happy to show you around once he takes over."

Fiona turned her eyes to the ceiling. "Now what is that silly mailman going to do with a fine old Victorian treasure, I wonder? Sell it?"

I leaned closer. "It's better for you if Seymour keeps the place."

She blinked. "What have you heard, Pen? Tell me."

I called Bonnie over and asked her to handle the check-out line. Then I spoke to Dilbert, who was assisting customers on the floor. "I'm going to set up the events room for the Feline

Friends reading group. Keep an eye on the counter and help Bonnie if she gets jammed up."

"No problem, Mrs. McClure."

I turned to Fiona. "Okay, follow me."

I led her through the archway to our events space, turned up the lights on the darkened area, and took down two folding chairs from the stack.

We sat down face to face, and I began to tell Fiona all about the Lindsey-Tilton group's offer to purchase the Todd place, with an eye toward transforming it into our town's second bed-and-breakfast—in direct competition to Fiona's already established inn.

"That's the trouble with being a pioneer," Fiona said. "You end up getting scalped! It took Barney and me fifteen hard years to establish Finch Inn, and now some international bunch with a big war chest is going to try squeezing us out!"

"Take it easy. Seymour probably won't sell. Or at least that's what he told Mr. Stoddard."

That did little to reassure Fiona. "A million bucks is a lot of money to a mailman who thinks a wise investment for thirty thousand in *Jeopardy!* winnings is an ice cream truck. Do you think he'll hold out?"

I took a deep breath. "Well . . . there's another reason Seymour might sell. One that's got nothing to do with money."

"What?" Fiona snorted. "Is the place supposed to be haunted?"

I let her quip hover in the air for a moment, and then I said, "Yes."

Fiona's eyes widened and (no surprise) the true-crime reader in her instantly came out. "Do you think Miss Todd's death is connected to the haunted house rumor?! Did you know that some in town are wondering if Seymour had a hand in scaring her to death?"

"Let me guess: The rumor came out of Chief Ciders's office?"

"Of course! I ran into Debra Lane in Leo Rollins's

electronics shop. She talked to her cousin Joyce, who's Chief Ciders's secretary. Joyce told her the chief nearly arrested the mailman for murder, and Ciders hasn't given up yet! He's waiting for the state forensics and the medical examiner's final report."

"Well, that's no surprise, but I already know what the town's M.E. is going to say. Dr. Rubino is ruling that Miss Todd died of natural causes. I doubt the autopsy will alter his opinion. And even if the state comes back with evidence that Seymour was in the house, it doesn't prove any guilt. He already admitted that Miss Todd permitted him to step inside to leave the mail on the foyer table."

Fiona smirked. "But you think something's wrong with the way Miss Todd died, don't you?"

"I'm no doctor, but . . ." I told Fiona about the state of Miss Todd's corpse when I found it, the expression of horror on her face, and about the weird cold spot that seemed to hover near the body.

"Goodness," she whispered.

"I'm sure 'goodness' had nothing to do with it. I know Seymour and I'm positive he had nothing to do with it, either."

"How does Seymour feel about all this?"

"As far as I can tell, he's stunned that Miss Todd remembered him in her will. And he can't wait to become a resident of Larchmont Avenue."

Fiona met my eyes. "That's good. Then he probably won't sell the estate."

"I know, and that's what worries me. I think maybe whoever had a hand in killing Miss Todd might have been trying to get possession of her place. Seymour's a wild card. Now that he has possession of it, I'm worried his life might be in danger."

"That's an awfully big leap, Pen. I mean, you said it yourself, the medical examiner doesn't even think there was foul play surrounding Miss Todd's death."

"Well, something else happened. Something you don't

know about. Last night, while Sadie and I were driving home . . ."

I told Fiona about the VW breadloaf bus losing its brakes. I mentioned the mysterious phantom car behind us, and Leo Rollins showing up right after the accident with an elaborate dagger that had the exact same markings as Todd Mansion's wrought-iron fence.

Fiona frowned and shook her head. "I don't know what to make of all that. I mean . . . are you saying Leo had something to do with those brakes failing?"

"No. I mean, I don't want to accuse the man . . . I don't have any evidence, and even Seymour thinks it's his mechanic's fault. He's waiting to hear from the garage on what went wrong."

"You mean, you're waiting to hear whether or not the brakes were sabotaged?"

I nodded. "If they were, then it's just too much of a co-incidence, don't you think? I mean, it happened right after he inherited the mansion."

"And right after he was accused of murdering Miss Todd. Don't forget that!"

"What are you saying?"

"That someone may be trying to exact revenge."

"Revenge?" I hadn't thought of that. "Who would want to avenge Miss Todd's murder—if she even *was* murdered?"

I thought back to our meeting with Mr. Stoddard. He'd mentioned Miss Todd having a sister, who insisted on remaining anonymous. I asked Fiona what she knew about that—after all, the innkeeper had dug up enough town dirt over the years to fill Quindicott Pond—but Fiona shook her head (which was obviously still focused on one thing).

"I didn't know the old lady except by reputation; and of course her property is well known. That Larchmont Victorian's a real jewel. And if Seymour Tarnish sells to the Lindsey-Tilton group, they'll turn it into our competition! When is he moving in?"

"He signed papers last night, and he plans to have a wake for Miss Todd on Saturday night."

Fiona bit her thumbnail. "That doesn't give me much time."

"Time to do what?"

"To bribe that stubborn mailman into staying at Todd Mansion, and *not* selling out to my competition!"


"DO YOU REALLY think that . . . that *thing*"—the woman punched her index finger at the Zara Underwood display—"is appropriate for our town's bookstore?"

It was now Friday afternoon; I *still* hadn't heard from Jack, but at least I'd made it to three P.M. before I received the first complaint of the day. This time it came from Binky Stuckey, wife of Quindicott's premier car dealer, Scott Stuckey of Stuckey Motors. Binky had just caught her eight-year-old twins ogling the provocative standee. After sending the boys scampering to the children's section, the angry mother called me to the front of the store to voice her protest.

Smiling politely, I shrugged. "I admit it's not wholesome, but it's not really offensive, either. Miss Underwood *is* wearing clothes, and we've both seen more exposed flesh at the beach."

"A *nude* beach, perhaps," Mrs. Stuckey countered. "Can't you get rid of that? Cover it up."

Dilbert Randall's head popped up from behind a stack of Stuart Woods's latest. "It wouldn't matter anyway, Mrs. Stuckey. The same author picture is on the book's cover."

Mrs. Stuckey glanced at the standee. "But she's so . . . so *big*."

I exchanged a glance with Dilbert. "Don't worry, Mrs. Stuckey," I said. "At the speed *Bang, Bang Baby* is selling, by next week we won't have enough copies to stock the display, and down it will come."

"That woman's book is pure rubbish," she huffed. "Neither the *New York Times* nor the *Boston Globe* chose to review it; therefore, it must not have *any* literary merit."

Dilbert raised an eyebrow. "Clearly you haven't read B. R. Myers."

"Who?"

"B. R. Myers, author of *A Reader's Manifesto: An Attack on the Growing Pretentiousness in American Literary Prose.*"

"Excuse me?"

I took a deep breath and did my best to channel my battle-hardened aunt. "You know what, Mrs. Stuckey? I'm not a book critic. I'm a bookseller."

"Fine, Mrs. McClure! I won't come back until next week, then." The woman gathered her boys and pushed them toward the exit. "Or perhaps I won't come back at all!"

As her boys stumbled through the front door, I heard one of them declare, "But I *like* the big girl's picture, Mommy!"

Dilbert turned to me. "She seemed pretty upset."

"We'll see Mrs. Stuckey again. I guarantee it."

"What makes you so sure?"

"I sold a copy of *Bang, Bang Baby* to *Mr.* Stuckey two hours ago."

Dilbert laughed and I automatically braced for a quip from my resident ghost, but none came. Jack had disappeared on me. *Completely* disappeared. On Wednesday I'd practically passed out the moment I hit the mattress. I didn't dream that night, but I wasn't all that surprised, given my level of exhaustion. Thursday night, however, was another matter.

Sadie and I had gone to the funeral home, where Miss Todd's remains were on view. I could have used Jack's opinion on what I'd observed there. But he hadn't made contact. He hadn't shown in my bedroom hours later, either, even though I lay there wide awake, just waiting to feel his cool breeze across my cheek.

This abrupt disappearance of my ghost had happened many times before, especially after an intense trip into his memories, but it had never been this long a lag.

I began to worry—*seriously* worry—that Seymour had contacted those Spirit Zappers people. He'd mentioned something about de-ghosting all of Quindicott. Maybe the

Zappers had visited Miss Todd's mansion in the dead of night, performed some exorcism ritual, and then moved on to zap all of Cranberry Street. Could they have turned on some sort of anti-haunting equipment and scared Jack into limbo for good?

I couldn't help choking up at the thought. The dead PI may have started out as an annoyance in my life but he'd become a comforting, cheering . . . okay, even an exciting presence. With my son off to camp, I was starting to feel abandoned. I even began to wonder whether Spencer had swiped that old buffalo nickel of Jack's, the one I carried with me outside the store to give his spirit passage beyond these walls. But when I checked the little pillbox on my dresser, I found the nickel still safely tucked inside.

The worst part about Jack's absence, I realized, was that I couldn't even tell anyone about missing him; and as I fretted in private, I began to open up the roadblocks on some old mental avenues: *Maybe the ghost isn't gone. Maybe he was never here. Maybe Jack Shepard was—and always has been—nothing but a construct of my imagination . . .*

The phone rang behind the checkout counter and Sadie called me off the selling floor. "It's Bud," she said, frowning as she passed me the receiver. "He wants to speak with you."

I nodded, happy at least to speak with a living man. "Hi, Bud."

"Pen, the city council just refused to rescind the parking permit they granted to Jim Wolfe's construction company. That damn equipment of his will block my business all summer unless we can do something about it!"

"Good news on that front. I've already spoken with the coordinator of the Seekers reading group and they're willing to leave the events space by nine. We can start the meeting then."

"Great!" I could hear the relief in Bud's voice. "Most everyone has agreed to show up. If the Business Owners Association presents a united front, we can push back against the council's move. Otherwise I'm bankrupt by the end of summer."

Out of the corner of my eye, I could see my aunt's worried expression.

"We'll fix this," I said into the receiver, loud enough for Sadie to hear. "I promise."

On the other end of the line, Bud sighed heavily. "I could end this mess tomorrow if I pulled out of the election and let Marjorie Binder-Smith run unopposed."

"But you're not going to do that, are you?"

"Damn right I'm not." His tone was steely. "Pass the word to any holdouts. The Quibblers meet Monday at nine."

I set the receiver on its cradle, and looked up to find J. Brainert Parker leaning against the counter, a frown on his fine-boned, patrician face.

"You heard?"

He nodded. "Bud told me all about it. He can count on me to help any way I can."

A professor of literature at St. Francis, J. Brainert Parker had been a friend of mine since childhood. Although he'd been involved with the Quindicott Business Owners Association (a.k.a. The Quibblers) since the organization's inception, Brainert felt himself above such petty concerns as zoning laws, parking restrictions, and littering fines. Or he *did,* until he and his business partner, Dr. Wendell Pepper, dean of St. Francis's School of Communications, refurbished and reopened the town's previously broken-down Art Deco movie theater.

Now, with one tenuous foot in the world of capitalism, Brainert (a proud member of the "ivory tower" set, as Seymour referred to the academic class) suddenly found common ground with the rest of us poor working stiffs who plied our trades on Cranberry Street. And it was just like my old friend to jump into the fray with both feet and arms swinging. In fact, Brainert was now the most vocal backer of Bud Napp's campaign for Marjorie's council seat.

"This will all be over when Bud triumphs in November," he crowed. "Now, on a stranger note, the reason for my visit. I found this bizarre missive in my mailbox this morning."

Brainert reached a slender, long-fingered hand into the pocket of his tweed jacket. I glanced at the letter he produced. It was an official invitation to Seymour's party on Saturday—"to honor the esteemed Miss Timothea Todd."

"Seymour certainly isn't wasting any time moving in on the new domicile, is he?" Brainert said.

"It's his prerogative," Sadie answered from behind me. "I'm sure Timothea would have been pleased to know that Seymour is holding a wake for her in her beloved Victorian."

Brainert shook his head. "I wonder why Miss Todd left such a valuable property to a guy like Tarnish?"

"They were friends," I said. "And she knew how much he appreciated the property."

Brainert shot me the inscrutable Mr. Spock stare he'd mastered in junior high. "Or perhaps *more* than friends."

I shook my head. "Are you saying what I think you're saying?"

"Seymour Tarnish is an unlikely gigolo, it's true. But he has a pulse, he bathes semiregularly, and let's face it: When you're over eighty, your romantic prospects have narrowed considerably. Even a wealthy woman like Miss Todd can't afford the luxury of being *too* particular."

"That will be enough of that!" Sadie snapped, hands on hips.

"You have to admit it's a puzzle." Brainert rubbed his chin. "What do either of you know about Miss Timothea Todd, anyway?"

I exchanged a glance with my aunt. "She was a nice woman who lived on Larchmont Avenue," Sadie replied. "What more is there to know?"

"What more indeed?"

"Sadie and I went to her funeral this morning," I said. "Did you know she's supposed to have a sister?"

Brainert shook his head.

"Well, she does, according to the lawyer handling her estate. Also, according to the lawyer, the woman wants to remain anonymous. *But* I may have found a clue to the woman's identity."

I leaned across the counter. "There was a viewing at Fontwell and Bradley Funeral Home last night. "When I signed the guest book, I noticed that two people had stopped by to pay their respects. One was a Mrs. Arthur Fromsette, who left a Larchmont Avenue address."

Brainert nodded. "Obviously a neighbor. And the other?"

"This woman signed the book 'A. Briggs' and left *no* address. I checked the phone book, and there are no Briggses listed in the Quindicott or Millstone directories, so she may have come from out of town. I'm betting this person is Miss Todd's sister."

"No mysterious strangers at the funeral service?"

"Only Mr. Stoddard, Seymour, Sadie, me, and Eddie Franzetti, who dropped by in uniform. The Reverend Waterman was there with a prayer group from church and he said a few words, but he said he really didn't know Miss Todd. I saw only three wreaths: one was sent by Seymour, the second came from this store, the third collectively from Miss Todd's Larchmont neighbors. I sighed, suddenly sad. "I can only assume the estrangement between the sisters lasted beyond the grave."

Brainert folded his invitation and tucked it into his lapel pocket. "I'll come to Seymour's wake for Miss Todd. Actually, I'm surprised he hasn't asked us to help him move his mountain of junk."

"I guess Seymour's housemate is helping him on that score—or I should say, former housemate."

Brainert sighed. "You haven't seen Harlan Gilman lately, have you?"

"Come to think of it, I haven't. He used to be a regular here, too."

"He also used to *work*, on the loading dock at Brier's Dairy. But the man hurt his back, so he's been living on disability payments for six months now." Brainert lowered his voice. "During that long period of inactivity, Gilman has become a bit chubby."

"Is that right?"

"Obese, actually."

"How obese?"

"Morbidly."

"You mean like the Pillsbury Doughboy?"

"More like the Stay Puft Marshmallow Man."

"I guess I shouldn't be surprised. Seymour's complained more than once that his housemate hasn't been pulling his weight—" I closed my eyes. "Did I just say that?"

"You're not wrong, Pen. Harlan is well enough to do light housework and do grocery shopping but Seymour says he refuses, and they're fighting like a couple on the verge of divorce. This change is probably good for both of them. So, are you going to this wake tomorrow night?"

"Wouldn't miss it, for a lot of reasons." I didn't want to let Seymour down, of course, but I also wanted to check out the house again.

"It's potluck, so I'm making fried chicken," Sadie announced.

I quickly calculated my free time. "I suppose I could mix up a batch of maple-pecan fudge tomorrow morning. Seymour loves fudge."

Brainert raised an eyebrow. "So does Harlan Gilman. Better make two batches."

# CHAPTER 13

## *No Place Like Home*

"This is a rich town, friend," he said slowly. "I've studied it. I've boned up on it. I've talked to guys about it . . . If you want to belong and get asked around and get friendly with the right people you got to have class."

—*Playback*, Raymond Chandler, 1958

"WELCOME TO TARNISH Mansion," Seymour said, dipping in a fair imitation of a courtly bow.

I gaped at the apparition greeting me on the columned porch of Miss Todd's Victorian. Seymour's pencil-thin moustache was so new it was barely filled out. A smoking jacket of royal blue silk was draped over his bulky, mail handler's shoulders, and an apricot-hued ascot circled his beefy neck. If I'd been met by the ghost of the late Timothea herself, complete with flowing shroud and rattling chains, I couldn't have been more stunned.

*What the hell happened to your letter carrier? He's decked out like a low-rent bed warmer stalking widows at a Bowery dance hall.*

"Jack!"

Seymour eyeballed me. "No, Pen. It's me, Seymour Tarnish." He grinned as he smoothed his lapels. "Didn't recognize me in my evening attire, did you? Well, I guess you'll just have to get used to the new me."

I nodded, swallowing my reply—at least to Seymour. Inside my head I couldn't wait to ask the ghost: "Where have you been?"

*What do you mean? I've been with you.*

"No, Jack, you haven't! I was beginning to think you'd been exorcised or something." I searched my mind. "What's the last thing you remember?"

*You and I getting cozy in Mrs. Dellarusso's Second Avenue lobby. I was just getting around to inviting you back to my place, where I figured we could—*

"That was three nights ago!"

"Maybe in your time, doll. To me it was just three seconds ago."

Beside me on the porch, Brainert Parker was now gazing at Seymour with a deadpan stare. Finally, he folded his arms and tilted his head. "That's a new look for you," he said dryly, then made a show of sniffing the cologne-scented air. "And a new smell, as well, unless I'm mistaken."

Seymour beamed. "You like it? Ralph Lauren Purple Label: the essence of elegance, custom-blended with notes of suede and tobacco flower." He adjusted his apricot ascot. "I wanted to blend in with my new neighbors, and Larchmont is *very* exclusive."

"What do *you* think, Pen?" Brainert asked, raising the old Spock eyebrow.

*Listen, baby, I got a new theory now. I think maybe your mailman pal might have been giving old lady Todd a joy ride through the tunnel of love.*

"I, uh . . ." I bit my cheek for a moment. "I brought fudge!"

"Ah, Penelope, how thoughtful." Seymour took the Tupperware container from my hands. "Won't you come in? Your aunt and her beau have already arrived. Everyone is assembled in the salon."

Brainert's eyes narrowed. "Why are you talking that way?" He gestured to the half-filled martini glass dangling by its stem in Seymour's hand, little finger extended. "And since when do you drink martinis? I hardly recall you drinking at all, and when you do it's usually Budweiser—from the can."

Seymour tossed Brainert a superior smirk. "I am now part of the *smart* set that lives on Larchmont. We do not swill cheap beer from an aluminum can. We savor blended cocktails."

Brainert glanced at me. "Tarnish seems to be channeling some sort of stereotypical Hollywood version of the wealthy class, gleaned from a Three Stooges short, no doubt." He sighed, returning his gaze to our martini-sipping host. "The reality is quite different, Seymour. I doubt even one of your neighbors owns a polo pony or a yacht, just as I'm sure plenty of them enjoy a cold beer."

"If you prefer the taste of hops, I've stocked imported Heinekens and Sam Adams Summer Ale." Seymour sniffed. "Otherwise, the bartender will be happy to mix you a cocktail."

*I'll take Scotch, baby. Straight up.*

"We're not in my dreams right now, Jack."

*I know. I was just getting into the party mood.*

"Well, we're not taking the night off," I told the ghost. "I've got a lot of questions for you—about that case of yours and that odd dagger we found."

*Shoot.*

"I'd like to know exactly what's connecting your case and mine."

*So would I, doll.*

"What's that supposed to mean?"

*It means I have some hunches, but I don't know for sure. We have to start looking for concrete evidence. This joint's gotta have some leads. Start sniffing around—that is, if you can smell anything besides your host here. What did he do, dump the whole bottle of tulip water down his pants?*

"Pen? Didn't you hear me?" Seymour said.

I blinked. "Oh, sorry, Seymour. Were you speaking to me?"

"Yes. I asked if you'd like the grand tour?"

"Oh!" I said. "Yes! That would be great!"

Seymour guided Brainert and me through the decorated foyer, past the cascading staircase, and into the main room, proudly describing what he loved about each space. The "salon" (really the living room, where I'd found Miss Todd's corpse) was crowded with Seymour's friends, most of whom I recognized. I doubted the mansion had hosted this many guests in decades.

But more than that had changed. The heavy antique chairs, love seat, overstuffed couch, dark wood end tables, doilies, knickknacks, and thick curtains were all still in place, but now twin halogen floor lamps glowed with enough brilliance to pierce even Miss Todd's gloomy Victorian clutter. On the mantel above the marble fireplace, a photo of Miss Todd in a silver frame was given a place of honor between two lava lamps, roiling in a violet glow.

I recalled the portrait that Miss Todd had kept over the hearth—a corpulent man in a three-piece banker's suit with a jowly face, large, dark, staring eyes, and rather longish black hair swept back off his face. I'd assumed the man was her father or some other Todd patriarch, but the formal painting was gone now, replaced with a vintage 1940s poster from a Fisherman Detective serial titled *Buccaneers of Fire Island*. I asked Seymour about the change.

"I hated the picture of that fat guy, so I moved it to the attic," said Seymour with a shrug. "The movie poster was the only thing I owned big enough to fill the empty space. So I bought a do-it-yourself frame from the craft store and voila! Problem solved!"

"I see."

But the picture swap wasn't the most dramatic change in the space. Neither was it the room's single concession to modernity (besides the purple lava lamps). A massive flat screen, high-definition television was now parked in the corner. It was obviously brand-new and just out of its carton—I noticed the packing material peeking out from behind the couch, along with part of Seymour's old lime green bean bag chair. The TV was mounted on a black steel platform, which also held a DVD player and a bank of audio speakers.

Standing on either side of the giant screen, Harlan Gilman and Leo Rollins bickered about the best place to position the entertainment system. I realized Brainert had been right about the girth of Seymour's former roommate. In the six months since I'd last seen him, Harlan had become so heavy he now had to lean on a cane to stand.

As for Leo, he obviously wasn't intimidated by the posh Larchmont address. Unlike our host, who'd dressed for the occasion, Leo wore the same flannel shirt and frayed jeans he sported at his electronics store every day, though I noticed his mountain man beard had been trimmed attractively short and was neatly combed. I couldn't help wondering if he was once again carrying that suspicious dagger with the odd pentagram design on its hilt.

"I'm going to put your fudge on a plate," Seymour told me.

"I'll go with you," I said.

I followed Seymour to a vast kitchen, which appeared to be state of the art for the 1940s. Okay, the refrigerator and range were modern, but everything else dated from a time when Miss Todd was young. The cabinets were white metal with chrome handles. The Formica countertops were cherry red. The linoleum floor sported a red-and-white checkerboard pattern. The red-and-white theme continued with the café curtains and the chrome-and-red kitchen table set. Metal bread baskets and canisters sat on the counter, and an old-style wash tub and hand-cranked wringer stood in the corner.

"Isn't this kitchen great?" Seymour said as he piled the fudge in neat rows on a rectangular party platter. "So retro!"

*Hmmm . . . looks to me like we never left Mrs. Dellarusso's apartment.*

I ignored Jack and asked Seymour, "What are the outbuildings like?"

Seymour shrugged. "One's just a big brick shed filled

with tools and a push-powered lawn mower. The other building looks like ruins."

"Oh. Too bad."

"No, Pen, you don't get it. The building's a folly. It was meant to look like ruins on purpose. Real gothic, you know." Finishing the platter, Seymour washed the sticky fudge off his hands. "Actually, a lot of English manor houses had fake ruins like that, back in the day."

A phone warbled beside the sink. "My hands are wet, Pen. Would you punch the speaker button for me?"

"Sure." I hit the switch.

"Hello!" Seymour called, drying his hands. A gruff voice spoke over the line with a heavy Rhode Island accent.

"Mr. Tah-nish?"

"Yes."

"This is Ben Kesey at Warwick Motors."

"You're calling about my breadloaf?"

"That's right."

"What did Paddy Scotch do to my vintage VW?"

"Gad knows Paddy's my competitor, but you can't fault him for what happened. Found two neat punctures in the brake fluid cylinder. That's why you lost your brakes, see, 'cause you lost your brake fluid. Be 'bout a week till I can fix it. Need a new cylinder, and parts for a VW this old are hard to come by."

I spoke up. "What about the punctures, Mr. Kesey? How did that happen?"

There was a pause. "Is that Missus Tarnish? Well, there's a funny thing 'bout those punctures, Missus Tarnish—"

Seymour chuckled when Ben Kesey pronounced us married, but I didn't waste time correcting him. I was too anxious to hear his reply.

"Those holes were real neat," the mechanic said. "Like they were made deliberate. You don't see that kind of damage from road debris."

Seymour looked at me with a mixture of worry and disbelief.

"In my opinion, those brakes were interfered with on

purpose. If you or the missus has an enemy, I'd think about lettin' the police know."

"Thanks, Ben," Seymour said. "Let me know when the VW's fixed." Frowning, Seymour ended the call and turned to me. "I can't believe anyone would want me dead!"

*Yeah, genius, that's what I thought, too, and look where it got me.*

"Someone might have a serious grudge against you," I told Seymour.

"For what?"

"Inheriting this house, for one—Miss Todd has a living sister. The two women were estranged for years, but the sister may have been expecting to gain this property. There could be another reason, too. Fiona suggested it to me the other day."

"Fiona? Fiona Finch?!"

"The rumor's already gotten around town that Chief Ciders suspects you of being responsible for scaring Miss Todd to death. Maybe someone thinks you really *are* responsible. He or she could be trying to exact revenge."

Seymour looked afraid for a moment. "I liked Miss Todd, Pen. I had nothing to do with her death. You know that, don't you?"

"Of course!"

"Well, I'm not going to turn into a paranoid rabbit over this." His eyes narrowed with resolve. "Nobody's going to spook me, do you hear? Nobody."

"But you *are* going to call the police, right?"

"You mean the very same police who tried to railroad me into a jail cell earlier in the week?"

"Not everyone on the force is guilty of that. You really should—"

Just then the doorbell rang. Seymour shook his head and grabbed the plate of my homemade fudge. "Forget it, Pen. At least for tonight, okay?"

"But—"

"Come on, let's party!" he exclaimed with a gaiety that sounded a little forced. "This is a wake for Miss Todd, you know. I insist you have a drink. Try the gimlets! They're superb!"

As Seymour headed out of the kitchen, I took a deep breath. "Jack?"

*The grease monkey wasn't wrong. There's evidence of a crime against your postal pal. On the other hand, the mailman wasn't wrong about the local badges, either. Chief Cornpone and Deputy Dawg aren't exactly at the top of my Law Enforcers of the Year list.*

"I'll call Eddie."

I pulled out my cell and punched in his digits. When he came on the line, I explained the situation.

Luckily, Eddie was on duty and cruising around in his patrol car. He said it was a quiet night so he'd head over to Ben Kesey's garage and take a look at the VW bus himself. I gave him the name of the state police officer who'd helped me and Sadie on the highway, and Eddie said he'd check in with the Staties, too.

"Pen, do you have any idea who might have done this?"

"I have a few theories, Eddie, but no evidence."

"Let's get together tomorrow, okay?"

"For sure."

Feeling relieved, I ended the call. Now I was ready to party—just as Seymour advised.

# CHAPTER 14

## Under the Rug

The first time we met I told you I was a detective. Get it through your lovely head. I work at it, lady. I don't play at it.

—*The Big Sleep*, Raymond Chandler, 1939

WITH MY WORRIES somewhat lightened, I headed back into the "salon" and wandered over to the small crowd gathered around Seymour's "bar"—really a mahogany table covered with liquor bottles, buckets of ice, and an industrial-sized blender.

"Borrowed the blender from Seymour's ice cream truck," Hardy Miles informed me when I asked.

Hardy was tonight's bartender. He was also Seymour's friend and fellow mail carrier. Sadie and I knew him as a good customer. He favored crime novels by Elmore Leonard and Carl Hiaasen. He also spent the busy summer seasons moonlighting weekends at the notorious girly bar out on the highway, so I wasn't surprised to see him moving swiftly and efficiently. The man knew how to mix a drink.

"What d'ya have, Mrs. McClure?"

"It's a little warm and I'm plenty thirsty. What do you suggest?"

His florid face grinned. "How about an iced tea?"

"Great. Sounds refreshing," I said—naively, as it turned

out. The first gulp singed my throat, and I realized Hardy had mixed me a Long Island Iced Tea. "Wow, this drink's strong."

*Hey, doll?* Jack piped up in my head.

"Yes?" I replied between multiple sips.

*Before you start heading down that short road to Stinko, you might want to consider a few things.*

"What things?"

*Just because your pal's taking the night off from worrying doesn't mean your perpetrator's taking the night off from reattempting murder.*

I sputtered, choking on my spiked tea.

"Let me freshen that," Hardy said, taking the glass from my hand.

"Okay, Jack," I silently whispered. "What's your theory? Do you suspect the sister? Or do you think Fiona has a point—that someone's got a grudge against Seymour?"

*The grudge theory's possible. But then, what would the person gain, putting the mailman six feet under?*

"Vengeance, I suppose."

*Vengeance don't buy new shoes for baby. I'm bettin' someone's goin' for the big prize.*

"You mean the inheritance? This house and land?"

*Don't you remember what that slip-and-fall jockey said? If your postal pal gets himself croaked before the title officially transfers, the house goes to Miss Todd's next of kin—which would be the old woman's—*

"Sister," I said.

"A twist?" Hardy said. "Of course you can have a twist, Mrs. McClure." He finished the drink and handed me the newly filled glass.

"Uh, thanks," I said, then quickly stepped away.

*Get a lead on the sister. Something just don't smell right with her trying so hard to stay anonymous.*

"Well, whoever she is, she can't be here now," I silently whispered. "I know everyone in this room. They're all friends of Seymour or town locals I've known for some time as customers."

*That doesn't mean they're clean, doll. Lift up the rug of most Johnny Do-Rights and you'll find some amount of dirt. Plenty of people will do just about anything for a big enough payoff.*

"Surely not anyone Sadie and I know."

*The person who sabotaged those brakes might very well be in this room.*

I noticed Seymour approaching with a well-built older man. He had a sturdy jawline and a thick head of salt-and-pepper hair, and gave off an air of affable confidence. His blue blazer, khaki pants, and open-necked button-down were neatly pressed and obviously expensive, yet he still appeared approachably casual. I recognized him immediately as the master of ceremonies from our recent Film Noir festival, but he was better known in Quindicott as the dean of St. Francis's School of Communications.

Brainert moved up to us, obviously surprised to see his superior at the party. "Dean Pepper? What are you doing here?"

"I dropped by to greet my new neighbor!" Wendell Pepper replied. "But then, we've already had a few rollicking conversations, haven't we, Seymour? Mr. Tarnish and I share a true love—old movies and film memorabilia."

Brainert turned to Seymour. "Anyone else from Larchmont dropping in?"

"I delivered invitations to every house on the avenue. Wait and see." Seymour faced Dean Pepper again. "Care for a drink, *Dr. Pepper*? Or maybe you'd care for *another* brand?" Seymour winked and Brainert cringed, but Dean Pepper laughed and slapped Seymour's back.

"I haven't heard that one in years!"

"Well, I'm not kidding about the drink." Seymour gestured toward Hardy. "Have a gimlet, or try a martini. My bartender's reputation is legendary."

"Cocktails! How civilized." Pepper's eyes lit up like a Broadway billboard. "Don't mind if I do."

As Dean Pepper crossed to the bar, Seymour leaned

close to Brainert. "See, I told you," he whispered, raising his martini glass. "Rich guys lap this stuff up."

Brainert smirked and glanced at me. "Seymour neglected to mention that his bartender's 'legendary' reputation was garnered among a collection of middle-aged, dollar-bill-waving men ogling half-naked women."

My reply was cut off by the regal *bing-bong* of Miss Todd's doorbell.

"Excuse me," Seymour said.

"Can't fault his manners," Aunt Sadie observed, offering Brainert some buttermilk fried chicken from a tray. "Have a piece. I got this recipe from Judy Tarnish before she moved to Florida. It's Seymour's favorite."

Brainert's eyes lit up as he looked over the crisp, golden-brown pieces of chicken. "Hmmm. Don't mind if I do."

I glanced behind Sadie but didn't see Bud Napp. "Where's your date?"

She and Bud had arrived early for the party so they could help Seymour set up. I'd stayed behind at the bookshop to help Bonnie ring up the last customers of the day.

Still holding the tray of chicken with two hands, Sadie gestured toward the large-screen television with her chin. "Bud's over there, playing with Seymour's new toy. You know men and their gadgets."

Suddenly the massive HDTV screen sprang to life. Russell Crowe appeared in Roman gear and began dispatching a horde of barbarians.

"Where's the sound?" Harlan Gilman complained.

Leo Rollins's bearded face flashed with annoyance. "I told you not to put in the DVD. I haven't attached the speakers yet."

Even without the sound, the widescreen images were hypnotic enough to draw the partygoers like zombies to a warm body. My aunt moved to another cluster of guests, tray of fried chicken in hand. I turned around and walked slowly in the opposite direction.

The movement of the people suddenly exposed the floor in the center of the room. I recognized the pattern of the lush area rug, and with a rather ugly jolt remembered what I'd seen less than a week ago at the center of this room.

Cautiously, I approached the spot where I'd found Miss Todd's corpse. There was almost no trace of the violent scene I'd witnessed; only a faint bloodstain marred the carpet. I wasn't surprised, and it didn't matter. I wasn't looking for *physical* evidence. I was searching for signs of something else.

I hovered over the spot where I'd found the dead woman and waited for the frigid stab of air I'd felt that awful afternoon. It never came.

I closed my eyes and shut my ears to the sound of laughter and buzz of conversation. I did my best to block out my physical surroundings, and tried to tap into a sixth sense. Finally, after a few moments of intense concentration, a trickle of cool air raised the tiny hairs on the nape of my neck.

*Nobody here but us spooks, dollface.*

"Shhhh, Jack. I'm trying to contact the spirit world . . ."

He laughed.

"Okay, the *rest* of the spirit world!"

*Knock yourself out.*

Again I concentrated. This time I tried to visualize the horrible tableau I'd stumbled upon: the blood-spattered corpse, the expression of stark horror frozen on the dead woman's face. I tried to recall every detail, and then I tried to imagine what had happened to Miss Todd in her final terrible moments.

"Can you hear me, Timothea?" I whispered in my mind. "Tell me what you know. Did someone or something really scare you to death? Do you know who's trying to hurt Seymour?"

There was a long moment where I sensed nothing. Then suddenly I felt icy-cold fingers touch my arm. "Ahhhhh!"

"Goodness!" Sadie stepped backward, nearly spilling

the chilled bowl of chocolate-covered strawberries. My aunt had snuck up on me with the stealth of an apparition!

"I only wanted to know if you'd like to try a hand-dipped strawberry. Mr. Koh's daughter made them."

I glanced at the bowl. The chocolate-enrobed fruit did look delicious, but considering my memories of this particular spot in the room, I couldn't raise much of an appetite.

"I'll have one later," I told my aunt.

Sadie gave me a strange look. "Are you okay, Pen?"

"Fine, Aunt Sadie, really. You just startled me. That's all."

My aunt nodded and drifted off.

*Looks like I'm the only haunter showing up for this soiree.*

"Looks that way." Disappointed, I headed back to the bar. "I'm not giving up yet," I told the ghost. "I'm going to try again later."

*That'll be good for a laugh.*

"Another iced tea," I told Hardy. "But this time just tea, okay?"

"What a lovely room!" Fiona Finch loudly announced as she swept into the party.

"Fiona!"

"Fiona's here!"

"Hi, Fiona! Come on over!"

Amid the din of greetings, Hardy cupped his ear. "Say again, Mrs. McClure?"

"Tea," I said, louder. He nodded.

Fiona quickly circled the living room, her eagle eyes scanning the walls, curtains, furniture, and fixtures. As a veteran antiques collector, she was obviously appraising each item in her head.

Hardy slipped a fresh glass into my hand. "Here you go."

"Thanks." I took a sip, tasted alcohol. I realized Hardy hadn't heard me ask for tea *only*. Unfortunately the bartender was swamped now, so instead of asking for a replacement I vowed to nurse this second cocktail for the rest of the night.

"Seymour, you are a lucky man," Fiona declared. "This place is glorious. A real treasure."

Quindicott's premier innkeeper had dressed quite strikingly this evening in a black lamé pantsuit and black silk blouse, the brooch on her lapel a shiny black raven perched on a bone-white skull.

"Fiona's dressed for a haunted house party, all right," whispered Sadie, as she passed by on her way to the kitchen.

Of course, my aunt and I had worn black outfits to Miss Todd's viewing and funeral, but this evening's wake was a celebration to honor her life, and we'd both decided to wear light summer slacks and pastel blouses. But then, Fiona hadn't made the viewing or the funeral. To her, the black was probably her way of showing respect for the dead.

"The dead," I repeated on a mumble, my mind trying to consider who'd want Seymour that way. I absently sipped my Long Island Iced Tea—gulped it, really. This stuff went down far too smoothly.

*Easy, doll. Go easy on the sauce.*

I frowned, not appreciating the nanny treatment. "You know what, Jack? You're starting to sound like a hypocrite."

*You're bananas.*

"You kept a bottle of Scotch in your desk." I took another sip. "You drank on the job all the time, didn't you?"

*I could hold my liquor, baby. You get blotto on three tablespoons of cough syrup.*

"Only once—and that particular brand had a sedative in it!"

Meanwhile, Fiona continued her buttering-up of Seymour. "The curtains, the décor, it's all *so* tastefully done. Miss Todd certainly maintained the authentic Victorian feel of the place. I'm glad you decided not to change it"—she spied the twin purple lava lamps and nearly gagged hiding her reaction—"too much."

Seymour stood behind Fiona, both hands clutching a

large painting in a frame of carved dark wood that perfectly matched the room's décor.

"Wait till you see what Fiona's brought me!"

The woman smiled and spoke to the rest of us. "I remembered how much Seymour admired the nautical paintings in the Finch Inn's restored lighthouse bungalow, so I bought this new work from the same artist as a housewarming present for him."

Seymour held the painting up and studied it. "Thank you! This is so amazing!" Beaming, he hurried across the room and propped the oil painting on an oak sideboard. A curious group clustered around to study the images: a tall sailing ship foundering in a terrible storm, massive waves towering over the broken vessel. There were no human figures, but if you gazed deeply into violet sky and green roiling waters, you could make out the ghostly faces of drowning sailors.

"A powerful rendering," Dean Pepper said. "Powerful and grim."

"Haunting," Brainert said, nodding his head. "The colors are so vibrant they're almost surreal, yet the overall effect is so authentic I can almost smell the sea." Brainert glanced at me. "Almost," he mouthed and pointed to Seymour's cologne-drenched form.

"Cool," Leo Rollins said, stroking his trimmed beard. "What kind of ship is that?"

"A nineteenth-century Yankee clipper," Dean Pepper replied. "I know because Bill Wheatley, another one of Seymour's new neighbors, is a real sailing buff. He's a retired importer. That man has a den full of nautical paintings. I'll introduce you, Seymour. Perhaps I can persuade Bill to take us out on his yacht."

Seymour shot Brainert another "I-told-you-so" look. Then he directed Fiona's attention to the bottom-right corner of the canvas. "The painting is only initialed 'RD.' What's the artist's name?" he asked.

"If she wanted to be known, the artist would have signed with more than her initials," Fiona replied.

Seymour's eyes widened with interest. "*She*. Are you saying a woman painted this? I've got to meet her!"

"Out of the question," Fiona stated flatly.

"Aw, come on, Finchy—"

A blast of sound exploded suddenly, filling the room with a howling roar and terrified screams. On the television screen, a man in a Nazi uniform melted like a wax doll.

"The climax of *Raiders of the Lost Ark* in THX," Harlan Gilman bellowed over the wall of noise. "This and the Death Star battle at the end of *Star Wars* are the two best audio checks known to man!"

"Turn that off!" Seymour yelled.

The roar vanished and the screen went black. Harlan Gilman smirked. "Just like I said before. The television should be over there." He pointed to the opposite side of the room with his aluminum cane. "Otherwise the sound reverberates in the stairwell like a cheap echo chamber."

Leo Rollins shrugged. "He's got a point. Let's move this thing."

"Okay," Gilman said, leaning on his cane. "Who's going to push?"

Seymour, Rollins, Bud Napp, and Dean Pepper each gripped a corner of the huge entertainment system.

"It has wheels so it's easy to move," Bud said. "But we have to get that rug out of the way so it will roll on the hardwood."

"I'll get it," Fiona said, dropping to one knee.

"Need help?" I asked.

Fiona grabbed a corner of the fabric. "That's all right, Pen," she said. "This rug is much lighter than it looks."

In a flash, Fiona pulled the carpet aside—and the room exploded with shocked gasps.

"My God! Look at that," Dr. Pepper cried, staring at the newly exposed floor.

"What is it?" Seymour asked, staring at the bizarre design etched into the floorboards.

I stepped forward, examined the strange circle on the

hardwood, and immediately recognized the familiar pentagram pattern with the fleur-de-lis center. The star design was surrounded with weird symbols.

"It's a magic circle," Brainert said in a tone of amazed disbelief.

"A magic circle?" Bud scratched his head. "Just looks like a star design to me. The same one that's on the fence outside. What the hell's it for?"

"People who practice the occult arts use the magic circle for protection against harm," Brainert replied.

Seymour's eyes bugged. "Protection? Protection from what?"

Brainert hesitated a moment, then answered. "Evil spirits. Demons from hell. That sort of thing."

Harlan Gilman leaned forward on his cane. "I have a bad feeling about this."

In silence, everyone gazed down at the weird design. I dropped to one knee beside Brainert.

"What are these symbols?" I asked. "They look familiar."

"Astrological signs. You see them every day in the paper."

"Oh, yes, I see."

He pointed. "And over there, those are the Greek symbols for alpha and omega."

"It looks like these designs were carved into the wood and then painted."

Brainert gingerly touched the edge of the circle, then sank his index finger into the groove. "No, it's not painted. I think it's burned in."

"Burned?" My aunt gasped. "How?"

"By Hell's fire—wooo-woooo," Gilman said in a spooky voice.

"Cut the crap, Gilman," Bud said. With one arm, he hugged my aunt's narrow shoulders. "The design was made with a wood burner, honey. Satan had nothing to do with it."

"How old is this?" Brainert wondered aloud. "I suppose

that it's possible Miss Todd didn't even know what was under her rug."

I rubbed my own finger inside a groove and it came away clean. "You're no housewife, Brainert. Look, there's no dust. And candles have been burned here." I pointed to dollops of melted black wax at each point of the star, then rubbed the wax with my thumbnail. "Recently. The wax is still soft."

"Ah . . . Listen, guys," Seymour said. "I saw this design somewhere else in the house, besides the wrought-iron fence out front, I mean—"

The doorbell rang, its *bing-bong* startling everyone.

"I'd better get that," Seymour said. He glanced down at the magic circle. "Cover that up, please!"

Seymour headed off to the foyer and Fiona reached for the carpet. I stopped her and pulled my cell phone out of my pants pocket. After snapping several images of the circle from different angles, I helped Fiona cover it up again.

A minute later, Seymour returned holding a black bottle with a velvet ribbon around its neck. At his side was that intense young woman who'd manned the front desk at Emory Stoddard's run-down law office.

"Hey, everyone, I'd like you to meet Ophelia Tuttle. Ms. Tuttle works for my lawyer."

Tonight Ophelia Tuttle wore a form-fitting sleeveless dress of crimson silk. Her dark hair was piled on her head and held in place by a gold clasp in the shape of a scarab. Around her long neck she wore a choker of black velvet. Her sophisticated hair, low-cut dress, black polished fingernails, bloodred lipstick, dark eye shadow, and heavy black liner beneath severe rimless glasses contrasted dramatically with Ophelia's pale complexion and obvious youth. I saw more than a few of Seymour's male friends take immediate notice.

I noticed one other thing about her—a very important thing. With her glossy raven hair in an upsweep, I could now see the shape of the tattoo on her upper arm. It was a gold ankh, just like the ankh ring Stoddard had been wearing.

Was it pure coincidence? Or had she gotten the tattoo because of Stoddard's ring? Had she given him the ring? Either way, it seemed to me Miss Todd's lawyer and his assistant were more than employer and employee.

"And what's she doing here anyway?" I silently wondered.

*The mailman invited her, remember?*

"I remember, Jack, but he invited her to come *with* Stoddard. I don't see him, do you? As far as I know, Miss Tuttle doesn't live on Larchmont and she only met Seymour the other day. Why would she come alone?"

*Maybe she's charmed by the size of Seymour's, uh . . . property.*

My eyes narrowed. "Which makes her a suspect, right? In fact, now that I think about it, didn't Ophelia Tuttle leave Stoddard's office before anyone else the other night? As far as she knew, Seymour would be driving himself home in his VW bus."

*You're right, doll. Ghoul Girl was in the perfect position to have sabotaged those brakes.*

"That's the opportunity—but what about a motive?"

*Think about it, baby. I count at least two.*

"You're right. If Miss Todd's sister wanted Seymour dead, then Ophelia Tuttle is in one of the best positions to help her do the dirty work. That's *one*. As for *two*: Ophelia's working for Mr. Stoddard. And it was Stoddard who appeared to be pushing for Seymour to sell this place to the Lindsey-Tilton group for their bed-and-breakfast plan."

*The slip-and-fall jockey would get a big, fat commission for handling that sale, wouldn't he?*

"Yes, which means Stoddard could be in on it, too. In fact, it could be a little conspiracy on the part of the estranged sister—"

*Sure, kill the old lady and make sure the sucker she left her property to also ends up six feet under.*

"It's a solid theory, Jack. But how do we prove any of it?"

*Just keep your pretty peepers peeled, baby. Criminals always give themselves away. You just need to set up some bait and wait for them to take it.*

# CHAPTER 15

## Unexpected Guests

A bleak house . . . a corpse . . . and three suspects—
that's the problem Detective Mike Hanlon faces!

—Teaser for "Hotel Murder,"
Steve Fisher, *Thrilling Detective*, 1935

"MR. STODDARD ASKED me to send his regards and his
regrets," Ophelia announced to Seymour. "Business forced
him to Newport, and he won't return until tomorrow."

"Sorry he couldn't make it." Seymour lifted the cham-
pagne bottle. "I'll have my bartender chill this. May I offer
you something in the meantime?"

Ophelia pondered the question. "Green tea on ice with
fresh lemon peel," she said at last.

"I . . . I think we have Lipton in bags."

The woman smiled. "That will be fine."

After Seymour scurried off to the kitchen to prepare the
Lipton's tea, I kept a wary eye on Ophelia. A minute passed,
then two, and no one approached her—even men who were
clearly interested seemed intimidated by her powerful aura.
Sadie offered Ophelia a fried mozzarella stick and she de-
clined. I watched while they chatted a moment. Then my aunt
moved on with the tray, and Ophelia began to slowly circle
the room. I kept moving, too, feeling uneasy about the
woman's ability to see my ghost.

*Relax, doll. Even if she knows I exist, what can she do about it? Conduct an exorcism?*

"Maybe. It does give me the creeps that she can see you, Jack. I mean, I can't even see you—unless I'm dreaming."

*Aw, you're just jealous there's another dame out there who can appreciate my mug. And she ain't a bad looker, either, if you can get past the sailor tattoo and Cleopatra makeup.*

"Well, if she can see you, maybe Ophelia can see other spirits. Maybe she summoned an evil spirit to frighten Miss Todd to death."

*And how you gonna prove that to Chief Cornpone and company?*

"I have no idea."

Ophelia paused in the center of the rug, where we'd found the hidden magic circle. The woman blinked in surprise. She stared at the rug under her heels. After a long moment, Ophelia scanned the faces in the room. Then she stepped right over the spot, in the middle of the circle, where Miss Todd's body was found.

I held my breath, waiting to see her reaction. Would the young woman feel the cold spot the way I did when I found Miss Todd's body?

It was obvious she didn't. After glancing at the faint bloodstains, Ophelia turned around and moved to another part of the room, where Seymour approached her with a tumbler of tea on ice. I moved close enough to eavesdrop.

"How do you like the place?" he asked.

Ophelia raised an eyebrow. "How do *you* like it, Mr. Tarnish? Have your nights been . . . restful?"

Seymour seemed taken aback by her frank question. Not Harlan Gilman.

"He hasn't seen any ghosts yet, if that's what you mean." Tottering on his cane, the heavy man moved closer to the woman. "If you ask me, it's only a matter of time before he does." His tone was snappish.

Seymour shifted uncomfortably and shot Gilman a dark look. "Don't be stupid, Harlan."

Brainert edged closer to me. "I'm not surprised Harlan's gone negative," he said quietly. "There's bad blood between him and Seymour since Seymour decided to move out."

*Bad blood? Did you hear that, doll?*

I frowned. "I thought maybe Seymour might reconsider the split and invite Harlan to move in, too."

Brainert shook his head. "Apparently Mr. Gilman took *Ghostbusters* and *The Exorcist* a bit too seriously. He's heard the wild rumors about Miss Todd being frightened to death in this house, and he says he won't take any chances."

*Ask him if ol' Harlan is in acute need of lettuce.*

"Brainert, do you know if Harlan is having any money troubles?"

Brainert nodded. "I'm sure he is. With Seymour moving out, he's asked Hardy Miles to be his housemate. Hardy's still thinking about it, but I hear Harlan's got some serious credit card debt."

I didn't like the sound of that and I took a harder look at the fat man. Was that cane just a prop? Could Harlan really get around much easier than he was letting on? Could he have been the one to cut Seymour's brakes for, say, a cash payoff from Miss Todd's sister?

My gaze drifted to Ophelia, who appeared to be wringing the life out of her tumbler of green tea. "Don't discount your friend's opinion so fast," she told Seymour rather loudly. "This house could very well be haunted. It's not outside the realm of possibility."

Seymour looked at her askance. "Do you really think it is? Haunted, I mean?"

Ophelia scanned the room again. Her eyes lingered on me—or Jack, I couldn't be sure. I shifted from foot to foot.

*Steady, baby.*

"There are spirits present," Ophelia finally said with authority. "I'm not certain they are connected to the house, however."

While everyone within earshot began to murmur uneasily,

I sighed with relief. The last thing I needed was for Ophelia to accuse me of traveling around with my own personal ghost.

"Well," Seymour said, "until I actually see an apparition, call me a skeptic. I mean, what does an actual ghost look like, anyway?"

"Maybe like the spook on that hokey movie the other night. What was it called?" Leo scratched his beard. "The one on Channel Ten—"

"Oh yes, that was *The Screaming Skull*," Brainert said before catching himself. He looked away, but it was too late.

Harlan Gilman snorted. "*You* actually watched *The Screaming Skull*?"

"I . . . I was only flipping channels," Brainert stammered. "I just happened to see—"

Seymour cackled. "One of the cheesiest horror films ever made. The ghost is just a lot of dry ice and a cheap anatomical skeleton. And I mean *cheap*! You can actually see the wires holding it together, and the saw line across the forehead where you can remove the skull cap and look inside."

Everyone giggled. Everyone except Ophelia Tuttle.

"Of course it all looked rather silly in the movie," Ophelia said. "But I'm sure your reaction would be very different if *you* actually saw a screaming skull in your bedroom one dark night."

The laughter faded quickly.

*Ghoul Girl here sounds like she's best friends with Skull and Bones—and I'm not talking Yalie social clubs.*

The conversation went dead for a moment (appropriately enough) and then (mercifully) the doorbell rang again.

"I'd better get that," Seymour said, running off.

"Ophelia seems convinced this house is haunted," Brainert said quietly to me.

I gulped my drink. "Brainert, what exactly do you think about that sort of thing?"

"Well . . ." Brainert stroked his chin. "Some of the greatest minds of Western civilization believed in the occult, even attempted to practice magic."

"Like?"

"The poet Virgil. He was said to possess supernatural abilities. Then there's John Dee, the English mathematician who was also the court astrologer for Queen Elizabeth the First. And did you know that Casanova, the legendary Renaissance lover, once summoned evil spirits inside the Coliseum? He wrote in his autobiography that malevolent ghosts followed him through the streets of Rome, bedeviling him for an entire night."

"Hear that, Jack?" I whispered.

*Back off, babe. It wasn't me.*

"Of course, that's just the ancient world," Brainert continued. "If you prefer more modern examples, there's the poet William Butler Yeats, who belonged to the Hermetic Order of the Golden Dawn, along with fellow scribblers Algernon Blackwood and Arthur Machen. Mark Twain was active in the Society of Psychical Research. Sir Arthur Conan Doyle believed in fairies and earth spirits and tried to communicate with them. And some of psychologist Carl Jung's writings about the collective unconscious could be mistaken for a mystical treatise."

"Really?"

"Oh, yes!"

For the next two minutes, my academic friend continued to talk—lecture, actually. The one-sided discussion included grimoires, alchemy, and highlights of the life story of Cornelius Agrippa.

I nursed my drink, which only slightly impaired my ability to follow his conversation. I do remember that at some point, Seymour swept back into the party like a Nor'easter hitting the Rhode Island shoreline.

"Everyone!" he announced with a huge grin on his face. "I'm pleased to introduce you to an unexpected guest. Ms. April Briggs."

All male eyes, once again, turned toward the new female arrival clinging tightly to the arm of Seymour's royal blue smoking jacket.

"Briggs," I silently repeated to myself. "Now why does that name ring a bell?"

*Maybe she's a Feline Friend or a Yarn Spinner or one of the other half dozen groups of yakking dames you've got traipsing through my habitat.*

"Oh, my God, Jack, I think I know who April Briggs is."

*Who?*

"There was an 'A. Briggs' who signed Miss Todd's funeral home guest book. No address, just the first initial and last name."

*So she knew the old woman?*

"She must have. Why else would she have come to the funeral home!"

*You better brace her then, doll, 'cause except for me, the spirits ain't talking in this haunted house and you need all the leads you can get.*

Having lived in Manhattan, I immediately recognized April Briggs as an obvious come-from-money type. So chicly thin she could have been a poster child for Tom Wolfe's "social X-rays," she possessed matinee starlet teeth, high cheekbones, and long, model-straight blond hair—which may well have been brunette and kinky before the salon got finished with her. She had runway height, health-club muscular legs, and leather sandals that were hand-tooled in Italy or my son doesn't have red hair and freckles.

April's crepe party dress appeared to be designer quality. The turquoise color perfectly matched her eyes—which may or may not have been sporting contacts to enhance the electric blue-green shade. Her tasteful string of pearls gave off the whiff of money, too. The woman's appearance was so polished I had to get a bit closer before I could pinpoint her age, which (once I saw the fine lines around the edges of her mouth and eyes) I pegged at closer to fifty than forty.

"She's not old enough to be Miss Todd's sister," I

whispered to Jack. "But she could still be related—a niece or cousin, some relative who has an interest in Seymour's inheritance."

Just then, an elderly woman strolled in. Her slender frame was elegantly sheathed in a finely tailored navy pantsuit of summer silk. Her eyebrows were lightly drawn in with pencil, her shoulder-length hair dyed a rich chestnut and smoothed into a neat ponytail, and a delicate black lace shawl was draped around her narrow but still-straight shoulders.

Dean Pepper approached her. "Ah, Mrs. Fromsette, how have you been?"

My eyebrows rose. "Jack, that must be the other woman who signed the book at Miss Todd's funeral: *Mrs. Arthur Fromsette*. She also wrote down a Larchmont Avenue address."

Though advanced in years, Mrs. Fromsette's blue eyes were bright and her movements vigorous. As Dean Pepper took the older woman's hand, I edged closer to the couple.

"I haven't seen you since, well . . ." His voice trailed off.

"Yes, Wendell, not since Mr. Fromsette's funeral. How are you, Professor? And how are things at Mr. Fromsette's alma mater?"

"Very well, thank you. And as always, St. Francis is on the move. Have you come tonight to greet our new neighbor?"

Mrs. Fromsette nodded. "My daughter saw the invitation I received and insisted we drop by. She's happy to see this old house lit up again." Lifting a wrinkled hand, she gestured to the attractive blonde attached to Seymour's side. "You know my daughter, of course, April Briggs. She's visiting again from Boston."

"Yes, April and I bumped into each other at the bakery and caught up."

I sighed with that exchange. "Another lead bites the dust," I told Jack. "Mrs. Fromsette is just an old neighbor, and A. Briggs is her daughter. No mystery there."

*Maybe she's more than a neighbor. Maybe she's the sister, too. Get her maiden name.*

Dean Pepper brought the older woman over to Seymour.

"Ah, Mrs. Fromsette," Seymour said. "Did you find the restroom then?"

"Yes, dear boy. It's been a long time, but I still remember where it is."

"Can I take your wrap?" he asked.

Mrs. Fromsette shook her head vigorously. "No!" She pulled the black shawl around her more tightly, her blue eyes suddenly looking like a wounded animal's.

Everyone around the older woman froze, Seymour included. His mouth went slack and he didn't appear to know what to do or say. Nobody did.

After a moment of silence, Mrs. Fromsette obviously realized her inappropriate reaction and shook her head. Her fingers twitching nervously, she forced a smile and changed the subject, gesturing broadly to the silver-framed photograph of Miss Todd.

"It's good to see this place so full of life again," she said with exaggerated cheerfulness—as if trying to will normalcy back into the moment. "Miss Todd was so reclusive."

"You knew her well?" I asked, stepping up. I quickly introduced myself.

"Pleased to meet you, Mrs. McClure. No, I didn't know her that well," Mrs. Fromsette replied. "She was always a very aloof, standoffish neighbor."

"Did you know she had a sister?"

"Yes, I did," the woman replied with a nod. "I never met her, but Timothea once mentioned her to me. She said they had a falling-out many decades ago."

*Listen up, doll. Could be the lead you're looking for.*

I leaned closer. "Do you know her name?"

Mrs. Fromsette shook her head. "I'm sorry, dear. I'm sure it was Todd at one time. But Timothea said her sister married and moved to Newport. Mr. Stoddard must know more. Emory Stoddard is the lawyer who handled all of

Miss Todd's affairs. He had an office in Newport until recently. Now I believe he's working out of Millstone."

"I know Mr. Stoddard. We've met," I said aloud, and to Jack, I silently said—

"Did you hear that? Stoddard *had* an office in Newport. That confirms what I already suspected."

*Yeah, it's a big step down for lawyer boy, all right, baby. Sounds like the man's in dire straights.*

"Dire enough to maybe arrange the death of his client? You heard Mrs. Fromsette. She believes Miss Todd's sister resides in Newport. I'll bet the sister's the one who hooked up Miss Todd with Stoddard's firm in the first place."

Mrs. Fromsette was still speaking to me. ". . . and I did want to meet Mr. Tarnish. I understand he was very kind to Miss Todd in her last days."

"She was a nice lady."

"And you're a very nice man," April said, still clinging to Seymour's arm.

Seymour blushed at the attention. Dean Pepper blinked in surprise. Brainert's Spock eyebrow rose.

"Is she flirting with him?" I whispered.

"Undoubtedly," Brainert replied. "Can't imagine why."

*New money's the oldest aphrodisiac. Seymour's grown real attractive since he's become landed gentry.*

Meanwhile, Dean Pepper glanced at his watch. "I'm sorry to say I have to go. I'm giving a lecture about John Milton at the Episcopal Church tomorrow afternoon, and I haven't even written it yet."

"Thanks for coming, Wendell," Seymour said.

April smiled and leaned closer to the mailman. "Would you mind showing me around?"

Seymour nodded like crazy. "Sure."

She pointed. "How about telling me about that poster above the mantel?"

"Love to!" Seymour grinned. "The actor is Pierce Armstrong. I actually met the gentleman . . ."

I have to admit, I was pretty surprised to see a woman like April looking up at Seymour Tarnish with flirty female interest—then again, I probably would have been surprised to see any woman doing the same. On the other hand, the mailman had transformed himself, and it wasn't just the smoking jacket and Ralph Lauren Purple Label. Cranky Seymour was virtually bubbling over with good cheer and masculine confidence. It *was* sort of attractive.

"You know, Jack, for the first time I can actually see marriage in Seymour's future."

*What the hell are you doing just standing there?!*

I jumped at the chill Jack had sent my way. "What do you mean?"

*I mean get your panties in motion and go brace that overgrown Yalie before he leaves!*

I didn't know what I was supposed to "brace" Dean Pepper about, but I didn't waste time arguing. I just handed Brainert my iced tea glass—empty now—and headed Pepper off in the foyer.

"Uh, excuse me? Dean Pepper?"

"Yes?" The dean turned and smiled—still affable enough, but strain at the edges told me I was holding him up and he wasn't happy about it.

"Uh . . ." I said.

*Ask him about the Fromsette broad! Haven't you noticed her acting squirrelly? Get a handle on that. See if there's more to her relationship with the Todd dame.*

"Mrs. Fromsette's very nice," I said, trying not to slur my words. "Why haven't I seen her around Quindicott?"

Wendell frowned. "She used to be quite active in the community. Head of the Larchmont Avenue Charity Drive, that sort of thing. All that changed when Mr. Fromsette went missing—"

"Missing?" That sounded odd. "But I heard you mention a funeral."

"There was a funeral," Dr. Pepper said. "But Arthur Fromsette's body was never found. Only his sailboat washed ashore, off Mullet Point. He enjoyed fishing. He'd started on Quindicott Pond and then followed the inlet out to the ocean. He did it every day for years. The Coast Guard concluded he'd fainted, had a spell, or perhaps even a heart attack, and fell overboard."

"How tragic."

"She never quite got over it," Wendell said. He leaned closer, lowered his voice. "That black shawl she refused to let Seymour take? She put it on for Mr. Fromsette's funeral and hasn't taken it off since. Wears it all day, every day, I understand."

"Is that why April's here? To take care of her mother?"

"Yes, but April usually visits every summer," Pepper said.

"From where?"

"Boston. She was married until recently."

"Oh, divorced, eh?"

"Separated, but I believe the divorce papers are filed. You should get to know her better, Mrs. McClure. She's thinking about making a permanent move back to Quindicott, to be near her mother."

"Really? Wouldn't that be a difficult commute to her job?"

"From what I recall, she runs her own bookkeeping business so she can probably relocate fairly easily."

I could certainly sympathize with April's situation. After my husband's suicide, I'd wanted to get away—not just from the memories of Calvin's unholy leap, but of the truth of how bad our marriage really had been. April was obviously on the rebound and looking for a summer fling. Seymour was single, available, and a brand-new, prosperous-looking Larchmont resident.

*Looks like your mailman's about to become the beneficiary of something a lot steamier than an old Victorian.*

Pepper glanced at his watch. "I'd better go."

"One more thing, Dean Pepper. I'm just curious. You don't happen to know Mrs. Fromsette's maiden name, do you?"

"Why yes, as a matter of fact. I believe her husband's funeral announcement listed it as Field."

*Hoping for Todd, weren't you?*

"Yes, Jack," I told the ghost. "It would have been a nice, neat package, wouldn't it?"

*Sorry, baby, but the gumshoe game's rarely that clean and easy.*

Pepper left and I watched him wander down the dark drive. "That's odd about Mrs. Fromsette's husband disappearing, don't you think, Jack?"

*Yeah, baby.*

"You think he's still alive?"

*It's possible. In my experience, faking your own death's usually linked to theft of a great deal of money or cheating the life insurance company.*

"Or he could just be dead."

*Either way, the Fromsette dame gave you the best lead on the case you're trying to crack.*

"Yes, you're right. Miss Todd's sister is married and lives in Newport—or at least she did. And now I'm almost positive I already got a glimpse of her."

*You're talking about the old dame you saw in front of Stoddard's run-down office?*

"Exactly. And remember when she climbed into that Mercedes sedan? There was a chauffeur driving—and wouldn't someone like that know all about cars and how to sabotage them?"

*Good call, baby. But you still don't have a name.*

"True, but I can tell Eddie my theories tomorrow. Maybe he can figure out a legal way to pressure Stoddard into revealing it."

*I have a better idea.*

"Well, tell me in a minute okay? I'm thirsty again."

I returned to the party and crossed to the bar. As if he'd read my mind, Hardy handed me a third ice-cold glass of tea before I even asked for it. Grateful, I took a long gulp, not caring anymore whether or not it contained alcohol.

*Got enough liquid courage now, baby?*

"For what?"

*I want you to brace someone else, someone who does*

*know the identity of Miss Todd's estranged sister, someone who you've been avoiding like the plague.*

"Who?"

*Ghoul Girl.*

"Aw, crap." I took another sip of spiked tea.

*Let's go, Penelope. You and me together. Let's find out, once and for all, whether or not this broad really can see yours truly.*

# CHAPTER 16

## *Now You See Him*

I've got to keep in some sort of touch with all the loose ends of this dizzy affair if I'm ever going to make heads or tails of it.

—*The Maltese Falcon*, Dashiell Hammett, 1930

"DID YOU KNOW there's a magic circle under this rug?"

Ophelia turned to face me. Her heavily lined eyes flashed darkly, but she said nothing.

"It's a pentagram," I said, "like the one on the gate outside, only it has a—"

"Fleur-de-lis in the center," she said flatly. "Yes. I know."

"You can see the circle then? You can see it through this rug?"

She rolled her eyes. "I've seen the gate *outside*. I don't have X-ray vision."

"Oh."

Ophelia swirled her drink. The ice tinkled softly against the tumbler. *Tink-tink, tink-tink* . . . It was mildly hypnotic, but then, I had consumed some pretty powerful fire juice.

"You know about magic circles, Mrs. McClure?"

"Not much. What do *you* know?"

"In rituals of ceremonial magic, the practitioner stands inside the circle, which forms a barrier against the demons and evil spirits the sorcerer hopes to summon and control. Bend to his will, so to speak."

I felt a chill, not the ghostly kind, more like the old-fashioned kind, right up my spine. "What can these demons and spirits do?"

Ophelia shrugged. "Whatever the sorcerer wants them to do. Turn lead into gold. Bring you the mate you desire. Grant power and influence, bestow eternal youth—"

"Could the spirits be employed to destroy another person?"

"That, too, I suspect." Ophelia sipped her green tea, met my eyes. "If you believe in such things."

I looked away, pointed to the carpet. "That's where I found Miss Todd's corpse. Right *there,* on the rug, in the center of the circle."

"*You're* thinking there are spirits in this house, and that the magic circle failed to protect Miss Todd, right?"

I took a gulp of my own tea and nodded.

Ophelia forced a laugh. "Which proves your fears are baseless. If this house really was haunted, and if those spirits suddenly menaced Miss Todd, shouldn't she have been safe from harm inside the magic circle?"

"Well, I guess . . ."

*But she died, anyway, which proves that witchcraft stuff is a bunch of hooey.*

Ophelia sighed like a patient teacher with a particularly slow student. "For starters, sir," she whispered to the air just above my head. "Ritual magic is not the same thing as witchcraft. Ritual magic is a conceptual system that asserts human ability to control the natural and supernatural world."

An exceedingly uncomfortable moment of silence stretched between us.

"Do you see him?" I whispered.

Ophelia nodded. "Don't you?"

"I just hear him. Unless I'm dreaming. He sometimes comes into my dreams, influences them. But then he disappears. He did that after our last dream."

"It takes energy to manifest. They draw it from the molecules around them. That's why the air's cold whenever they're present. A dream like the one you're describing probably took a lot of energy from him."

I glanced uneasily around us, making sure no one could overhear our discussion.

"You mean he has to rest after expending a lot of energy?"

"Just like we do." Ophelia studied me closely for a moment. "You suspect me of something, don't you, Mrs. Mc-Clure?"

"You're a psychic, right? Not just a medium or whatever you call yourself?"

"I call myself Ophelia." She sniffed. "Listen, I can see spirits, which is obvious, right? And I can read emotions of maybe six out of ten people. You're easy to read. You're an open book."

Jack laughed.

"Okay, Ophelia, if I'm such an open book, then you must know *what* I suspect you of."

She shrugged. "Not really. I just know you suspect me of something. Why don't *you* enlighten me on the *what*?"

"I need to know the name and address of Miss Todd's living sister. It's important."

"Why?"

"I think she's trying to hurt Seymour."

Ophelia's eyebrows rose. "What makes you think that?"

"A lot of things make me think it, but I'd rather not go into all of that right now."

*Just spill, Cleo. Give up the name.*

"Cleo?" Ophelia frowned and glanced around. "Who's Cleo?"

"You," I informed her. "Your makeup reminds Jack of Cleopatra."

*She's not Egyptian, is she, doll?*

Ophelia rolled her eyes. "The 'smoky eye' look is in, sir."

*Don't call me sir. It makes me feel old.*

"As opposed to dead?"

This whole thing was freaking me out. I drained my glass, which began to impair my ability to stand completely straight. Whoa.

*Listen up, raccoon eyes! Answer the questions and lose the attitude!*

"It's my attitude. Live with it. Oops. You can't, can you?"

*Show some respect for the dead!*

The room began to spin a little and suddenly got a whole lot colder. I shivered. "Stop pissing him off," I warned, knowing instinctively it was Jack creating the chill and not some other spook.

"Sorry," she said, but her tone was still insolent.

Then Ophelia's handbag rang—or rather the cell phone inside it. She fished it out and took the cell call in front of me (and Jack).

"Yes?" She glanced at me, then higher up. "I'm at Mr. Tarnish's," she told the other party. She listened some more, then looked back at me. "Excuse me."

She walked away, her voice a whisper. After a minute, she closed the phone, threw me an uneasy glance, and approached Seymour, who was laughing with April Briggs on the red velvet, claw-footed loveseat in the corner.

"Alas, I've got to go," Ophelia announced.

Brainert wandered over to say goodbye to Seymour as well. As I bid him pleasant dreams, I noticed Leo Rollins had finished working on the television and was drinking a bottle of Sam Adams. His gaze appeared preoccupied with Ophelia. Did he know her? It sure seemed to me she threw him a nod of recognition when she'd first walked in.

I addressed the ghost: "I was just thinking . . ."

*Considering your inebriated state, that's a miracle—*

"No, not thinking." I shook my head, trying to clear it. "More like remembering. Leo Rollins has that suspicious knife with the Todd Mansion pentagram design. And Leo was on the road that day I found Miss Todd's corpse. Don't you recall? I heard that Harley motor of his first, and then I saw him pass me going in the opposite direction."

*So?*

"So Leo was coming from Larchmont. He could have been at Miss Todd's house. He could have been involved in her death!"

I passed Bud Napp, who was loudly complaining about the construction vehicles parked in front of his business. As I approached Leo, I noticed him glance at me, then nervously shift his bottle from one hand to the other.

"He's looking awfully uncomfortable, Jack."

*Could be he's just bashful around attractive redheads.*

"Who, me?" I pushed up my black-framed glasses. "Get a grip!"

"Hi, Leo," I said, a little too loudly. (The Long Island Iced Tea was most definitely talking now.) "I wanted to thank you *again* for helping my aunt and me on the highway the other night!"

"No big deal," he grunted, then lowered his eyes.

"So, are you having fun?"

"Sure," he said with a shrug.

"Really something about that pentagram design on the floor, huh?" I pointed to the rug. "It looks *just* like the one on *your* dagger."

Leo's head bobbed once. "I guess."

"Tell me *again* where you got that—"

"Hey, Leo," Bud cried, interrupting.

"Yeah," Leo said, looking past me.

"You know Jim Wolfe, right? You did work for him last year. Can't you ask him to move his trucks?"

"I haven't seen him much, not this summer. He cut back—having a bad year, I think. I'm not on his payroll. Anyway, I'm just an independent contractor. He's not going to listen to me." Leo drained his bottle, and before I could speak with him again, he whirled and headed for Hardy Miles and a refill.

Sadie appeared just then, and offered me the last pass on the tray of fried chicken. I wolfed down two wings, suddenly ravenous, and realized eating might help me sober up. I found more snacks, then headed to the bar again and ordered myself a soft drink. "Dr Pepper!" I giggled. "Oops! He already left!"

"Here you go, Mrs. M., have a nice cold Coke, okay?"

I nodded and sipped. The drink was sweet and cold and sadly bereft of that sweet little stinging buzz.

*Get a grip, doll. Don't turn into an alkie on me.*

About an hour after Brainert departed, Seymour said goodnight to April Briggs and Mrs. Fromsette. Then the doorbell rang again. The party was winding down, and I was surprised anyone would arrive so late. But the *bing-bong* appeared to reenergize Seymour and he moved quickly to greet the newcomers.

He returned with a bundle of flowers under his arms and a bemused expression on his face. I understood Seymour's reaction when, seconds later, Councilwoman Marjorie Binder-Smith strode past her host and into the room on patent leather power pumps.

Newly svelte after a monthlong spa vacation, Quindicott's longest-sitting and most powerful political player wore a form-fitting scarlet suit and floral scarf. Her dyed brown hair framed a suspiciously dewrinkled forehead. Appearing jovial (her one and only job skill, as far as I could see), a wide smile remained plastered on her middle-aged face despite the coolly calculating look in her eyes.

"I think . . ." Seymour began, a bit uncertainly. "I think you all know the councilwoman."

The room fell silent—except for the sound of Bud Napp choking on his Sam Adams. I figured the councilwoman was in for a hailstorm of grief, but then a brassy voice cut through the tension.

"What a charming place! Absolutely charming."

A fortysomething woman swept into the room—and I do mean *swept*. Knee-length white halter dress flaring around her tanned legs, the woman strode to the center of the space like Jackie O. making her debut.

"Hey, everyone," Seymour announced. "I'd like you to meet—"

"I'm Charlene Fabian!" the woman interrupted, offering us all a wave. "What a pleasure it is to meet you all. This town is just so quaint, and it's wonderful to see this old rickety house filled with life!"

Ms. Fabian spoke with a vague, English accent, her eyes obviously bypassing the people to appraise the room, the furniture, and all of the fixtures. She continued to chatter as she circled the space, gushing about the marble fireplace, the brass lamps, the chandelier, the handmade doilies, the magnificently preserved wainscoting.

When Ms. Fabian strode past Fiona Finch, I saw my friend blink with something like recognition. Then Fiona's eyes narrowed like a seasoned cop who'd just spotted a known crack dealer. She glared openly as Ms. Fabian plopped down on the red velvet cushions of the ornately carved claw-footed love seat.

"You must be very proud of your acquisition, Mr. Tarnish," Ms. Fabian said, crossing her tanned legs. "And you must also feel very fortunate to inherit such a lovely and valuable property."

"Uh, yes. Yes, I am," Seymour replied. "Would you like a drink, Ms. Fabian?"

The woman tossed her short, black, perfectly layered do and batted her eyes at Seymour. "Johnny Walker Blue. Straight up."

Seymour cleared his throat. "I'll see what I can find."

Across the room, Fiona stared at the stranger with naked hostility. Then I watched as she set her cocktail down on a mahogany end table and approached Ms. Fabian.

"Hello, I'm Fiona Finch. The owner of the Finch Inn on Quindicott Pond," she said, crossing her arms. "Are you one of Seymour's new neighbors? I'm asking because you seem very *familiar* to me. Like I've seen your *picture* somewhere."

Charlene Fabian barely acknowledged Fiona's presence.

Instead she ran her French-tipped fingers along the velvet upholstery.

"This rosewood love seat is genuine Victorian," she murmured. "And I'm certain that solid mahogany cabinet against the wall is a valuable antique, too."

Fiona's eyes narrowed. "Actually, the love seat is a *copy* of a Victorian, manufactured in the 1920s. And that 'solid' mahogany cabinet over there is anything but. It's veneered, and shoddy work at that. By the way, the cabinet also dates from the twenties, as does most of the furniture in this house, which is Depression-era *mock* Victorian!"

Ms. Fabian's face went rigid. Everyone was staring at the two. Seymour practically bolted from the bar to the loveseat.

"Your Scotch!" he said.

The woman accepted the amber liquid without thanks. She sipped and made a face. "Ugh. You don't have Johnny Blue, I take it?"

Seymour's shoulders sagged. "Dewar's White Label. Sorry."

"So, Ms. Fabian." Fiona's small hands went to her hips. "We've determined that you don't really *know* much about antiques, but we still don't know *why* you're here."

Before the woman could reply, Marjorie Binder-Smith stepped forward. "Charlene and I are old friends. We attended Brown together. She's visiting from California and staying at my home, just down the block."

Fiona frowned. "California? Santa Monica, by any chance?"

For the first time, Ms. Fabian met Fiona's gaze. "Why, yes," she answered in an icy tone.

Fiona snapped her fingers. "I knew I recognized you. I saw your face on the cover of a magazine. Recently, too."

Inside of a nanosecond, Ms. Fabian's expression moved from stormy to bright. "Last month's *Woman Entrepreneur* ran a feature. I was on the cover."

Fiona shook her head. "No, that's not the one. I'm thinking about the story in *Modern Innkeeper* about the Lindsey-Tilton group. 'Here Come the McBed-and-Breakfasts,' I think the article was called. And it was all about *you*, Charlene *Lindsey*-Fabian."

Ms. Fabian fluffed her hair but said nothing.

"So, are you here to do a little shopping? Looking for the next hot property to exploit?"

Seymour practically leapt between the women. "Come on now, ladies, let's not argue. This is a wake for Miss Todd. How about we do something she would have enjoyed? Let's team up for charades!"

But Fiona wasn't listening. She poked her head around Seymour's large body. "You've got a lot of nerve showing up here, sniffing around like a predator—"

Seymour held Fiona back. "Or Pictionary. Everybody loves Pictionary!"

"Now, now," Councilwoman Binder-Smith said, wagging her finger in Fiona's face. "That's no way to treat a guest in our community—"

"Wheel of Fortune?" Seymour cried, his grin strained. "I have the home edition!"

"Fiona's right!" Bud exploded, slamming his bottle down on a side table. "Both of you have got a lot of nerve *parking* your rear ends here, if you get my drift. Maybe you should ask Seymour for a *permit*!"

Seymour snapped his fingers. "I've got it! Six Degrees of Kevin Bacon!"

"If this were my home, I'd throw you bums out on your collective ears, but I guess that will have to wait until November." Bud rose and adjusted the waistband of his pants. "Unfortunately, this isn't my damn house, or my damn party, so I'll just say good night."

He strode to the foyer without a backward glance. Stricken, Sadie caught my eye. "I promised Seymour I'd help clean up, but—"

"Go," I insisted. "Take care of Bud. I'll help Seymour."

Sadie hurried to catch up with her man. Marjorie Binder-Smith watched them go. When I saw the triumphant smile on her face, I wanted to slap the councilwoman myself.

*Go on, knock her one, toots. Give her the Jack Dempsey treatment. You can blame it on the pickle juice.*

"Couldn't I be charged with treason or something?" I stifled a hiccup. "I mean, if I assault an elected official?"

*Maybe. But sometimes it's just good sense.*

After the front door slammed, the frowning councilwoman faced Ms. Fabian. "I'm sorry that had to happen, Charlene. I've never been so mortified."

"Really?" Hardy Miles said, his eyes a little glazed from the drink. "Guess you don't get around town much!"

Seymour dropped into a chair and buried his face in his hands. "Why can't we all just get along?"

"Well!" The councilwoman tossed her head. "I guess I know when *I'm* not wanted."

"Wanna bet?" Hardy said.

"Let's go, Charlene!" Marjorie took Ms. Fabian's arm.

"Yes, go!" Fiona said. "And don't let those mock mahogany doors hit your Johnny Walker Blue rears on the way out!"

# CHAPTER 17

## *Ghost Hunting*

We're ready to believe you!

—*Ghostbusters*, 1984

"IS THAT THE *doorbell*?" Washing the last martini glass in the joint, I turned from the sink. "What time is it?"

Seymour checked his watch. "Twelve fifty-five."

*Bing-bong!*

The second regal ring shot a stream of adrenaline through my dragging limbs. My ears pricked; my spine stiffened. "Who'd be coming to your party at almost one in the morning?"

"I'll get it. You stay here."

"I don't think so!" Drying my damp hands on a checkerboard dishtowel, I followed Seymour's fast-striding mailman legs out of his newly inherited retro kitchen and down the long hallway that led to the foyer.

The party guests were long gone. As I'd promised Sadie, I remained behind to help clean. I was in no condition to drive myself home anyway. Not that I was seeing double, but things were definitely fuzzy around the edges, and I figured I could use the time to sober up.

I also wanted the chance to look around. While Seymour was still entertaining the last remaining guests, I'd poked through the first-floor rooms, opening closets, rummaging drawers. I found grocery lists, recipes, batteries, pens. The closets held mothballs, vintage clothes, and hats upon hats from the '40s and '50s, all preserved in their original round boxes.

*So this is where haberdasheries go to die,* Jack quipped.

There were no easy answers. No clue to Miss Todd's living sister, the alleged haunting, the magic circle, or anything else beyond an old woman who'd lived in this house for many years.

I had another drink.

When the last of the guests were gone, I began helping Seymour clean—until this one A.M. arrival.

"Be careful!" I called. Ben Kesey's phone call was fresh in my mind, even if Seymour didn't want to remember it. But then, he hadn't been the one to put his foot down on a brake pedal and feel nothing but spongy impotence.

Waving off my admonition, my mailman snapped on the porch light. Without even bothering to check through a window, he yanked the front doors wide.

Standing on the small, columned porch was a short man in his midtwenties. The prominent Adam's apple was the first thing I noticed; then sunken cheeks; long, skinny sideburns; and sleepy, half-closed eyes. He wore neon-green overalls with a fully-stocked pocket protector. A matching baseball-style hat was turned backward on his brown hair, and a clipboard was tucked under his arm.

"Are you Mr. Tarnish?" the stranger asked.

I poked my head around Seymour's bulky form. "Why are you here? What do you want?"

"Easy, Pen. Take a chill pill."

I threw the dishtowel over my shoulder and folded my arms.

Seymour faced the stranger. "What's up, dude? Who are you?"

"My name is Kenny Vorzon. And *you* called *us,* remember?" He jerked his pen toward his backward cap.

Seymour's brows knitted. "Huh?"

Kenny frowned a moment, then realized. "Oh! Sorry!" He reached up and turned his hat around. The cap's brim sported a glowing yellow lightning bolt with two words on either side of it: *SPIRIT ZAPPERS*! Below the logo, a motto was scrawled in small embroidered script: *Your entity eliminators*.

I froze in semiterror. "Jack, go away!" I shouted in my head. "Now! Before he sees you!"

*Why? Who is this Alvin?*

Beside me, Seymour clapped his hands and grinned at the newcomer. "I thought you looked familiar. You're one of the guys from the Alternative Universe network." He extended his hand and pumped the man's arm. "Great show! Never miss it."

Kenny nodded. "Thanks."

Seymour stepped forward to scan the driveway. "Where's your van? The ghost-busting crew? The cameras?"

"Whoa, dude, you're a long way from seeing any of that. You have to pass the audition first. And this is it."

Thank heaven, I thought, praying the Spirit Zappers needed more equipment than a clipboard and a pocket protector to "eliminate" an "entity" as stubborn as Jack.

Kenny raised his clipboard, pen poised over paper. "First question—"

"You want me to answer questions now?" Seymour scratched his head. "At one in the morning?"

"Apparitions tend to manifest between midnight and four. That's one of the two reasons we work between those hours."

"I see," Seymour said. "And what's the other reason?"

Kenny shrugged. "We all have day jobs."

"Right." Seymour folded his arms. "So where's your posse working tonight?"

"Millstone." Kenny jerked his pen over his shoulder. "Their high school's supposedly haunted."

"No kidding," Seymour said, eyes wide. "What's the story?"

"A deceased lunch lady in a hairnet's been seen floating

through the hallways carrying a chafing dish full of Sloppy Joe meat."

Seymour glanced at me. "Sounds like a scary enough vision even without the ectoplasm."

"Anyway, since we were right down the highway from you, they sent me on over to check you out. Now, are you ready to give us some background on your alleged haunted house?"

Seymour nodded. "Ask me anything you like."

"Is this the aforementioned infested residence?" Kenny pointed his pen through the front doors.

"Yep. Want to come in?"

"Ah . . ." Peering past us into the foyer, Kenny scratched his temple with the pen tip. "To tell you the truth, confronting entities alone is not my area of expertise. I prefer to have a crew with me whenever I cross the threshold of a suspicious domicile."

*What a worm!* Jack snorted. *You want me to scare this goomer into next week?*

"No!" I silently whispered. "And will you *please* go away! Ophelia saw you. What do you think would happen if this guy did, too?"

*I don't know. Why don't we find out . . .*

"No, Jack!"

But my stubborn ghost was on a mission. His mildly breezy presence began to whip up a furious chill. I rubbed my arms, my gaze fixed on Kenny Vorzon, whose attention remained on his clipboard.

"How has the spiritual presence manifested itself since you've been here, Mr. Tarnish?"

"Well . . ."

As Seymour crossed his heavy arms, thinking it over, Jack's chill became downright arctic. Kenny actually began to shiver. "Sure is cold tonight for summer, isn't it?"

"I guess so," Seymour said. "As for the spirit world manifesting, I haven't seen or heard anything yet. But my friend Penelope Thornton-McClure here found a cold spot in the salon."

Kenny nodded and scribbled vigorously. "Cold spots are good."

"It's gone now. Like it was never there," I added quickly. The man frowned. I could feel Jack's cold presence flowing more energetically around me and right toward Kenny.

He reached up and closed his collar. "Brrrr!"

"It *is* getting chilly tonight," Seymour said, glancing at the night sky. "No storm clouds. Must be a front coming down from Canada."

"So what leads you to believe the property is haunted?" the Spirit Zapper asked, reading from the canned question sheet.

"Well, by reputation, mostly," Seymour said. "And the fact that a number of people believe the woman who lived here before me may have been frightened to death."

"Frightened to death!" Kenny's sleepy eyes suddenly woke up. "The network will love that!"

"The medical examiner didn't rule that," I warned. "He said she died of natural causes."

"Doesn't matter. We can challenge the local medical examiner's opinion, cast doubt on his findings. We can bring in our own experts, too."

"Wow," said Seymour.

"Next question," said Kenny, his voice more animated.

For the next ten minutes, Kenny went down his list, asking Seymour about strange noises, electronic voice phenomenon, mysterious movement of objects, and ectoplasmic manifestations. I got the distinct impression that Seymour's answers were starting to disappoint the newly enlivened Spirit Zapper, which was fine with me. I certainly didn't want the "entity eliminators" anywhere near Quindicott, my bookshop, or my ghost.

*Aw, baby, you that sweet on me?*

"Shut up," I told Jack. "And will you cut the refrigerator act. You're drawing attention to yourself!"

"One last question, Mr. Tarnish."

"Hit me."

"Have you noticed any increase in pest problems. Rats?

Mice? Ants? Termites? Swarms of bees on the property? Even trouble from bats, birds, squirrels, or raccoons? Think hard before you answer."

"I haven't done an inspection of the property yet. I've only just moved in." He leaned forward, lowered his voice. "Are these things indications of supernatural activity?"

"Nah!" Kenny waved his hand. "By day we're exterminators—you know, the regular bug kind—and we want you to know we can handle any pest problems while investigating your alleged haunting."

"Oh."

"Be sure to keep Spirit Zappers in mind for all your pest-control needs! Here—" He handed over a business card. "In the meantime, our exec producer will review these notes and someone will get back to you."

"Great," Seymour said. "How soon?"

"A couple weeks. Then we'll begin the vetting process, and our lawyers will contact you to sign the releases and waivers—"

"Waivers?"

"Sure," Kenny said. "Spirit Zappers needs permission to bring in digital cameras, recorders, temperature gauges, EVP and volt monitors, ultraviolet and infrared lights, electromagnetic detectors, not to mention the cameras, lights, and our camera crews."

"I see."

"But I do think you've got a good shot at being approved for a segment. Your frightened-to-death story's a real grabber. And the look of this house is fantastic, real *Dark Shadows* creepy."

"Thanks!" Seymour said.

"After the papers are signed, we should get around to filming in, say, six to eight months."

"Six to eight *months*!"

"We only do thirteen shows a season, Mr. Tarnish, and two segments a show. We've got a huge backlog."

"Thank goodness," I muttered.

Kenny waved and headed for the steps. "So long," he called. "We'll be in touch."

Seymour closed the door and faced me. "I need action now. Not in six or eight months." He slapped his forehead. "Damn, I forgot to tell him about the magic circle!"

I touched his arm. "Don't worry about it. You heard Kenny. He said you were a good enough prospect anyway. But now that you mention it, didn't you say something earlier? Something about finding that fleur-de-lis pentagram design in another part of the house?"

He nodded. "Upstairs."

"Show me."

We climbed the wide wooden staircase to the second floor, passed through a long, dim hallway dominated by a suit of armor at one end and a loudly ticking grandfather clock on the other. Seymour guided me through a door and into the master bedroom.

"Check out the front of that nightstand," he said, pointing to a boxy piece of furniture beside a massive canopied bed.

About the size of an old-fashioned television set, the stand appeared to be mahogany stained in black. Bolted to the front of the piece was a sterling silver relief the size of a serving platter. Just as Seymour said, the relief's design was that odd fleur-de-lis pentagram. I bent down to touch the metal, and discovered the design had a use. It was a handle.

"This isn't just a nightstand, Seymour. It's a cabinet." I tugged the handle and the front opened wide.

"Holy secret compartment, Batman!"

Inside the cabinet were three glass tiers. A delicate tiara made of silver rested on the top shelf; the middle held a silver hatbox. A leather-bound book rested on the bottom shelf. Embossed in silver on its cover was the fleur-de-lis pentagram. There was no title above the design, and the spine was blank. I lifted the book and paged through handwritten incantations and drawings of magical circles as well as other occult symbols.

"Did Miss Todd write that?" Seymour asked, peering over my shoulder.

I shook my head. "The person who scribbled these notes had a much bolder hand. Heavier, too. See the large size of the letters and numbers? I'll bet this was written by a man."

Seymour took the book from my hand and paged through it. "I see some Latin in here and some Greek, but almost everything else is gibberish. I can't make heads or tails of it."

"It must be important, because Miss Todd wanted you to have it."

"Huh?"

"Don't you remember the 'special book' she cited in her will? I have a pretty strong feeling this is the book."

Seymour glanced at the cabinet. "What's in that hat box?"

As I pulled out the box, my eyes drifted to the object behind it—a polished steel dagger with the pentagram design on its hilt.

"Leo Rollins has a dagger like this one!" I lifted the blade and examined it. "It looks exactly like the one J. J.'s mother had, too."

"Whose mother?"

*Watch it, baby. You're speaking of things long past.*

"Not so long," I silently replied. "This very dagger—or Leo's, for that matter—could be the very same one you showed me from your case."

"Earth to Pen? Who is J. J.?"

"J. J.? Oh, he's, um, a—"

*A customer, doll.*

"A customer, doll," I repeated to Seymour. "I mean, a customer of the bookshop! Anyway, don't you think it's odd that Leo has a knife just like this?"

"I guess." Seymour took the knife. "I wonder where Rollins got it."

"According to him, an antiques store in Newport."

I pulled out the hatbox, moved it onto the bed, and opened the lid. The box contained a tape recorder. I took it out.

"There're audiotapes in here, too." Seymour grabbed the tapes and scanned them. "They're all dated recently—a few days apart."

I shuffled through the four plastic cases and recognized Miss Todd's tiny, precise handwriting on each label. The tapes were time coded, each starting at around nine or ten P.M. and ending at midnight or later.

"There's a tape left in the machine, too." I pointed.

Seymour read the label. "It's dated June 8."

"That's the night before Miss Todd's body was found."

We exchanged glances. Then, by silent consent, Seymour pressed Play.

No sound greeted us. After a minute, my fingers spun up the volume control and we suddenly heard the whispered thoughts of a person now dead. This was far from a unique occurrence for me, but it clearly unnerved Seymour. He swallowed hard.

"I am now inside the circle where the spirit cannot harm me." Miss Todd's voice was quiet, tremulous yet determined. "The candles burn and I am holding the sacred dagger in my hand. I am waiting for the spirit to make itself heard . . ."

After a protracted silence, there was a shuffling sound as if the woman were repositioning the tape recorder. More silence. Then—

"Still quiet, yes! But I know he will come because he hates me so. Hates me for what I've done. When he does come, I'll record the noises he makes on this tape and play it for that dolt Bull McCoy. Then that oafish policeman will know I'm not just some delusional old woman!"

"You tell 'em, Timothea!"

"Shhh, Seymour."

But no sound followed. Once or twice, Miss Todd could be heard clearing her throat. Then came the sound of a car rolling by outside, followed by more silence.

Impatient, Seymour grabbed the tape recorder and fast forwarded. When he hit Play again, we heard a loud rushing noise, like a high wind battering the walls.

"Turn it down!" I shouted.

Even after Seymour lowered the volume, the noise was obviously deafening. Miss Todd had to yell to be heard: "Eleven fifty-five P.M. and the spirit is attacking now! Listen to it roar!"

The noise abruptly ceased. I heard Miss Todd's gasp of surprise, and then: "You're clever, but not clever enough! You realized I was recording you, but it's too late. I have you on tape again!"

Seymour rewound the tape and found the place where the weird sound began. "I can hear him now," Miss Todd whispered. The rushing noise built slowly, becoming louder until it ceased. Seymour turned off the machine and his bugged-out eyes scanned the other tapes.

My own head was spinning, and it wasn't just the residual effects of those Long Island Iced Teas. Miss Todd had recorded evidence that this mansion was haunted. So—

"Why in the world did she stay here?"

Seymour exhaled. "You heard Mr. Stoddard. She had an emotional attachment to this house. The noises only started a few weeks ago. Seems to me she was trying to use magic to get rid of this spirit, or whatever it was. Or maybe there's a logical explanation for these weird sounds."

I shook my head. "However you want to explain it, she had to be frightened, and to face that kind of fright alone for all those nights? Imagine the strain. It's no wonder the poor woman's body gave out."

"I *wish* she would have said something to me!"

"Seymour, do you realize what we have here?" I held up one of the audiotapes. "This is proof that the strange sounds Miss Todd heard were real. Not some figment of her imagination."

Seymour nodded dumbly.

"We have to call Eddie! We have to turn this over to the authorities—"

"No!" Seymour grabbed the tape from my hand and

threw it back into the box. "These tapes will only make things worse."

"What! How?"

"Dr. Rubino claimed Miss Todd was suffering from dementia. He ruled her death to be from natural causes. But Chief Ciders is still convinced I frightened Miss Todd to death with fake noises. The only thing these tapes will prove is that Miss Todd wasn't suffering from dementia! There really were noises." Seymour grimaced. "I know Ciders is just waiting for some kind of evidence like this. If he gets hold of these tapes, he'll just say I made the noises to kill Miss Todd so I could inherit her house. He'll use these to frame me for murder!"

*Listen to the mailman, baby. The lettuce he's handing you ain't funny money.*

I closed my eyes. "My God, Seymour, you're right. But we should at least listen to every one of these tapes."

"We will." Seymour stifled a yawn. "Just not now. In the morning when the sun is up, and the house won't seem so . . ."

"Creepy?"

Seymour nodded and returned the tape recorder to the hatbox. He put the lid on the box and shoved the thing back into the cabinet, right next to the dagger. As he closed the cabinet up again, the grandfather clock in the hallway gonged the hour.

"Ouch," I said. "Two in the morning and my head's still fuzzy."

"Then you better sleep over."

"I couldn't impose, really," I said, even though I was pretty sure my blood-alcohol level was high enough for a DWI charge. The thought brought a vision to mind: Bull McCoy pulling me over and demanding I walk a straight line. *Eesh.* That did it.

"Where would I sleep?"

"Right here in the master bedroom. The same guys who delivered my new king-sized mattress also transported my bed from my old place. I set that one up in one of the guest rooms." He jerked his thumb over his shoulder. "I can sleep in there and you can sleep here in the king canopy bed. It's where Timothea slept."

Just the answer I *didn't* want to hear.

# CHAPTER 18

## *Things That Go Bump*

I hear voices crying in the night and I go see what's the matter. [But] You don't make a dime that way.

—*The Long Goodbye*, Raymond Chandler, 1953

LIKE THE LIVING room below, the master bedroom held all the cheer of an upholstered coffin. The windows were covered with bulky brocade, the four-poster bed was topped with a thick velvet canopy, and the weak bedside lamp barely held off the oppressive shadows. Surrounded by dark-stained, ornately carved furnishings, I felt like a fly caught in a gloomy cobweb.

Seymour pointed to the massive bed set against the wall. "You'll be sleeping on Superman sheets," he warned in a sheepish tone. "They're the only ones I had that were big enough to fit this sucker. Sorry. I should have had king-sized sheets delivered with the mattress."

"That's okay. I always liked the Man of Steel. I feel bad kicking you out of your own bedroom, though."

Seymour glanced around. "I actually prefer a northern exposure. I'd planned on moving this bed into the guest room next door, but guess what." He grabbed one of the bed's stout mahogany posts with both hands and shook it. The canopy quivered a little, but the bed didn't budge. "It's bolted to the floor! The moving guys couldn't understand it, and they couldn't move it, either. Saved me some money though." He tapped the baseboard and grinned. "I didn't need box springs. It's a platform bed."

He lifted the mattress to show me the wooden planks underneath. "Don't worry. Even without the springs, the bed seems comfortable enough."

"*Seems?* Haven't you slept in it yet?"

"This is actually my first night in the mansion. I was supposed to stay here last night, but I was packing up my collection at the old place and it got so late I just crashed on the floor of my old room."

I got the distinct impression from Seymour's shaky tone that he wasn't all that eager to be alone in Miss Todd's house tonight. This eased some of my guilt about displacing him from the master bedroom—but it failed to mitigate the creepy vibe I was feeling from this space.

"Most of the drawers and stuff are still filled with Timothea's things, and my crap is still packed up in bags and boxes." As he spoke, Seymour fumbled through a pile of clothing on top of a chest of drawers. He tossed me a white T-shirt still wrapped in its original plastic. "It's extra large, big enough for you to sleep in if you like."

"Thanks, Seymour." I stifled a yawn as I tore open the plastic wrapper around the big shirt. "Well, goodnight."

I expected him to leave right then, but he didn't. He didn't say anything, either, just stood there in the middle of the bedroom staring at me for an awkward minute.

"Something on your mind?" I finally asked.

He shifted from foot to foot. "You've been a good friend to me, Penelope."

"Thanks. You've been a good friend to me, too."

"Do you think that you and I should maybe—" He glanced away, then back to me. "I don't know, maybe be more than that?"

*Uh-oh,* said the ghost in my head.

My entire body went rigid. Maybe sleeping over wasn't such a good idea. "Um, Seymour, I don't really feel that way about you."

Seymour blew out air. "Oh, good! I mean . . . I really like you and all, Pen, don't get me wrong, but as a *friend*. I just don't feel that romantic chemistry thing, you know?"

"Chemistry, right."

"See, I didn't want you to think I was insulting you or anything."

"Insulting me?"

"By not making a pass."

*Oh, brother.*

"Listen, Seymour, I think you're a great guy." I took his arm and began walking him to the door. "But I wouldn't want us to put our friendship in jeopardy, you know? That's too important to me."

*Good line, baby. You think that up all by yourself?*

Seymour nodded. He stopped in the doorway and looked down at me with an excessively sympathetic look in his eyes. "I agree with you, Pen. Let's just keep things on a friendship level between us. It'll be better for you in the long run. You'll see."

I gritted my teeth. "*Anyway*, you have other romantic prospects to think about, don't you? I mean, April Briggs was all over you tonight."

"You noticed, too, huh?" Seymour waggled his eyebrows. "She couldn't keep her hands off me, but you know, there was still something missing with her."

"Missing?"

Seymour shrugged. "That chemistry thing again. I told her all about my comic collection, my pulp magazines, too, and she wasn't even impressed. Hardly knew what to say."

"Well, not every couple has everything in common. On the other hand, Seymour, maybe April's not the one for you. Aunt Sadie always says there's someone for everyone, and I'm sure your soul mate's out there somewhere. You'll know her when you meet her."

*Nice, baby. That's a much better line.*

"Well, maybe you're right, Pen." He smiled and walked into the hall. "Pleasant dreams, okay. I'll be in the next room if you need me."

I closed the door behind him and collapsed against it. "Lord, what a night." With a sigh, I moved back into the center of the shadowy room and glanced around. All of a sudden, I felt very alone.

*What did I tell you before, doll? With me around, you're never alone.*

"I'm glad you're here, Jack," I said as I changed into the oversized T-shirt. "Even though you really should have listened to me and ducked out. You dodged a bullet tonight with that Spirit Zapper guy, you know?"

*Dodging bullets was always my specialty. Until the last one, that is . . .*

"My point exactly. You can't be too careful."

I yawned as I pulled down the bedcovers and climbed into Seymour's Superman sheets. I yawned again as I switched off the bedside lamp. Still sitting up, I looked around. With the light off, this room was much darker than my own room on Cranberry Street, where ambient light from the street seeped softly through my thin curtains. The closed brocade drapes on Miss Todd's tall, narrow windows blocked even the moonlight.

They seemed to block all sound, too. Not that there was much to block in the first place. Up here on Larchmont, car traffic was minimal, pedestrian traffic was practically non-existent, and Miss Todd's mansion sat high on a hill, a fair distance from her nearest neighbor.

I swallowed. The silence felt tomblike.

"Jack?"

*Yeah?*

"You want to talk?"

*Get some rest, baby. You've had a long day.*

"But, you've been gone the last few nights. This is a good time to catch up—"

*No, it isn't.*

I stifled a yawn. "Why don't you tell me more about that case of yours?" I yawned again as I settled myself under the covers. "Did you ever find"—(yawn)—"little J. J. Conway's mother?"

If Jack answered, I didn't hear. I passed out as soon as my head hit the pillow.


"WHAT THE—?"

A noise woke me from the sleep of the dead. I lay on my side, stiff and still, peering into the inky dark.

"Where am I?"

The mattress didn't feel like my own. I glanced around and saw four posts, a thick canopy draped overhead. That's when I remembered: I was in Miss Todd's room. Then the noise came again—

*BOOM!*

The thunderous explosion shook the massive bed. Another one came and then another.

"My God!"

More booms came in rapid succession, until the sounds overlapped like the mechanical roar of a freight train running right through my head. I sat up and screamed—

The noise abruptly ceased.

A moment later, the master bedroom's heavy door slammed open. By the light of the hallway I saw Seymour standing there in pea-green Incredible Hulk pajamas.

"Pen! Are you okay? I heard you screaming!"

"Did you hear it?" I asked, clicking on the bedside lamp.

Seymour blinked. "I heard *you.*"

"Not *me*! Those booms! Like a giant stomping through the mansion! Then it started running. The rumble was so loud the bed was shaking!"

Seymour's expression was no longer alarmed, and I stopped chattering. He shook his head. "Listen, Pen. I think you had a—"

"Don't say it!" I folded my arms, lowered my voice to a rational volume. "It wasn't a nightmare. I heard it, I tell you."

"Right. Okay. Maybe you did hear a, uh, giant, but he's gone now." Seymour was now gazing at me with excessive sympathy, as if he were once again breaking it to me that we had no romantic chemistry.

"So where did he go?" I asked flatly.

"Maybe back to the Valley along with the original Jolly Green Giant to grow more vegetables. Ho. Ho. Ho!"

I knew the man was just trying to lighten the tension, but I wasn't in the mood for Chuckles the Clown.

Seymour noticed my scowl. "Sorry. You want me to stick around?"

I shook my head. "I'll be fine."

Seymour bid me goodnight again and closed the door. Warily, I lay back down, but I didn't close my eyes, just peered unhappily at the thick velvet canopy above me.

"Jack, where are you?" I whispered.

*I'm here, baby.*

His voice sounded far away, but I held on to it like a lifeline. "Stick close, huh?"

*Easy does it, doll. Remember, you got nothing to fear from the dead. It's the humans still walking around on God's green earth who should scare the living crap out of you.*

"At the moment, I'm scared of both, okay? Did you hear the noises?"

*You're my ears, doll. That's the way it is.*

"So you did hear?"

*I heard. But I can't explain it to you.* The ghost breezed past my ear. *Get some sleep. I can tell you need it.*

"I can't sleep. I'm too freaked out."

*You want me to sing you a lullaby?*

"You know any?"

*Take me out to the ballgame, take me out to the park—*

"That's not a lullaby."

*It's the only ditty I know all the words to.*

Quiet descended.

"I still can't sleep."

*Okay, then get your keester up and start working.*

".Working?"

*Sure, baby. I don't have arms and legs. You do. Start searching this dump for more clues.*

"Fine," I said, throwing the covers aside. But before I got out of bed, I heard what sounded like a sob.

"Did you make a noise just now, Jack?"

*Not a peep.*

Then I heard it again: a woman's sob. The sound was filled with misery, a cry of anguish. I switched on the bedside lamp, fully expecting the sob to vanish. But it only got louder. I swung my legs over the side of the bed and stood up. Then I crossed the rug in bare feet, trying to locate the sound. It seemed to come from everywhere.

"Miss Todd? Is that you?" I called. "Why are you crying?"

The sobs intensified.

"If it is you, Timothea, please show yourself!"

The sound faded until I had to strain to hear it. Finally all I could hear was the accelerated beat of my own heart. Then I heard heavy footsteps in the hall outside my door. I pulled my slacks on, tucked in the oversized T-shirt, and shoved my feet into my flat sandals.

I tiptoed to the door and pressed my ear against it. There was definitely someone or something on the other side of the wood. I held my breath, closed my fingers around the glass handle, and ripped the door open.

I heard a scream a split second before I was blinded by a blazing light. Then I screamed, too.

"Pen!" Seymour cried. "You scared the hell out of me, opening the door like that! I thought you were——"

"The flashlight! It's shining in my eyes!"

"Oops. Sorry."

Seymour lowered the Maglite until its beam illuminated the carpet that ran down the center of the hall.

"What happened to the electricity?" I asked, trying to rub the white spots from my eyes.

"The lights flickered and then went out."

"The light in my room is working fine——" I faced the bedroom I'd just left and saw it was now completely dark in there, too. "Well, it *was* working. When did the electricity fail?"

"Right around the time I heard what sounded like a woman crying."

"You heard it, too?"

"Listen!"

The sobs began again. Then the lights flickered in the hall and came on. "Thank goodness! At least we don't have to stumble around in the dark—"

"Holy crap! Look at the clock!"

I followed Seymour's flashlight beam to the old grandfather and gasped. The hands on the face were spinning like propellers. Then the clock began to chime, its repeated gongs filling the narrow space.

"Let's go!" Seymour began pushing me toward the stairs. He didn't have to push hard; I'd definitely seen enough! I turned and together we raced to the end of the hall.

As we ran, the sobs intensified, until the wretched sound of crying was louder than the noise of the gonging grandfather clock. When we reached the bottom of the staircase, the clock finally stopped making noise. That was when I noticed lights flickering in the living room and strange wisps of white rolling through the door. Seymour saw it, too.

"Holy smoke!" he said. "Is that a fire?"

"No. There's no smell, no heat."

Taking a deep breath, I pulled away from Seymour and moved through the doorway to the living room. Seymour had left two lamps on, but as soon as I moved over the threshold, they went off. I continued forward in the dark.

The sobbing suddenly ceased. I stopped dead.

"Miss Todd?" I called and waited. But everything in the house remained silent and still. I took another step forward—and gasped. A shroud of frigid air suddenly enveloped me.

"Pen?" Seymour's voice sounded shaky. I turned to see his flashlight beam at the door.

"Over here," I called.

Seymour's flashlight moved closer. The chilly curtain of air still lingered, but now I could see my breath forming little condensation clouds in front of my face. I looked down and realized I was standing in the exact spot where I'd found Miss Todd's corpse.

"The cold spot's back," I whispered.

"Great," Seymour said.

The lamps in the room suddenly snapped on, and the cool air began to dissipate, along with all traces of the mysterious smoke. Seymour turned off his flashlight and scanned the living room.

"Maybe it's over," he said, setting the flashlight down on a table.

I took a deep breath. "Maybe."

Then the lights went out again, and the room felt darker than a graveyard on a moonless night. Seymour must have lunged for the flashlight and missed because I heard the heavy object clatter to the floor and Seymour shout a curse. A few seconds later, the flashlight beam was on again— and shining right in my eyes!

"Ahhh! Watch it, Seymour! You did it again!"

Between the alcohol and the second flash of that Maglite, my night vision was now pretty much shot. So it was Seymour who observed the phenomenon first.

"The room's filling up!" he cried.

"With what? I can't see!"

"With some kind of ectoplasmic fog!"

I rubbed my eyes till the white spots faded, and finally saw the strange fog. It rolled like the odorless smoke, but it was much thicker. Like an early-morning mist, it felt cool and wet as it descended on us.

That's when we saw it: the apparition.

Shimmering and semitransparent, the image of a corpulent middle-aged man drifted silently across the living room. The specter's broad, jowly face appeared waxy; his longish black hair was swept back off his face; and his large, dark eyes were glassy. His clothes were old-fashioned—a three-piece, pinstriped banker's suit with a handkerchief blooming from a breast pocket and a silver watch chain hanging from his bulging vest.

The spirit looked familiar for some reason, but I was in too much shock to place it. For a moment, Seymour and I stood transfixed. Finally, I called out.

"Hello! Can you hear me?"

But the specter didn't answer. It simply continued on its path across the room, until it faded away. A few seconds later, the sobbing began again.

"That's it!" Seymour cried. "We're getting the hell out of here!" Then my mailman grabbed my arm, dragged me through the front doors, and delivered me to the purple dawn.

# CHAPTER 19

## *Light of Day*

I looked over to the left and saw ghosts . . . They
looked like ghosts at any rate.

—"Brother Murder," T. T. Flynn,
December 2, 1939, issue of *Detective Fiction Weekly*

"PEN? WHAT ARE you doing here?" The whispering
voice slipped into my sleep but failed to rouse me. It was
the sharp knocking against the glass that did it. "Pen! Wake
up!"

My slumping body came to upright attention. By now,
the sun was fully up, too, and glaring at me through the
wide windshield. I squinted, glanced around, and realized
I'd dozed off in the front seat of Seymour's ice cream truck.

The last few hours had felt close to surreal. After fleeing the haunted mansion, Seymour and I had stood on the
damp lawn in the murky light debating what to do. Since
I'd left my keys in Miss Todd's bedroom, he piled us into
his only set of working wheels—his ice cream truck. We
drove from Larchmont to Primrose and parked in front of
Eddie Franzetti's house, a modest three-bedroom ranch
circa 1952, where he lived with his wife and kids.

"What's wrong, Pen? Why are you here?" Eddie's face
now replaced the sun; his lean Italian features peered at me
through the truck's passenger-side window.

I rolled down the glass. "Morning, Eddie." I stifled a yawn. "We're here because—"

An explosive snort-snore interrupted me. I glanced across the seat. Seymour was still sleeping, his body sprawled behind the truck's steering wheel. I popped my passenger door and stepped down onto the curb.

Eddie stood barefoot on the sidewalk. His blue jeans looked as if he'd pulled them on quickly since the top button was still undone. He wore a dress shirt, also unbuttoned and hanging half open. Dangling around his neck was an untied tie.

"I was getting ready for Sunday mass when my youngest asked me for an ice cream cone."

He jerked his thumb over his shoulder and I noticed his littlest girl looking curiously at us from behind the house's screen door. I smiled and waved. She waved back.

"How long have you two been out here?" Eddie asked.

I squinted at the cloudless sky. "What time is it?"

"Seven."

"We had a scare a few hours ago. But it was so early, we didn't want to disturb you or your family."

"What was your scare? A burglar?"

I shook my head. "I spent last night with Seymour in Miss Todd's mansion."

Eddie's big brown eyes appeared genuinely surprised. He glanced back into the truck at the snoring mailman in Incredible Hulk pajamas. "I didn't know you two were more than friends. How long have you and Seymour been—"

"We're not!" I cried—a little too loudly. I closed my eyes, took a breath. "I just had too much to drink at his wake for Miss Todd. I was in the master bedroom. He was in a guest room. Got it?"

"Oh, I see. Sorry. Guess I jumped to the wrong—"

"Anyway! We heard noises. Loud booms—well, technically, I was the only one who heard those—but we *both* heard the sobbing. We both felt a mysterious mist, a cold spot, and then we even saw—"

I paused and swallowed, gathered my nerves.

Eddie was staring at me with a perplexed expression. "Yeah? What did you see?"

"A fat man. We didn't recognize him at first—we were both too shocked at the time. But on the drive over here, we remembered he was the man in the portrait over Miss Todd's mantel. He was transparent, and he floated across her living room."

Eddie shook his head, stared down at his bare feet.

"It *happened,* Eddie. I'm telling you it was real. Don't say you don't believe me."

"Pen . . ." He paused. "I believe that *you* believe you experienced something. But you said it yourself: You had a lot to drink. And the Todd house *is* pretty creepy."

I folded my arms, gritted my teeth. This was exactly why I hadn't told a soul about Jack. The mixture of doubt and pity on Eddie's face was almost as hard to take as Seymour "breaking it to me" why he wasn't going to make a pass.

"Tell you what. I'll tell my wife we'll go to the later mass. Let me grab my gun belt. I'll follow you two back to the house and check it out, okay?"

"Okay. Thanks."

"It's not like I don't owe you, Pen. You're the reason I got my promotion. I haven't forgotten."

I nodded and pointed at his naked feet. "Better not forget your shoes, either."


EDDIE FOLLOWED US to the mansion, checked out the living room, the staircase, the bedrooms. Nothing appeared out of the ordinary. (Of course.) In the light of day, the house seemed to be nothing more than a quaint old Victorian filled with antiques and moth balls.

I was beginning to understand what Miss Todd had gone through. Like us, she obviously experienced the manifestations, even reported them to the police. But they didn't believe her then any more than Eddie believed me now.

"Dr. Rubino's explanation for the noises was dementia," I said, pacing the foyer. "Chief Ciders's explanation was a prankster or maybe even a killer. But neither man considered another possibility."

Eddie put his hands on his lean hips. His QPD gun belt had been hastily buckled on over his jeans. He'd exchanged his Sunday-best dress shirt for a Franzetti Pizza T-shirt and laced a pair of scuffed Nikes onto his bare feet. Unfortunately for me, he hadn't put on a new frame of mind.

"Pen, you're not seriously claiming—"

"This mansion is actually haunted. That's one mystery solved. There really *is* a ghost here." I faced Eddie. "Tell me something. Miss Todd started reporting strange noises fairly recently, didn't she?"

Eddie nodded. "Only a few weeks ago."

"Nothing before that, right?"

Eddie nodded.

"Don't you find that suspicious?"

"What?"

"An old Victorian *suddenly* starts showing supernatural activity—activity so obvious that the elderly owner who's lived there for decades contacts the police about it. Activity that becomes so disturbing it scares her to death."

Seymour came down the steps just then. He'd changed out of his Hulk pajamas and into an avocado-green knit polo over tailored beige shorts.

"I don't believe it," Eddie said, folding his arms. "Tarnish in a polo? Where's the superhero T-shirt, Seymour?"

The mailman rolled his eyes. "This is Larchmont, Franzetti. Haven't you ever heard of blending in to the neighborhood? Or to put it in your native-land lingo, 'When in Rome'?"

Eddie pointed to Seymour's suitcase. "Is that where you're going? To see the pope about an exorcism?"

"No. I'm checking in to the Finch Inn."

"What?" I said. "I thought you were calling your former housemate, asking him to put you up for a few nights."

Seymour shook his head. "Gilman's already convinced Hardy Miles to move in—his girlfriend threw him out a few weeks ago, and he's been crashing with his sister and her husband. He couldn't wait to get out of their basement. He's moving his stuff in today. No room for me."

"Give me a minute," I said. "I'll give you a ride over to Cranberry."

"Thanks, Pen."

I headed back upstairs, changed back into the rest of my party clothes from the night before, ran a brush through my hair, and grabbed my handbag, where Jack's buffalo nickel had been safely stashed.

*Where you been, baby?*

"We went to get Eddie."

*That badge isn't gonna truck with your haunting story.*

"Tell me something I don't know."

*Don't let the copper set you back, doll. When I was alive, I was just like him, didn't swallow anything that wasn't clear as a glass of gin. Not even those tapes will change his mind.*

"The tapes!" I ran to the cabinet, pulled out the hatbox, and stuffed all five cassettes into my bag. That was when I thought of one more thing I'd need.

Downstairs I asked Seymour to haul out that portrait he'd removed from the living room, the one of the fat man over the mantel. When he produced it, I pulled out my cell phone and took a digital photo.

Seymour locked up the house and the three of us headed into the driveway. Eddie stood beside me as I unlocked my car door. He pointed to Seymour's parked ice cream truck.

"Weren't you two worried about the brakes on that thing?"

"*Pen* was. Big-time," Seymour said, waiting for me to pop the Saturn's trunk. "She made me drive to your place at about five miles an hour."

"*And* I made him stop every twenty feet, just to be sure."

"Good." Eddie nodded, folding his arms. "Because the sabotaged brakes of Seymour's VW worry me a lot more than this alleged haunted house."

"The brakes," I said. "That's right. You were going to stop by Ben Kesey's garage."

"I did. Ben had Seymour's bus on a lift, showed me the damage. I took digital photos, picked up some prints under the vehicle, too."

Seymour frowned. "But you'll just get Ben's greasy fingerprints, won't you?"

"I took Ben's prints so we can eliminate him, sent what I got to the state police. They're analyzing them now. It's a long shot but you never know. The undercarriage was unusually clean."

Seymour nodded. "I clipped a coupon a few weeks ago for that new Auto Wash by the Sleepy-Time Motel: half-price engine and undercarriage steaming with the purchase of a hot wax."

"Well, it's a good thing. I'm pretty sure I got some prints that weren't Ben's. In the meantime, watch your back, Seymour. You be careful, too, Pen."

I nodded. "I will."

As Seymour stashed his suitcase in my trunk, I stepped closer to Eddie. "If you want my theory," I told him quietly, "I think Miss Todd's living sister has the most to gain if something happens to Seymour."

"You know her name?"

I shook my head. "Emory Stoddard does. But he won't divulge it. He says she wishes to remain anonymous and he's under no legal obligation to reveal it at the moment. All I know is that she may be living in Newport under a married name."

Eddie frowned, remained silent for a minute. "Let me see what I can find out."

I thanked Eddie and slid behind the wheel of my Saturn. Seymour climbed in beside me. I noticed Eddie didn't go back to his own car until we drove away. And yes, even though it made Seymour crazy, I braked the car every ten yards for the first half mile, just to be on the safe side.

I drove slowly after that, turning onto Dogwood from Larchmont. We didn't say a word as we rolled under the shade trees, along the stone wall, and past the gates of the "Old Farm." Finally, we left the site of the town's graveyard and continued on the road to Cranberry.

I drove to the far end, just past the business district, and turned onto a long drive lined with century-old weeping willows. The Finches' bed-and-breakfast stood at the end, its brick chimneys, bay windows, shingle-covered gables, and corner turret making for a much cheerier picture than the Todd mansion—to my relief.

Fiona and Barney had researched their Queen Anne thoroughly, even repainting the house in its original high-Victorian colors: reddish-brown on the main body's clapboards, and a combination of olive green and old gold on the moldings and the spindlelike ornaments that served as a porch railing.

There were four floors of rooms, each with its own fireplace and most with breathtaking views of Quindicott Pond, a good-sized body of saltwater fed by a narrow, streamlike inlet that raced in and out with the nearby Atlantic's tides.

A nature trail circled the pond, stretched into the backwoods, and branched off to paths that led all the way to the shoreline. The inn rented bicycles for the trail and rowboats for the pond, which was usually pretty well stocked with fish. A dozen or so local fisherman even docked small boats here and used the inlet to reach the open ocean.

The inn's French restaurant was housed in a separate, smaller building, which featured a large dining room partially built right over the pond. Chez Finch was a little too pricey for most of the town's residents, but the raves from papers in Providence and Newport were bringing in plenty of foodie tourists with deep pockets.

As I climbed out of my car, the June sun felt warm on

my face. Seymour joined me and we walked across the small parking lot, feeling the breeze off the pond—brisk and fresh with the tang of brine. We ascended the Queen Anne's six long steps, moved across the wide, wraparound porch, and through the open stained-glass doors.

Fiona noticed us strolling past her palm trees in her dark-paneled entranceway and waved us over to the inn's hospitality table. "Morning, you two! Care for a snack?" She was just transfering the last breakfast pastries from the white bakery box to a decorative plate. "I stopped by Cooper's after church."

Without a word, Seymour dropped his suitcase and stuffed a hot glazed circle of fried dough into his maw. "Thannns, Finnna," he mumbled between chews.

Unfortunately, my stomach wasn't up for Milner Logan's lighter-than-air doughnuts, mouthwatering maple-glazed banana muffins, or any of the delicious-looking fare from Cooper Family Bakery. Coffee was about all I could handle. So I moved to the urn on the table and helped myself.

*Have two, baby,* the ghost advised. *Between last night's drinking and your funhouse scares, I'm surprised you're still walking upright.*

"Me, too," I whispered, stifling a yawn.

"Now, tell me exactly what this is all about," Fiona said, pointing to Seymour's suitcase.

"I told you over the phone. I need a place to stay for a little while," Seymour said, his thick fingers selecting an apple turnover even before he'd swallowed the last of the doughnut.

"Seymour and I had an experience last night," I said quietly. "It started in the bedroom."

Fiona's eyebrow arched. "You and Seymour?"

I could already hear the ghost laughing.

"*Listen,* Fiona. Todd Mansion really is haunted." I pulled out my cell phone and showed her the digital photo of the old portrait. "Seymour and I saw the ghost of this man. Miss Todd must have seen him, too. That's what scared her to death."

Fiona's jaw dropped as I went through the entire tale, including the audiotapes we'd uncovered. ". . . and I want to find out more about this dead man. Do you recognize him?"

Fiona shook her head. "He's likely a Todd patriarch, don't you think? Miss Todd's father or grandfather?"

"Would you look into the history of Todd Mansion for me? I know you have the connections with the historical society."

"Of course."

"Find out everything you can. Who built the house, who lived there before Miss Todd, everything. And while you're at it, ask around. See if you can find anyone who knows or remembers Miss Todd's sister."

"I promise I'll find out what I can." She eyed me. "Stick around a few minutes, okay?"

I nodded, downing another cup of java as Fiona showed Seymour to his room upstairs. When she came down, a few of the inn's guests were eating pastries and drinking coffee. She smiled, greeted them warmly, and took me by the arm.

"Let's step outside," she whispered.

We moved through the stained-glass doors, clomping across the floorboards, and stopped in the far corner of the wide wraparound porch. The day was growing warmer but the awning kept us well shaded.

"Tell me the truth, Pen," Fiona said quietly. "What's going on with Seymour? Has he been spooked enough to give up the mansion? Is he going to sell to that vampire who crashed his party with the councilwoman last night?"

"You mean Charlene Fabian?"

"*Lindsey*-Fabian," Fiona noted. "Of the Lindsey-Tilton group; let's not forget that."

"The McBed-and-Breakfasts, I know."

"You should also know that I don't buy that ridiculous story Marjorie Binder-Smith told about Charlene being an old friend staying with her for a visit. That woman might be a college chum, but she was there last night to get a good look around. Probably would have greased the wheels with Seymour, too, if I hadn't been there to run interference."

"I'm sure you're right."

"Of course I am! And I'll bet dollars to doughnuts that there's a financial reason Marjorie's involved—probably a political contribution or even a quiet kickback under the table if the councilwoman agrees to steamroll through rezoning of Larchmont for a B and B."

I nodded.

Fiona shook her head. "You know, I saw her again this morning."

"Who? Marjorie?"

"No, Charlene Lindsey-Fabian. She was going into Cooper's as I was heading out. It took every ounce of willpower for me to bite my tongue and not tell her off again."

"Listen, Fiona, after last night, you better prepare yourself for the possibility. Seymour may decide to sell. He's pretty upset about the whole haunting business. Even before we witnessed the manifestation, he contacted the Spirit Zappers." I explained who they were and what they did. "But they're backed up for months. And right now I'm more worried about someone trying to hurt him—even kill him—over that property. Eddie Franzetti confirmed what Ben Kesey found: The brakes on Seymour's VW bus were sabotaged."

Fiona's eyes bugged a moment. Then she folded her arms and tapped her foot in thought. A cool breeze off the pond blew the line of Shaker rockers back and forth as if a group of ghostly guests were taking it easy, biding their time till midnight when they'd rise up and haunt the town.

"What the Todd house needs is a séance," Fiona finally said. "An authentic medium might be able find out some key information from the spirit or spirits lodged there."

"A séance . . ." I thought it over. "That's not a bad idea. The house is very old, yet the manifestations began only recently. Why? What's behind it? What made the activity start?"

"If a medium can help Seymour answer those questions, maybe even exorcise those spirits and prevent him from selling, then I'm going to introduce him to one."

"*You* know a medium?"

"As a matter of fact, I do. She's going to be leading a séance in my restaurant tonight at midnight."

"Chez Finch?"

Fiona nodded. "She belongs to a spiritualist group based out of town. A small number of them are coming to stay the night at the inn." She glanced at her watch. "They're all due to check in before sunset."

"But why hold a séance at Chez Finch? It's too new to be haunted, isn't it?"

"It's not the restaurant they're interested in. It's the pond, which the dining room is partially built right over."

"Why is that significant?"

"Apparently they're going to try to reach the spirit of a man who may have drowned in the ocean waters connected to the pond."

"I see. And what's the name of this group?"

"I don't know yet. It's all very secretive. The reservations and arrangement were made by the medium herself: Rachel Delve. I actually know Rachel from another business transaction. She's very nice and quite trustworthy. She's the real thing, Pen. Maybe she can help Seymour."

I nodded. "Introduce the two then, okay?"

"I will. I'm sure once Seymour explains his situation, Rachel will find a way to help."

I stifled a yawn. "When is this Chez Finch séance due to start?"

"Midnight tonight. Would you like to come?"

"I'll be there."

*Better get some shut-eye first,* Jack warned in my head.

*Or you'll be dead to the world long before that broad starts
trying to raise them.*


JACK WASN'T WRONG about my needing sleep. The
drive to my bookshop was a short one, but I nearly nodded
off behind the wheel. One passing glimpse along a sidewalk,
however, quickly woke me up again.

"Jack!" I whispered. "Do you see what I see?"

*I always see what you see, baby.*

Strolling out of Cooper Family Bakery looking chummy
as can be were Charlene Lindsey-Fabian and an older,
heavier woman in a tailored gray suit.

"That's her! That's the woman Aunt Sadie and I ran into
coming out of Mr. Stoddard's office!"

I well remembered the fleshy face with patrician features,
the short brown curls shot with gray, the chilly blue eyes, and
the haughty expression. I even recalled the expensive handbag of quilted leather, which seemed out of place when I first
saw her carrying it in Millstone.

I immediately slowed my car and just as quickly heard
a horn honk behind me. Sunday mornings were far from
sleepy in Quindicott. Two churches near the commons
brought plenty of traffic onto Cranberry, and Cooper's always had a line around the block for Milner's legendary
doughnuts. No surprise, there wasn't a parking place in
sight.

"Darnit!"

I checked my rearview mirror. Charlene and the mystery
woman were walking right up to a parked sedan. I remembered in Millstone, the older woman had gotten into a silver Mercedes with a driver. But this car was white and
appeared to be Charlene's, because she was the one who
unlocked the doors and helped the older woman inside.

The driver behind me beeped again.

*Just dump the car anywhere, doll!*

I raced my motor, quickly turning off Cranberry. I
pulled over a few seconds later, illegally blocking the first

driveway I saw. Grabbing my handbag (and Jack's nickel), I popped the door and ran full speed down the sidewalk. But it was too late. Charlene's car had already pulled out. It was blocks away now and turning out of sight. The mystery woman was gone again—and I was illegally parked!

Wheeling abruptly, I took a blind, frustrated step, right into a brick wall.

"Whoa, there, Mrs. McClure!"

I looked up to see Jim Wolfe standing there—all six-foot-three of him. The blond-haired, dimpled-chin Viking smiled down at me, a Cooper's bakery box dangling from his work-callused fingers.

"Jim! You came from the bakery? Just now?"

He laughed. "Yeah, what's wrong with that? You afraid I'll get fat eating too many of Milner's doughnuts?"

I almost didn't recognize the man. Most days around Quindicott, the head of Wolfe Construction was wearing dusty jeans, a denim shirt, and a hard hat. Today he was cleaned up and sharply tailored in a Sunday blue suit.

"Sorry, Jim." I shook my head clear, feeling like an idiot. "I was just wondering if you'd happened to bump into Charlene Fabian."

"Yeah, I did. You know Charlene?" He reached out then and touched my hair. "Your hair looks nice like that."

"Like what?"

"Down around your shoulders. Whenever I see you, it's always tied back."

Jim's eyes were blue but I'd never noticed just what shade—this close they looked cobalt, like an early autumn sky. It was distracting. I swallowed, trying to remember what I was going to ask the man.

*Whether he knows the name of the old battleaxe. Whether the broad is Miss Todd's living sister. Whether she's in league with the innkeeper's mortal enemy to off your pal the mailman for a million-dollar payoff. Get a grip, baby.*

"Uh . . ."

Jim smiled. "You trying to ask me something, Mrs. McClure?"

"Yes!"

"Let me make it easy for you, okay? You want to go to dinner or a movie with me sometime? Is that what you want to ask?"

"No, no! You're misunderstanding—"

"Hi, Jim!"

"Hey, there, Bob."

It was then I noticed a few passersby were glancing our way with more than a little curiosity. The whispering women on the street seemed especially interested in what Jim and I were discussing so intensely. I closed my eyes took a breath.

"I'm not trying to ask you out, Jim," I whispered. "What I'd like to know is if you knew the name of the older woman with Charlene Fabian."

"Oh, I see . . . Uh, yeah, actually I do. Her name's Mrs. Beatrice Ingram. I just had a short meet-and-greet with those two inside."

"Meet-and-greet?"

"Uh-huh. We had coffee together. Mrs. Ingram's planning to invest in a property with Charlene, turn it into a bed-and-breakfast. They need some work on the place and I've done work for Charlene in the past." He shrugged.

"Where is this place?"

"Newport."

"You have an address?"

Jim shook his head. "No. They said they're not ready for me to see it yet, but in a few weeks they'll have me take a look. Like I said, this was just a meet-and-greet. I'm sure they're talking to other construction guys, you know?" He shrugged. "I did my best to charm them. What else can I do? You win some, you lose some."

"But you hardly ever lose."

Jim smiled. "Thanks for saying that. I'm good at under-bidding. It's true."

"Okay. Well, thanks for the name." I was about to walk away when Jim lightly touched my arm.

"Wait."

*Get away from this stormtrooper, baby. He's just gonna lay a line on you.*

"What?" I said.

"That's it?" He laughed. "Use me and toss me aside?"

*Oh, brother.*

"It's nothing personal, Jim. I just wanted the woman's name because there's a very good chance she's Miss Todd's sister."

"Miss Todd? The old woman who was—" He glanced around. "You know what the rumor is, right? That she was frightened to death."

"I know what the rumor is. But I have my suspicions that the frights were manufactured."

Jim's blond eyebrows rose. "You sound like a private eye." He smiled. "But then, that's what they say about you around here. You do more than just sell those detective books. You like investigating, too. It's kind of a hobby of yours, right?"

"I've solved my share of puzzling cases around this little town. Let's leave it at that."

"Let's not." Jim smiled again, bigger this time. The man's teeth were nearly as dazzling as his eyes. "Let's go out sometime. How about it? You can tell me more about your, uh, puzzling cases."

"I hardly know you."

*You tell him, doll!*

"That's the point of going out, right? Getting to know each other better?"

"Well, stop by my store sometime. Maybe we can go out for coffee."

"Will do, Mrs. M." He reached out and touched my hair again. "It's Penelope, isn't it?"

"Pen."

"See you next week then, Pen. Maybe I'll even break down and buy a book. Three of the guys on my crew are enjoying books you sold them just this week." He gave me a little wink.

"Really? What books are those?"

"Not books—book. They're all reading the same one. They say it's really hot, too." He waggled his eyebrows. "Sounds like it from the title. It's called—"

I gritted my teeth, already guessing.

"—*Bang, Bang Baby*."

# CHAPTER 20

## *Past Is Present*

Now let's add it up and don't interrupt me.

— *The Long Goodbye*, Raymond Chandler, 1953

"NO WONDER HE asked me out! He thinks I'm a loose bookseller, peddling pornographic fiction!"

Aunt Sadie smirked at me over the check-out counter. "He asked you out because you're an attractive redhead who ran into him on the street."

"Yes, *literally*!"

"Don't look a gift horse in the mouth, dear, especially when it's six-three, has sky-blue eyes, and owns its own business."

I glanced at my watch: eleven thirty A.M. We were due to open in thirty minutes, and I was dead on my feet. I'd already called Eddie and Fiona to tell them the name I'd uncovered (Beatrice Ingram); and with one marathon running of the mouth, I'd brought my aunt up to date on the haunting, Miss Todd's audiotapes, tonight's séance, and Jim Wolfe.

Sadie's reaction wasn't surprising. My romantic prospects always drew more commentary from her than my investigative ones.

"I'm going to catch a few hours' sleep," I finally told her. "Are you sure you're okay to manage without me this afternoon?"

"Of course. Dilbert's coming in at one. Then you can relieve us both at five, close up shop at seven, and have plenty of time to attend your séance." Sadie shook her head. "You really think a medium can help Seymour?"

I was about to tell her that I needed all the help I could get since the only spirit that would talk to *me* was Jack Shepard, but I bit my tongue. "It's a strange situation. I need to speak to someone who understands more than I do about how this occult stuff works."

Jack laughed.

"You don't count," I whispered. "Since you *are* occult stuff."

Upstairs, I opened the apartment door, automatically glancing into the living room for Spencer—and then I remembered.

*He's at boot camp, baby.*

I walked down the hall and into my son's bedroom anyway. The room was so empty and quiet, with the baseball bat leaning against the wall, the bed perfectly made. Bookmark was sleeping soundly at its foot. I picked up the little orange cat, cuddled her close, and carried her to my own small room.

*Miss him, huh?*

"Of course." I rubbed Bookmark's ears. She yawned and purred.

*But you know he's having fun with his pals.*

"I know. He's a different boy now than a few years ago. Not like his father anymore. He's happy, energetic. Full of love . . . and a love of life, thank goodness."

*That's right, doll. The kid's just spreading his wings.*

I sighed. "That's the trouble, Jack. Once they learn to spread their wings, they fly away."

*Flying away is good, baby. It's how boys become men.*

"I don't care. I still miss him."

I thought of Spencer as I changed into my nightshirt, turned down my bedcovers, closed my curtains. My little boy's auburn hair and freckles were still on my mind as I fluffed my pillow and hugged Bookmark close.

*There's plenty of ways a boy can lose his mother, honey. Believe me, your way's better.*

"My way?" The kitty's purr was soothing; the breezy brush of Jack's presence more so.

*Close your eyes, doll*, the ghost whispered. *Close your eyes and I'll remind you . . .*

"HEY, MRS. McCLURE! What do you know, what do you say?"

I opened my eyes. A little freckle-faced boy was standing in front of me, but it wasn't my little boy. It was J. J. Conway. His ruddy cheeks appeared freshly washed, his brown hair looked newly trimmed. His shirt and slacks were clean, too, the small tears neatly sewn. He had a big smile for me— and Jack, as it turned out.

I glanced to my side. My bad-boy partner was standing there in his sharply tailored double-breasted, a fedora slanted over the hard planes and angles of his lived-in face.

"Find my mom yet?"

"Not yet, kid," Jack replied.

His slate gray gaze slid over me. Self-conscious, I glanced down at myself, saw I was now wearing a cute little navy suit with matching round-toed pumps at the end of my stocking-clad legs. I touched my hair, felt the rolled bangs, the sleekly styled pageboy.

Jack gave me a wink and addressed J. J. again. "How's things working out with Mrs. Dellarusso?"

"Swell! She sure is a good cook!"

"Pack on a few pounds then, kid. You can use it."

Glancing around me, I recognized the busy Third Avenue street corner where J. J. Conway had worked in 1947. Mac Dougherty's newsstand stood a few feet away.

"So, Mrs. McClure, you got any leads?" J. J. asked.

"Uh . . ." I looked to Jack.

"We're on the job today," he told the boy. "We'll get back to you."

"Okay," J. J. said with a little military salute.

"Got that photo I asked you for?"

J. J. nodded. He dug a hand into his pocket. "Here it is, Mr. Shepard. A picture of my mom, Mable Conway."

"Thanks, kid." I moved to look at the woman's picture, but Jack quickly stuffed the small photo inside his jacket. "See you later, J. J."

"Not if I see you first!" He smiled, then turned his voice to the sidewalk crowds. " 'Killer Fire! Accident or Arson?' Read all about it!"

Jack took my arm and pulled me up the block.

"Where are we going?" I asked.

"Remember my case?"

"Barely."

"We're heading to the jewelry store, doll. We found an empty box in the bedroom of the kid's mother. It had a card inside—"

"That's right! The mother's boyfriend was Frankie Papps. He bought her a pair of pearl earrings. The jeweler's card was in the box."

"Broadway's Best Jewelry," he said as he pulled me along. "Shake a leg."


"THE GREAT WHITE Way" is a phrase supposedly coined in 1901 by an ad man named O. J. Gude, who foresaw the awesome possibilities of the electric display. It started with one sign on Broadway—an advertisement for an ocean resort. By the early twenty-first century, digital billboards half the size of skyscrapers were flashing real-time images from cable TV.

At the moment, however, we weren't that far in the future. We were in Jack's time, mid-twentieth century, and the ads weren't quite as massive in size, but they were plenty ubiquitous in scope. As we skirted crowds of pedestrians to cross the intersection of Broadway and Forty-second, a field of billboards urged me to chew gum, drink beer, and eat Planters Peanuts.

Nighttime was always magic in Times Square, with the

glow of theater and movie marquees giving everything a glittery, electric feel. Daytime wasn't quite so spectacular—and right now it was high noon.

The midday sun's unforgiving spot exposed the dinginess of the old buildings here. The side streets appeared drab, the ticket offices tired. Grand hotel lobbies and theater entrances were dark; life swarmed instead around cheap lunch counters, cut-rate haberdasheries, and novelty concessions.

Broadway's Best Jewelers sounded like a glamorous shop, but when we arrived at the address—closer to Eighth Avenue than the actual Broadway—we found a dingy storefront with a faded sign. A bell clanged loudly above us as we pushed open the glass door.

The place smelled of must and old wood with theater posters covering the paneled walls. There was a counter—not glass but scarred oak—and no jewelry of any kind was on display; no watches, rings, or pendants, just fat catalogs with plain covers. The shop ran deep. Behind the counter, a number of men and women were bent over craft tables, bright lights shining on their work areas.

"I'm Dolly. Can I help you two?"

A heavyset woman in a black suit and wearing horn-rimmed glasses approached us from the other side of the counter.

"We're private detectives," Jack said. He showed her his license. "We're looking for Frankie Papps. Know him?"

Dolly shook her head. "I haven't seen Frankie in weeks."

"Two weeks?" I asked.

"Yeah, why? What's it to you, miss?"

"To me, nothing," I said. "But there's a little boy worried about his mother. She disappeared two weeks ago. Frankie gave her pearl earrings, which you sold to him." I showed her the card we'd found inside the jewelry box.

The woman frowned. "You're talking about his girlfriend, then? The burlesque dancer? She has a kid, huh?"

I exchanged a glance with Jack. "J. J. said his mother was a schoolteacher," I whispered. "Do you have that photo J. J. gave you?"

Jack pulled the picture out, showed it to the woman behind the counter. She shrugged. "Sorry, I never saw her. Just heard Frankie mention her a few times."

When she handed the photo back, I finally gave it a look. The picture showed a stunning platinum blonde no older than twenty. She wore a huge smile and a tight, low-cut sweater—very low-cut. The woman wasn't built like any schoolteacher I'd ever known. She wasn't dressed like one, either.

"Did Frankie have more than one girlfriend?" I asked.

"How should I know?" Dolly said. "He buys a lot of stuff from us, but it's usually for the shows, not the showgirls."

"Shows?"

"The shows!" Dolly gestured to the Broadway posters on the walls. Then, as if I were thick-headed, she rolled her eyes and shoved over one of the catalogs on the counter. "We make costume jewelry for the theater people—legit, burlesque, magic shows. You name it, we make it."

I paged through the catalog, seeing tiaras, fake strands of pearls, diamond chokers, even stage weapons—fancy swords and daggers.

"Did Frankie ever have you make daggers for him?" I asked.

"Oh, yeah. We made daggers for him, tiaras, costume jewelry—"

I glanced at Jack. "Sounds like all the stuff that burglar was trying to steal from J. J.'s basement apartment."

"Did he pay you in cash or with some kind of check?" Jack asked.

"He didn't pay. He bought his stuff for whatever theater he was working for."

"Wait. He was an actor?" I said, glancing at Jack again. "I thought he was supposed to be an electrician."

"He works stagecraft, miss," Dolly said. "Does lighting, special electric effects, whatever the show's director wants."

"Who was the guy working for lately?" Jack asked.

She shrugged. "Some big producer. Don't know his name but he gave us a lot of business through Frankie. He was the man who paid the bills for the props. It was Frankie who placed all the orders and picked up the stuff. He said their show was still in rehearsals."

"Can you give us the address where the bills were sent?" Jack asked.

"Maybe. If there's something in it for me."

Jack slid a five-dollar bill across the counter. Dolly slid an address over to him. We left the dim interior of Broadway's Best Jewelers and stepped into the blazing September afternoon.

I squinted up at Jack, my white-gloved hand shading my eyes. "Where's the address?"

"Great Neck."

"Guess we have to take a train ride." I started down the block. Jack stopped me.

"Your *next* move is all the way out to Long Island? You're all done with your business in the city? Is that right?"

I smirked up at the man. "From that tone, I'm guessing I'm not."

Jack tilted back his fedora. "You sure got a lot to learn, honey."

"Give me that photo!"

Jack raised a sandy eyebrow but he didn't argue, just handed it over.

"Come on!" I said. This time, I grabbed his arm and tugged him up the block. I turned into the first burlesque show I saw. There were girlie pictures plastered under the marquee; billboards with half-dressed cuties; and a big, ugly-looking bouncer at the door. He stopped us with a giant hand, pointed to the ticket booth.

"We're not here to see the girls," I said. "We're looking for this woman. Know her?"

The big man frowned at the photo of Mable Conway and shook his head. Then he pointed to the booth and folded his massive arms. "Thirty-five cents each."

"Come on!" I pulled Jack to the next theater.

The burlesque houses were mostly clustered along Eighth

Avenue and Forty-second. I showed Mable Conway's photo to the next bouncer and then a third. None of them recognized her. But the fourth one said she looked familiar.

"She ain't a blonde, though. She's a brunette. And she's about fifteen years older than that photo."

"Did she work here?" I asked, excited to find a lead.

The bouncer nodded. "You should talk to the girls inside."

Jack flashed his PI license and the bouncer waved us in. A sultry brunette was onstage, peeling off opera gloves to a slow-playing sax. Men sat in the dark, sipping drinks, hats pulled low.

We found our way backstage, and I showed the photo around.

"Yeah, I know Princess," one of the performers finally said. The woman was stunningly tall and very well built, wearing what looked like nothing but a robe, and smoking a cigarette. Her face was heavily made up, probably to hide her age. From a dim distance she looked maybe twenty-nine; in stronger light, she was closer to forty.

"Princess?" I repeated.

"That's what she called herself. Her real name's Mable."

The woman confirmed everything. Mable Conway had a little boy. She lied to him, telling him she was a teacher, didn't want him to know what she was really doing.

"Mable was a legit dancer back in the day." The woman took a long drag, blew out a white plume. "Couldn't make it out of the chorus line, you know? A real looker so she did leg shows, then waited tables, then ended up here."

"Did you know her boyfriend, Frankie?"

"Sure. Frankie and her were cozy and all that mush. He's the one got her out of this hole. Got her some job working a legit show again. Don't know much about it. Just that some rich guy on Long Island's producing."

I glanced at Jack. *"See,"* I whispered. "Long Island again."

Jack nodded. "Keep going, doll."

"Got any idea where we can find Frankie?" I asked.

"Why?" the woman asked. "He disappear or somethin'?"

I nodded. "He disappeared two weeks ago, along with Mable."

"He probably skipped town," the woman said. She paused and frowned at me at Jack. "You're not working for Curly, are you?"

"No," Jack said abruptly.

"Curly who?" I asked, but Jack was already pulling me toward the stage door. "Thanks," he called to the stripper and two seconds later, we were out in the alley.

"What's the big idea?" I demanded, straightening my little blue suit.

"Every yegg in this neighborhood knows who Curly is, baby. You don't need a lead on him. I'll take you."

Then we were off again, hurrying down the block.

CURLY THE BOOKIE took illegal bets in a run-down apartment on Ninth Avenue. Jack was an occasional client, so he got us in easily. We climbed three flights of a narrow staircase and Jack knocked a certain way. A bolt slid aside in the door like a speakeasy. Eyes peered through then the door opened and a muscle-bound guy with a crew cut and an anchor tattoo greeted Jack with a handshake.

The men exchanged words about some big boxing match. Then Jack grabbed my gloved hand and pulled me along like a little coal car behind a massive steam engine.

The apartment was shotgun style, with one room leading into another. Each was full of smoke—cigarette and cigar. A radio was playing loudly somewhere, the announcer calling a horse race. A dozen men were sitting around on easy chairs, reading papers and drinking. A half dozen more sat around a table playing cards, also drinking. We plowed through room after room until we came to a closed door. Jack knocked three times.

"Come!"

Curly the Bookie didn't have any curls. He didn't have any hair, either. In an irony that didn't get past the Three Stooges, "Curly's" head was shaved clean as a billiard ball. He had a bulky, half-muscular body, as if he'd been a boxer once and had gone a little to pot—but only a little. The man's bulldog face and ham-sized biceps didn't look worth challenging in the ring or out.

He greeted Jack with a stern but not unfriendly, "Howya doin', Shep?" The men exchanged some views on a race-horse and more on the same boxing match Jack had discussed with the muscle-bound doorman.

". . . but I'm not here to lose my money today, Curly," Jack said all of a sudden. "Got a girl partner here today wants to ask you a few questions. That okay?"

I tensed. Curly's bulldog face didn't move but his black eyes narrowed on me from behind his desk. "Depends on the questions."

Jack stepped back and pressed me forward. "You're on, baby."

"Crap," I muttered.

"Excuse me?" Curly said.

"I was wondering, Mr. . . . uh, Curly, if you know a man named Frankie Papps?"

"Why?"

"I, uh, need to find him for a little boy who wants to lo-cate his mother. Frankie was the woman's boyfriend. And she's disappeared. Can you help me find Frankie?"

Curly took a long time looking me over. He took a long drag on the stub of a cigar. "Frankie places bets here," he finally said. "Does it once a week, like clockwork. He ain't been here in two."

"Do you have any idea where he might have gone?"

"He mentioned his boss owed him a big cut of back pay and he was sick of waitin' for it. He was going out there to collect so he could place a nice big bet on Graziano vs. Zale at Yankee. Frankie don't show soon, he's gonna miss the book."

"You said he was going 'out there'—where is that? Long Island?"

Curly nodded. "Said his girlfriend worked for this rich guy, too, and they were both going to get their cut, quit while they were ahead."

"What does that mean? What were they doing for this man?"

"From what Frankie told me, they were running some kind of elaborate scam. There were whales involved, a big payoff."

I glanced at Jack. "Whales?" I whispered.

"Rich people were being scammed, baby. *Very* rich people."

"So that's it," Curly said. "That's all I know."

We were clearly dismissed and Jack led me out again, back through the shotgun rooms. We were almost to the door when someone stopped him.

"Well, if it isn't my favorite slugger. What brings you here, Jack? A bet or a case?"

"I'm done talking to you about cases, Brennan. Unless you want another shiner?"

My ears pricked at the name. "Timothy Brennan?" I leaned my head around Jack's wide shoulders and my jaw dropped. The famous late author of crime novels (in my time) was standing in front of us, now very much alive—much younger than I remembered, too, and about a hundred pounds leaner. But then, the man wouldn't be keeling over at my in-store appearance for another sixty years.

"Who's the cutie?" Tim Brennan winked at me. "Introduce me, Shepard. Don't be a cad."

"This is Penelope. She's helping me out today."

"Charmed." Brennan winked again, but this time it was more of a leer. "And what exactly are you helping our Mr. Shepard with, Red?"

"The case of a missing mother." I sniffed.

Beneath a boyish shock of hair, Brennan's eyes lit up. "Really? Sounds like great copy."

"Don't tell him a thing," Jack warned.

"Okay, then," I said. "I guess we're off to Great Neck then."

"Great Neck?" Brennan echoed as we began to move past him. "You two investigating the deaths in that fire?"

"What fire?" Jack asked.

Brennan slapped a newspaper into Jack's hand. "Read all about it, buddy. Eight dead in mansion land. Rich guy's place burned to the ground. Could be arson. And if it is, it's eight counts of homicide."

"I'll read it," Jack said, then hustled me out of the bookie's lair.

When we hit the street, I asked Jack how we were getting to Long Island. The weather was looking pretty lousy by now; clouds were smothering the sun. The daylight was dying.

"Close your eyes, baby. We don't have much time left."

"We're not done, are we? I still haven't solved the case!"

"Close your eyes."

I did and all of a sudden the balmy September weather felt much colder. The hard street under my pumps turned soft, as if I were now standing on damp earth. A chilly wind blew and I smelled the acrid scent of charred wood. I opened my eyes and gasped.

I was no longer in Manhattan. I was standing in front of the Long Island mansion that had burned to the ground. The stone foundation was left, but the structure itself was a smoldering wreck. I glanced around, looking for Jack, and noticed the wrought-iron fencing around the property.

"Oh, my God."

The design in the fence was wholly unique—a series of pentagrams, each with a fleur-de-lis at its center.

Jack walked up to me, took off his double-breasted coat, and draped it around my shoulders. For a moment, he hugged me close from behind, and then he turned me in his arms.

"The officials on the scene are still assessing the damage," he said quietly and pointed to two men in suits and three in uniform. "They pulled eight bodies out of here. The way they found six of the bodies, they suspect they may have been drunk or drugged. The last two were found in the basement tied to chairs—a man and a woman."

The weather was getting colder, the evening darker. A low mist began rising off the damp grass. I shivered. "Was the woman who died in the fire—was she J. J. Conway's mother?"

Jack nodded. "She was. Her body was identified within the week."

He handed me a newspaper, the same paper Brennan had given him, the same newspaper J. J. had been peddling earlier. There was a small photo with the article about the fire. It showed the owner of the home that burned to the ground.

He was a fat man in a three-piece banker's suit with dark hair brushed off his forehead. He was the man in Miss Todd's portrait. He was the ghost in Miss Todd's mansion.

The caption gave me a name: GIDEON WEXLER.

"But I still don't understand, Jack. What does it mean? Who is this man? And what's his connection to Miss Todd's place?"

I looked up, but Jack's solid form wasn't near me anymore. He was just a silhouette, at the edge of the grounds, fading into the fog.

"Keep digging, baby," his voice called from the rising mist. "The case is in your time now . . ."

"Wait, Jack, don't leave me! I need you! Jack!"


"PEN? PENELOPE!"

My eyelids lifted. Sadie was sitting on the edge of my bed. "What century is it?" I asked, feeling disoriented.

My aunt smiled. "It's the twenty-first, dear. And the day is Sunday and the time is nearly five. Do you feel up to working in the shop?"

"Oh, yes." I nodded. "No problem."

"Good. I'll see you downstairs in a little bit then." Aunt Sadie smiled, stroked Bookmark, and got up to leave. Sensing a snack in the offing, Bookmark jumped off the bed to follow her.

I rubbed my eyes, feeling groggy. Part of my mind was still stuck in the past—Gideon Wexler was the name of the man in the portrait. But that name didn't mean anything to me. And it made no sense. Who was Miss Todd to this man? A relative? A friend? A lover? And what did it matter, anyway?

I called silently to Jack, but he was gone. Once again, reliving his past memories had exhausted him.

"An envelope came for you, by the way." Aunt Sadie called from the doorway. "I left it on the dresser."

"An envelope?"

"Yes, Dilbert found it earlier, stuffed in our door's mail slot."

"But this is Sunday. We don't get mail on Sunday. And we're open. Why didn't the person who delivered it just come inside?"

"Yes, it's a little mysterious, isn't it?"

I could tell my aunt was curious, if not a little worried. I threw off my bedcovers and went to the dresser. The envelope was white and plain with MRS. MCCLURE typed on the front—no address, no stamp, no other markings. I opened it, unfolded the paper inside. There was only one sentence typed: nine black words on a field of white.

"What is it, dear?" Aunt Sadie could see something was wrong from my expression. She moved back into the room, took the paper from me and blanched at the simple message:

BRAKES AREN'T THE ONLY THINGS THAT CAN GET CUT.

# CHAPTER 21

## *Happy Medium*

She looked a little pale and strained, but she looked
like a girl who could function under a strain.

—*The Big Sleep*, Raymond Chandler, 1939

"A LITTLE MELODRAMATIC, isn't it?" I pointed to the
burning candle in Fiona Finch's hand.

She shrugged. "No electricity. That's the way they
wanted it."

"Who's they?"

"RIPS—they're the ones conducting tonight's séance."

"RIPs?" I repeated. "Rest in—"

Fiona cut me off. "It stands for Rhode Island Paranormal
Society. Rachel explained it all to me after checking in this
evening."

It was close to midnight and I was standing with Fiona
in the foyer of Chez Finch. Despite the threatening note, I
was determined to attend this séance.

Of course, I'd already notified Eddie Franzetti about the
threat. He'd raced over to the shop as soon as I'd called,
impounding the letter as evidence. I doubted he would get
any useful fingerprints. He said the state forensic lab could
analyze the paper and ink, but I didn't put much faith in
that getting us anywhere, either.

Aunt Sadie and Dilbert insisted on staying with me until

we closed the store. I agreed, but I wasn't going to cancel my plans for the night. One stupid note wasn't going to stop me—if anything, it made me more determined than ever to keep digging into this case. My one concession was asking Eddie to have a patrol car include the Finch Inn on its watch as long as Seymour was staying there.

"RIPS?" I repeated to Fiona.

She nodded her head. "The group's been around since the 1920s and the current membership takes this all quite seriously." She gestured toward the archway that led into the restaurant's large dining room—completely dark now except for a single taper burning on the room's largest round table. Two human silhouettes were standing near the wall of windows overlooking Quindicott Pond.

"Are you going to this thing?" I asked her.

"Not me. But you can fill me in after the séance is over. I have some other things to discuss with you, as well—"

Girlish laughter echoed loudly through the darkened dining room, followed by a very familiar guffaw: my mailman.

"Sounds like Seymour's getting along pretty well with someone in there."

Before Fiona could reply, we both heard the honk of Barney's electric golf cart. "The other guests are arriving." Fiona waved me forward. "Go ahead inside, Pen. Seymour will introduce you to Rachel."

Beyond the restaurant's wall of windows, the pond appeared black as outer space, the inn's solar-powered footlights marking nearby trails like tiny stars in the distance. The moon was full tonight, its glow rippling on the dark water and providing much-needed ambient light in the murky room.

I found Seymour chatting with a young woman dressed casually in a denim skirt and high-top yellow sneakers.

"Hey, Pen!" he called with an energized grin. "This is Rachel Delve. Rachel, this is my friend Penelope McClure."

Smiling, the woman took my hand. Rachel was petite, shorter than me—and I wasn't very tall to start with. Her freckled face, framed by a tangle of reddish-orange hair, was so round it was almost cherubic. Even in this dim light, I could see her complexion was rosy from laughter.

"Nice to meet you," she said, taking my hand.

At first I doubted Rachel was part of the RIPS group. She seemed so normal, so bubbly. She came off more like a member of the restaurant staff—until I noticed the ankh symbol dangling from a gold chain around her neck.

Jack might have had an opinion, but I'd deliberately left his buffalo nickel back home. He'd disappeared after our dream—which was par for the course —but I wouldn't have brought him anyway. I'd never been to a séance, and I didn't know what to expect. After Ophelia Tuttle's little display, the last thing I needed was a public gathering where someone might announce that Penelope Thornton-McClure secretly lived with a bad-boy, sandy-haired PI last seen breathing in 1949. And that wasn't even the worst of it—how did I know what these people had in mind? Jack could be accidentally exorcised or spook-zapped or something.

Anyway, I was on my own. So I took a deep breath and greeted Seymour with a smile. "Sounds like I interrupted a funny story."

"We were talking about the old Popeye cartoons, the ones featuring Goon Island," Seymour explained. "Check out Rachel's watch."

She presented her wrist to me.

"That's a vintage Popeye timepiece," Seymour informed me. "Turns out Rachel's into the Sailorman, big-time."

"I love anything connected to the sea," Rachel said. "Probably because I fell in love with Popeye when I was six years old."

"Well, blow me down," Seymour joked, with a wink to Rachel. "If you like seafaring stuff, you should see the amazing painting Fiona gave me. She has more of them hanging in her lighthouse. The artist is awesome."

Rachel listened with amused interest while Seymour described his painting. That was when I noticed Ophelia Tuttle sitting alone at the big round table, hands folded in her lap. Seeing her there, I took a deep breath—on the one hand, I was surprised and alarmed, but then I realized it made perfect sense, given her obvious ability to see the dead.

She wore a long dress of ebony. It was sleeveless and with her hair twisted high, I could clearly see her gold ankh tattoo.

"Good evening, Ophelia," I said.

She observed me for a long, silent moment. "Decided to come alone tonight, I see."

"Actually, Pen isn't alone," Seymour piped up, not understanding the young woman's remark. "She's here with me. We both experienced something weird last night. *Supernatural*."

"Really?" Ophelia sniffed. "Well, you should talk to Rachel about it. I have my own concerns." She looked away after that, clearly not wishing to talk anymore.

I wasn't surprised. I didn't trust Miss Tuttle. Not one bit.

"Is there anyone else here I know?" I asked, glancing into the dark room.

"Yeah," Seymour said. "You know Leo."

"Leo Rollins?"

I turned to see his shadowy form sitting in a dim corner, far away from everyone else. He nodded a silent greeting, one hand stroking his trimmed beard. Then he turned away, to stare out the wall of windows.

Ophelia *and* Leo? Neither of the two sat well with me; seeing them here together made me even surer that something was up. The threatening note came to mind again— the word *cut* had been prominent—and Leo's dagger remained highly suspicious to me. I swallowed hard, trying to assure myself that there'd be too many witnesses here tonight for anyone to hurt Seymour or me.

As Seymour and Rachel went back to their conversation about Popeye, sailors, and comic books, Barney Finch ushered a new guest into the dining room.

"Hey, Mr. Stoddard!" Seymour called. "Are you here as my lawyer?"

Emory Stoddard shook his head. "Tonight I'm here to represent the society, Mr. Tarnish." Then the lawyer offered me his hand. "Good to see you, Mrs. McClure. Fiona told me about your experience last night."

I did my best to cover my reaction. Something was *definitely* up here. He offered me his hand, and I shook, once again noticing the ankh ring.

"You lied to me about this ring, didn't you?"

Stoddard frowned.

"This symbol has something to do with your affiliation with the Rhode Island Paranormal Society, doesn't it?"

"Yes," Stoddard admitted. "When the society was founded by my great-grandfather and others, they adopted the ankh as their talisman. For them, the symbol represented the gift of life, both on the physical plane and eternally, in the realm of the spirit. It's too hard to explain to unbelievers, so we don't even try."

"And Miss Tuttle is also a member of your group?"

Stoddard lowered his voice. "She came to our Newport headquarters several years ago, a troubled spirit seeking a way to cope with her burgeoning psychic gifts. I have been guiding her way ever since."

"I was under the impression Miss Tuttle was your employee."

"Ophelia is much more than that," he said. "She's the most gifted medium I've ever known."

I raised an eyebrow. Now I knew where a reserved and mannered lawyer like Mr. Stoddard crossed paths with a young woman as dark and edgy as Miss Tuttle. Apparently it was somewhere on the astral plane.

"You said the society is headquartered in Newport? Didn't you have an office there, Mr. Stoddard?"

"And I will again, once the building our group has purchased is refurbished. My Millstone office is only temporary."

"Inconvenient for your Newport clients," I noted, wondering whether to believe him.

"There are so few of them nowadays," he replied. "I've

given up most of my practice to devote more time to the society. Our architects are creating a facility that is specifically designed to aid our psychic investigations. My legal offices will be on the premises."

"I see Leo Rollins is here." I gestured to the dark corner. "Is he a member?"

"Leo is working on our facility in Newport, and he's assisting us tonight with the electrical system." Stoddard frowned. "You see, electrical fields interfere with communications from the astral plane, so we banish all such devices from our psychic sessions."

It was *also* a neat dodge to avoid having the results of such sessions verified by recordings and video, but I kept my mouth shut. We all turned when two more guests entered the room.

"Ah. There you are, Mrs. Fromsette."

I was stunned to see the woman from Seymour's party, black mourning shawl still swaddled around her narrow shoulders. Her daughter, April Briggs, was here with her—which was what stunned Seymour. He suddenly found himself caught between two eligible women who both obviously liked him.

"Er, hello, April," he said, shifting uncomfortably. Rachel had been reading his palm. His hand was still cradled in hers and it didn't appear she was letting it go anytime soon.

April's face flashed with obvious jealousy. She quickly masked it with a tight smile. "Good to see you again, Seymour. I didn't know you were interested in . . . all of this psychic stuff."

From the way April was glaring at Rachel, I didn't get the impression she'd actually meant "psychic stuff."

"Well, I guess I could say the same about you," Seymour replied.

April rolled her eyes. "It all seems silly to me. No offense, but I'm not here to commune with the spirit world. I'm here to support my mother."

"Perhaps we'll change your mind," Stoddard said, "for

tonight we're going to attempt to contact the spirit of Mr. Arthur Fromsette—" He glanced at Seymour. "And if we can, we'll also seek an answer to your vexing mystery, see if we can't get in touch with the spirit of Miss Todd."

Mrs. Fromsette blinked back tears. "I know my Arthur is gone, but I hope to learn what really happened to him. I feel very hopeful about tonight because Miss Delve comes highly recommended."

I tensed, my mind racing. Stoddard and his group operated out of Newport, a place with old family histories as well as old money. Could this be a brand-new version of what Gideon Wexler was most likely doing on Long Island back in the 1940s: bilking wealthy, gullible people out of their fortunes—only this time, using real spirits instead of fake scares?

Miss Tuttle strolled past me, a smirk on her pale face. "It's time to start."

I moved to sit down at the big table. Instead, Mr. Stoddard told me to stand back. Ophelia and Leo Rollins then moved the table out of the way. They placed the chairs in a tight circle. Ophelia set that single burning candle in the center of the darkened dining room.

"Please be seated, everyone," Stoddard said. "Take any chair."

Rachel Delve sat down beside Stoddard, feet together, hands folded in her lap. Seymour tried to grab the seat beside her, but April was faster and snagged it.

"Sit here, Seymour," she said, patting the empty seat on her opposite side. I saw a flash of relief on Seymour's face when April's mother took that chair instead. I grabbed the spot beside Mrs. Fromsette, and Seymour sat beside me. The circle was uncomfortably tight. I had to be careful not to knock over the candle.

When everyone else was seated, Miss Tuttle sank into the empty chair beside Emory Stoddard. To my surprise, Leo did not join the circle. Instead, he closed the heavy draperies, covering the wall of windows. The ambient light was completely cut off. As Leo melted back into the shadows, the only illumination was the candle inside the circle.

"Let us begin," Stoddard said, barely above a whisper. "Everyone, please gaze into the flame. Imagine that it is the glow of existence, burning bright in the void of the universe. That's it . . . Keep watching the flame . . . Keep watching . . ."

He droned on for a few minutes, until I began to suspect Stoddard was trying to hypnotize us—so, rather than concentrate on the flame, I glanced at the other members of the circle. Most everyone was following Stoddard's cues. Everyone but April Briggs. Instead of watching the flickering flame, her eyes were closed tight, her full lips pinched into a tense frown. Finally, Stoddard ceased to prompt us, and addressed Miss Delve directly.

"Can you hear me, Rachel?"

"Yes," she replied, wide eyes fixed on the flickering flame.

"Are you in contact with the spirit world?"

"I am."

Stoddard leaned forward. "Mrs. Fromsette, you may speak now."

"I wish to commune with Mr. Fromsette, my late husband," she said in a voice hoarse with emotion. "He vanished right here in Quindicott Pond, last September, nine months ago today."

There was a long and very tense pause. Finally Rachel broke the silence. "Arthur is with me now," she whispered. "Your husband is here."

I let out a breath. So did everyone else.

"He wants to know how Tutu is doing," Rachel said in a voice that seemed suddenly hollow.

Mrs. Fromsette gasped. "Tutu is Arthur's African gray," she told us. I saw April Briggs tense.

"Tutu is fine, Arthur! I bought a much larger cage for the parrot and he seems very happy."

Another long silence followed.

"I . . . I wonder about you, Arthur," Mrs. Fromsette continued. "What happened that day on the boat? Why didn't you come back to me?"

I watched as Rachel's formerly relaxed features twisted into a mask of torment. "I . . . I can't hold on," she stammered in a low voice.

"What's happening, Arthur?" Mrs. Fromsette cried. "Tell me!"

"The boat," Rachel rasped. "Trying to hold on, but the oar—it keeps hitting me. Why? Why are you hitting me?!"

Rachel writhed in apparent torment, until I felt Seymour tense in the seat beside me. I thought he was going to bolt to Rachel's side, but he remained in his seat, fists tightly clenched.

Mr. Stoddard watched the medium closely, his eyes wide. "Quickly, Mrs. Fromsette, ask your questions," he urged. "I must bring her back soon!"

"Arthur? *Who* is hitting you?"

"I know! I know who it is," Rachel gasped, and her arms flew outward. She jerked them as if she were fending off blows, then her fingers clawed the air as if she were trying to hang on to something.

April Briggs reared back to avoid Rachel's flailing. I heard her scream the same moment the candle toppled and the room went black.

Then I heard another scream. Seymour brushed my leg as he lurched out of his chair. I heard a meaty smack, then a crash!

"The lights, Leo!" Mr. Stoddard shouted. "The lights!"

It seemed an eternity before the lights came up, and when they finally did, Seymour was on the floor, cradling a bloodied Rachel Delve in his arms. The woman's nose was smashed; blood dribbled down her cheek and flowed from her gaping mouth. Her eyelids fluttered wildly.

"Rachel, can you hear me?" Seymour called, shaking her.

He touched her face, adding to the gore that already stained his hands, his clothing. Finally the woman heard

Seymour's frantic calls, and tried to focus. Then her head lolled limply to one side.

"Call 911," Seymour shouted. "Get an ambulance here!"

THE AMBULANCE CAME and went, spiriting the medium to the emergency room. Seymour wanted to follow Rachel to the hospital, but was detained by an angry Chief Ciders who, after interviewing the séance members for less than five minutes, promptly arrested Seymour Tarnish.

"This time, I *know* it's the victim's blood on your clothes," the chief declared.

Seymour pleaded his innocence even as he was cuffed and dragged away by Bull McCoy. Stoddard was torn between going to the hospital to be with Rachel or arranging bail for Seymour.

"I'll be fine. I've spent the night in Ciders's hoosegow before," Seymour told the man. "You go to the hospital. Make *sure* the docs take good care of Rachel!"

Miss Tuttle and Stoddard left immediately for the ER, and the other séance members departed. April Briggs was sobbing and clinging to her mother on the way out.

"I was just so frightened," she said, sounding like a believer now.

I looked around for Leo, wanting to ask why it took him nearly thirty seconds to turn on the lights after Stoddard called out. But before I could locate the man I heard his Harley cough to life in the parking lot. He was speeding away as I stepped outside.

I found Fiona standing there, her face unnaturally pale.

"I can't believe Ciders arrested Seymour," I told her.

"It's awful what happened," she said. "Rachel's such a sweet girl."

"You don't think Seymour did it, do you?"

"No, of course not. But the chief can't hold Seymour long. He'll make bail in the morning. Let's just hope Miss Delve revives quickly and can tell us whatever she can about who really assaulted her."

"How long have you known Rachel, anyway?"

"Over a year now. I met her when I purchased her beautiful set of seafaring paintings. You've seen them, in our lighthouse bungalow. Seymour liked them so much that I bought one for him, too, as a housewarming gift."

"So *Rachel's* the mysterious artist 'RD'?"

Fiona shrugged. "I didn't want to introduce her to Seymour for fear he'd make an ass of himself. Who knew they'd hit it off?"

I glanced at my watch and groaned. "I can't believe it's nearly two in the morning—"

"You can't leave yet." She took my arm. "We have to talk. Remember you asked me to find out what I could about Todd Mansion?"

"Yes!"

Fiona led me back up to the inn and into her private office. "Sit," she said, pointing out a comfortable old leather chair.

As I settled in, I noticed she had a pot of jasmine tea already brewed and sitting on a small service cart beside her mahogany desk.

"I did a bit of snooping," Fiona began, as she poured our tea and handed me a bone china cup and saucer. "The local library's records weren't any help, but I called a friend at the Rhode Island Preservation Society in Providence. Folks there have long memories—"

"And?"

"And she e-mailed me a number of documents from their records. I printed them out." Fiona settled herself behind her desk, placed a pair of delicate reading glasses on the tip of her nose, and shuffled through a pile of papers. "The real history of the Todd house began back in 1948. Before that, the house was owned by the Philips family. Old Jeremiah was a banker hit hard by the Great Depression. Then he lost both boys in the war. He managed to hang on to the family homestead until he died in 1946, when the mansion fell into receivership."

Fiona paused to sip her tea. "The house was purchased

after that but my contact is still digging for a copy of the deed."

"Who purchased it? Timothea Todd?"

Fiona shook her head. "My contact believes the purchaser was a man named Gideon Wexler."

My spine stiffened. "Did you hear that, Jack!" I shouted in my head and then remembered. Because of the séance, I'd intentionally left his buffalo nickel on my dresser. Swallowing, I simply repeated the name aloud: "Gideon Wexler, you say?"

"Yes, apparently there was a chapter written on Wexler in a book about Newport spiritualists. It's long out of print, but it's in the Preservation Society's library and my contact scanned some relevant pages. Now let's see . . ." Fiona shuffled more papers. "Apparently, after the Second World War, Gideon Wexler was a big hit among high-society types in New York City. Here's his photo—"

She handed me a printout. Wexler was the fat man in the portrait over the mantel, all right, as well as the ghost I'd seen floating across Miss Todd's living room. He was also the man in the newspaper Jack had shown me—the one whose mansion had burned, killing eight people, including J. J. Conway's mother.

"He told fortunes," Fiona explained, "helping wealthy war widows contact their dead spouses—for substantial fees. His occult group, called the Order of the Old Ones, was so popular that Wexler purchased and refurbished an estate on Long Island. It became the group's 'spiritual retreat.' And according to witnesses, strange things happened at that house. People reported hearing odd noises, cold spots, ghostly lights, and frightening apparitions."

"*That* sounds familiar." I pointed to the papers. "Is there anything in there that shows that symbol on the Todd fence—a pentagram with a fleur-de-lis in the center?"

Fiona nodded and handed me one of the papers. "It's the symbol for their order, Pen."

I frowned, seeing the design and caption, thinking again of Leo's dagger.

"Wexler claimed he had the power to raise spirits of the dead to act as his personal supernatural guides," Fiona continued.

"But he operated in New York, right? And then Long Island. What brought him up here?"

"I'm getting to that—in 1947 his mansion on Long Island burned to the ground." Fiona flashed a familiar-looking newspaper clipping. "Several of his employees died in the fire, along with a few of the wealthy folks who had joined his group. The fire was deemed suspicious, but Wexler was out of town when it happened and was never charged with a crime."

"That's when he came to Quindicott?"

"Not directly," Fiona said. "After the fire, Wexler resettled in Newport—lots of money there, so it was a good location for him to start pulling in rich widows again. He started his Order of the Old Ones up in a town house but it wasn't big enough. He wanted a fresh location, a big place with lots of grounds and somewhat isolated, much like the house he'd refurbished on Long Island. That's how he came to purchase the house in Quindicott. He began remodeling it, put up the fence, and made other improvements. But within a year of moving in, he died of a heart attack."

"So Gideon Wexler bought Miss Todd's mansion. But how does Timothea fit in? How did she come to live there? Did they have a relationship? Or did she purchase it after Wexler?"

"Unfortunately, I don't know any of that, but my contact is still digging, trying to find a record of the latest deed. As soon as she comes up with any new information, I'll get it to you."

I thanked Fiona and asked Barney to walk me to my car. Then I headed back to the bookshop and locked myself in—glad that Seymour was locked in, too.

I hated that he was under arrest, but at least I could be sure he'd be safe, for tonight at least. There were a lot of pieces to this ghostly puzzle, and I still couldn't put it all together.

"Jack?" I whispered into the dark bedroom air.

But the air didn't stir and his voice didn't answer. I closed my eyes again, disturbed by the image of my PI partner fading into the fog.

# CHAPTER 22

## *Quibbling*

Dike was firmly opposed to the granting of contracts
and concessions to those who enjoyed political pull.

—*Honest Money*, Erle Stanley Gardner,
*Black Mask*, November 1932

THE FOLLOWING EVENING, Bud Napp hadn't even
banged the gavel (or in his case, the ball peen hammer)
on the Quindicott Business Owners Association meeting,
when the subject of the gathering sauntered in to Buy the
Book's Community Events space. As Bud's hammer hung
in midstrike, I turned and gaped with everyone else at Jim
Wolfe's six-foot-three form striding down the center aisle.

The contractor wore tight denims, spotless white sneakers, and a beige summer sport jacket over a V-neck black
T-shirt. "Hello, everyone," he said with a friendly smile.

"Hello, back!" called Joyce Koh, daughter of the local
grocer, her voice full of naked flirtation. Sitting next to her,
Mr. Koh scowled and whispered something—then they
quietly began to argue.

Jim cleared his throat, continued up to the raised dais,
and faced Bud. "I think I have a solution to your problem,"
he said loud enough for the entire room to hear.

"I'll be happy to hear you out," Bud replied warily.

"Councilman Lockhart and I have worked out a plan, but I want to hear your input before it gets implemented."

I was surprised to hear that. Previously, Brockton Lockhart had always backed Councilwoman Binder-Smith. Was what passed for a political machine in Quindicott actually breaking down? If so, then Bud's announced candidacy had already made a difference.

For the next ten minutes, Jim Wolfe outlined a plan to shift most of his construction fleet to an empty lot owned by Lockhart. "The generators will have to stay," he warned. "But we'll park them so they won't block your entrance. Line them up catty-corner, maybe."

"What's Lockhart getting out of this?" Bud asked suspiciously.

"Brock doesn't want to be used as a political tool by a certain councilwoman," Jim replied. "Frankly, neither do I."

Bud rubbed his chin. "Can I get a permit to paint yellow lines on the street—lines that'll keep your vehicles in their assigned spots?"

"I've got Lockhart's permission to do just that." Jim smiled again. "But you'll have to supply the paint."

Bud chuckled and extended his hand. "It's a deal."

Scattered applause broke out, increasing in tempo. Jim Wolfe smiled again and I heard female voices whispering— no doubt a few hearts were fluttering, too. Jim noticed me then and gave me a little nod.

My heart might have fluttered, if I hadn't been missing Jack so much. My PI spirit hadn't reappeared this morning. In fact, he hadn't reappeared all day.

I knew the dream he gave me would have drained him, but I was beginning to worry there was more going on. Ophelia Tuttle was obviously a powerful psychic and medium—and she knew about Jack. Could she have done something to push him into a cosmic limbo permanently? The image of my PI partner fading into the fog continued to haunt me, along with the words of that threatening note someone had left for me.

BRAKES AREN'T THE ONLY THINGS THAT CAN GET CUT.

Did Ophelia or someone else in her RIPS group cut Jack loose from me and my bookshop forever?

"I apologize for not dealing with this sooner," Jim was now telling Bud. "I've been pretty distracted, trying to replace an electrician I lost in an accident. Sal Gillespie was a good guy. Tough shoes to fill."

"Why don't you hire Leo Rollins?" Bud said. "He's a licensed electrician and he's worked for you before."

Jim shrugged. "I actually made Leo an offer the other day and he turned me down flat. Said he had found a better-paying job moonlighting. I don't see him here tonight." Jim glanced around. "Maybe he's already working."

I was surprised Rollins hadn't shown up for our "Quibblers" meeting. He was as angry as everyone else about Councilwoman Binder-Smith's so-called "green" initiatives, not to mention Bud's parking dilemma. But Leo wasn't the only absentee Quibbler. Seymour Tarnish hadn't shown, either, despite the fact that I'd heard he'd made bail sometime today. And Fiona Finch—who usually came early and spoke often—had yet to arrive.

Jim jerked his thumb toward the door. "Why don't we check out your storefront right now, Bud? You can show me where I can park my generators, and I'll have my crew paint lines in the morning."

Bud slammed his hammer on the podium, declaring the meeting adjourned. The mob of local business owners stood and moved quickly toward our exit. It was after ten o'clock by now and everyone wanted to get home. Bud and Jim Wolfe followed the crowd to the front door.

Jim pointed at me before leaving. "Coffee this week, Pen," he mouthed with a wink. "Remember?"

I nodded politely, but Jim's offer didn't make my pulse flutter—not even a little bit. Jim was a living, breathing hunk, no question. But my heart was already taken with someone else. The fact that the man I cared for was no longer flesh-and-blood didn't make a difference. Love wasn't something that stopped for a little thing like death.

If Jim ever did come by for our coffee date, I'd simply

break it to him that I was a confirmed widow, and he was better off taking out one of the half dozen females who were presently giving him the eye all the way out the door.

The crowd was nearly gone when I felt Chick Pattelli's callused hand touch my arm. "So, will it be a spring wedding?" the garden store owner asked with a smile. "I can hothouse-grow any flowers you like for the big day."

I blinked. "Excuse me?"

"Let me know," Chick said before he walked out. I was baffled, but the answer came a moment later.

"When are you and Seymour Tarnish getting married?" Joyce Koh asked, walking up to me.

"Must be soon," said Milner Logan, joining us.

Quarter-blood Narragansett Native American, Milner was our town baker. He was also a good customer, with a penchant for thrillers and noir crime novels, as well as anything penned by Tony Hillerman and Margaret Coel. A trained pastry chef, he'd fallen in love with an old friend of mine, Linda Cooper, while teaching her in a cooking class. It was Linda's family who'd started Cooper's. Now she and Milner ran it as a married couple.

"What gives, Pen?" Linda demanded, the bangles on her wrist jangling as she ran a hand through her short, spiked, Annie Lennox–style platinum hair. "My mechanic at Warwick Motors mentioned you're already calling yourself 'Mrs. Tarnish.' How could you not tell me what was up with you two!"

"Whoa!" I told Milner and Linda. "The only Mrs. Tarnish I know lives in Florida, and I doubt there'll be another one anytime soon."

"Just going to live together?" Linda asked.

"No!"

"Methinks she doth protest too much," Brainert Parker quipped from behind me.

Milner laughed and shook his head, his wiry black-and-gray ponytail shaking in the process.

I scanned the expectant faces around me, shocked to realize they all believed this crazy rumor. "Just because I spent the night at Seymour's house—I mean, as his *guest*. Okay, I slept in his bed, but Seymour stayed in another room—" I threw up my hands. "You're all mistaken. You're putting me into some kind of an *imaginary* relationship."

I bit my cheek, thinking of Jack. What would their reaction be if they knew the real truth? *Oh, God.*

"Come, Joyce!" Mr. Koh called.

The Kohs left and Sadie locked the door behind them. Then she joined me. I glanced around. Everyone was gone except our closest circle of friends—Milner and Linda, Brainert, and Fiona Finch, who must have arrived while all the others were leaving. She stepped up to me with arms folded and lips pursed.

"I tried to straighten them out, Pen," Fiona insisted. "But apparently I'm no longer a reliable source of gossip."

"What does Pen expect after that crazy ghost story we heard she was telling?" Linda asked.

"But it's true," I said. "I know Todd Mansion is haunted because I've seen the ghost with my own eyes."

Stunned silence and wide eyes greeted my statement. *Great.*

"Okay. You've got our attention," Brainert said.

It took twenty minutes, but with Fiona's help I brought Brainert, Milner, and Linda up to speed. I told them about Miss Todd's will, the mysterious Ophelia Tuttle, the sabotaged brakes, Seymour's wake for Timothea, the magic circle under the rug, and the aggressive moves by the Charlene Lindsey-Fabian on behalf of her Lindsey-Tilton group.

I described the supernatural events of the other night, told them about the weird tapes Miss Todd recorded, and the hidden history of Todd Mansion that Fiona uncovered. Fiona stepped in at that point and told them about the house's connection to spiritualist Gideon Wexler, the séance she hosted at Chez Finch, and the assault on medium Rachel Delve right before she was about to name Arthur Fromsette's killer.

When Fiona was finished, I saw only dubious expressions on everyone's face.

"If Seymour were here, he'd back me up," I insisted.

"Where is Seymour?" Sadie asked.

My aunt had been quiet up to now, but I knew she was worried. That threatening note addressed to me had really gotten her back up. She'd wanted to help catch whoever had written it (no doubt the same person who'd put our lives in danger on the road out of Millstone), so I handed her the audiotapes that Miss Todd had made. I still hadn't listened to them all, and I asked her to play them and make notes of anything, well, *noteworthy*.

"After he made bail, Seymour came to my inn around two o'clock today to pick up his things," Fiona informed us all. "He told me he was driving to Providence to pick up equipment. Special equipment, he called it. Seymour mentioned something about not waiting six months for help, and that he'd solve his ghost problem himself."

"Pen, what do you think is happening?" Brainert asked.

I took a deep breath. "As crazy as it sounds, I believe someone is manipulating the ghosts in that house. I saw the specter of spiritualist Gideon Wexler floating across the living room. I didn't imagine it. And I'm convinced something frightened Miss Todd to death."

Brainert frowned. "Who would be manipulating these spirits and for what purpose?"

"I believe Ophelia Tuttle is doing it—or someone else in her Rhode Island Paranormal Society. Mr. Stoddard may even be involved. I also believe Miss Todd's living sister is behind this, too. Her name is Mrs. Beatrice Ingram. She lives in Newport and had a meeting just yesterday with Charlene Lindsey-Fabian and Jim Wolfe about doing work on a 'property' to turn it into a B and B. I think that property is Todd Mansion, and she's arranging to either scare Seymour out of it or kill him so the property will legally fall to her and she can sell it for a million dollars to the Lindsey-Tilton group."

"Wait, Pen. I think you're wrong about Mrs. Ingram. You need to see this."

"What?"

Fiona handed me a sheet of paper. "The preservation society e-mailed me a copy of the latest deed to Todd Mansion." The photocopy wasn't the best, but the signatures were legible. "Along *with* Gideon Wexler, the house's owners were Timothea Todd and Wilomena Field."

"Oh, my God. Mrs. Fromsette's maiden name is Field!"

Fiona nodded. "And her first name is Wilomena."

"So Mrs. Fromsette is the mysterious sister?" I said. "But she has a different name."

"She's a half-sister—" Fiona said.

"She's *also* active in a spiritualist community," I broke in. "Mrs. Fromsette *must* be the one who arranged the manipulation of the ghosts in that house! She has the most to gain by her sister's and Seymour's deaths."

Milner shook his head. "But spooks don't sabotage brakes."

"And no spirit put poor Rachel in the hospital," Fiona reminded me.

"If Mrs. Fromsette had inherited the house in the first place, none of this would have happened," Aunt Sadie said. "I wonder what could have come between the sisters to estrange them so?"

"I believe I know the answer to that!" Fiona proudly declared. She produced a copy of an old black-and-white photo from the preservation society's files. It showed Gideon Wexler flanked by two adoring young women. The three of them stood in front of the open wrought-iron gates of Todd Mansion.

"That must be Timothea on the right!" Sadie cried. "I saw her wearing that very tiara once."

Fiona nodded. "The other woman is Wilomena Field— the future Mrs. Arthur Fromsette. This photo came from a pamphlet about Gideon Wexler's spiritualist society. In the caption, the women are identified as Timothea Todd and her *half-sister*, Wilomena Field! Both met Gideon in Newport and clearly fell under his spell. Just look at the way those young women are gazing up at the man. Look at the way his arms are around them both. I think there may have been a love triangle. I think Miss Todd and her sister may have fought over Gideon Wexler's attentions, and that's why the sisters had their falling-out."

"I guess Miss Todd got her man—or got his ghost, anyway," Milner said.

Sadie shuddered. "You wouldn't take this so lightly if you heard Miss Todd's tape recordings."

Brainert practically jumped out of his seat. "You've heard the tapes?"

Sadie nodded. "I've been listening to them all day."

"For heaven's sake, play them for all of us!" Brainert said.

Milner, Linda, and Fiona nodded with fascinated interest.

Sadie brought out the tapes and played them back through the Community Events PA system. In stereo, coming through recessed speakers around us, the creepy, unnatural sounds were even more unsettling. Sadie cued up some of the most dramatic sections. They obviously left an impression on the skeptical group.

As Sadie fast forwarded through the final tape, she stopped too soon and the room filled with a familiar, high-low rumble.

"That again," Sadie said, annoyed. "At first I thought it was part of the supernatural phenomena because it's on every tape. Then I realized it was just traffic noise."

"Play that again, Aunt Sadie," I said.

Sadie did, and my suspicious were confirmed.

"That's Leo Rollins's Harley!" I realized.

"Sure is," Milner said. "That's his customized engine. I'd recognize it anywhere. And didn't you say that Leo was at the séance, too?"

"Yes," I said.

Milner nodded. "Like I said. No *spirit* slugged that medium."

"But Leo's got no stake in this property fight," I said. "And it was Mrs. Fromsette who was seated inside the séance circle. She was closer to Rachel than Leo—"

"Pen, Mrs. Fromsette comes into our bakery all the time. And I can tell you that old woman could hardly give someone a black eye, let alone knock them out."

"But I don't think Leo could have been close enough to do it. The room was pitch-dark after the candle was knocked over. How could he have found Rachel to punch her?"

"Actually, Leo served with the 160th Special Operations Aviation Regiment during Desert Storm," Milner said.

Linda faced her husband. "How do you know that?"

"Guys talk." He shrugged. "Especially when they drink."

Linda scowled. "You went to that girly bar again, didn't you?"

"I, uh—"

"So Leo was a pilot, then?" I cut in before we got off the subject.

Milner shook his head. "Leo was an infantry scout, a Night Stalker. They're specially trained to fight in the dark."

"It was Leo who found us when the brakes failed on the highway, remember, Pen," Sadie quickly noted. "He said he was just passing by, but he might have been stalking us to see what happened after he sabotaged the brakes!"

"You said Leo doesn't have a stake in this, but someone could have *hired* him to kill Seymour," Brainert reminded me.

"That would explain what Jim Wolfe said to Bud earlier," Sadie said. "Remember? Jim offered Leo work but he turned it down. Leo said he was making more *moonlighting*."

Milner raised an eyebrow. "A hit man *would* earn more than an electrician."

"And what about that dagger Leo has?" Linda said. "If it looks exactly like the one you found in Todd Mansion, then there must be a connection, right? Maybe Mrs. Fromsette had the dagger all these years and gave it to him to use!"

Milner nodded. "That's got to be it. Mrs. Fromsette hired Leo."

"But all of this stuff is just conjecture," I pointed out.

The ghost of Jack Shepard may not have been with me now, but I could hear his voice echoing through my memories, railing about getting hard proof. Eddie Franzetti and his State Police colleagues would need conclusive evidence—facts that were *clear as a glass of gin.*

"All this stuff is circumstantial," I continued. "There's no presentable legal evidence against Leo. And the police aren't going to make an arrest based on our theories."

The group glanced at one another sheepishly. They knew I was right.

"Perhaps we should listen to more of Miss Todd's tapes," Brainert suggested. "We might hear something more substantial that implicates Leo."

While Sadie cued up another sound bite, I told her I needed to use the phone.

"Who are you calling at this hour?" she asked.

"Seymour! He's in danger. Concrete proof or not, we all *believe* we know who's guilty. Someone has to warn Seymour to ignore the stupid haunts in his house and watch out for Leo Rollins!"

# CHAPTER 23

## *Things That Go Boo*

Perhaps you have the solution. A few persons of unusual intelligence and scientific knowledge might be
able to guess.

—*Nightmare Alley*, William Lindsay Gresham, 1946

I DIALED SEYMOUR'S home phone and got a busy sig-
nal. Cursing the mailman for being too cheap to invest in a
cellular plan, I grabbed my keys and drove out to Larchmont Avenue myself. My handbag was with me, too, Jack's
nickel tucked inside.

"Jack? Jack Shepard!" I called into the night. "I need
you! Can't you hear me?"

No answer came. I didn't hear his voice. I couldn't feel
his presence. He was gone, and all I felt was cold inside,
empty and alone and scared. I swallowed back tears in my
dark car, forcing myself to believe that my spirit would
come back again.

"You can't be gone from my life, Jack, you can't . . ."

It was close to midnight when I pulled through the
wrought-iron gates of Miss Todd's mansion. Rising up on
the hill, the hulking Victorian appeared pitch black; not one
window showed a light burning. The regal doorbell didn't
*bing-bong* when I pressed it. I pressed again. *Nothing.*
Frowning with worry, I gave up and knocked.

Seymour appeared almost immediately, flashlight in hand. He was surprised to see me. "I just called Bud Napp's cell fifteen minutes ago," he said. "Surely he didn't send *you* to fix my electricity?"

"I called you around the same time."

Seymour shrugged. "Guess I was on the line with Bud."

"What's the problem?"

"The new equipment I rented blew a fuse, and—" He shrugged sheepishly. "I can't find the damn fuse box. I called Bud for help, but he just sat down to have a drink with Jim Wolfe at that new girly bar on the highway, Gentlemen's Oasis. What's up with that?"

"Long story."

"Anyway, Bud said he'd send someone by." Then Seymour brightened. "Come in and I'll show you my stuff."

I was nervous about crossing the threshold of Todd Mansion, but I followed Seymour to the red-and-white-checkerboard kitchen, now illuminated by the flickering glow of a dozen candles. I hadn't seen Seymour since he was hauled off to jail, and he looked tired. There was also a fresh bruise under his left eye.

"Courtesy of that moron Bull McCoy," he explained before directing my attention to an array of electronic devices piled on the counter.

"What's this stuff for?" I asked, dreading the answer.

"It's everything you need to track down ghosts. Here's an EMF detector." Seymour displayed a small, handheld device. "And this is a temperature gauge to locate cold spots— I have a handheld model, too. Here's a set of infrared cameras and a bunch of voice monitors and stuff to record electronic voice phenomena. The guys at Tech Squad even rented me a laptop to track my results."

"What are you planning to do?"

"Find the damn ghost and record it," he declared. "I'm going to *prove* that it wasn't *me* who made those noises and scared Timothea to death. It'll get Ciders off my back for good and he can stop arresting me for trumped-up reasons.

My only problem is this old house. I'm not sure it can handle the voltage I need."

That was when I heard an engine. With a sick twist of my guts, I realized it was the familiar high-low rumble of a customized Harley.

"Oh, my God," I rasped. "Leo Rollins is here."

Seymour peered through the window. "You're right! *He'll* be able to fix my electrical problems!"

"Seymour, no! Leo's dangerous! Stay away from him!" I grabbed a handful of his polo shirt.

"Are you kidding, Pen? I need all the help I can get!" Seymour broke away and hurried to admit the electrician.

I dug out my cell, called Eddie, and (thank goodness) got him on the second ring. "Come to Todd Mansion with your gun," I pleaded. "Can't explain. I think Seymour's life is in danger."

I didn't know how long it would take Eddie to get here, but I was determined to protect my friend. I glanced around and noticed a Maglite on the counter. My fingers closed around the heavy black flashlight like a cop gripping his nightstick. Then I moved through the darkened house to the front door.

"Thanks for coming, Leo," Seymour said.

"No problem," Leo's deep voice grunted in the foyer. "It's a short drive from the bar on the highway."

I cleared my throat. "You were drinking?"

"I was working. Been moonlighting for a couple of months at Gentlemen's Oasis. I operate the stage lights, play the music, talk to the ladies." He shrugged. "It's a pretty nice part-time gig."

Seymour nodded. "Glad you're here. I got a problem."

"Yeah, Bud collared me at the bar. Told me you blew a fuse," Rollins said, smirking.

"I'm not a moron, Leo. I could fix it if I knew where the damn fuse box was," Seymour said.

"It's most likely in the basement, probably along the south wall, because that's where the main comes in off

Larchmont. Show me how to get downstairs and I'll get your juice back."

Holding my breath, I decided that Leo had changed his plans to hurt Seymour. Seeing me here must have made the difference—after all, I'd be a *witness*.

I followed the pair to the kitchen, still gripping the Maglite tightly. We walked through a narrow door and down a rickety wooden staircase. The musty basement had a low ceiling and an uneven dirt floor. It was damp and cool, too, like a root cellar.

Leo produced a high-powered flashlight of his own and beamed it around the tight space. He smiled behind his trimmed blond beard when his light centered on a wooden cabinet mounted on the south wall. Inside, Leo found two large fuse boxes and the glass-domed electric meter.

"You blew a fuse all right, but the dial on the meter is still moving."

Seymour shrugged. "So?"

"So juice is still flowing. Somewhere in this house anyway."

"But nothing works, upstairs or down," Seymour insisted.

Leo shined his beam on three silver pipes bolted to the fieldstone wall above the fuse boxes. "The electrical lines are inside those aluminum conduits. Two of them run upstairs to power the house, but the third one goes sideways." Leo shifted the beam until we saw the point where the silver pipe seemed to vanish into a blank wall. "What's on that side of the house?"

Seymour rubbed his chin. "The folly."

Leo blinked. "The what?"

"The fake ruins in the garden," he explained.

"That's a pair of two 240-volt lines in there. That's *a lot* of juice. This folly must have some pretty powerful floodlights."

"That doesn't sound right," Seymour said.

Leo frowned. "If you don't have floodlights out there,

then your neighbor could be leeching power. Let me fix the fuse. Then we'll check out this folly thing."

"SEE, NO FLOODLIGHTS," Seymour said.

Even with Todd Mansion's lights now blazing away, things were pretty gloomy out here among the overgrown lawn and tall weeds. I watched Leo carefully as he inspected the faux gothic archway and the artfully tumbled-down walls.

"What's the point of this place?" Leo said. "It doesn't even have a roof."

"It's decorative," Seymour replied.

Leo grunted and pushed his way through the brush, to the opposite side of the structure. Seymour followed in his wake—and so did I, still tightly gripping the Maglite.

My handbag and cell were with me, too, and I glanced toward the road far away, anticipating Eddie's wailing siren, but I didn't hear a thing, just quiet night sounds, crickets chirping, and a dark sedan driving by—and then I realized, it wasn't driving by; it was slowing down and stopping.

A figure climbed out. I couldn't tell who he was from his dark silhouette, just that it was a leanly built man in street clothes. This was no cop in uniform. He stood there staring in our direction, but then, it would have been easy to notice us with our flashlights.

Meanwhile, Leo Rollins was gazing at Seymour's nearest neighbor. The house was half the size of Todd Mansion. It sat at the bottom of the low hill, at least a quarter mile away and separated by a stretch of overgrown grounds.

"Your neighbor's pretty darn far away to steal power," Leo concluded.

"Mrs. Fromsette lives there," Seymour replied. "She's too nice to steal electricity."

"Mrs. Fromsette lives *next door* to you?" I said.

"Yeah," Seymour said.

"I can see a clear trail here," Leo said, pointing. "Leads from the Fromsette place right up to this folly thing. Come on, Seymour, let's have a look inside, get to the bottom of this power mystery."

Leo moved through the shattered arch to the folly's interior. Seymour started to follow.

"No, Seymour!" I hissed. "Don't follow him in there!"

Just then I noticed the dark figure that climbed out of the parked sedan wasn't standing by the side of the road any longer. He was moving across the mansion's grounds, heading right for us.

"Seymour!" I whispered. "Listen to me!"

"Pen, what the heck's the matter?"

"Look!" I pointed at the figure of the man now running full speed toward us.

At last, Seymour appeared alarmed. "Stop!" he shouted. "Who are you?!"

The man shined a flashlight on us. The bright light blinded me. I screamed.

"Freeze! Everyone freeze!" shouted the man. "Hands where I can see them!"

"*Eddie*?" I called, holding my hand against the bright light beam. "Is that you?"

"Of course, Pen. You called me, said Seymour was in danger!"

"I thought you'd be in uniform! I thought you were coming in a patrol car with a siren!"

"You caught me off-duty. And from the sound of your call I figured a siren might put you and Seymour in jeopardy."

"What the hell's going on?" Leo demanded, finally coming back out of the folly.

"You tell us," Eddie said. His gun was now trained on Leo.

I closed my eyes, took a breath, and began to explain. When I finished, Eddie lowered his weapon and said—

"Leo didn't sabotage Seymour's brakes, Pen. I know that for a fact."

"I know something else for a fact," Leo said before I could ask how Eddie knew. "Something that looks criminal. You want to see?"

Eddie nodded. "Show me."

The grounds were a mess inside the tumbled-down walls of the folly. Leaves, debris, dirt, and dried vegetation lay in heaps and gathered in corners. Then Leo's heavy boots clunked hollowly and he played his beam on the ground at his feet.

"There's a trapdoor here," he said and pulled the metal handle. The door opened easily on well-oiled hinges. Behind it was a flight of worn stone steps, which led to an underground tunnel.

"Holy hidden cave!" Seymour cried.

We followed Leo down the steps and into the underground tunnel, which led to a secret room under the mansion. It was a cramped space, no bigger than a walk-in closet, and it was filled with state-of-the-art electronics devices including three surveillance screens, a sound system, CD and DVD players, all operated by a complex control panel.

"What the hell is this?" Seymour demanded.

Leo touched the control panel and the television screens sprang to life with black-and-white images of the mansion's interior. "Hey, that's my living room!" Seymour said. "And there's the bedroom and the hall."

I touched another button and the secret room echoed with the same sobbing and rushing sounds Seymour and I heard inside the mansion the other night. I quickly switched the CD player off.

Seymour pushed a button labeled VAPOR and we watched the den inside Todd Mansion fill with fog. I toggled the switch beside it, and the flickering image of Gideon Wexler appeared on the surveillance screen. We watched the ghost float across the room and then vanish.

"A projector's hidden somewhere in the den," Leo explained. "That's just an old newsreel image of some guy projected onto the mist to make it look like a ghost."

"Where did this stuff come from?" I wondered aloud.

"From *my* store," Leo said, frowning. "I special ordered this equipment last year for one of my best customers."

"You mean Mrs. Fromsette?" I asked.

Leo shook his head. "It was Jim Wolfe."

Eddie laughed.

"What's so funny?" I asked.

"Leo just blew my big reveal."

"What are you talking about?" I demanded.

"Remember those prints I lifted from the undercarriage of Seymour's VW? Well, I got a beauty of a thumbprint off the brake cylinder that was punctured and the state just confirmed the match. Apparently Mr. Wolfe has a prior arrest and his prints were on file. I was going to take him in anyway."


TEN MINUTES LATER, we were back inside the mansion. Once Leo knew what to look for, the electronics hidden throughout the house were easy to locate.

The smoke machine was tucked away in the attic, the mist pumped into the den through a pipe in the chandelier. The projector was in the light fixture, too. The cold spot was created by a hidden air-conditioning unit, and dozens of tiny speakers were secreted in the house, four of them inside the columns of the four-poster bed.

"That's why you heard the noise before I did, Pen," Seymour said. The four of us were standing in the master bedroom. "Those speakers directed the noise right to your ears."

"This is so twisted," I said. "All these devices just to drive poor Miss Todd crazy."

"It takes days of work to set this stuff up," Leo said. "And you can't do it in secret."

"Jim Wolfe had almost two weeks to do it!" I recalled the story Mr. Stoddard had told me in his Millstone office. "After his backhoe 'accidentally' ruptured the gas main on Larchmont late last summer, Miss Todd was evacuated.

While she was suffering a mini-breakdown in a Newport hotel, Wolfe was installing the equipment to push her over the edge."

Leo shook his head. "Two weeks isn't enough time to dig that tunnel or build a secret room."

"I think the house's previous owner, Gideon Wexler, built all of that back in the 1940s," I said, remembering Jack's case and Fiona's research. "I'm betting he tricked his followers using the same basic ploys, just with older equipment."

Seymour scratched his head. "What did Jim Wolfe expect to gain from this stunt?"

"Wolfe had to be working *with* someone or *for* someone," I said. "Most likely Mrs. Fromsette."

"Why not the Lindsey-Tilton group?" Seymour asked.

"The haunting was too personal," I said. "The newsreel footage of Wexler tells me someone who knew Miss Todd intimately was involved. It *has* to be Mrs. Fromsette. Remember that trail leading to her house? It wasn't overgrown. Someone's been using it."

Eddie frowned and folded his arms. "And how are we going to *prove* that she paid off Wolfe?"

I thought about the vicious tricks Mrs. Fromsette pulled on her sister and decided the woman needed a taste of her own medicine.

"I have an idea, but I'm going to need help to pull it off."

"What are you thinking, Pen?" Eddie asked.

"I'm thinking that turnabout is fair play."


IT WAS NEARLY three A.M. when we finally made the call using Buy the Book's telephone. Mrs. Fromsette's phone rang once, twice, three times.

"You're sure this is the right number?" I whispered.

Seymour nodded. "April told me that she and her mother have separate lines. This is Mrs. F's private line."

The phone clicked. "Hello?" said Mrs. Fromsette's sleepy voice.

I hit the switch on Sadie's recorder and the tape Leo hastily edited worked like a charm. "Why are you tormenting me?" the voice of Miss Todd asked, seemingly from beyond the grave.

"Who—who is this?" Mrs. Fromsette demanded. She sounded wide awake now.

I lifted the Pause button and let the tape continue to play.

"Why are you tormenting me?" Miss Todd's voice repeated.

"Timothea? Is that you? But how can it be?" Mrs. Fromsette's voice was tight with fear.

Once again, I lifted the Pause button.

"Why can't you leave me in peace?" Miss Todd's recorded voice demanded.

Leo did his best to eliminate background noise. He wasn't entirely successful, but the rushing sounds that remained were eerie and added to the overall effect.

Now I turned up the volume. "WHY ARE YOU TORMENTING ME?" Timothea's voice boomed.

"It wasn't me!" Mrs. Fromsette shouted. "It was April!"

*April*, I thought. *April Briggs?!*

"It was my daughter and that man—"

I glanced at Eddie. "That man?" I mouthed.

"April wrecked her marriage over her affair with him—that man Jim Wolfe," Mrs. Fromsette went on. "Now the two want your house!"

I hit the tape player again.

"Why?" Miss Todd's recorded voice now asked. "Why? Why? Why?"

"April believed that despite what happened between us, you'd still leave me the house. That's why she did it."

"Why? Why? Why?" Timothea's voice repeated.

"Anything I inherited, April knew I'd share with her. It's not her fault what happened. That man Jim Wolfe put her under his spell!"

"WHY ARE YOU TORMENTING ME?" Timothea's voice boomed.

"I told you, it wasn't me! I'm so sorry, Timothea. Arthur tried to tell me what April was planning. He tried to stop her. Then he had his accident, and after that, the will to care about anything anymore went out of me . . ."

The woman's voice trailed off. I hadn't played the tape for a few moments, so I could hear her torrent of words. Now, in the silence that followed, Mrs. Fromsette began to become suspicious.

"Timothea? Are you there? Is that really you?"

I hung up and dropped back in my chair. Eddie and Leo visibly relaxed, too, but not Seymour.

"*April* was behind all this?" he said. "But she told me she *liked* me!"

Leo grunted. "Women are fickle, Tarnish. Get used to it."

I rolled my eyes. "Seymour, you said April has her own phone line, right?"

Seymour's brows knitted. "Yeah. So what?"

"So I have another idea," I replied, thinking about what Jack once told me: Criminals always give themselves away. You just need to set up some bait and wait for them to take it.

"But first we have to set some things up back at the mansion," I told the men. "And, Eddie, we're going to need a little more help, too."

IT WAS NEARLY dawn when the mansion's doorbell rang, but it was still dark enough for our purposes. At the sound of the regal *bing-bong,* a nervous Seymour jumped out of the love seat.

"Calm down," I told him. "You know what to do."

Seymour nodded, then hurried to the front door. I stayed in the den with our other guest, close enough to eavesdrop on the conversation in the foyer.

"What's going on, Seymour?" I heard April ask. "You sounded frantic on the telephone."

"I'm sorry to bother you so late. I mean, so early," he said, locking the door behind her. "Things got really weird around here, and I didn't know who else to call."

"You can always count on me," April replied, her tone sincere. Then, after a pause: "You said you found something really valuable in the house. Is that right?"

"Yeah. Come into the salon and I'll show you."

April rounded the corner a moment later, and stopped dead, her beautiful turquoise eyes wide at the sight of Jim Wolfe and me sitting on the couch. The man was still wearing the same clothes from the Quibblers meeting, but they were rumpled now and he smelled like a gin mill.

"You should have told me you had guests, Seymour. I'm hardly dressed to meet polite company."

After Seymour's call, April had pulled a pair of tight jeans over her long legs, stretched a T-shirt, sans bra, over her model-slender torso. Despite her haste, I noticed the woman had taken the time to fix her sleek, sun-kissed hair and perfectly apply her makeup.

"Hello, April," I said, rising. "How have you been since the séance the other night? I was worried about you."

She didn't answer. Instead, her turquoise gaze shifted to Jim Wolfe, who refused to look up or even acknowledge her presence.

"Who's your other guest?" she asked.

"Oh, come on, April," I said. "You know Jim Wolfe. In fact, you used to do Jim's bookkeeping when you lived in Boston."

April shook her head. "No, you're mistaken. I never met him before."

"In fact, Jim was just telling us a funny story about how you convinced him to sabotage Seymour's brakes the night you learned that Mr. Tarnish here inherited Todd Mansion instead of your mother."

"I'm leaving." April took a single step and bumped into

a wall of Seymour. "Sit down," he said, backing her into a chair.

"No, I—"

"Sit down!" Seymour barked, and she dropped into the seat.

"What's this all about?" April demanded, submerging her obvious fear with some quickly mustered arrogance.

"It's about murder, Mrs. Briggs," I said. "The murder of your aunt, Miss Todd. It's also about Timothea's restless spirit, which still haunts this house."

April's glossy mouth twisted into a disgusted sneer. "Don't be ridiculous."

"I saw the ghost, April," Jim Wolfe said, speaking for the first time. "Miss Todd is with us now. She won't rest until you admit your guilt."

April's eyes narrowed. "This is some sort of sick joke, isn't it?"

Just in time, I heard a rushing sound, like a wind blasting through the room. Yet we felt no current of air and no curtain stirred.

"What's that noise?" April asked.

Jim Wolfe met her nervous gaze. "She's coming," he said ominously.

"Who's coming?" April's voice cracked.

"Why, Miss Todd, of course," I said.

"What!" she cried, her voice just on the edge of panic.

The lamps in the room flickered and then went out. Now the crimson blaze in the fireplace was the only illumination.

"Miss Todd wants you, April," Seymour said. "She told me so herself. Timothea won't rest until you confess your crime."

The howling intensified, and over the noise we heard the sound of a woman's sobs.

"Look! It's Miss Todd's ghost!" Jim Wolfe shouted, pointing to the staircase.

April whirled and her eyes went wide when she saw

the silhouette floating down the steps. She gasped. "It *can't* be."

"It's her, I tell you!" Wolfe cried. "Look at the clothes. The tiara on her head! It's the ghost of Miss Todd!"

On cue, an eerie, scarlet glow illuminated the figure on the staircase. Not enough light to reveal any detail, just enough to give the impression of a supernatural presence.

Jim Wolfe shrank back on the couch. Then he clutched his throat with both hands. "She . . . she's killing me," he rasped. "April!"

"Jim, this is a stupid trick!" April cried. "Can't you see that?"

"My heart," Wolfe gasped, reaching into his jacket as if to clutch his chest. "You have to tell them or I'll die!"

"Jim! Snap out of it!" April shouted.

"Confess!" he demanded.

"What's happening to you?" April howled. She tried to get out of her chair but Seymour pushed her back down again.

"No," she rasped, staring in horror as Jim Wolfe began to choke and cough. Then he brought his hands out of his jacket and covered his mouth with them.

"He needs help!" April shouted at Seymour. "Call an ambulance!"

Seymour held April back as she watched Wolfe wail and convulse and slump back onto the couch. His hands dropped limply to his side, and bloodred gore gushed out of the man's mouth and rolled down his chest.

"No! No! Help him! Please!" April shouted.

"You know what the spirit wants!" I said. "We know already, April! Jim told us!"

"Yes! All right! Yes!" April yelled. "I *killed* Miss Todd. I used the stuff in the secret room under the house to frighten her to death. Now *please*, get Jim an ambulance!"

Suddenly the room was filled with light. April jumped up and lurched toward her lover. Strong hands reached out and grabbed her before she could make it to Wolfe's side.

"What! Who?" April sputtered.

Eddie Franzetti snapped handcuffs around the struggling woman's wrists. Chief Ciders stepped out of the darkness, joined by Deputy Bull McCoy from the steps.

"April Briggs, you're under arrest for the murder of Miss Timothea Todd. You have the right to remain silent . . ."

As Ciders finished reading April her rights, Jim Wolfe opened one eye, then both. He glared at Eddie. "Am I *done*?"

Eddie shook his head. "Not by a long shot. We're going to book you, too—*and* get a statement."

Jim Wolfe smacked his bloodred lips and ran the back of his hand along his gore-soaked mouth. "What is this stuff anyway?"

"My family's pizza sauce," Eddie replied. "Delicious, isn't it?"

"Come on," the chief said to Wolfe.

Sheepishly, the construction hunk rose and Bull McCoy cuffed him. Without an escort, Jim simply followed Chief Ciders out the front door.

I stepped under the chandelier and gave a thumbs-up to the surveillance camera. "Good job, Leo. You can come in now." Then I faced Eddie. "You were great, too. I couldn't have done this without you."

Eddie smiled. "Face it, baby, we make a good team."

My eyes widened. "*What* did you say?"

But Eddie was interrupted by Bull McCoy. "We found Wolfe right where you said he'd be, Mrs. McClure. He was boozing it up at the girly bar with Bud Napp."

"Oh, jeez," I muttered. "Do me a favor and don't tell my aunt Sadie about the girly bar part."

*Your auntie's been around the block, doll. She don't need mollycoddling.*

"Jack!" I shouted in my head. The sweet breeze was back! I couldn't believe it. His presence was swirling around my body, brushing coolly past my cheek. "You're here! You didn't fade away!"

*You ought to know me better than that, baby. I always watch my partner's back.*

"Oh, yeah? Since when? I've been trying to reach you all night!"

*And I was with you all night, too, honey. Came awake when all those "Quibbling" friends of yours were spouting theories.*

"Why didn't you say something? Why didn't you answer me?"

*'Cause you didn't need me, that's why. Just like that little boy of yours, I figured it was time you took a test flight all on your own.*

"I get it." I raised an eyebrow. "So how did I do?"

*You passed, partner. With flying colors.*

I smiled wide just then and Eddie caught it. "Gotta go, Pen," he said with a smile of his own. "I want to be in on April's interrogation." Then he pointed at the cardboard cutout on the steps, the one dressed in Miss Todd's clothes, wig, and tiara. "You want that back?"

"The Zara Underwood standee? Why? You need that for evidence?"

"No. I'd like to have it."

"I don't think your wife would be too happy about that."

"She won't see it. I thought the guys at the station would get a kick out of it. Most of them are reading *Bang, Bang Baby*."

"I guess I'm in the clear now," Seymour said. "Hey, Eddie, thanks for your help."

"Don't mention it," Eddie said.

"Oh, and Bull!" Seymour called. "One more thing. Something I owe you."

"What is it *now*, Tarnish?"

I heard a smack, and saw Bull's wide butt hit the plush area rug. Seymour stood over him, shaking his just-used fist.

Stunned, Bull rubbed his chin.

Eddie glanced at Seymour, then glared at Bull. "What are you laying around for, Deputy?" he barked. "We've got work to do!"

# EPILOGUE

Don't hurry away, old man. We like you around. We get so few private dicks in our house.

—*The Long Goodbye*, Raymond Chandler, 1953

"OKAY, MOM, THE dumps are stocked up. What do you want me to do next?"

Spencer's face was red, this time from exertion and not the mild sunburn he'd brought home from camp last week. He'd been busy since eight this morning, first hauling regular and recyclable garbage to their respective bins, then restocking the picked-over displays.

"A new standee arrived yesterday," I said. "You can put it together."

Spencer grinned and saluted. "Okey-dokey," he said before bounding off to the stockroom.

Sadie appeared at my shoulder. "Where'd he get 'okey-dokey?' That's not the sort of slang I've heard youngsters use. That's an old-fashioned phrase."

"Oh, he's probably just watching those classic black-and-white cop shows again on the Intrigue Channel."

"I see," Sadie said.

The front door buzzed before I could give it any more thought. I moved to the front of the store and saw Eddie

Franzetti in a sharp blue suit, waving at me from the other side of the glass.

"You're out of uniform," I said, unlocking the door.

"Like it?" he adjusted the silver-and-blue silk tie. "I'm driving to Providence to give my final deposition on the Briggs-Wolfe mess. Lots of state officials and lawyer types." He smiled. "Just like Seymour, I'm blending in to my environment."

"Come on in." I led him to the counter, where Sadie greeted him and he helped himself to a warm, glazed pecan roll from the Cooper's bakery box.

"So what's the *almost* final verdict?" I asked, pouring him black coffee from our thermos.

"Plea deal all the way," he said between bites of buttery roll. "Jim Wolfe cooperated, so he'll do less time. But he'll *do* time, and that's what counts."

"And April?" I asked.

"She'll probably plea down to manslaughter on Miss Todd's murder. 'Frightened to death' is a tough count to prove. But her stepfather is a whole other ballgame. When she confessed to killing him on the boat, that put her away. There's a psychological evaluation pending, but I can't see the shrinks helping her."

I didn't, either. It seemed to me April's sickness came from an overdeveloped sense of entitlement and a whole lot of greed. The psychologists haven't identified those traits as pathologies. Not *yet*, anyway.

"So what exactly was the story on April and her stepfather?" I asked.

Eddie washed down another bite of roll with a gulp of coffee. "Arthur Fromsette got curious about what April was doing, taking that path from their house to Miss Todd's folly so often. One day, he followed her. The scheme to scare her aunt to death came out. April admitted that she expected her mother to inherit Todd Mansion. Mother Fromsette always had been generous to a fault with her daughter—loaning her money, paying off credit cards close to the point of personal bankruptcy. So April figured anything her mother inherited was as good as hers. But Arthur was appalled. He knew about her affair with Jim Wolfe, too, and probably the fact that April was cooking Wolfe's books with the tax man to keep his business going."

"Wolfe Construction was in financial trouble?"

Eddie nodded. "Jim Wolfe underbid on so many contracts around the region that he ended up in debt. The upshot is that Arthur Fromsette wanted to convince his stepdaughter to change her ways by threatening to go to the authorities. It didn't work. She killed him."

"Then it was April who attacked Rachel Delve at the séance?"

"According to April's confession, she believed Miss Delve was about to reveal the truth to her mother about her stepfather's murder." Eddie shook his head. "The act was good enough to convince April, even though it sounds like a lot of voodoo hooey to me. Talking to the dead! Can you imagine?"

*Maybe I ought to send a little chill Eddie's way.*

"Shhh, Jack."

Eddie shrugged. "In any case, April was the one who doused the candle and struck Rachel in the nose with the heel of her palm. Rachel was lucky she survived—Mrs. Briggs learned the technique in a martial arts class. If that single blow had been a little stronger, it could have killed the woman."

Sadie cleared her throat. "Explain the timing to me again, Eddie. Those electronics were installed late last summer, weren't they?"

"Yeah," said Eddie. "Pen was right about that. Jim Wolfe set all the special effects up during the two weeks Miss Todd was in Newport."

"But they didn't use the devices to frighten Timothea for nine months," Sadie noted.

"With Arthur Fromsette's disappearance, there was a police investigation and Jim Wolfe got scared. But as the months passed, Wolfe got deeper in debt, and more and more desperate. Finally, when April moved back in with her mother for the summer, she convinced him to go forward with their original plan."

I glanced around to make sure Spencer was out of earshot. "And what about that other matter?" I asked quietly.

Eddie leaned close. "We buried Gideon Wexler in his real grave on the Old Farm early yesterday morning. Nobody noticed."

"What was in the original coffin?" Sadie asked.

"A bag of rocks," Eddie said. "God knows how Miss Todd pulled that one off."

I shivered, recalling the night I slept on that platform bed in Miss Todd's master bedroom. Who knew I was sleeping over a mummified corpse?

*What's the matter, baby, lose your interest in dead guys?*

"Funny, Jack."

*How the heck did they even discover the body after all those years?*

"Seymour decided to redecorate the master bedroom," I whispered to the ghost. "He had to move that four-poster platform bed into the other bedroom to paint. That was when he found Miss Todd's secret diary, hidden with Gideon Wexler's corpse."

*Talk about ghoulish.*

"I returned the diary to Seymour yesterday," Eddie told us. "I know Miss Todd wanted him to have it."

"She did," I said. "I believe *that* was the book she mentioned in her will. She must have known Seymour would eventually find Wexler's body along with her written confession."

"No offense to the authors on your shelves, ladies, but I think that diary was the most fascinating thing I've ever read."

"I'd have to agree," Sadie said, shaking her head.

So did I. Miss Todd's story was downright operatic. According to her diary, Timothea lived in thrall of Gideon Wexler since the day they met, despite the fact that the man was thirty years her senior. Wilomena also loved Wexler. But the romantic triangle was not the reason for the rift between the half-sisters.

During their time together in Newport, Timothea learned of Gideon Wexler's guilt in engineering the 1947 Long Island fire that killed J. J. Conway's mother and seven other innocent people. Just like Todd Mansion, Wexler had rigged his Long Island manor with an elaborate setup to fool guests into believing the house was inhabited by spirits.

Ectoplasmic mists, ghostly apparitions, weird lights and sounds had been set up on the Long Island estate courtesy of Frankie Papps, who used his knowledge of stagecraft to create the effects. Frankie recruited Mabel Conway to act as a phony medium for Wexler, too. But their arrangement fell apart when Frankie and Mabel threatened to expose Wexler unless he gave them the big payoff he was continually holding out on them.

When the couple went out to his Long Island house to collect, Wexler drugged and imprisoned them until the time was right to stage the fire. I shuddered to think of the horror J. J.'s mother experienced as the flames roared around her.

Because Timothea was intimate with the man, she finally realized what kind of monster Wexler really was. She knew it was only a matter of time before he killed again. To prevent that from happening, she placed enough poison in her lover's tea to kill him on the spot. In those days, when a fiftysomething man, who pushed the scale at three hundred pounds, keeled over dead, no one questioned it. No one but Timothea's half-sister, Wilomena Field. She knew what really happened and made a pact with her sister to never reveal the truth. The two never spoke again—about that or anything else.

In the end, Miss Todd's own guilty conscience made her a prisoner. She served a life sentence for murder in her own home. And after years of isolation, the fake haunting unhinged her completely. She really believed that she was battling the ghost of Gideon Wexler, who'd finally risen from the grave to exact revenge.

"Well, Eddie," I said. "Truth is stranger than fiction, and Miss Todd's case is certainly strange. I can't believe you kept it out of the news."

"I had plenty of help, Pen. Councilman Lockhart. The chief. Doc Rubino. Even Bull McCoy. Nobody wants Quindicott to become a stomping ground for lunatic spiritualists or television spook hunters."

*You can say that again, pal!*

Eddie glanced at his watch. "Well, I'd better hit the road."

I walked Deputy Chief Franzetti to the door. "How's Zara Underwood these days?"

He laughed. "She's wearing a police uniform now, courtesy of the policewomen on staff. You should stop by the station and check her out."

"I will. Good luck in Providence, Eddie." I unlocked the door to let him out.

*Admit the truth, baby. You couldn't wait to get rid of Miss Underpants.*

I grinned, happy to hear Jack's voice again, happy he was with me still.

"Well, you know, Zara sold a lot of books for us, and she even helped solve a crime or two. And these days the public's pretty unforgiving: It's out with the old, in with the new."

*Guess it's only a matter of time before you toss me aside for some blue-eyed Viking with a dimpled chin and an easy line.*

"Never, Jack."

From across the floor, Spencer called to me. "The new standee's finished. Check it out!"

*Yikes! Who's that Alvin?*

"That's no Alvin, Jack. That's one of the biggest-selling authors in the country."

And that wasn't the only upside. The cardboard cutout

of a distinguished author wearing a tailored suit wouldn't stir an ounce of controversy in this little town, unless maybe someone objected to the color of the man's tie. Lucky for me, James Patterson wasn't going to be posing in lingerie anytime soon.

"Nine thirty," Sadie announced. "Time to start a new day!"


THE APARTMENT WAS quiet again. But it was a good kind of quiet. Not empty or cold, just the kind of quiet that comes after the sun sets on a long day of work, a day of feeling useful and alive.

*I'm glad you feel that way, baby. I wish I could have when it counted.*

"You didn't?"

*I was too busy, sweetheart.*

"Doing what?"

*Chasing phantoms.*

"Phantoms?"

*Today was never good enough. Tomorrow was always coming. And then one day it wasn't.*

I turned over beneath my bedcovers, stared into the silvery silence of the moonlit room. "Tell me something, Jack," I said, "what happened with your case?"

*You mean the kid?*

"J. J. Conway. You had to tell him, didn't you? That you found his mother."

*Yeah, baby. Not one of my happier memories.*

"Sorry to remind you. But your memory was a huge help to me."

*I know, doll. That's why we used it.*

"So did the little boy go into a foster home?"

*Heck, no. Mrs. Dellarusso adopted him. You remember? The woman on Second Avenue who'd lost her only son over there.*

I smiled into my pillow. "J. J. said she was a swell cook."

*She was a swell mom. And, if you ask me, J. J. was bet-*

ter off with her. *Not that the fat piece of scum who burned Mable Conway alive doesn't deserve to burn in hell, but J. J. was a good kid. He deserved better.*

"Sounds like he got it."

*Yeah, baby. I hope you got it, too.*

"What does that mean?"

*Your boy's lucky to have you.*

"What are you talking about? I'm lucky to have him."

*You have each other, that's all I'm saying. The kid'll grow up, move away, get a life. You won't be seeing him every day. He won't be seeing you. But maybe it's the things we can't see that matter. Maybe those are the best parts of who we are to each other.*

I turned over again and thought hard about that. I decided I couldn't argue. So I didn't. I just yawned and closed my eyes.

"Thanks, Jack," I said.

*Good night, baby,* he whispered back. *I'll see you in your dreams.* Then the ghost's breezy presence receded again, into the fieldstone wall that had become his tomb.

# ABOUT THE AUTHOR

**Alice Kimberly** is the pen name for a multi-published author who regularly collaborates with her writer husband. In addition to the Haunted Bookshop Mysteries, she and her husband also write the bestselling Coffeehouse Mysteries under the pen name Cleo Coyle. To learn more about Alice Kimberly, the Haunted Bookshop Mysteries, or the Coffeehouse Mysteries, visit the author's virtual coffeehouse at www.CoffeehouseMystery.com.

*Don't Miss the Next*

*Haunted Bookshop Mystery*

Join Penelope and her ghostly PI as they team up for an all-new spirited mystery. To learn more about Pen and Jack's upcoming cases, visit the author's website at:

www.CoffeehouseMystery.com

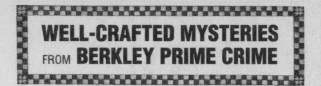